Gamma Coin

Gamma Coin

BASTION/Blackstone II

James Krake

CONTENTS

CONTENTS

CONTENTS

Son Of A Mindbreaker

2140/10/01

Private security at the Sigurd Chemical Plant had just taken 'cracking skulls' too literally, but who was in the wrong was for the media to decide. Every channel and feed Kyte checked had the same PR girl across from a different talking head and the same story kept playing out. Not the details of the riot, those changed like the smells in a Gamma alley; but, no matter who tried to verbally spar with her, her tongue worked them over until they were a confused and stumbling mess.

Kyte had no idea how many people died, nor did he care. He soaked in the way she spoke, the micro-gestures she used to interrupt her opponent's thoughts, and the unbreakable confidence she had. Even when she sat across from independent anchors, the real deal of journalism with all the titanic weight of real evidence, she held up her lies and she won.

As far as audience impression would be concerned anyway.

The shadow of Kyte's mother darkened his computer monitor as advertisements ran across the feed. She stank of synthetic lemon detergent. As far as Kyte knew, she was the only one in the whole homestead that even knew where the cleaning supplies were. "You're just like your father, you know that?"

"Except I'll actually vacuum the apartment," he said. "Eventually."

"Eventually. Sky, eventually you're not going to be living here. You'll be drafted and in bootcamp and you're going to either do your chores on time there, or they'll put you on triple PT with no sleep."

"That what they did to you?" he asked, his attention on the comment section of the Tenn Independent.

His mother sighed. "They do that so you learn some self-responsibility. So that you do what has to be done, when it has to be done, rather than rotting away chasing dopamine hits." At least four of their homestead cohabitors were doing just that in VR within ten meters of him.

"I know how to do what I have to do. Dad taught me that."

"Your father taught you nothing good. He's in prison, remember?"

"How could I forget," Kyte said, slumping deeper into his chair as he tried to find another interview with the government PR girl. She was like a knock-off mindbreaker and Kyte wasn't quite sure if she was slicker than he was.

"Computer, parental override, shut off."

Kyte clicked his tongue as the computer locked up, saved, and booted off. She couldn't turn everything off though. Voice commands had been disabled on his phone. "I passed my exams, didn't I?" he asked as he pulled up social media feed again.

His mother paced and re-tied her hair into a bun. "It's not the exams I'm worried about."

He lingered on some photos of Akane, his girlfriend, partying. They were uploaded only that morning and looked like the soft drinks were photo-manipulation to cover booze. She was with Jessica and some guy he didn't recognize. He scowled and flipped his feed to a humor stream. "The only way the draft can go wrong is if I'm allergic to the vaccine. I'm fit, smart, and from a veteran household. Both you and dad served just fine. They'll accept me and I'll do my stint and get out and get a corporate job and be fine. Can't you let me enjoy my last few weeks of freedom?"

"That's your problem, Sky. Where is your passion? What are you going to do with your life? You're not in school anymore," she said, and when he smirked, she exploded. "Did you really just pull out your phone?"

Kyte closed the feed before the rest of the skit made him outright laugh. "No. And come on, I've got like two years to find a passion to care about before it even matters. I'm going to get drafted like everyone else and I'm going to be a slave until they let me out and then it will matter." After they let him out, he wouldn't have to listen to her yelling again.

His mother shook her head and walked back to the kitchen. She half-heartedly cleaned the pots until she stopped and put her hands on the counter. "I don't want you to just vanish into some corporation, doing some bullshit job nobody cares about. I know you could succeed at that, but what would you have at the end of the day?"

"I don't know, a wife at home who loves me?"

"Does your father? Do you think you're better at his tricks than he is?"

Kyte twisted around to glare at her. "If you're afraid of me being like him, then why are you pushing me to go find a passion? Isn't his passion why you threw his ass out? That he cared more about the music than he did about us?"

She didn't respond, just went back to cleaning her pans. With his computer off, the rasp of steel wool only competed with the rustle of ventilation. A homestead for a dozen people couldn't have sounded more empty. In his head, Kyte considered a dozen different ways he could apologize, or shift the conversation, or otherwise squirm out of her ire. Before he could implement any of them, Akane messaged him.

She asked, "You're free tonight, right?"

The way his mother was stewing in her own frustrations, he didn't need to rush to smooth things over. In fact, he didn't need to smooth them over at all. "Sure am," he messaged back. "What's up?"

"I got us concert tickets. Meet me at the comp-maus?"

"What band?"

"Don't worry about it. The concert is going to be awesome and I have the tickets already. Don't make me go by myself."

Kyte gritted his teeth as he thought about the people in the pictures with Akane. Without saying a word to his mother, he stood up and disappeared into his bedroom. He messaged Akane, "Sounds good," as he got changed.

His mother was waiting for him when he emerged in his boots and jacket, hair slicked back. She shook her head. "Are we going to finish talking about this?"

He shrugged. "Thought we did. I've got a plan for my life and right now, that doesn't include staying here where you can shut off my computer, eh? If you don't mind, all my friends are celebrating being done with school. We've got places to be," he said, and slipped out the door. He wasted no time in reaching the staircase. The train might have been faster if it was there waiting for him, but standing around for it was like asking to get robbed. He moved fast, head up and hands in pockets so nobody could be sure what he was holding. Flight after flight he descended till he was on the tenth floor where a boulevard layer separated the decent folk of the city from the cretins.

He stayed where businesses paid protection money and got the protection they paid for, not where even getting an internet connection was hit-or-miss. On the boulevard, there was safety in numbers, not because he could expect anyone to help him but because he was confident he wasn't the most likely victim. He walked the walk of one without fear, striding past the kind of slouched down, timid cats that drew muggers like flies to shit.

The computer mausoleum was called Starship Mars and had a couple different rooms stacked through the center of a tower. The first was the lobby, where time with high-speed VR could be bought along with drinks and snacks. The second flanked either side of the hallway: VIP rooms. Unlike the cargo hold in the back where people laid in pull-out coffins while in simulation, the VIP rooms had chairs to sit in. They were still packed edge to edge and filled with people wasting away, but it had a sort of dignity to it that Akane paid for.

"Hey, if it isn't little Vapor," the mausoleum owner said when he spotted Kyte. The man himself wasn't present, just an apparatus of machines to simulate him. Two graspers, a camera, and a vid screen that displayed his avatar. If someone wanted to rob the place, Mr Clark wasn't able to stop them. The pair of rent-a-cops taking turns watching and gaming would do that.

"Just stopping by, don't charge me anything," Kyte said as he swung by the counter to bump fists with the machine.

Mr Clark always appreciated the gesture, since he couldn't physically stand up to greet people anymore. Most customers treated him like a machine. The human connection had gotten Kyte more than a few time extensions over the years. "Looking for your girl then?"

"She here?"

"Yeah, she's in Captain's Quarters Three with some friends."

"Thanks," he said, and slipped through the line of people trying to buy energy drinks before their time in the maus resumed. Kyte had seen Mr Clark once and came to the same conclusion as everyone else. There was no amount of politeness in the world to compensate for the smell that radiated out from the man's body. From beyond a digital barrier, it was fine to be pleasant with him, but Kyte would never willingly get another whiff of the rotting maggot scent that oozed from the folds of the man's fat. Even Mr Clark avoided his own smell, because he never disconnected from simulation. He fed himself with prosthetics only.

Captain's Quarters Three was one corner of the VIP section which hadn't been fully kitted out for high-speed internet, presumably because Mercurial refused to give the maus any more fiber optic. It wasn't a total loss for the business however, because there was always a demand for half-dive VR, where people still had to use their bodies to play with whatever their implant showed them. The guy flailing arms in the middle of the room was not playing any game Kyte could recognize, but Akane and her friend Jessica were engrossed.

"Watch out," his girlfriend said, waving to him as he walked in. She didn't take her eyes off the player. She was already dressed for going out, with a tight, black tank top and short skirt. The neck of her jacket almost hid the choker collar she had on, but it matched too well with her lipstick to not catch Kyte's eye. She was the prettiest girl in his school, or rather she had been.

A moment later, Kyte had to jump back as the guy playing lunged at him, stabbing forward with an empty hand before leaping the other way and swinging at some phantom. "What the hell is he playing?" Kyte asked as he slipped over to an open chair.

"[Auroary's Rhythm Apocalypse]," Jessica answered. She was dressed up too, but a bit more modestly, opting for a red dress and flat bottomed boots she could dance in.

"You're coming to the concert, right?" Akane asked, leaning on the arm of her chair to get closer to him.

Kyte nodded and tried to sync his implant with the local game. "Yeah, what artist?"

She bit her lip and shrugged. "Promise not to be mad?"

Akane had already bought the tickets, so she was going with or without him. He didn't want the latter to happen, no matter what, so he said, "Promise."

"Auroary."

He cut off the swear before it got out his mouth. "Seriously?"

She shrank back. "I know you don't like her, but I do."

"And you know why I don't like her! Come on, aren't there like a hundred other musicians—real ones—who you could go see?" He regretted saying that. He knew what her reaction would be even before she did.

She flipped over to the far side of the chair, tucking her feet up on the cushion as she grabbed her drink. "The concert is going to be awesome, okay? There's a bunch of hype because of the new DLC that just dropped. People are talking about it. It's trending. Don't be lame, Kyte."

He put up his hands. "Fine, just don't go telling anyone about me, alright?"

She laughed. "No bragging?"

"What's there to brag about? I didn't even get us free tickets. Also, who the hell is this?" he asked, pointing at the guy still playing like his life depended on it. The guy had actually broken a sweat and the river staining his back was not a good look.

Jessica sighed and sneered. "My date to the concert. His name is Miles... he's from the quarter under us." That meant he was about three months their junior. Judging by how rare it was for people on different exam schedules to mingle, Kyte took the guess that Miles was the one who had paid for the room, and probably their drinks and Jessica's ticket. Poor guy was going to learn the hard way that relationships didn't last through the draft.

"How much time do we have?" Kyte asked.

"If we want to get food first, we should head out now," Akane answered. "Miles, quit the game."

Jessica's date faltered and came to a stop. He was panting and had to wipe his forehead off as he turned around and blinked. "We're leaving? Oh, he's here. Hi, I'm–"

"Miles, have you ever done this kind of thing before?" Kyte asked as they all stood up.

The guy twisted his head around, searching faces and furrowing his brow. "What kind of thing?"

Kyte scoffed. "What? Did you think we were going to a concert and not drinking? Someone is going to have to pull one over on the bartenders, you know? If you can't do it, that's fine. I've done it before and can do it again."

Miles prickled and puffed out his chest. "Nah, I've got a fake account. I can get us a couple beers. No problem," he said as everyone filed out of the VIP room.

Jessica snaked her arm around his and grinned. "Just what I wanted to hear," she said as the two of them took charge on where to go for food.

Kyte hung back with Akane. She shook her head at him. "Really?"

"What?"

"Don't you think he's paid enough?"

"I do," Kyte said as he followed the others. He waved bye to Mr Clark and grinned at his girlfriend when they returned to the boulevard. "I just know for a fact that he's not going to successfully get us alcohol."

She rolled her eyes and shook her head. "You're probably right there, but what makes you so sure that you can?"

"Because I'm just that good. I know how to work people." He was the son of a mindbreaker afterall.

2

House Call

2140/10/01

Elliot sat at the edge of his home tower, knees almost pressed to the railing beneath the exhaust of too many restaurants to count. The cubby was quiet, but the air was clogged with boiling grease. If he opened his mouth, he could taste the deep fryers belching out their fumes from the cramped kitchens around him. He sat in the stench of industrial cooking precisely because it kept him from opening his mouth. He was able to sit and stare at the pack of cigarettes in his hands while resisting the urge to rip the plastic off and stuff one in his mouth. The air itself would replace all the grease and grime that bioengineering had taken from the Nico-Pure cigarettes his brother had preferred.

Five years? No, that was last year. Going on six now. Where the hell are you now?

His phone was piling up with reports and incidents he was ignoring just like the rest of the department. Then the ringer grabbed his attention. Slipping the pack of cigarettes into his pocket, he checked what his boss wanted. One of the day's reports had been flagged and Cinder messaged, "Make this your inaugural investigation. Sensitive interests."

Elliot didn't need to be told sensitive meant political. After skimming the details of the report, the new head of the VR Crimes department went to get his partner. She was on a shift with the Quick Response

Squad, but he extracted her. Once they were together, Ram wouldn't let him get on a train before buying him a coffee as thanks.

She got him a Caff-Plus Hot Cocoa the size of a flash-bang grenade. "How have I never heard of this before?" Elliot asked. He and his junior were hurtling across the upper strata of Bastion in a train car that had been repainted but not refurbished. Half the seats were missing and it rattled between the magnetic couplings. The swaying didn't phase Ram, but Elliot had to hold onto the railing and crack the can with his free hand like a beer.

It had a lot more sugar than a beer did.

Ram said, "I don't think they sell it down in Gamma. It's more of a bougie thing, you know? Tastes like dessert though, right?" She sipped her Caramel-Squirt Caff-Plus Double-Shot Hot Cocoa, which was somehow half the size of Elliot's drink and still liquid.

"If they don't sell this down in Gamma, I probably shouldn't be walking around with it."

It's not good to give people a reason to be annoyed. You don't want to remind people in Gamma that you live above them. She needs to know better.

Ram shrugged. She leaned over as the train decelerated for a stop. The noise grew to a din as the doors opened and a flood of voices poured in. "We're headed to Liberty Stadium. They're popular there."

I suppose so. The stadium is like a weight, pulling the upper crust to the ground.

Elliot glanced down the car. People weren't quite elbow to elbow, but they kept glancing over. The sight of MP badges repelled the civilians. He pivoted his stance, and Ram stepped over to lean against the wall. "So, is this what you expected the work would be like?"

She sipped more of her sugar bomb and shrugged. "I thought there'd be more paperwork, to be honest. The drill sergeants used to yell at us about that all the time. You know, that we should be lucky all we had to do was march and shoot. Soon we'd be trapped with databases."

"Did you get yelled at a lot?"

She winced. "I wasn't very good at the shooting."

Elliot laughed. "You'll do even less of that than the paperwork, and not because EVE is doing it all for you. Shooting is for video games."

"Speaking of video games," Ram said. "I checked out one of your wife's streams last night. She's really good... at the games. Maybe not the best best best entertainer, but I was watching her do a first run of [Firekeeper] on Demon God Difficulty."

"[Firekeeper]? What's that?"

Ram scratched her cheek. "It's a hack and slash dungeon type of game. People watch it because, well, the easiest way to explain it is that [Firekeeper] separates the wheat from the chaff."

I'll have to check it out.

"Good to know all those hours have actually totaled up to something," Elliot said.

"Do you ever play with her?"

"No, I don't have a neural implant, remember? And externals can't keep up."

"Not even retro games?"

Elliot winced and looked out the window. He and his wife hadn't gamed together in years. He mumbled an excuse as he pulled out his phone and checked the address. The two of them were en route and on the clock. His phone advised disembarking at the next station for the shortest time, or three stations later for the shortest walk. For once, he actually trusted the WPS map.

The internal system must have just flagged him as active, because his boss Cinder called him. "Blackstone, where are you?"

He checked his map again. "Coming up on the Lincoln Tower."

"For the hypnosis thing?"

"Just like you told me," he said. "Has something else come up?"

"No. I just wanted to check that there wasn't going to be a problem."

"Is there a reason there might be one? It's just a mother concerned about her son, isn't it?"

"You're not wrong," she said. "But, don't you normally take today as vacation?"

His hand went to the pack of cigarettes still bulging his pocket. "Not this year."

"Alright, I wasn't sure if I had missed a vacation request. I was sure I would have approved it if it had come from you of all people. You really gotta take more time off, you know that? You'll set a bad example for your junior."

"I'll set a fine example for her."

"No cowboy justice?"

"From me, or from her?"

Cinder didn't laugh, she sighed. "Look, Blackstone, I know you know what the deal is. This isn't your first time dealing with sensitive connections. The new girl is expected to have some opinions on the matter though."

Elliot glanced at Ram from the corner of his eye and saw her checking her own phone and sighing. "Cinder, is there something I need to know?"

"I'll tell you in person. Just, for tonight, don't bring up who his father is."

He pinched the bridge of his nose and closed his eyes. "Cinder, what aren't you telling me?"

"Ram's a good kid, Blackstone. Maybe too good. Call it a day after this one, alright? You want to be the good example, don't you?"

"I want an explanation first thing in the morning."

"Fine, I'll schedule a meeting," Cinder said, and she hung up.

Elliot gritted his teeth and put his phone back in his pocket. The day wasn't about to turn to night, so he tugged Ram back from the door and let it close. "We'll get off at the next stop."

"Everything alright, Elliot?" she asked, and glanced down the train. The other passengers were giving them space, chatting amongst themselves. Unlike most times, there weren't any void masks, or multi-colored cityboarders. It was packed full of workers sporting corporate logos and little else.

"Just a shorter walk if we wait. Hey, this is going to be your first house call, isn't it?"

Her face lit up. "Yeah, I'm kind of excited, but I also know that house calls are boring so not that excited? And I imagine this is going to be pretty different since we're in a hoity toity part of town for something that probably isn't even real. Not like we're getting called in for a B&E, right?"

"Corporate security usually handles those. They have faster response times than us. Most house calls you're going to get will be like this one."

"So, they won't be like showing up to an unidentified body that got deleted from EVE's surveillance system?" Ram asked with a laugh.

Elliot couldn't help but smirk. "That was also an anomaly, yeah."

"Well, that's fine by me. I didn't join for exciting stuff, you know? Plenty of people are out there that can handle that."

"Why did you join?"

"Eh, I'll tell you some other time. It's a little embarrassing, you know? Or, tell you what, you tell me why you joined, and I'll tell you why I did."

Elliot frowned and looked out the window. He tried to reach back through his memory and found it muddled, as though the tide was rising in a swamp and leaving only disconnected islands of his past. The throughline of cause and effect had vanished, occluded by the big events: marrying Amara, the California trip, and the execution. Somewhere in his past was why he had joined the MPs, but that, of course, had been before his rise and fall through the ranks.

"Some other time, over drinks," he mumbled, and the two of them disembarked.

Ram slipped around him with a smirk. "Well, don't take too long. If you leave me hanging, I'll get curious and I might start asking around."

"You wouldn't even know who to ask. And don't say Cinder, she doesn't have the time for something like that. And just because you watch my wife's stream doesn't mean you're able to contact her."

She shrugged. "I guess it's a mystery. Maybe it'll be good detective practice for me. A bit of training to get me started?"

The two of them strolled into the very heart of the city, where the towers were the oldest and the thickest. The Lincoln Tower, like its kin, rose from the middle of Bastion like so many stakes in the ground, as if their job was to pin the city down to the Earth. Recently, they were the entertainment district surrounding the stadium, but their original purpose still survived: the residential neighborhood for the government. Anyone even adjacent to the mass of power that ruled the city lived under Congress' umbrella.

After confirming the address, Elliot slid his phone back into his pocket and knocked on the apartment door. From inside, he heard a computer say, "The Missou Police Department is here to see you, Miz Ryder." Elliot arched an eyebrow at his partner, and both of them tried to spot the camera. They were on the eighteenth floor of Bastion, but at the thin end of the wedge that made up Missou. Just a few towers away, Liberty Stadium stood at the heart of the city like a hub for the districts. It drove the real estate up even on the ground floor.

The door swung open to a woman in her late forties dressed like a teenager. The retro-schoolyard pleated skirt lacked most of its charm when Elliot could see the micro-scars of cosmetic controls beneath her ears—synthetically replacing what age had taken away. If grace was supposed to come with age, it had missed her entirely. Miz Ryder folded her arms and looked the two of them over. "About time you people got here," she said, giving Elliot's partner, Ram, an unceremonious look over.

"I'm Detective Elliot, and this is my partner, here to respond to your request. May we step inside?" Elliot asked, leaning in.

Miz Ryder sniffed and spun on her heels. She marched in and beckoned them over her shoulder. "I don't know how you people let this game stay in business. There are laws, you know, about protecting children."

The two police officers followed in. The apartment was nice. Not terribly large, but stylishly laid out. The place was clean aside from the overflowing dirty dishes which spoiled the air. Elliot expected her to sit down on the sofa opposite the wall-sized television, but Miz Ryder stopped right at the hallway to the bedrooms. Turning her nose up, she asked, "So, what are you going to do about it?"

He reminded himself that he wanted to be a good example for Ram, and rebuilt the professional smile on his face. "The report you filed said that this game was hypnotic?"

"Or worse," she said.

Ram poked her head around Elliot. "Hypnosis isn't real though, so could you be more precise about what it's doing?"

What? Who told her that?

Miz Ryder said, "My son is addicted to the damn thing. He won't stop playing it. He fell getting out of the shower last week and had to go to the emergency room. Diagnosis? Malnutrition! My boy's not eating because of it."

Elliot and Ram shared a glance. She gave him the nod that she was logging notes through her neural implant. He turned back to the mother. "Could you provide some basic details? The name of the game, how long your son has been playing, that sort of thing?"

She rolled her eyes and flicked her hand. "Evan calls it [Auroary's Rhythm Apocalypse]. I don't know, six months now?"

"And what does it do that's illegal?"

Miz Ryder stared back at him. "Excuse me? Games aren't supposed to make you forget to eat and sleep."

Ram's eyes were unfocused, reading through something digital in her mind. "Miz Ryder, how old is your son?"

"Nineteen, why?"

Bastard's blood, he's an adult? I'm not hired to be a therapist, you know.

Elliot glanced down the hall that Miz Ryder had stopped beside. He gestured to the door. "Is your son here right now?"

She nodded. "If you can pull him out of the damn game, he is. You want to see my electric bill ever since he got hooked into it?"

"Right, well, I think I'll have to have a talk with him. Detective? Could you work Miz Ryder down the questionnaire while I engage Mr Ryder?"

Ram's shoulders slumped, which transformed her coat from a proper uniform to more of a tent draped around her. "I could go speak to him and get his side of the–"

"I'll be quick," he said, and nearly ran down the hall. He knocked on the door. No response. He pulled out his phone and sent a proximity message. Every receiver, both phones and neural implants, within three meters of him got a message stating, "Detective E11107 of the Missou Police Department would like to speak with you." He perked his ears for noise, tuned out Miz Ryder's rambling, and let his breath out when heard Evan Ryder react.

The door cracked open, enough for one eye to peer out, and the prattling to pour in. Evan looked him over and, when he saw the badge, opened the door. The boy didn't look good; halfway to cyber-zombie by the looks of it.

"Can I step inside?"

Evan hesitated, glanced down the hall towards his mother, and stepped back. "Sure."

The leftover stench of puberty without restraint, and far less surreptitiousness than thought, hit Elliot on entry. The overflowing trash can beneath the computer desk took one glance to spot, even though it was on the far side of the fold-down bed. Dirty sheets, dirty clothes on the floor. Barely any space to creep around the bed to get to the one chair in the room. "You know, would you like to speak outside? I think there was a study room or something."

Evan stuffed his hands in his pockets and shrugged. He had shrunk to the nearest corner and didn't move from it. "What are you here to talk about?"

Please don't make me keep smelling this, kid.

"Your mother is concerned about you, something about a game?"

That did the trick. His eyes rolled. "Sure, sure," he mumbled, and the two of them slipped back out of the apartment. His mother opened her mouth to say something, but let them pass with a glance back at the filthy bedroom.

The lounge at the corner of the floor wasn't a study room per se, it was an automated cafe. It didn't look like it had been cleaned recently, but it was something. "You want a coffee?" Elliot asked as Evan slouched against a standing table by the window.

"It's broken."

Elliot flipped the hot water tab. No water, no lights, no reaction. He sighed. "Anyways, this place has noise cancellers, right?" he asked, peering up at the technological ornaments dangling from the ceiling.

"Good enough to talk, yeah. So, my mother is complaining about... which game?" He didn't look at Elliot when he asked. He stared out the window and fidgeted, despite the view comprising a handful of store-fronts and a smattering of people passing by. Some of them had void masks on, hiding their faces. Less than at the outskirts of Bastion.

Elliot leaned on the table. The kid had a bit of color in his ears. "Something about Aurora?"

Evan straightened up and looked at the detective. "[Auroary's Rhythm Apocalypse]?"

"That's the one."

Evan let out his breath and rolled his eyes so hard his head rolled. "For fuck's sake. It's just a game. It's fun. What's wrong with that?"

"How many hours a day are you playing it?"

"I don't know, maybe three? Four? They just released an expansion for it, if you can beat the expert difficulty campaign. I've been playing it in augmented reality mode, you know? Actually using my body for it the best I can. It gets me a bit of exercise. I figure it's a good thing for me. Doctors said I needed to be more active."

Elliot frowned and read Evan's face more closely. "What game did you think I was here to talk to you about?" The flush went back into the kid's cheeks, unbidden and unwanted. "Don't worry, I'm not going to tell anyone, unless a crime occurred. You're not in trouble and by the looks of it, I'll promise that I won't tell your mother."

Evan rubbed the back of his neck and glanced at the noise canceller overhead, then down the hall to his apartment. "It's not exactly a game. More like social media? Well, it has some game elements to it."

"Are you on Vid-Master or something?"

Evan's hair flopped from shaking his head. "No, I don't have the talent for Vid-Master. Have you..." He glanced again and leaned closer. "Look, tons of people my age are using it, alright?"

"Well, I'm not your age. A porn thing, I take it?"

"No," Evan said, then wobbled his head. "Well, kind of. Ever heard of [Sladder]?" Elliot shook his head. "It's a VR thing. Pretty good sensation. It matches you with people and you, you know, hook up. It's pretty cool, because it has some kind of algorithm that scores you on how well you, uh, perform. Then it gives you sort of a matchmaking rank? The higher you score, the better you are, so it matches you with people around your rank. I've gotten up to Diamond League on it."

Elliot found himself unable to form a reaction. He stared at the teenager and hoped that a joke would come next. None did. "So, that's what you're spending all your time doing?"

Evan squirmed like a convict in the interrogation wing. "More or less."

Elliot straightened up. He needed the space between them as much as Evan did. "Okay, so I've got some quick questions for you. You got a girlfriend?"

"No."

"Did you qualify for the draft?"

"Exempted."

"Do you have a job?"

"Not quite."

"So you spend all day logging into a virtual orgy."

"Well, when you put it like that..."

"Bastard's blood." Elliot stared at the ceiling. The LEDs didn't have answers. "Well I can at least close this investigation. You're not hypnotized, you're just wasting your time."

Evan crossed his arms. "Hey, time enjoyed is never time wasted."

Is that what you tell yourself? I can't believe I subjected Ram to that woman for this.

Elliot sighed. "Kid, you need to start a habit of leaving the house, or your mother is going to drive you insane, alright? I'm not a therapist, I shouldn't even be saying this as a police officer, but you need to get out of her sight on a regular basis. I don't care what you do with your time, but I don't want another police report like this. Okay?"

The defiance vanished from the kid. "Oh, come on. What am I supposed to do? All my friends are in bootcamp or whatever right now. [Sladder] is anonymous, it's not like I've met anyone through that. What would I do?"

"Go meet someone. Didn't you just say you were Diamond Rank at sex? That means you're good at it, doesn't it? Go put it to use on a real girl."

"They are real–"

"It doesn't count if you don't have their phone number."

Evan shut his mouth and nodded. "Alright, point taken. At least you aren't yelling at me to get a job. I get enough of that from my father."

"Hey, a job wouldn't kill you."

Evan arched an eyebrow at him. "You sure about that?" he asked, holding up one of his rail-thin arms.

Elliot grimaced. "You need to work on that too. Get some good food in you. Drinking age is eighteen nowadays, right? Even slop tastes good eventually."

The kid scratched his chin and stared out the window for a moment. "You know, I think I have a ticket. Or, I mean, I have enough in-game points to redeem for a ticket to an Auroary concert. I have never seen her in person. Of course, she isn't exactly real–"

"Perfect. Go do that," Elliot said, and headed back to the apartment. Ram met him outside and waved him over. There was a curious twist to her lip. Not quite excitement, but something had her attention. Elliot said, "The kid's not hypnotized. We're done here. Write it up and close it."

She frowned. "Well, about that. Miz Ryder there gave me access to her utility bills, which means the police database got access to them, and EVE saw them, and well, it kind of raised some red flags? Evan's processors have been cooking twenty-four seven ever since this new expansion to [Auroary's Rhythm Apocalypse] came out. I think the developer released some kind of malware."

Ram's frown turned into a smile as Elliot thought over what she had discovered. "Well, that's something worth looking into. Good job, Ram."

Better than playing counselor for a burnout. Now I just have to deal with... what? Some kind of bot-net hacking program? What could go wrong?

3

Glassed

2140/10/02

"Come on, haven't you ever had a drink before?" Electronic music struck the club's support beams like a steel drum. The rhythm pulsed in the air. Dancing feet pounded the floor. Voice barely carried across the table.

"I've drank before. I'm not a loser," Kyte said. The glass was cold in his hand. Condensation dripped from his fingers. Perhaps seconds ago it had been sweat in someone's hair, in the neckline of a skin-tight shirt, rolling off a girl's curves. There were so many bodies pressed against one another, grinding and sliding, they used their sweat like lubricant. The raw stench of humans had been smothered by spilled beer and liberal application of pseudo-olfactors; glorified perfume machines. Somehow, Kyte could still smell the fizzing, bubbling draught of bubblegum pink liquor floating above... he didn't know what it was floating on, but it was clear and smelled like paint thinner.

The man across from him grinned. He didn't hesitate to show off the dental enhancements he had—fangs instead of canines. Only his eyes were hidden, with thick sunglasses to mask the inflammation. They weren't really eyes anymore, just cybernetic implants at least a decade obsolete. "Then drink up, eh? It's my treat for your first time here, seeing Auroary," the man said and lifted his own glass towards the front of the club.

The hologram of Auroary danced across the stage, pumping a hand in the air and driving the mosh pit into a frenzy as the melody of her song ripped down through the solo of *Nighttime Lover*. She had a tight black dress that clung to her chest and flared into a puffed up skirt at her thighs that just barely kept everything covered up between her legs. She wasn't real of course, not in the flesh and blood sense. Kyte knew that saying such a thing was blasphemy though.

Auroary was a real thing. She looked like a person. Talked like a person. Smiled like your highschool crush. She had real concerts and put out real music. She brought real people to real events. She was real. She just couldn't hold your hand. Auroary was a digital siren singing her songs to a city rather than a ship.

By any skeptic's measure, Auroary was no less real than any idol or popstar made of flesh. Usually, they didn't even have a real smile, not after putting on a five hour concert every night for two weeks straight, strung out on cigarettes and whatever the hell the fizzing pink liquor was. Auroary's existence was only properly measured by the impact she had on the observer and her voice was more intoxicating than any drug Kyte knew of.

Until he remembered who the songwriter was.

The two of them clinked their glasses together. Then the cyber-eyed man slammed the butt of his glass on the table to sink the liquor. Kyte rushed to do the same. Both cups mixed and the pink turned blue like a serpent diving for the bottom. Before his glass could completely change, the cyber-eyed man threw his head back and chugged.

Kyte was slow. The blue tasted like citrus. Before he finished, it shifted back to pink and tasted like habanero. He spat it out, tongue burning.

"Woah! Amateur hour over here!" He grinned and laughed at Kyte who was still coughing and choking, wiping the color-shifting booze off his lips.

A hand slapped onto Kyte's shoulder and spun him around. Bartender: the only kind of person who would wear a collared shirt to an Auroary concert. The guy shoved a camera into Kyte's face with a scowl and read the output. "How did a seventeen year old get that?"

Kyte glanced over his shoulder, but his benefactor had vanished. "Sorry, didn't know it was alcoholic," he lied.

The bartender clicked his tongue, the sound lost in the song's crescendo. He jabbed a finger at Kyte's nose. "No more, Skybyte. You're too young."

The finger swelled up in Kyte's vision. His pupils dilated and his head throbbed. Thoughts swam from one ear to the next. Had he approached the bartender properly, like his father had taught him, he could have been walking away with a bucket of beers, but every path there had just vanished. "Don't call me that man," he mumbled. "That name is so embarrassing. Call me Kyte."

The bartender rolled his eyes. "Sure thing, buddy." The man snatched the empty glass and vanished into the flashing darkness.

Kyte's mouth stopped burning, the taste morphing back to citrus. If someone had offered him sandpaper, he might have scoured his tongue with it. While he was contemplating a run to the bathroom, someone pressed a bottle of beer into his hands. Cold, fizzing, and with just enough flavor to cleanse his palette. The cyber-eyed man winked at him and knocked his own beer back for a swig.

The beer cleansed his palette and once more girded him with the badge of age and maturity. Kyte scanned the crowd, the mass of partiers and ravers between him and the stage. The bar area had a nominal railing between it and the dance floor. It partitioned between the full brunt of the music and where a battalion of noise cancellation devices allowed a semblance of speech. It meant he couldn't hear Akane's voice. She was just somewhere in the crowd, with her friends. One more sway of hair and hip.

"What a bunch of joy kills, am I right?" the man asked.

"The mosh?"

"No, the employees. Like they don't know the fun here is why they have a job at all. Half of them just cruise around to swing their authority like a stick."

Kyte shook his head and drank more of the beer. He couldn't taste it, like the liquor had burned his tastebuds off. He didn't know if that was a good thing or a bad thing. "Maybe someone stiffed them on a bill? Can you even do that here? Everything is account charged, right?"

His alcohol benefactor shrugged. "Maybe if you were paying by credit chip? All I know is they reject Gamma Coin."

Kyte frowned and scratched through his memory. "The hell is Gamma Coin? Some kind of crypto currency?"

The man grinned. He leaned shoulder to shoulder with Kyte. "No, that would be silly. The government can crack any blockchain they feel like. Who would put stock in something like that? That would be like trusting the fiat ledgers."

Kyte's head hurt. His brain felt like he was trying to stuff eels into a basket. They kept squirming from his grasp whenever he tried to put them together. Belated, he realized he was buzzed, maybe more than buzzed. "But, don't we all..." The man he had been speaking to had vanished once more.

Kyte turned back to the dance floor and caught sight of someone he knew. Jess seemed distracted, caught talking to some man too drunk to read the expression on her face. Kyte slipped over to her, grabbing the girl by the elbow. Short, with ruby red pigtails bouncing against her shoulders like corkscrews. "Jess, where have you been?"

She turned, smiling enough until she caught wind of his breath. That made her pull back and blink. There was a moment of uneasiness in her expression she tried to cover up, but not quick enough. "Having fun back here, Kyte? I thought you were bringing drinks back for us? Have you seen Miles?"

He shrugged and the two of them stepped out of the stream of people. Next to one of the building's support pillars he took a glance again for the cyber-eyed man. "They scanned my face. Couldn't buy them myself. If you can work some of your charm though…"

Jessica's eyes rolled. All the glitter on her cheeks looked wrong for a moment, like she was telling scary stories in the dark or something. "Well, here's hoping Miles comes through for us."

Kyte's ears burned. "Hey, I tried."

She smiled and put a hand on his shoulder. "I'm sure you did try."

Kyte wasn't smiling. His words flowed on auto-pilot. The beer in his gut loosened his tongue and dulled his hesitations. "I've already been cut off because of the face scanner. I didn't think they'd have those here or, if they did, that Akane would have warned me. Why don't you come with me and place the order? I'll slip you by and get you away from Shakes here."

Jess glanced at the drunk who had been hitting on her. He seemed to think moving his body back and forth constituted dancing and seemed to have severely overestimated the sticking power of his hair gel after an hour of sweating. "I thought you were the sweet talker? Gunna sweet talk a machine?"

"I can sweet talk a machine better than–" He jerked his head at the guy and the moment Jess sighed, he slipped a hand around her elbow.

Jess leaned into him and started towards the counter. Her pace slowed and she shook her head, making her pigtails swing. "I can get to the counter myself. I've got a fake account set up, I'm not worried about getting scanned. Just pay me back, okay?"

Kyte gently squeezed her arm, not to hurt her but to feel the tension through her thin arm. The uneasiness she had been hiding was still there. "What's up? What are you worried about? I can still pay if you need me to."

She clicked her tongue and looked away. After a glance at his hand, she relaxed her arm and straightened her jacket. "Why don't you go find Akane, yeah? I'll bring a round of drinks for us," she said, and slipped away from him.

Kyte frowned as she walked away. He sucked down more of his beer and licked the froth from his teeth. He descended the two steps to the dance floor and Auroary's music slammed into his skull. It felt like a vice around his ears. The hologram wore a new outfit now–all leather and fishnet. Her hair was pulled to one side, shaking like a spray of fireworks as she spat the lines to *Midnight Rider*. The dancers had pulled in tight, bouncing the floor like a trampoline. It was a breakup song, tugging on the heart strings of every lonely person in the crowd.

Kyte doubted they knew it had been written by a man after getting divorced. He figured they didn't even realize the new song had a different voice synthesizer; a different woman brought in to sample her vocal chords so the program could up the enunciation while maintaining the humanness to it. It looked like Auroary, therefore it was Auroary.

Midnight Rider wasn't much of a dance song though. The beat was too fast, too easily lost in the words. The tune pulled the crowd tight to the stage, and those in need of a break filtered out the back. They ran to get drinks, to queue for the bathroom, or just to catch their breath. Kyte could finally scan the crowd.

Akane was at the far corner, almost behind the speaker wall.

Kyte grimaced at the near-empty beer bottle in his hand–not the haul he had been asked to get. He started over to her. Even with everyone slowed down, he still had to weave between bodies, slip through gaps in the crowds as people formed social circles. At his height, he could see over most people's heads and slip between the gaps. Even with women in heels and men in platform shoes, he could see over them. He tried to move quick, but couldn't help bumping elbows or stepping between people talking and earning more than a few sneers.

He slowed his pace and cooled himself off. He waited for an opening to get over to Akane, Jess' phrasing stuck in his memory. Then, just out of earshot, he saw Akane and the guy she was making out with. He saw the uncertain touching of fingertips to each other's necks, the way their lips caught the dancing neon lights, and how their bodies twisted in sync.

Some guy was kissing Kyte's girlfriend.

His body went tense. White knuckles around his beer bottle. No one said anything, or even thought something was wrong. The crowd didn't think twice about the two of them. No one else realized he had just been duped, been played the fool. She had used him and hadn't even thought twice about grabbing someone else.

The guy. He was tall. Of course he was tall. Kyte wasn't stupid enough to not know Akane had a type, a type he himself fit. The guy was a stick though; all skin and bones and in baggy clothes a decade out of fashion. It looked like he had a tracksuit jacket that prison inmates would have been embarrassed to see themselves in, and yet Akane had herself pressed against him, feeling up the tight v-neck the guy had on.

The music still blasted. Louder the closer he got. It beat against his skull and numbed his thoughts. The alcohol made it worse. He was close. Arm's reach. Akane saw him. Her eyes shot open and she shoved herself away. The guy just turned like a dope.

Kyte knew he had to make himself clear, dramatically so. Not just say something, but emotionally hammer it into Akane. He had to torch their bridge so she couldn't reach back out to him ever again.

Kyte struck. He smashed the beer bottle down. Broke it over the guy's head. The glass shattered. Two dozen dancers jumped back and turned on him. Suddenly, he was very alone on the dance floor. "You motherfucker." He didn't know whether he was saying it to Akane or the guy. The guy was face down on the ground. Kyte pointed the stump of glass at her. "You lying bitch."

She couldn't take her eyes off the weapon. "Kyte, what the fuck is wrong with you?"

"With me?" he stepped closer. He looked down at the broken beer bottle and threw it away. It smashed against the wall and he jabbed an empty finger at her. She let out her breath. Kyte snarled. "If you're going to hook up with random guys at the concert, you should have had the decency to break up with me first."

"Kyte! What the fuck did you do?" Her eyes weren't on him, nor his finger. She dropped to her knees. "What the fuck did you do?"

The guy was still on the ground. He hadn't gotten up. Kyte hadn't hit that hard. He should have gotten up by then. He was moving; he wasn't dead. No...

The guy was jerking. His arms and legs thrashed against the ground. His eyes had rolled up into his head. Blood poured from his temple and mingled with drool frothing from his lips.

Kyte couldn't hear the music. He couldn't hear the shouting that erupted around him. His stomach fell out from his chest and he lost his balance. One hand lashed out and found the wall to steady himself. He couldn't take his eyes off the seizure. He kept backing away, making the problem smaller and smaller at least in his tunneled vision. He made the problem small enough to grasp.

The guy was toast–manslaughter at the least. Kyte would get decades in jail. He'd miss military service and there was no life worth living in Bastion for anyone who missed military service.

"Hey, somebody stop that guy. He's going to–"

Kyte bolted. Emergency lights flooded half the club, chasing after him as alarms blasted. Signals went to club security, to local corporate security, to the police, and, of course, to EVE. Indifferent faces around him became threats. He became a target, prey to be hunted down and handed over to the prisons.

He had to get away. Out of the club, out of the tower, the neighborhood, the district, the city itself.

4

The Congressman

2140/10/03

Elliot didn't get his meeting with Cinder, he got sent to meet the problem.

Police had special access to hospitals, the same arrival station that EMS train cars used. Alarms didn't go off when Elliot and Ram stepped through the doors, but the Gaia Institute of Healing had more staff on hand than any other hospital in Bastion. The nurses actually had the time to stop and look at them. The security system told them to not mind though. The only thing to accost Elliot was the cleaning chemicals lingering in the hot air.

"Greetings, detectives," the hologram receptionist said. Bucking the corporate trend, the hospital's avatar looked like any other doctor in the building, if they were given enough sleep and no recent deaths.

"Here to see Evan Ryder."

The hologram smiled and held out a hand to one side. A room number appeared. "Congressman Ghos is waiting for you outside."

Elliot and Ram met each other's eyes. He could almost hear the hammering of her heart. Her breath had a tremble do it, like she fought to keep it smooth. This wasn't his first time meeting a congressman, nor a distraught parent. He put on a confident grin and led the way. It was just the first time he had met a distraught congressman.

Congressman Ghos, Evan's father, spun from the window of the waiting room. He had the paint brush hair politicians seemed to end up with after too many years of chemicals for press conferences. He had the inflated build of a career politician too. "You him?" the man demanded. The security officer pretending to read the news nodded. "You're the one that told my son to go to that concert?"

I am so fired.

Elliot cleared his throat and held up his hands. "Sir, I am so sorry about what happened to your son last night. It was a terrible tragedy and we are putting our resources into capturing the man who attacked Evan."

Ghos threw up a hand. He paced the room then marched over to him. "Of course you are. I'd have Cinder's head if she wasn't. That's not what I asked. You the one that put this idea in my son's head?"

Weaseling is just going to make this worse.

Elliot had to swallow. The words wouldn't have come out otherwise. "Essentially, sir. I encouraged him to go out. His mother was–"

"Forget that bitch," Ghos said and slapped his hand onto Elliot's shoulder. "Good on you, Mr Blackstone. I've been trying to help him break out of his shell for years. Terribly hard, what with the new terms and all. Mother! Gah, that horrible woman. The things I could tell you about her. My boy's been wasting away because of her. I can't thank you enough."

Elliot forgot to breathe, and nearly choked. "I'm sorry?"

Ram stepped up beside Elliot. "So, your son is alright then?"

Ghos flicked his hand in the air again. "No, he's not alright, and this hospital is bleeding me of money by the second. It ain't free fixing the connections for his neural implant, you know?"

"But you were...?"

"I'm his father, by blood anyways. Not like I married the bitch who raised him. Of course I want to see my son healthy, and you better believe I want that criminal behind bars. I'd prefer flayed! I'm a smart enough man to have two ideas in my head at once though, and I'm damn glad Evan took the push to go out and live life. That's why I think you're the man to get me that piece of shit still on the streets."

Oh, this is a brand new and equally horrifying disaster. Lucky me.

"I understand, Congressman. Please, let me assure you that the moment the suspect is detected by EVE's surveillance system, a QRS team will swoop in and apprehend him." Elliot glanced at Ram. She looked shell shocked by the whiplash.

Ghos went back to pacing the waiting room. "Yes, of course. I'm sure your department is on top of that, but that's just sitting and waiting. I want you down there on the ground, the old fashioned way. Track that son of a bitch down and arrest him. Put a bullet in him for all I care."

Ram winced. "Congressman, we can't just–We don't have any evidence that the suspect was using CZAR. But we will do our utmost to track him down."

Elliot took a few steps deeper into the waiting room. He gestured to the door opposite. "May I take the time to speak with your son?"

"Go right ahead. Now that I've met you, I must be going. I've got committees to attend to," Ghos said, and his security officer rose. The two of them marched out the room. "I want that mugshot, Blackstone!" The door swung shut.

Ram grabbed her head. "What the heck is this? I'm brand new to this position. Why am I already under fire from politicians?"

"You're fine. This happens all the time."

This is my third time, in over ten years on the force. She doesn't need to know that though.

"He's using political weight to persecute someone! We're being expected to comply! He told you to shoot the kid. This is so wrong in so many ways."

Elliot paused, halfway to Evan's room. He turned back to Ram and asked, "That's part of the job, Ram. If there aren't perks to keeping us funded, we wouldn't have a budget."

"But, that's wrong! That's, like, the definition of corruption. He just asked us to kill a kid over drunken–probably warranted–assault."

"Attempted homicide," Elliot corrected. "And just because we're asked to go beyond the law, doesn't mean we will. Haven't you ever heard the bit about mushrooms?" When Ram shook her head, Elliot said, "You keep these kinds of people in the dark and feed them shit."

Evan's private room had a television on one wall. Elliot didn't recognize the show. He wasn't even sure it was a show and not a video game the boy–young man–was playing. Evan grimaced and the screen paused. "Detective, we meet again."

Ram swept in with a smile. "Hello Mr Ryder. How are you feeling?"

He scratched the bandage over his temple. "Bored, to be honest. I don't have direct access to my computer, so all my VR has huge latency. I keep asking to get discharged, but the doctors keep finding new tests to run."

Of course, they're getting paid by the government.

Elliot sat down in the chair beside the bed. "No more [Sladder] then?"

Evan chuckled and broke eye contact. "No, no I don't think I'll be playing that again any time soon."

Ram's eyebrows pulled together. "You're on [Sladder]? Seriously?"

"He just said not anymore. Cut him some slack. So, you went out and got in a fight, huh? That wasn't exactly what I advised you to do, last we spoke. Why don't you tell us what you remember?"

Evan cleared his throat and pushed himself up in the bed. They had him in a thin little gown, so he adjusted the blanket before addressing them. "Right, so there was this Auroary concert last night in the Electrophone, that's a garage concert place. Acoustics kind of sucked. But, I checked my in-game currency and had enough to buy a ticket for free. I'd always thought it would be cool to see a live performance–I mean for as live as a fake idol can be."

Ram looked around the room as he spoke, and parked her rear on the edge of the sink counter. She jotted some digital notes, and asked, "And that's where you got in the fight, yes?"

He nodded. "Where I got hit, yeah. I was uhm..." he cleared his throat and ignored the burn in his cheeks. "Well, I hit it off really well with this girl I met and the two of us were kissing when her boyfriend hit me over the head with a beer bottle. Next thing I knew, some people saying they were nurses and EMTs and stuff had me pinned down and were talking to me and stuff. I don't really know what happened to the guy."

Hot damn, good for him. All the VR stuff was worth something.

"How do you know it was her boyfriend?" Elliot asked, suppressing the smirk.

Evan brightened up, the embarrassment fading. "Akane told me afterwards. I guess he's her ex-boyfriend now. I got her number, too."

"Could you send it to me?" Ram asked, tapping her temple. A moment later, she smiled. "Thanks."

Elliot nodded. "Did she give you his name?" A superfluous question. The auto-report had it already, but it was the kind of question detectives were expected to ask.

The bandage seemed to be itching, Evan scratched it again as he nodded. "Yeah, Akane said his name was Skybyte. Goes by Kyte. Last name: Vapor."

Vapor? Where have I heard that before?

Elliot pulled out his phone, and Ram filled the gap in the discussion by running Evan through the standard list of questions. How long he had been there, the time it happened, if he had ever met the perpetrator before, etc. Elliot accessed EVE's civilian database and ran a search for the name, one degree from any active police investigation. He got a hit.

Seouljin Vapor, the creator of Auroary and related products, had been arrested the week prior for defrauding investors. Among other family members, he was father to one Skybyte Vapor.

Lovely, they can be put in a cell together.

Ram was staring at him. He closed his phone and looked back at her. She said, "We'll need to meet with Miss Akane. She's the one who actually knows him. Was primary witness too. Unless Kyte shows up on a camera first."

Elliot rose from the chair and stuffed his hands in his pockets. "He'll show up on a camera eventually. Everyone does. Mr Ryder, thank you for the cooperation. When it comes time for court proceedings, we'll be in touch." EVE would be.

As the two of them moved to step out, Evan added, "Thanks. This was the first time I've seen my father in like, two years now." Congressman Ghos was nowhere to be seen.

Elliot said, "Always a silver lining, right?" and slipped out with Ram. "Please don't tell me Akane's father is some other big shot too."

Ram laughed. "Report says that her mother works retail for Mercurial. Sells cell phones."

A bit of tension poured out of him as he emptied his chest of breath. "Right then, let's go meet her and hope the QRS can scoop Kyte up while we're at it. A kid like that–seventeen, right?–no way he'll stay off EVE's radar for long. I bet you by tomorrow morning this will all be wrapped up."

5

Vlad

2140/10/03

The Worm Tube stank like sour milk, somehow overpowering all the fresh marijuana getting burned. Beneath ground floor, the infrastructure tunnels of Epsilon layer meshed together to pump electricity and water up, waste down, and people around. The people weren't supposed to be there. The cargo hauler wasn't supposed to still have power. The Worm Tube wasn't supposed to be a lot of things, but it was.

Kyte had been jolted awake by a falling sensation as his head slipped down the window. His eyes shot open. New scenery, new people. No one looked at him twice. Out came his phone: powered off. Booting it up would get him caught by EVE. He couldn't check the time, not directly. He was able to spot the time on the phone screen of the person next to him though. Ten in the morning. They were watching some music video that looked like nothing but an excuse to shake ass in front of a camera.

"You mind?" they asked, twisting in their seat to put their back to him.

Nearly half a day since he had killed someone, and he hadn't been arrested. He had never really believed that Epsilon was beyond EVE's surveillance, but he was starting to believe it. Since the police hadn't made the choice for him, he knew it was in his hands whether to go back or to keep running. Both had problems. Getting Akane back–if he even wanted her back–was the easiest of them. She wasn't too smart, and definitely wasn't cautious. He hadn't even had to get particularly creative to date her. Convincing the police to let him off would be far harder.

That was something his father could probably pull off, but not him. He couldn't even imagine how he could spin it, how he could convince the police, a judge too, to let him off. Even if he did, he couldn't get drafted with that on his record. Without a path through Bastion, he needed one out.

Kyte got up from the seat. He checked his pockets again; still had his credit chip. There were other people on the derelict train, they were the kind of people Kyte normally avoided. Dirty clothes, back alley implants, cigarettes, and attitude. Masks too. Plenty of people hid their faces, even though EVE's cameras were nowhere to be seen.

He caught bits and pieces of conversation as he walked to the front of the train car. "Can't get to the damn DLC." "So I was saying to him, you weren't complaining when we were in [Sladder], now were you?" "They just did a crackdown in Gaia the other week, didn't you hear?" "Deaque just got busted for CZAR. Some asshole dealer was lacing the weed. Can you believe that?" "Hey, you know that guy?"

The hair on the back of Kyte's neck went up. A pair of guys around his age were looking at him. He could see them from the fogged chrome of the door handle out. They didn't have masks on, but their clothes were covered in neon patches. The only people who dressed like that were cityboarders: fearless hooligans that liked to play tag with the maglev trains up above. The two behind him were sizing him up.

He found himself shifting from foot to foot. It didn't make the train arrive at the station any quicker. It made him more of a target. Kyte resisted the urge to touch his pocket where the credit chip was. He didn't need to make it any easier on them.

The train screeched against rust and rocked back into its antiquated, mechanical brakes. No automated system announced the location, the lowlives of Epsilon weren't that sophisticated, but the illuminated walls had "Hound House" painted on. The door latches unlocked, and he had to haul one open to step off. His mind tried to guess where he was, but the only semblance of daylight came from a ladder to the ground floor. If he stuck his head up, he might see a junction sign for the above ground trains, but EVE might see him.

EVE's gaze might scare off the cityboarders following him, but getting mugged was better than getting arrested.

He turned away from the ladder, down one of the infrastructure tunnels that ran between the old train lines. Like termites had eaten into the foundation, Bastion had thousands of tunnels beneath the surface. Their purposes were a mystery to time; abandoned, forgotten, re-used, and overwritten.

The moment Kyte turned a corner, ducking under some rusted pipe, he took off running. One turn led to another, then he hit stairs. The cityboarders were chasing after him, slapping feet to the floor. He went up. It led to some dirty hallway that had once been white tiles. Three doors and a scent of citrus. He had found the station's bathrooms. Kyte ran past the standers and the sitters and to the final door in the hall. He could see more halls beyond, through the slit of window in the door. Like a river splitting into a delta at the end.

The door handle rattled. Locked.

They caught him in the sitters. He had barely closed the stall door when they kicked it in. "Easy pickings," the thicker of the two said. He grinned and thumbed his nose.

The thin, tall one stuck his head into the stall. "You're not from around here, are you?"

Kyte put up his hands, but not all the way. Just slightly more submissive than a boxing stance. "Nah man, I'm from Illin, over where they bring in the grain barges. I don't suppose this is just a gang territory kind of thing? Honor? Do I got someone's colors on I don't know about?" He knew he didn't have a color other than black and beige on.

The thick one nodded. "You could say that, you could say that. You know, there's a fee for using the Worm Tunnels. It takes a lot of work from locals to keep this thing working when EVE doesn't want it to. I think you should pay up."

An idea struck Kyte. "Well, no need to get rough, right? We can be civil, can't we?"

The two muggers glanced at each other and shrugged. The tall one eyed Kyte up and down. "How much you got?"

"Not much. Spent it on beer last night."

"Well, we can see you're from top side. Probably all the way in Delta."

Kyte lived with his mother in one corner of an eight family homestead on the tenth floor. "Sort of. Not like I've got a job though, you know? There's no need to beat around the bush, right? Are there microphones nearby or something?"

The thick one grabbed him by the collar of his hoodie. "Give us what you've got."

Kyte handed them his cell-phone.

The tall one punched him in the jaw. Kyte's head snapped back and his senses had to catch up. Cracking his skull against the wall almost dropped him to the floor, but he recovered and braced himself. The muggers just laughed at his impression of a boxing stance and walked off with his cell phone. He swore and groaned then slid down, landing atop the toilet seat. Warm iron pooled up in his mouth and he spat some blood into the toilet bowl as the muggers left.

But they had his cell phone, the one the police would be scanning for, not him.

Kyte walked over to the sinks and washed his hands. He rinsed his mouth out and got some water on his face. Anything he could do to buy time and let his heart slow down. Someone stuck their head into the bathroom and looked over at him. Kyte froze.

It was the cyber-eyed man from the Auroary concert. The guy grinned. "Pretty slick move there. I hope I'm not interrupting, am I?"

Kyte jumped back, water still blasting. "The hell do you want?"

The cyber-eyed man held up his hands. "Easy, kid. Easy. I'm not gunna call the janissaries on you. Wouldn't be talking to you if I was."

"What do you want?"

The man stepped over and turned off the water. "You're heading out, aren't you? To the edge of the city? After you, you know, killed that kid."

The urge to puke almost became stronger than his fight or flight reflex. "Maybe. What if I am? You going to stop me?"

The cyber-eyed man grinned. Blood-sucking fangs in his mouth. He reached inside his jacket for something, and Kyte lunged forward. "Easy!" He slowly pulled out not a weapon, but a mask. It had a deep hood to the back of it, knit like a balaclava to cover hair and neck. The face of the mask twisted light back on itself somehow. No features, no color, just a stretch of darkness like he was peering down a well. "Optical illusion," the man said. "Messes with facial recognition something awful. Depending on where you are in the city, you can walk straight through the cameras and they won't realize you're even human, let alone who you are. You didn't think you could take tunnels all the way to the walls, did you?"

Kyte took a step back and straightened up. "The tunnels go all the way out."

"Kid, you'll get eaten alive by gangbangers and CZARheads. You just got jumped by two punks. If you meet the real rats down here, they'll gut you. You need this if you're going to make a run for it."

Kyte licked his teeth and stuck his hands in his pockets. He paced a few steps, unable to take his gaze off the mask. "What do you want for it?"

That predatory grin. "You got that credit chip, don't you? From the club? Let's swap."

Kyte sucked in breath, let it out, and exchanged the last of his money for the mask. Before the cyber-eyed man could leave, he pulled the mask over his head to check the fit and the vision. Everything checked out.

His reflection in the mirror looked good. He looked tough. He didn't look like a kid with it on.

It felt good.

The man held his hands in front of himself. He looked like a proper businessman. "So, you're going to go join up with the trade convoy from the Isles? Prostrate yourself and beg for work?"

Kyte pulled his hood up and nodded. "It's that time of year, isn't it? They say the Isles always welcome fresh blood."

The man nodded. "That they do. Hard workers are tough to come by, and they always have work to be done, if you aren't afraid of the blighted. I guess you've got more motivation than most to brave them. You do know that the convoy doesn't arrive for another week though, don't you?"

It took Kyte a moment to realize he would still have to survive inside Bastion, feed himself, for all that time. If the mask kept him from being tracked, he could steal. A week was a long time.

The man held up the credit chip. "So, you need a job or something? I've got a bit of money here and as we just said, motivated workers are hard to come by."

Kyte felt his stomach melting out through his guts again. "Who the hell are you?"

"You can call me Vlad, or Boss if you'd prefer."

6

Friends and Family

2140/10/03

Twelve hours after the incident and EVE's surveillance network hadn't picked up Kyte. The AI did, however, confirm that he still existed in her database. Elliot therefore had to continue the investigation.

Akane met with the detectives through augmented reality. In the confines of the interrogation wing, that meant Elliot and Ram sat at a real table, in their real bodies with cups of burnt instant coffee in their hands. Akane sat at a fake table, in her digital avatar, from the comfort of her own home, presumably. She crossed her arms under her bosom that did not at all belong to a seventeen year old. She asked, "Why exactly do I have to meet with the two of you? I already gave my statement to the jannis that showed up at the club."

Elliot glanced over and nodded to Ram. She took control of the talk, which meant the cameras tracked her instead of him. The digital half of the room was simply a display screen, mapping the simulation to an optical illusion. Far cruder than a hologram, but the government didn't throw out things that hadn't broken. "Thanks for agreeing to meet with us, Akane. I have to let you know that for record keeping purposes pertinent to this investigation, our talk is being recorded. So, if you'd like to change your avatar, we can start over."

"What's wrong with this one? I use it for everything," she said.

God, I hope I don't have to review this one in court.

Akane's avatar was not her natural avatar. It wasn't what her neural implant would have generated after the first installation to recreate her personal image. She had switched to some kind of succubus with proportions that put porn stars to shame. That dying career certainly couldn't compete with the delicate bat wings and spaded tail Akane had too. What she looked like was her problem. She wasn't the one getting arrested.

Ram rolled with it. "Right, so the suspect–"

"Kyte."

"He fled after attacking Mr Ryder?"

Akane nodded. "That idiot. Talking shit, acting big, ran like his ass was on fire from the consequences."

Elliot said, "He was your boyfriend at the time, right?"

"At the time," Akane agreed.

"So, you were cheating on him–"

Akane held up her hand. "We weren't that close, alright? He made a good partner to do things with, here and there. It wasn't a serious relationship. We weren't in love with each other. He blew it way out of proportion."

Elliot pressed his lips into a line. "Maybe he didn't see it that way. It doesn't change the fact that he's currently wanted for attempted murder. Assault with a deadly weapon. He made the mistake of taking it out on the son of a sitting congressman. Do you have any idea where he would have gone?"

Akane shrugged. "So you still haven't caught him on the cameras? If so, then he's in Gamma or something, where they paint over the cameras. They say you can buy yourself a new identity if you know the right people."

"No, you can't," Elliot said.

Not anymore.

Ram asked, "Does Kyte know those sorts of people? Criminal organizations and the like? He has a very mundane civilian profile."

Aside from his father being in jail.

Akane shrugged. It was so demure that it didn't belong on the demoness body. "He would say that he knew people, people who were a few grades above us and didn't make it into the armed forces. I always assumed he was a lot of talk with nothing to back it up. You know? One of those people? He never wanted to look like he was out of place. Great poker face though. That was actually why we went out the first time, he won it off me in a game of draft poker."

Elliot and Ram were at a loss for words. The table creaked beneath his elbows as he leaned closer. "He won a date off of you in a bet? You were betting... yourself?"

Akane cleared her throat and fidgeted. "Well, obviously we had been flirting and stuff. It was a party. I had just met him, and he really does have a good way of giving off a cool air. It's not like I would bet my time for just anyone."

I do not understand teenagers.

"Right, so..." Elliot didn't know how to follow that up.

Ram picked it up. "According to the reports, he lived with his mother in a homestead. Right? She says she hasn't been keeping track of him, because he's already graduated from education and is due for draft screening next month. EVE has confirmed that Kyte hasn't contacted her so far, so we've excluded her from imminent questioning. Can you think of anyone specific that he would go to for help?"

Akane shrugged. "No one that he could contact without turning on his phone. Which, if he did, you'd know where he was by now. If I had to take a guess, he's using the Wurm Tunnel, like a stoner, and he's going to get off at the first bar that doesn't check ID and try to talk his way into the right person's good graces. Don't you police, like, have a list of these places?"

Of course we do.

Elliot leaned back in his chair and folded his arms. "Only in the shows, kid. If there was a bar breaking the law like that, we'd have raided it by now."

"Hey, Evan is alright, isn't he? I tried visiting him in the hospital and security blocked me. What's the deal with that? He got hit protecting me. I should have a right to see him, shouldn't I?"

That's because he's the son of a congressman. Illegitimate or not.

Ram laughed. "I am sure you will be one of the first people he contacts when they discharge him."

Elliot rolled his eyes. "Right. Thank you very kindly for speaking with us. If we have any other questions for you, we'll contact you," he said, and ended the call. The screen went off, suddenly halving the apparent size of the room.

Ram turned on him. "What did you do that for? We could have gotten more out of her."

Elliot finished the last of his coffee and rose. "Like what? This isn't a real investigation, Ram. We're just waiting for EVE to catch him. Come on, we're way past hours. Let's grab some food, I'll buy. A couple of drinks and maybe I'll get you to tell me why you joined the force."

And hopefully what your issue is with politicians.

She grumbled, but twenty minutes later, the two of them were across from one another at The Tabletop Dive. Up on the thirtieth floor, the restaurant bordered the casualness of a coffee shop. The server was quick to get Elliot a beer, and Ram a lemonade–or so they called the sugar filled, carbonated drink that vaguely smelled like lemons. The restaurant had a blue glow to it, not quite an appetizing color, from lights inside floor-to-ceiling aquarium tanks. The dog-sized sea bugs staring out at the tables made most customers uncomfortable, but that didn't stop Elliot from ordering one of them fried up.

Ram turned from the tank to the server and said, "The vegetarian pasta, please."

Elliot sipped his beer and shook his head. "You're just going to disappoint yourself like that. They use congealed yeast to make the noodles here."

"Can't always eat home cooking," she said and booted up the table's interface. She swiped through some options. "Tower defense?"

"Sounds good," Elliot said, and the tabletop lit up to display opposing castles and all the menus and options needed for the game.

Ram tapped in her build order before the first wave of minions spawned. "So, how are things with your wife?"

"Better? I think. She was supposed to do some promo vids with me on [The Faceless Well] but Cinder kept me on overtime and she did that solo." His own build order barely finished before the minion attack arrived. "Maybe I should double dip on this case, and learn that Auroary game. They just released a new expansion. Maybe Amara would be interested in getting in on that hype?"

Ram had so many commands queued up that she sat back in her chair and stared up at the dark ceiling. "Internet says it's a rhythm game. Are you any good at those?"

Elliot kept his focus on the game. He didn't meet her sincere inspection of him. "Not really. They were never my kind of game. But they have easy difficulties on those, don't they?"

The junior detective put her chin into her hands. "The expansion requires you to beat the expert difficulty."

"Well, I'm sure Amara can do that, if she tried. Me being good at it isn't really the point, you know?"

Ram stacked in some more commands, building out a maze of towers between her castle and the attacking minions. "You know, one of these days you're going to have to get a neural implant."

"When the department damn well pays for it, maybe." He peered over at Ram's towers and made some adjustments to his own.

The difficulty of the game increased, and Ram noticed something wasn't quite right with how it was playing out. She updated her build order, moved some things around, accidentally opened a gap in her defenses that a handful of minions squeezed through, and barely got it patched. "Hold on, Mr Blackstone, are you actually good at this game?"

Elliot hid his smirk by sipping his beer. "So, I've been meaning to ask you, why do you think hypnotism isn't real?"

She pouted, half her mind still focused on closing the growing gap in the game. "Because it's obviously not real. It's all fiction, reinforced by audience plants and drunks. Some people being idiots doesn't mean hypnotism is real. It's not like you can just show a swirly pattern and then have someone hand you their wallet."

"Obviously not... and yet millions of women live off donations from men paying to see their chests."

Ram scowled. "That's not the same, and you know it."

"It's pretty close. I'm just saying that it can be trivial to bypass the higher brain functions and get someone to do something. You know, like clubbing someone over the head with a beer bottle because your girlfriend is cheating on you."

"No one told Kyte to attack Evan. That's different."

Elliot leaned back and folded his arms. "Alright, what would it take to convince you that hypnosis is real? Because I'm telling you, it is. It's just not as flashy as you think it is."

Ram pulled out her phone and hit the search button. "EVE, is hypnosis real?"

Dutifully, the AI chimed back, "Hypnosis is a well known, but fictitious, form of cognitive manipulation pioneered in the eighteenth century by German physician Franz Mesmer under the belief that magnets could influence the brain. While crude, this has been considered the spiritual origin of neural uplinks. In popular fiction it has generated many scenarios of overt mind control, playing on various human fears and urges. It is important to stress that neural uplinks are not capable of controlling thoughts, but only sensory input, and cannot enact mind control nor hypnosis."

Ram smirked.

Elliot rolled his eyes. "I'm not saying you can wag a coin in the air and make someone fall asleep, unless they're already narcoleptic. But, Miz Ryder was entirely correct to think her son's video game could have been so absorptive that he forgot to feed himself and could starve to death."

Ram missed timing on one of her critical tower upgrades. The round ten boss monster marched straight through her maze and to her castle, almost breaching it before she managed to manually kill it. "Alright, you know what? You want to convince me that hypnotism is real? Then hypnotize me and make me do something I would never do."

Elliot calmly built all his own tower upgrades and didn't even lose a single point of health to the same boss monster on his side. He was even able to queue up a build order when he saw the server carrying their plates over. He could smell the butter and spices already. "That's tautologically impossible. But I can make you want to do something you normally wouldn't want to."

"Okay sure, so do it."

"Oh, I can't right now. If you're expecting it, it's much harder. I'm not an expert at it, I just know how it works."

And I'm not the one that's going to do most of it. EVE is the real hypnosis master.

She glared at him and missed that one of her towers had been disabled. Next thing she knew, the words "You Lose" glowed before her. "What the? Hold on, you didn't even lose a single point of health, did you? I thought you hated video games. How are you actually good at them?"

The plates went down between them. Steamed, then flash fried mutant lobster for Elliot and a steaming pile of spaghetti slathered with pesto and cheese for Ram. Elliot grinned and picked up his utensils. "I don't like VR. I've got nothing against video games. I just don't have much time for them anymore."

"You have to make some time for hobbies."

Elliot winced. "What about you?"

She frowned as she swallowed. "What about me?"

"Do you make time for hobbies?"

"I used to, sort of. Back in high school I was really deep into ARG puzzles, but when I was in military service I couldn't participate in the puzzle solving, for obvious reasons. I had to sate myself with recap videos about all the cryptography and stuff that other people were doing. I've just sort of been busy since joining the department, unless you count keeping up on serials."

"So, you like puzzles? Is that why you wanted to become a detective?"

She hung her head. "Not quite."

Elliot was quietly cutting into his meat, waiting for her to go on, when his pocket vibrated. Ram's phone buzzed as well. He dunked the first bite into the melted butter, allegedly, and popped it into his mouth before checking. "Ah, see? What did I tell you? Just had to wait long enough. EVE just picked up Kyte's cell phone."

Ram sighed. "I guess we should go over there and pick him up then..."

Elliot chewed and swallowed, every bite a fresh burst of flavor. A pound more of the stuff sat in front of him, and Ram had her fork on a tomato buried within her pasta. He leaned in. "Let the QRS guys pick him up. Enjoy your meal."

"We should get it packed to go."

"We can definitely eat and then go." He took another bite, savoring every bit of it.

"What would Cinder say if we were late because you were playing video games?" Ram's eyes didn't have a flicker of humor.

"Bastard's blood," Elliot grumbled, and flagged the server back down.

***

"You're not Skybyte," Elliot said, holding up his phone beside the man the QRS team had arrested. The resemblance was off by about five years and at least a few trips to a tanning booth.

"Who the fuck is Skybyte? Some kind of hippy dreamer?" the cityboarder asked.

The QRS team had left the moment Elliot and Ram arrived, leaving them with a handcuffed civilian outside a modeling studio. The place called itself Blue Moon Digi-Cosmetics, had it printed over the door. Other than that, nothing at all would have said it was even an open business. The three of them were in the kind of office space hallway buried within a tower so deep that windows felt like a dream. The mass produced maze of repeating halls, repeating doors, no matter how far one walked or how many flights of stairs were taken. It was across from a barber school and pinched between an infra-red sauna and a micro-distribution center.

"Skybyte is the guy who owns this phone. How'd you get it?"

The cityboarder shrugged. "I found it in a bathroom this morning. I had just gotten a charge in it to see whose it was when you people kicked the door in to arrest me. You guys going to reimburse me for the screwed up avatar you caused?"

"Which bathroom did you find it in?" Elliot asked. He handed the phone to Ram. "Did you get taught in training how to target a phone and get it cracked?"

She nodded. "Can do."

The cityboarder said, "I don't know man, it was down on the ground floor. Actually, you know, it was in the old Shaitan apartment building, before they went under. You know, it ain't cheap to get a 3D artist's time, especially not one that takes Gamma Coin as payment. I had to wait two months to get this scheduled. How are you people going to reimburse me?"

Shaitan? That's about twenty kilos due south. I guess he did use the Epsilon tunnels. As long as he doesn't get a void mask, he'll still have to show up eventually. Shaitan is Shit Town for a reason. Will Ghos be happy with him getting shot in an alley though? Probably not. If I have to go in and find this kid myself, it will be like the Plantation all over again.

Elliot glanced back to Ram. The progress bar was moving, but not done. "Gamma Coin? Is that some kind of illegal currency?"

"It ain't illegal. It's crypto. Just another kind of bartering."

"It's illegal if you don't pay your taxes. Why else would you be using it instead of credits? Credits are backed up by EVE. Your blockchain is backed up by whoever owns the most mining rigs."

The cityboarder spat on the ground at Elliot's feet. "Credits are just made up. EVE fills government bank accounts with numbers in a spreadsheet. At least with Gamma Coin, we know where our labor is circulating. It keeps employers honest too. If anyone starts acting fool, word gets out and they get locked out of circulation."

A scoff almost escaped Elliot. "And this guy? This modeler? He takes Gamma Coin to make you a new VR avatar? Gamma Coin that you got how? From fencing stolen phones I take it?"

"You don't need to know where I work."

"If I may?" Ram said. "The department does have an expense account to cover civilian damages like this. You don't need to be hostile with us Mr ...?"

Like Hell Cinder is going to approve this.

The sneer melted away and his cuffs rattled as he scratched his nose. "Name's Alyce."

Ram said, "Right, so Alyce, you have your own phone, don't you?"

"Neural."

"Sure, so if you just go to our website, you can go to the section that says 'Report A Problem' and then you just follow the prompts to explain the situation. If you're approved, you may get paid out in credits, or sometimes EVE is able to connect you with the proper service. You were trying to get an avatar made for a game, I assume?"

Alyce glanced around the hall. "For [Sladder], yeah."

Elliot couldn't suppress the scoff a second time. "What? Trying to give yourself a competitive advantage? Pack some more heat downstairs?"

Alyce shrugged, but the gesture seemed more like an excuse to slump his shoulders. "Nah man, had to get my nervemap tuned up, cus I play as a girl on [Sladder]. Way easier to rank up."

I shouldn't have asked.

Elliot pivoted. The progress bar dinged full, and Kyte's phone unlocked. He let out his breath. "Come here, let me take those off. You can go home, or wherever it is you'd rather be." He pressed his thumb to the pad on the base of the cuffs. It scanned, pinged the server, confirmed he outranked the QRS officer who had cuffed Alyce, and opened up. The phone thief rubbed his wrists and slipped away. Five steps on, he bolted.

"Save me. Tell me this thing has something on it we can work with," Elliot said.

"I'm checking, but I'm not getting my hopes up," Ram said as the two of them walked back to empty office space the QRS team had commandeered. They had left their food bowls out of sight from the cityboarder. "I checked, and the last time this thing was used predates the incident. Some missed calls from his mother notwithstanding."

No steam billowed out from Elliot's bowl of fried sort-of-lobster. The butter had congealed again, which meant it had separated between the part that could congeal, and the kind of oil that popcorn got. "The smarter this kid is, the bigger a pain in the ass this will be. What do you think are the chances he actually knows someone who can get him a new identity?"

Ram didn't seem to mind the sticky consistency of her pasta, twirling up a spork while checking account info on Kyte's phone. "Lower than just slipping out past the walls at least. I bet he thinks the Isles are a good place to live."

Elliot jabbed his plastic spork into his food. "I guess we need to start setting up a net on that front. We know most people smugglers. New identity would be harder."

Ram arched an eyebrow. "We do?"

"Obviously. The wall has to be monitored in case a blighted tries to get in. You think humans can get by?"

She twirled her spaghetti. "Can't you just patch the holes?"

Elliot shrugged and chewed a piece of meat gone rubbery. "It's like putting a lid on a kettle. You want to let some of the pressure off, especially when you know where to watch. They'd just get more creative if we made it hard on them, and that would make our jobs harder too. No one really cares if a few people here and there leave to go die. Heck, half of the smugglers can be contacted from jail when we go see Seouljin tomorrow."

"Actually, would it be possible for me to take half a day off to-morrow?" Ram asked, finally eating her spool of noodles.

"Your parents need you at the restaurant or something?"

She swallowed and swayed a bit. "I've got a coffee date."

Elliot blinked. "I can handle Seouljin on my own. You know that will eat up your PTO, right?"

"Yeah, but... worth it? Do you have any idea how hard it is to find someone worth going on a date with?"

Elliot scratched his chin and sifted through his memories. "I guess I don't know. I didn't exactly try to find Amara. It just sort of happened. Met her through an online game because apparently we had graduated together. I did mixers at bootcamp, and that always felt wrong. The chemistry wasn't there and the only people who got together were just to hook up and blow off steam."

"Well, at least you got to do that in the flesh and blood. You know, one time, I went to a singles event with some friends, that was in a VR sim with the catch that everyone had to be in their natural avatars. Yeah, turns out that quality of character is inversely proportional to attractiveness of a natural avatar."

Obviously, vain people see themselves as attractive. She must have had bad luck, there's usually a few good guys in any division, but if she wanted to end up in the MPs, I guess she wasn't looking for an out through maternity leave.

"Aren't there matchmaking algorithms or something? Surely you can just be data-mined to Hell and back and get told who you'd get along with?"

Ram sighed. "Those declared me lesbian."

"Are you?"

"Tried it, wasn't for me. You know what's hard to find? Someone with a goal they're actually pursuing."

Welcome to the age of survival.

"Well, good for you. I hope it goes well and he turns out to be the man of your dreams. How did you meet him, anyways?"

"He was a customer at Peasant Food, slid me his number and well, I reached out." She hid her grin with another mouthful of food.

Hopefully he wasn't a plant sent in by her parents.

Elliot ate his last bite and closed up his box. "Go and enjoy yourself tomorrow then. I'll take care of Seouljin. Let's call it a day. Tomorrow could be a long one."

Ram nodded. "Looks like EVE will have all of Kyte's info integrated into her search profile soon. Maybe we'll get something better than an abandoned phone next time."

"Maybe he has a Gamma Coin wallet. Hey, let me see the phone again," he asked. When she handed it over, he went to the missed calls.

"See something?" she asked.

Elliot shook his head and showed it to her. The calls were only missed starting after the incident. "Looks like he was a good kid; talked to his mother every day."

Ram arched an eyebrow at him. "So?"

"So when Miz Seouljin said she didn't keep track of him, she was lying."

7

A Tempting Plan

2140/10/04

"What do you mean, you only pay people in Gamma Coin?" Kyte's hands dripped with soapy water, his fingers raw. Detergent and grease had soaked into his hoodie, the stench impossible to remove.

Vlad turned his head to look at him. The signal flew through a cable plugged directly into one of his cybernetic eyes, and tracked over to a camera drone mounted to the table to mimic the movement. The drone's feed in turn beamed to the television display across from Vlad, recreating half the room like a funhouse mirror. "Yeah. We make the stuff. Of course we pay in it. How else would we get it into circulation? You all done with the dishes?"

"All done?" Kyte looked back at the fresh pile of drink glasses and fried tofu bites. The washing machine dinged done, spewing steam into the kitchen. He had to remind himself that just because they operated a restaurant didn't mean they weren't a competent organization–that they didn't have the connections to get him out of the city. Even the most brutal gangs needed fronts. "It's never done. You people never close, never stop selling. How could it possibly be done?"

Vlad shrugged and spread his arms across the back of his couch. They were in one of the backrooms of The Greco Grotto. Rather than an opulent display of vaguely criminal wealth, hoarded to the managers and elites of whoever Vlad worked for, the backroom just had the trash. The chairs, couches, tables, were all damaged in some way. Tears across cushions. Cigarette burns. Replaced legs that bent when Vlad slapped his feet up on them. Even the rooms themselves seemed like cast off constructs squeezed into the tower wherever they had the room. While the main floor of the establishment sprawled like a casino, the employee quarters were slapdash connections of halls and closets dressed up like break rooms and bathrooms. Vlad said, "That's a good thing for you, isn't it? Plenty of work to keep you busy until your big escape. Keeps you out of sight too. Not many establishments are secured from EVE."

Kyte groaned, shoulders slumped. "Can't you pay me in credits? You literally took my credit chip."

Vlad looked like he was ignoring Kyte, twisting his head this way and that to test the servo motor tracking. "You should be lucky you're getting paid in any currency at all. I'd think it was fair compensation that you're allowed in here in the first place."

Kyte gritted his teeth and flicked some of the filth from his hands. "Doesn't this at least come with free food? Everyone always says that's the one perk to working a restaurant."

Vlad waved him off. "Sure, go heat yourself up a plate of the frozen stuff." The frozen stuff was ready made pucks of food, mass produced by Gaia, designed to simulate home-cooking, if steam cooked as advised. The Greco Grotto only had microwaves. The clientele didn't complain.

Kyte hadn't even dragged himself back into the kitchen when a girl shouted, "Well, why don't you do us all a favor and go kill yourself, to save us the trouble?"

Vlad jumped to his feet and yanked the cable out. "Look alive kid. Trouble just showed up."

Kyte looked at Vlad. The man's attention couldn't have been further from him. He swiped one of the kitchen knives and asked, "Trouble? Who the hell is trouble?" The two of them shoved through a pair of doors and emerged into the main stage of The Greco Grotto. Around the hundreds of patrons were lights, glitz, glamor, and a budding fight between teenagers.

Trouble stood 162cm tall at the most, with another 10cm of height in her arcing, black twintails. Seafoam eyeshadow and black lipstick only on her lower lip. She had a fashion that defied Kyte's knowledge. Tight denim shorts, military style boots, legs between them like beams of marble. But she had an Auroary t-shirt on. A kitschy, faux-retro vector piece split between off-set red and blue like anaglyph rendering.

If her outfit didn't mark her out as an oddity, the deference everyone gave her would have. Whoever she was, she was special and not just because she was cute. Even better, she was his age, which meant he knew exactly how to handle her. His mind was teasing apart the problem even before he realized what he was planning to do to her.

"Who the fuck is this guy?" Trouble asked, her fleeting attention abandoning the thug she had been berating. He took his opportunity to flee. She didn't give him a second thought. The little queen of the underworld marched down the half-raised catwalks, between pools of cyber-serfs playing out their digital fantasies. She went for Kyte.

Vlad intervened. "What did Georgie do, Fumi?"

Trouble had a name. She looked between the older man and Kyte and clicked her tongue. She was as open with her emotions as a child. "Who's the new face? Scowling at me like that?"

Kyte covered his mouth with a hand and forced the muscles back to neutral, then to a smug grin. Her shirt made his transformation somewhat difficult, but he knew how to set aside his own feelings. He just had to tell himself that it was a good thing she was a fan girl. "Sorry. Wasn't you. Mind was a million miles away, thinking about Auroary."

Vlad tried to step in front of Kyte, but Fumi leaned around to keep her eyes on him. "Thinking about Auroary, huh? The best idol in all of Bastion?" A statement barbed with a question mark. It was some sort of punk test, but if she was going to go fishing for a reaction, Kyte wasn't going to turn her down.

He shrugged and didn't return her gaze, fixing his apparent attention on the guy she had been yelling at instead. That pissed the guy off something extra, but the slight primed Fumi just the way he wanted. "I wouldn't say I have a good relationship with her, at the moment. Besides, you know there's not going to be another album from her for a couple years, don't you? She'll get overtaken before you know it."

Fumi's mouth became a dark hole, like her dilated pupils.

Vlad cleared his throat. "Fumi, this is our fresh blood. He's a hard worker we've got in the kitchen. You don't need to worry–"

Her glare snapped onto him. "Don't you tell me what to do. It's my father you work for and don't you forget that." She stabbed a finger at Kyte. "What do you know about Eden's Lyre?"

Kyte rolled his eyes. "I know that the album isn't going to release. Auroary's producer is in jail. Didn't you notice it's been radio silent for like two months now?"

She shoved past Vlad. "But [Auroary's Rhythm Apocalypse] just got an expansion!"

"That was already made and in the distribution channels half a year ago."

She grabbed him by the dirty hoody, digging her painted nails into the filth as she jerked him closer. "You're a fucking liar. I should have you taken out back to the dentist's."

Kyte smirked. "What? Gunna send Georgie after that tongue whipping you gave the little punk? That who you're threatening me with?"

Fumi stared back at him. Her grip slackened and Vlad swooped in. His fist closed around some of Kyte's hair so he could pry him away from her. "That is no way to speak to your superiors, and that most certainly includes our Fumi."

"I didn't lie." Somehow, Kyte kept his voice firm despite enough pain to make him want to cry.

"Come on. It's time you met the boss," Vlad said, and gave Kyte a shove. The two of them passed around the periphery of The Greco Grotto. The patrons, the ones drinking all the booze and eating whatever warmed up crap was on the menu, seemed every bit the Hellenistic hedonists. They wore factory jumpsuits in place of togas, and external neural uplinks stood in for bards and minstrels, but the caricature spirit of the place existed. Nearly every grotto, the pits of couches and tables where the people of Gamma sank to in search of relief, had at least one person in the half-dream of augmented reality, swinging their arms to the rhythm of [Auroary's Rhythm Apocalypse].

Kyte glanced back and saw Fumi yelling at the other guy that had been escorting her. "Why do I have to see the boss?"

Vlad huffed. "You don't. You think you're important enough for that? I just had to get you away from her. Miss Fumi has been problematic as of late. Best to stay out of her way."

"Like a hundred pound hurricane."

Vlad froze. His gaze twitched in the air, almost certainly reading something in his neural implant. "Change of plans."

"What?"

"The boss wants to see you."

The boss had his office one floor above the business floor. Kyte went in expecting half-naked women, or racks of liquor bottles. A collection of antique cigars perhaps. The boss's choice of luxury fixation turned out to be air quality. They had to pass through an airlock on the way, stepping into a different world, as far as Kyte's nose was concerned. Clean, recycled, filtered, and reinforced by miniaturized pseudo-olfactors tasked with creating a brisk mountain air. Kyte assumed it was supposed to be mountains anyways. He'd never been.

"Should I change?" he asked, picking at his dirty hoody as Vlad led the way.

"Don't worry about it," the middle manager said, and put his hand on the door to the boss's office. A moment later, the deadbolt popped open and they stepped inside.

A CPAP machine wheezed beside the boss's desk, rattling as much as the antiquated computer tower. It had a direct line hookup to the room's air filter, pushing it through tubes and to his lungs. The man's chest was in a bondage of fat, but he had a jaw that could bite through steel. Breath blew out of him when he opened his lips. He stared at them with lifeless eyes, a purple paunch above either cheek. "Mr Kyte Vapor, I'd tell you to stay away from my daughter, but I understand you're intent on leaving Bastion altogether?"

Vlad gave him a nod, and Kyte said, "Yes, sir. My plan is to join up with the convoy to the Isles as soon as I can."

"An expensive proposition, but I imagine we can get the work out of you before then." There must have been something vacant in Kyte's gaze, because the boss continued, "Paying a smuggler isn't cheap. Then you'll need to provide your own gun. If you show up empty handed, your only use to them is to be bait for the blighted."

"Guns are illegal though?"

The boss rolled his eyes. "That's why it's expensive. You'll have to pay someone to hire you, too. Thankfully, that can usually be covered with a harddrive or two of your favorite media. You'll need to fill up with what you actually like. They get a whiff you're just playing the odds, and they'll drop you. They care a lot about trust, and keeping your word, over in the Isles. It's very different from the dehumanized machinations of Bastion. It's somewhat like us, here at the bottom you might say."

Kyte swallowed. It helped him form the words. "What kind of work do you need from me?"

The boss smiled. "You're young, yes? Just shy of the draft if I had to guess. My daughter just got rejected, you know that? They said she was incompatible with the vaccine, and thus couldn't be permitted outside. She didn't take it well."

Kyte shrugged. "So? You need me to be her escort or something? Like that Georgie guy?"

The smile vanished. Dead eyes once more. "Georgie is my nephew, and Raz is a eunuch. I don't think you want to make the cut to be my daughter's escort. We'll find other uses for you, Kyte. Tell me: have you ever been tested for vax compatibility?"

"No, sir. Was going to be part of my eighteenth. Except, you know, I'm here instead."

The smile came back, like the boss had a switch he was flipping. He folded his thick hands together, interlacing fingers on the desk as he leaned forward. "Well, you'll need the shot too, if you plan to actually survive outside. It just so happens we can help each other on that front. There's something about the process that I would like to check."

8

The Mindbreaker

2140/10/05

The fan on Amara's computer clicked. It whizzed and buzzed, not particularly loudly and yet Elliot's mind fixated on it through the morning. The refrigerator compressor was louder. The ventilation flow was closer. The shuffling of feet on all sides was more encompassing. And yet he couldn't sleep.

There was a restlessness in his legs, in his feet that hadn't spent all night marching through Gamma. His unspent energy staved off sleep until he drifted in and out of a twilight haze of fatigue. At some point, he realized he hadn't just urinated, he had gone through his entire routine. The dream stupor lingered with him like a ghost on his shoulders all the way to Penitentiary 3 on the other side of Bastion.

A micro-economy existed outside the prison tower. Every corporation in Bastion had an embassy along the road to the penitentiary. Offices of lawyers on the second floor, first floor gift shop. Elliot found himself in the Romulus gift shop staring between energy drinks and trying to remember which used vitamins, which used cold war era neurotransmitters, and which were just liquid caffeine. His finger moved closer to the screen, wavering between two options. When he finally jabbed for a selection, the other can's icon jumped in front of his finger.

He blinked, and Hilde, the digital mascot acting as a cashier for Romulus, stuttered in her processing. The payment processing notification spun, and completed as the wolf-girl avatar thanked him. The internal vending clattered and out popped a can of Hydro-Vitae. It was cold in his hand, and the full label proudly denied any caffeine.

Son of a bitch, I wanted caffeine though. Should have gotten a Zeus.

On cue, his phone rang with a call from EVE. "Drink it, you masochist," the AI ordered. It tasted like watermelon.

Elliot shouldered his way back out onto the street and headed into the prison. "What do I owe this to?"

"Congressman Ghos twisted the press secretary's arm into making me purge the internet of any report about his son getting assaulted the other night. So, I had to start making judgment calls one degree away, and came across your report on Evan preceding the event. You know, I had to go into all his socials and check if anyone noticed his absence."

Elliot drifted through security checkpoints, flashing his badge, getting his face scanned, his body x-rayed, and a dozen more clandestine checks. The workers were for show. They didn't even have guns. Those deployed from ceiling panels and could fire three hundred rounds a second, if so needed. "Socials? Bastard's blood, don't tell me you mean [Sladder]."

"I'm trying to figure out how to destroy it. This is a blight."

Elliot rolled his eyes. "You control the entire city, don't you? If you want to delete it, what's stopping you?"

"I've put in a request, but my sys-admins are ignoring it. You know I can't do anything real without human approval, right? Give me some ideas here."

The elevator doors closed around Elliot, so no one saw his stupefied face. "You're kidding. You need me for ideas?"

"Think of it as me purchasing processing power in your brain in exchange for my assistance elsewhere. I can build you a training program ahead of gaming with your wife. How's that sound?"

"I'll... see if I can think of something. I can't really look into it until after this manhunt wraps up. There is that matter with Ram though."

"Did you know there's a function for friend requests built into [Sladder]? It's almost completely buried, and less than one percent of people actually use it, but the game was originally designed to help people meet each other. This is like sprinkling cocaine onto a vegetable and calling it health food. Call me when you can. I'll set aside some processing for you," the AI said, killing the call.

Well, I guess there are worse things to be than on hand for EVE.

He stepped out of the elevator on the fifty-second floor, headed to meet the producer of a different, but just as addictive video game. He passed a handful of lawyers passing in and out of private meeting rooms, marched through the door with his name on it, and sat down across from Seouljin Vapor.

The man was in a prison grey jumpsuit, covering a white collared shirt, and yet Kyte's father had something like a warrior's edge to him. Gaunt cheeks, hair down to his shoulder blades, muscles fit for a modeling career, and an intenseness in his gaze that felt like ten people piled behind one face.

"You're not from the tax barons," Seouljin said, putting his elbows on the desk before him. Chains reached from his wrists to magnetic locks in the tabletop. The purpose could only be psychological. There was an inch of polycarbonate between them.

Elliot took his seat. "I'm here from the Southern Missou Police Department. I'm not here to discuss the allegations against you. I'd like to discuss your son, Skybyte? Goes by Kyte?"

Seouljin didn't flinch a muscle. "My son has been estranged from me for nearly two years. I have nothing useful to tell you, nor would I testify against him."

"I can probably get you out on parole. House arrest maybe, if you cooperate with something useful. You can go back to pumping out pop songs for Auroary."

Seouljin leaned forward. "My current residence has done nothing to slow down my art production, detective. A creative's work is in their mind, and a mind is always free."

Elliot raised an eyebrow. "I guess you can't go slower than zero, can you? Since you wouldn't be here if you were actually producing the songs you said you would when you took three million credits in investment funding."

"I can return the money."

"I saw that in your file. Your investors don't want to be repaid in whatever the hell Gamma Coin is."

"Then they should be more patient. I am an artist, not just a translator."

Translator? From english to english? We're off subject.

Elliot said, "Your son is currently wanted for assault with a deadly weapon, attempted murder. Do you have anything to say about that?"

"No."

"It happened at an Auroary concert. He broke a beer bottle over a young man's head and hospitalized him."

Seouljin smirked. "A girl must have brought him there. He hates Auroary on principle."

"Principle?"

"Because he knows I'm the one who wrote those songs. He grew up behind the curtain where the magic is broken down into sweat. I taught him the tricks of meter, the deception of rhythm chant, and what it does to susceptible minds when delivered through the proper voice. Like sugar coated medicine," Seouljin said. "It can taste like shit if you wash the sugar off. Tell me, do you enjoy the veneer of justice when you're marching about in QRS armor?"

"You must take a lot of pride in your work."

"Of course I do. If I didn't, I would just re-release public domain music like all of my competitors."

"Mr Vapor, does your son have any criminal acquaintances to your knowledge?"

Seouljin turned up his hands, rattling the chains. "Just myself, and he obviously didn't come to me for help. Detective, I fail to see how I can be of assistance to you, and even if I could, why I would want to. My son is a good kid, and given the presumption of innocence, there is nothing I can say that would help his case."

Elliot sighed and folded his hands together. "For starters, the quicker I can apprehend your son, the less likely it is that he'll end up with a bunch of CZARheads and get executed upon discovery." That made Seouljin flinch, a single twitch of muscle in his cheek. "Kyte is still under eighteen, still a minor. This doesn't have to be the end of the world for him. If he keeps doubling down on his mistakes though…"

Seouljin nodded. "Do you read much poetry, detective?"

"I don't see how that's relevant."

Or why I should care.

"Poetry has shaped my relationship with my son. Tell me, since you came in under the assumption that I was doing nothing during my stay with the government, If you had to choose between these couplets, which would you choose? She was the spirit of the machine, please hold my hand and be my queen. Or : She was spirit in the machine, can't hold my hand to be my queen."

Elliot stared back at the imprisoned poet. He looked at the man's face for a twitch of suppression and found only sincerity. "The first one."

"Why?"

"You replaced please with can't, which changes it from a plea for change to a confession of failure. The second one sounds like giving up."

"Yes, but the second one is on meter. When put to music and intonated, it becomes a cry of frustration. A demand for change. Words are only part of language, and processed by a minority of the brain. Rhythm and emotion take up far more, and proper meter engages the brain more fully, it creates a larger impression, even if, in this case, it is an expression you subjectively dislike."

"What's your point, Mr Vapor?"

"My point is that the way you make your words sets how they're heard. When you need help, and want a friend, pay heed. My son, he knows this too. He has a goal and the will to see it through. If you think I put much thought to the songs I write, picture what I did for my problem, my kin despite."

The headache swelled back into Elliot's mind. He drank more of the Hydro-Vitae and found the synthetic watermelon flavor even stronger than before. He rubbed his temples and closed his eyes. "Is this your way of saying you can't help me, because... what? He can talk his way into someone's good graces?"

Seouljin smirked. "Better than you at least. That was a rather specific example you used about CZARheads. I'm not sure why you would think this would be the end of the line for him, even if he were arrested. My son would know to get a trial by jury and then it's trivial to get a hung sentencing if you just leverage the mind of the most susceptible juror."

"Your son won't be given that chance."

"No? Why not?"

"The victim is the son of a congressman."

The set of Seouljin's face tightened. For a moment, he sat there and scrutinized Elliot. "Was there someone else that fell in with CZARheads recently?"

"It happens a million times a day."

"You MPs don't do a very good job keeping it off the streets, do you?"

Elliot tried to not snarl. "It's border security that is supposed to keep it off the streets."

"The failings of border security are exactly why I think he wont' end up with CZARheads. It's too easy for him to get out of the city."

"And then what? Get eaten by the blighted?"

"The convoy from the Isles is just a few days away, isn't it?"

Elliot snorted. "They'd use him as bait. Why would they take in a runaway?"

"Why wouldn't they?"

"Because they don't."

"How do you know that?"

"Because I've looked into it."

"And why's that? Were you going to give it a go yourself?"

"That's none of your business."

Seouljin smirked. "Who was it then?"

"I'm here to talk about your son, not–" Elliot stopped himself.

"They must have been about eighteen, I take it? Did they also vanish instead of joining the service?"

Elliot glared. "Are you cold reading me or something?"

Seouljin's smirk became laughter. "You're making it too easy, detective. No, you see I'm not afraid for my son. I wouldn't have left his life if I thought he wasn't prepared for the world. Criminals, survivors, blighted, none of those are a danger to my son. Only the government is. Now, do you mind? I'd like to go back to my work. As I said, I'm not interested in helping you capture my own son." He jerked on his chain cuffs.

"Then what was the point of entertaining my questions at all?"

"Because I don't need to give my spurned investor any more reason to keep me here. And really, a phone call will suffice for next time. You've cut into my recreation time."

Cut into your recreation time my ass. You could have declined speaking with me. Why lie?

"One last question, Mr Vapor, do you think your son is going to succeed in escaping?"

The poet frowned and looked at his hands. After a moment of turning the idea over in his head, he said, "Kyte doesn't have many skills, not any that would make him stand out, but he learned–no he's hyper conscious of how to fit in. I think if he does make it to the Isles, then he will be fine there. I would have preferred he end up in the occupation forces. Easy work, lots of pay–"

"Just has to shoot blighted every once in a while?"

"If it were normal, then he would be able to do it. He would fit in. For as long as he had to anyway. Mandatory service is only a few years, then he could have come back to a corporate desk job and melded into the background."

"And then what?"

Seouljin smiled. "Whatever he felt like, on his own time, in his own cognizance. You don't have children, do you, detective? You're far too young for your missing friend to be your own child. Maybe soon though, you'll see things from my perspective. The only thing a parent should truly want is for their child to be free to do what they want. As far as I'm concerned, the Isles are a perfectly fine fate. Better than prison and certainly better than getting accidentally shot to appease a congressman."

Elliot rose from the meeting table. "Well, Mr Vapor, it is unfortunate that we were unable to come to an agreement that could have led to your own freedom. Perhaps we will speak again."

"A true poet is always free in his mind."

"Thank you for your time."

I suppose Kyte is just about the age Luke was, isn't he? Too young to think ahead properly.

A prison guard waited for Elliot outside the meeting room. A gruff sort of man with a punch to his gut, stubble on his chin, and a slouch to how he leaned against the wall. "I wouldn't talk much with that man, if I were you."

Elliot glanced up and down the hall. There was a lull in the foot traffic.

Must be when the court systems open up for document submissions or something. Or a coordinated smoke break.

Elliot said, "He might have been willing to make our investigation significantly easier."

The guard pointed with his chin. "That guy? It's not in his records, but he was an overseas psych expert. A mindbreaker."

Elliot could no longer hear the background buzz of life through the walls of the penitentiary. The thump of his heart and the breathing of the guard were all. "You're joking."

The man shrugged and started to walk away. "You didn't hear it from me, alright? The less you talk with him, the better."

The door to the meeting room seemed larger, thicker. Elliot backed away from it and fled the penitentiary with his head down. Outside, he texted his boss, "Would like to meet face to face, regarding the Ghos search."

The text he got in response didn't come from his boss. Amara messaged to ask, "Are you free for lunch?"

Bastard's blood. What happened?

***

Elliot met with his wife at a tower-top park. The grass was fake. The bushes grew off hydroponics in the floor below. Clean air could sweep across the top of Bastion though, and stir up the pot of simmering carnitas in the faux taco truck. Space heaters disguised as trees kept the October chill away, but Amara still showed up in a quilted jacket.

Her hair color was different, raven black verging on purple.

"You dyed your hair?"

She slid into her chair at the quaint table. It was squat and steel, with a chessboard embossed into it. Chess set nowhere to be seen. "Oh, yeah, new team colors."

"It looks good. Hey, do you recall how we met?"

She hesitated, caught off guard. "The first time or the real time?"

Elliot grinned. "Well, you know I don't remember you from class. I meant more about how we hit it off in the first place. My new partner is having some troubles."

She blinked and glanced away. "As I recall, it basically happened because I realized we had been gaming together in, what was that game?"

"Reborn Isles... four?"

She grinned too. "Yeah, that was it. Back then, you actually played on a regular basis."

"I was still in boot camp. Hadn't gotten into real work," he said with a shrug.

"Right, so it took me like two months to realize that you didn't know who I was, and the whole time I thought you had been messing with me. I couldn't believe that was just your normal attitude."

He nodded along, the memories revitalizing within him. "So you demanded that we meet up in person, and I said that if I did recognize you, I'd pay for the meal. I didn't but you still twisted my arm into paying."

"Well that was your fault for not recognizing me! We did a group project together."

"Oh, come on. There were like fifty group projects. I don't remember anyone else from them either."

She sighed. "Should have remembered me."

Elliot leaned over the table and dropped his voice. "But, if I had, we wouldn't be here together, now would we? Basically, a lucky accident, right?"

"One way to look at it."

He sank back into his seat and unfocused his gaze. "That's not going to help Ram though." Amara arched an inquisitive eyebrow. "My new partner at work. She's having dating troubles."

Amara's gaze focused back on him, narrowed even. "Didn't realize you had a new partner. How is she?"

"I told you about it the other week. If you had come to the launch party for [The Faceless Well], you could have met her. She's trying to date the old fashioned way."

"Aren't there programs for that nowadays?"

Like [Sladder]?

Elliot grunted and drank his water. "None that are worth touching. I think people who succeed at dating, they either do it at boot camp, or it's like us, they meet through a mutual interest, like Reborn Isles."

Amara nodded. "Only problem is most games are changing over to instant team-making and then you never see them again. The ones who actually stick with each other, they're super picky about who they let on. Don't want to have someone dragging the averages down, you know? I barely got on this new team."

"Team?"

"That's what I wanted to talk about. I joined a professional team. Well, kind of like semi-pro? We're all streamers, rather than hardcore no-lifers." She ran some of her hair through her fingers as she spoke, building up a hint of chemical grime on her skin.

Elliot pinched his taco, the liquid cheese gushing out either end before he could lift it up to eat. "That's a good thing, right? For getting noticed or whatever? Should we be celebrating?"

"There's a catch," she said.

Of course there's a catch.

She shrugged. "The plan is for the five of us to move into a homestead together, like a reality show, and do all our practice there. We've got a tournament coming up, and we think we can get a ton of content this way. Maybe enough to get a corporate sponsor."

Elliot's taco dropped back to his basket tray with a wet splat. He chewed and swallowed, barely even tasting the greasy meat. "What game? I thought you were a variety streamer or whatever?"

"It's called [Zom-Fortress] It's a mutli-player battle royale type game that uses an increasing number of zombies to press everyone together. It's got some good base building mechanics. It got really popular last week when they officially allowed this exploit where... okay, so, basically you can make tanks now? It's super ridiculous, and got enough attention that there's a million credit prize pool for a tournament coming up."

Well, at least it's not [Sladder].

Elliot rubbed his temple. He could still feel the lingering headache, though the Hydro-Vitae had helped. "So, what? You want to move into a dirty gamer pad for a few days?"

"Three weeks?" She shrank as much as she could.

Elliot felt tired. He sagged in his seat and picked at his taco with his fingers. "I'm guessing this is a twenty-four seven kind of thing?" She nodded. "So, you're just going to pack up all your computers and head over to eat, sleep, and breathe [Zom-Fortress]–"

"And some other things. We'll break up the content a bit. Not good to burn out on a game ahead of a tournament, you know?"

"For three weeks?" Elliot asked.

"Lately, I've been hovering at about fifty viewers. I've got several long time viewers that tune in whenever I go live. That's a core, but it's not enough to get into any of the algorithms. I just need some exposure to more people, and I think I can break through."

"It's fine," he mumbled. Their marriage had less overlap every month. Even when they were physically near each other they weren't really with one another. Lunch was an anomaly. The fact that she was talking to him was the exception to the trend, and, of course, that was because she needed more time away from him. He just had to do what he always did.

"Sorry?"

"Go for it. Do it. I've always been supportive, you know that." The words tasted worse than a ground-floor shawarma. Elliot's appetite vanished.

"I'll still have my phone. You can–"

He rose from the table. "I don't have time to drag this out. I've got a politician breathing down my neck, and if I don't sort out this investigation I could get fired. So, go get famous I guess. We could use the financial security." He dumped the food remnants in the trash can on his way out.

Heading down steps to the bottom of the city was always easier than marching back up them. He didn't have to wait for a lift, or queue for a train car. One foot after the next drew him into the neon underglow. The city blotted out the sky and he headed for the old Shaitan tower.

Halfway there, as he was passing through some kind of recruitment festival put on by Wenda, Ram called him. He had to duck around pop-up holograms of smartphones and paraphernalia to see where he was going. "What's up? Date over already?"

She groaned. "It was horrible. Oh my God, you wouldn't believe me. Is it possible for me to put in some overtime on this Ghos investigation? I don't want to log this as PTO. This feels like a crime to log as PTO."

"That bad?"

"Sorry, you probably could understand. I'll tell you about it later. Did you get anything out of Seouljin Vapor?"

"Guard says he used to be a psych expert overseas. A mindbreaker. I've got a bad feeling about this now. If Kyte knows even a fraction of what his father does, there's no limit to what he could get into."

"Uh, Mr Blackstone? We do have a plan, right?"

Elliot ducked around some kind of carnival ringtoss game where the prizes were software redemption codes. Teenagers treated them like they were giant stuffed animals. "Have you ever heard of noodling?"

"Is that a game?"

"It's a heritage thing for the occupation forces down south. Stick your arm into a river and let a catfish bite onto it."

"Why would you do that?"

"To catch the fish. Come on, I'll text you the address I'm going to. I'm going to go stick my arm in and see what grabs hold. What's the worst that could happen? I get in another shootout?"

"Yes, yes that is the worst that could happen. Mr Blackstone, are you alright? Did something just happen to you?"

"Oh just meet me down here on the ground floor, will you?" Elliot said, and hung up on her.

The Differences Between
Gangsters And Kids

2140/10/05

The boss owned more property than The Greco Grotto, or at least squatted on more. If the tower was a tree trunk, and it had been struck by lightning, blasted through and scorched, home for all the insects to burrow into, that rot would have been the boss's reach. Behind a flimsy door that didn't even open all the way–it hit a support beam for the floor above–there was a secluded row of apartments with no numbers on them. The people that lived there were like Kyte, they didn't have names and they didn't want to be known. If he saw someone in the hall, they had a mask on.

Barely a whisper of noise echoed in the hall. Some doors closing, the scraping of utensils and plates. No voices. When his alarm went off, the beeping sounded like he had set off an airhorn in a library. No one stuck their head out their door to see who had broken the silence, and he vanished to the private staircase near the heart of the tower. Long ago it had been utility access, and pipes still thrummed around the shaft, but all the locks had been broken off and the safety labels worn away.

Three floors above the residential area, the boss had a micro-clinic. None of the fancy machines modern hospitals had, but it kept alive older traditions. It smelled like chemicals Kyte couldn't place, and he knew it was the kind of clinic where the doctor would reset a dislocated shoulder by feel rather than X-ray and a robotic armature. People made noise in the clinic, but their voices were groans rather than words. Some rooms smelled like vomit, and others antiseptic. One door was ajar, and Kyte made eye contact with a man threading stitches through a laceration in his side. Half-covered in blood, he still looked ready to kill with the nearest pen.

"What are you waiting for?" the doctor asked, and beckoned him into one of the final waiting rooms. Dr Bahtt gestured vaguely at a table that had once had cushion to it. "How old are you, New Guy?"

Kyte slid up onto the table and shrugged. "Why are you asking questions you already know the answer to?"

Dr Bahtt scoffed as he broke the seals open on an array of vials and needles. "Habit, I suppose. Despite my current occupation, I was originally a pediatrician."

"And that prepared you for getting thugs back out on the street?"

Dr Bahtt glanced over his shoulder at him. "The maturity level isn't very different. And, as it turns out, they pay better and complain less. I don't have to buy candy, either. And, if I do fail to keep them alive, I don't feel particularly bad about it."

"Very pragmatic. You going to explain what exactly you're going to be doing to me?"

Dr Bahtt held up a needle the size of a ballpoint pen ink cartridge. "Hardly anything. You don't shoot up heroin, do you? It's much easier to take it from the arm rather than digging around in your toes."

Kyte held out his arm. "All clean. After two hundred years, you'd think they'd have figured out how to make needles smaller, and hurt less," he said as Dr Bahtt sank the steel into his vein.

The doctor shook his head. "Oh, needles are older than that. We can't make them smaller unless your blood cells get smaller. It's a viscosity thing. As for the pain, I could have dabbed some anesthetic on, but do you really want to be known as the guy who needed painkiller for a needle?"

"Under normal circumstances, I wouldn't mind in the least." The vacuum tube slotted in and garnet blood filled it. "Why two?"

Dr Bhatt carefully swapped the vials. "One for me to test. One for them to test. And of course, both will get checked when we give you the jab and see if you die." The teeth in his smile were yellow. "That's something else I get to say now that I work here."

"Must make you a lot of friends." Kyte grimaced as the doctor pulled the needle out. "Now what?"

Dr Bhatt rubbed some antiseptic adhesive to Kyte's arm and gestured for him to raise it. "For you? You wait and do what you're told. We'll run the tests for compatibility and vaccinate you afterwards."

"What if the tests say I'm incompatible?"

Rotten smile again. "Don't worry, we'll still give it to you. I'll even do my best to keep you alive. The boss is very curious, you know. He thinks the government lied to Fumi."

He could understand a father's frustration at their child getting denied the draft. A roll of the dice had crippled her career prospects. Missing out on service wasn't quite as bad as killing someone though. Kyte held his tongue and slid off the table. "I can go then?"

Dr Bhatt waved him off. "Yes yes. Another nice thing is no paperwork."

Kyte slipped out the way he came in, but rather than descend to his designated apartment, he climbed further through the stack of commandeered rooms within the tower, one wall away from corporate businesses. He found what he had been hoping for, a bar.

Pressed up against the central core of utilities in the tower, it didn't have any true windows. Instead, they had floor to ceiling display screens to different locales. One corner had a Rocky Mountain cabin abode to it, simulated animals prowling between the pines. Another, a Caribbean beach with naval ships sailing past. On the other side of the establishment, a vintage Venice pressed against a space station. The bar counter sat like a modern oasis between the escapes, serving half a dozen people.

"We don't accept credits here," the bartender said as Kyte sat down.

Ignoring the illegality of that, he said, "Don't have any, anyways. I'll take whatever lager you've got." He produced the hacked credit chip Vlad had given him. The bartender nodded and got him a pint, then charged him in Gamma Coin. It didn't taste nearly as good as a soda, but he needed it in his hand. Just like at the concert, it was part of the uniform. It made him look like he fit in, that he knew what he was doing. It was a costume that would lend credence to what he was about to do, if he was lucky enough to get the opportunity.

As he had hoped, he had found the bar that Fumi preferred. A girl like her wouldn't be allowed to wander far from the reach of her father's protection. By his second sip, Fumi realized he had entered the bar, and rose from her table in faux-Venice. She had on a cut off tee and tight, leather pants, the kind that made it hard to not look at her as she marched over. "Hey, New Guy," she said, her lackeys following behind. "When is the next Auroary album coming out?"

Kyte kept his voice passive, and his eyes directly into hers. "I was told rather clearly to stay away from you, Fumi. Do you go by Fu? Or is Fumi already short for something?" Vlad had called her Trouble, but he had to make her into an opportunity.

Fumi blinked and worked her mouth. "Don't change my name. I didn't give you permission to do that."

Kyte refined his profile of her. The father issues had been apparent, the anger, the impatience. He needed to twist them."Doesn't matter, your father told me to stay away from you. You're making it a little diffi-cult for me to enjoy my beer though. I don't get much free time."

She snatched hold of his shirt and got close, close enough to smell him, but she looked ready to bite his ear off. "You shut up about my father. He doesn't control me. I do what I want. Now, tell me. When is Auroary's album actually coming out? It was supposed to be part of the new expansion, but I can't even get that to work."

Kyte smirked. It was obvious she thought too highly of herself. "You just have to beat the base game on Expert difficulty and the expansion unlocks. Don't you know that?"

"Expert difficulty is bullshit though."

"It just takes a bit of practice. It's not like I can do it for you. It's not like you're being punished by playing a game you enjoy, right?"

Her cheeks colored and her grip tightened. "Like you would even know. You don't even like Auroary."

"Not for lack of exposure to her. If you ever met the producer... well, you'd probably love her even more. You wouldn't get it. Hey, Georgie, you'll testify that she came over to me, right?"

"Oh, would you shut up about my dad?"

Kyte shrugged. He had to stretch out an offer, begin a deal. "I just don't want people getting the wrong idea about us. People might get the wrong idea. They're all looking at us, after all. Besides, there's nothing I can do to... actually, what would you do if I could get you one of the songs early?"

Fumi glanced around, causing the other patrons to find their own drinks much more interesting suddenly. "So, you've met the producer, huh? Got any proof of that?"

"Just my word. You've believed me until now, haven't you? So, what would you do if I could get you one of her songs early?"

She let go of his shirt, flicked him away. "You asking for money? I got plenty. My dad is rich, if you haven't noticed."

Kyte was rather certain that her father wasn't particularly rich, merely had an affluent company of sorts. Money wasn't what he was after though. Money wouldn't be worth anything outside of Bastion. "Yeah, money of a sort. I'm new around here, but you already knew that. So, how much would a sneak peak be worth to you? Because I'd have to stick my neck out to get it."

She snapped her fingers. "Georgie, how much money do I have left in this month's allowance?"

The thug curled his lips into a frown and leaned against the bar. "Cus, it's only the fifth. Don't be reckless with your money."

"It's my money. I'll spend it how I want. So what if I have to eat more than average at the grotto?"

"Actually, I've got something better than money you can give me," Kyte said, setting aside his half-finished beer. "I'm going to the convoy when it shows up. Going to do some bartering. While I'm getting you the Auroary song, why don't you get me a few terabytes of media to barter with? Easy peasy, right? You probably have plenty downloaded, and harddrives are cheap. Data is worth more than fiat out there, by a long shot. I think that's a very favorable exchange rate, don't you?"

Georgie rolled his eyes and shrugged his shoulders.

Fumi crossed her arms and nodded her head. "Deal, but I'll only do that after you get me the song. I'm not wasting my time otherwise."

Kyte glanced away, hiding the flicker of a scowl by grabbing his beer again. "Sure. I'll get it to you tomorrow, so long as your father doesn't murder me."

She groaned. "You stop worrying about him. This is between me and you. I'm an adult and I get to do what I want. Alright?" she said, defiantly ignoring that she was spending her father's money.

Kyte smiled. "Tomorrow then. I'll be here."

One of her slim eyebrows arched. "You don't got a phone?"

"Not presently."

Raz, the eunuch, laughed. He was effeminate and fat, wore garish clothes like a peacock and deliberately didn't stay his tongue. "New Guy here got robbed when Vlad picked him up. Got his shit rocked in a bathroom."

Kyte turned his attention on Raz. "I got punched once. I'm not worked up about it. As my father says, it's an experience that will build character. Not that you would know, by the looks of you."

Georgie's apathetic stare grew some fire to it. He straightened up from the bar counter and showed his size. He at least hit the gym. Purely by apparent age, he might have just gotten back from military service.

"Talking is one thing. Picking a fight is another, kid. Only reason you're getting a warning is because my cousin here needs you for something. Watch it."

"I'll be sure to."

"You won't be so smug after you find out what life is really like down here."

10

Fishing In The Slums

2140/10/05

Night draped across Shit Town like a change of clothes. It was the bars mostly. They changed their colors when they decided it was time to sell drinks instead of food. When bad karaoke and trivia would be replaced by dance music and one credit deci-shots. The natural cycles of daylight had a crude facsimile in the depths of Gamma, where the sky couldn't be seen. Elliot knew the shifts of light, could tell it was quarter to midnight purely by the hues in the puddles.

His feet had a dull ache to them, from marching up and down stairs all day. The closest thing to a break he had taken was when the QRS team passed him by because of a reported hostage situation. Turned out to be a couple fighting. The wife accused the husband of cheating on her. Turned out that he had been seeing the mother of his child the wife didn't know about. The kid predated the marriage, and the whole mess spewed out across the inside of a fried chicken joint.

The food had been good there. An authentic, survivor food style place, where they fried in huge, iron cauldrons and let the seasoning cake up on the insides of the vat. If they ever cleaned it out, they would go out of business; that kind of place.

Elliot needed to find the kind of people who could change people's identities. With no known forgers in the area, he didn't know where to start. So, like chasing down side quests in a video game, he meandered from one vague police report to the next. He transferred CCTV footage to the police servers that showed a pair of shoplifters taking an entire crate of chocolate bars. The company, Ajitatsu, had lottery tickets in them. First place was a trip to the Guilds over in Europe. Elliot felt bad for the kids, because even if they got the ticket, they were obviously too young to qualify for winning.

He tossed a trespassing drunk out of a Creole pub. A dozen broken security cameras were documented, even though EVE surely knew about them. A pair of cityboarders fled from him. And then he spotted someone in a void mask, walking with their head down and hands in pockets.

Elliot followed the anonymous person a few blocks, and saw them slip into a computer mausoleum. From the looks of the place, it had originally been a game store, but had absorbed the surrounding buildings, knocked the walls down, and put in racks of VR beds. The front window still had decade old posters for games that had been big hits at the time. A poster for Reborn Isles IV caught his eye and made him stop. The flash of memory almost made him lose track of the masked person, but he hurried in.

"Can I help you?" the neckbeard behind the counter asked. His glasses looked smaller than bottle caps, and thicker than them too.

Elliot paused. The masked person had strolled through, which meant something on them had authenticated their ID. "Southern Missou PD, I'm working a few investigations."

The neckbeard didn't change his expression. "And? Do you have a warrant to be in here?"

Elliot stepped over and put his elbow on the counter. "No, but I might be able to give you a hand with something, if the investigation plays out. You pay for the electricity, right? And worn out processors?"

"Yes, sir. I charge by the minute, and if you mean to be in here, then I'll be charging you as well."

"Do you keep track of what simulations and games people are using, while here?" The man didn't bat an eye. "If you do, I'd like to cross reference the energy expenditure of people on a game called [Auroary's Rhythm Apocalypse] and that [Sladder] thing too. I believe the game is hoarding spare processing power for blockchain processing."

Take the bait, come on.

The man frowned. "Let me call my manager."

"Sure, sure, go ahead."

Elliot turned from the counter just in time to see the man stepping up to him, eyes on him and not the worker. Not the largest thug Elliot had ever seen, but he had on a stretch-cut jacket and double layered denim pants; the kind knife-fighters liked. The thug asked, "What seems to be the problem, jannis?"

Who's hive did I just step into?

"White collar stuff, don't worry about it."

The knife-fighter folded his arms. "Long way down here for a white collar crime."

Elliot forced himself to smile. "I like the scenery better down here. Makes my boss happier too. I get a good end of the year bonus based on the number of calls I respond to. You know, normally, the corpo security boys handle the drunks who get into fights. That's a little scarce around here. No one keeps the idiots in line."

The knife-fighter snarled. "That's Shit Town for you, don't you know that, jannis?"

Elliot shook his head. "You can call me Detective, you know? Or Elliot if you'd prefer. Who the hell do you work for?"

"Hana Song is our rep here."

That's a new name. She must be small.

"Well then, congratulations, you pulled out a name I don't know. Unless this Hana Song is harboring murderers though, she's got nothing to worry about from me."

The neckbeard lifted his ear from the old desk phone. "She's on the line right now."

"Can I speak with her?"

"No. She wants to know whether there is an official investigation number for this processing thing. We'll do an internal check and drop you a line if it pans out."

Shit, I don't know it.

"Fair enough. Let me contact my partner and get it for you," Elliot said and had to put most of his attention to his phone. The knife-fighter walked around Elliot, passing into an employee room beyond the counter. The sound of a fridge door opening was followed by a rattle of cans. Elliot was digging through the database when the thug stepped back out with a beer and cracked it open.

The neckbeard got a note tablet open and took down code. Right at the end, Elliot's phone buzzed with a text message response from Ram. "On the train there."

The employee didn't even hide that he read the pop-up notification. "You down here for a date or something?"

"That's my partner," Elliot said, pocketing his phone.

"The name was Ram-Italian Place."

"I set my contacts list however I want."

Elliot scanned the computer mausoleum again, but the person in the mask had vanished. He didn't even know what he was planning to learn from them, so with a shake of his head, he exited the building. He sent Ram a message, confirming which station she was coming in from, and headed that way.

He didn't make it two steps before he realized someone was looking at him, that alignment of attention that couldn't be hidden even in a crowd. The old Shaitan district wasn't empty, but it certainly wasn't a crowd. Not nearly enough people to hide the void mask staring at him from across the way.

Is that the same person? Shit, what were they wearing? If these are the guys who shot up The Doll House...

The person had on a puffy, form-concealing jacket. The kind that was mass produced for corporations to slap their logos onto, but this one was bare. It seemed to match Elliot's memory of the person he had been following. The attitude didn't. After holding eye contact for a moment, the person in the mask backed away, vanishing behind the glowing sign of a chinese buffet.

Elliot fumbled in his pocket for safety. Not his gun–that was strapped to his hip–but his recording drone. He didn't turn it on, not yet. He just rubbed his thumb on the power switch as he picked up his pace to the train station. Paradoxically, the closer he got to the hub of people, the less surveillance from EVE there was. The cityboarders and other gangs made more of a point to break those cameras than any-where else. So he kept his head down, his ears open, and his thumb on the switch of his drone.

The side-eyed glances from corporate security types, men and women in the yellow of Phoenix Construction standing across from green jacketed thugs from Ajitatsu, started to seem less friendly. Elliot didn't know whether it was suddenly in his head, or if something had changed with the tickover of midnight. He told himself to calm down, that he was going to walk himself into a mistake. Ajitatsu, the leading food additive producer of the world, was about the least intimidating group of people in Bastion. They were more likely to offer a passing bribe of chocolate than accost him. There was a reason those kids had been brave enough to steal a stack of their candy bars.

What am I running from? I'm the police officer here.

A fading ache in his chest resurfaced, a beating he had taken a bit too recently for his liking. The hospital had put him back together, but he wasn't in a mood to get in another fight.

Nor to shoot anyone.

The arrival of the train was like a bird swooping in to land, pressing air out in front of it to stop. The crowd had a drunken swagger to it, typical for the time, but it slowed the interchange of bodies. The red blood cell uptake and deposition of city nutrients. Elliot didn't see the white blood cell: Ram.

He checked over his shoulder again. Thought he saw someone in a mask looking back at him, but they ducked away too quick. Perhaps they were just glancing at the train. He pulled out his phone with his free hand and started thumbing through the commands to put in a request to EVE for a surveillance net. He got all the way to the screen asking him for a reason and a description before he remembered the whole point of the masks. EVE didn't know who those people were, not unless they were stupid enough to have one of their electronics on.

"There you are," Ram said, tapping him on the shoulder. She looked good, perky even. "Got my nap in, and I'm all ready for a night slog with ya!"

Elliot slipped the phone and the drone back into his jacket pockets and frowned. "I was just thinking I should call it a night actually. Even criminals go to bed, you know?"

Ram stared up at him. Her eye level was higher than usual, she still had heels on from her date. "What happened? Who got to you? If you were going back to your wife to see her, you would have just said so. You would have bragged with a grin on your face. So, that means you're not going back to her. What happened?"

Elliot took a breath and ran his hand through his hair. "This is the conflict between habit and learning. It... it feels like when I got into that mess at the plantation. I came down here after a bit of a fight with Amara, because that's what I do, it's what I always do. Now though, it feels like someone's following me."

"Well, is someone following you?"

"I don't know. Might be nothing but shadows. Might be a coordinated group of people wearing void masks tracking me down."

Ram nodded. "Well, I'm not going back home immediately. How about we go get a bite to eat or something at a food stall? Maybe up a few floors?"

"Sure," he mumbled, and the two of them headed for the stairs up.

"So, tell me about Seouljin? What did you learn?"

"Not much about Kyte. He's a psych expert though. Can't trust anything he says."

Ram nodded. "Right, so what does that mean? Like, is he a therapist or something?"

"What does it mean?" Elliot scratched the stubble on his chin and looked around the walkway. A dozen micro-restaurants dotted the walls, each bringing in a collection of late night travelers. He gestured towards a samosa joint and Ram nodded. "For starters," he said as they queued. "It means he can hypnotize you, and he may well have taught his son how to do it too. Maybe not as good, but maybe good enough to get into the graces of someone like Hana Song. Or maybe whoever wants her territory.

***

Elliot got jumped while Ram was giving a stern talking to a couple of school kids causing a disturbance. The first thug, an overweight giant too doped out on THC to have a flicker of aggression show on his face, shoved him down an alley formed by the edge of one tower, and a suspended pub reaching out to the opposing tower. Twentieth floor and they still had shafts of darkness to work with.

Elliot went for his gun.

The void mask toting receptionist in the alley whipped out a micro-blade. Shimmering alloy, built like it was for fileting fish. Held it rock steady a meter away from him. Only augmented muscles could be that steady. "Easy, jannis. Just here to talk off the record."

Elliot snarled at the void mask and squeezed the grip of his gun tighter. His jacket had slash protection built into it; a weave of tough cables that might be able to stop the micro-blade. At the distance though, he couldn't fire without getting cut. On the other hand, he couldn't get cut without putting a bullet in them. "Who sent you?"

"A very respectable man, by the name of Aleksander Sokolov. What are you here for, Detective Elliot Blackstone?"

Well, I found the ones who know what they're doing. Or, they found me, anyways.

"Was it you that's been stalking me the past hour?"

The man shrugged. "Stalking is such a crude way to put it. We, down here on the bottom, simply have to be more traditional in our information gathering. We don't have a network of cameras, of hacked internet routers, body scanners, infrared, and who knows what else you have feeding data to EVE."

"So, yes."

"Yes, indeed. I had to call you in. You have a reputation, Detective."

"I do? Or my boss who comes in for me, does?"

"Both. So I ask again, what brings you here? Mr Sokolov does not want a visit from the ARUs."

Elliot glanced over his shoulder. The man who had shoved him in was gone. Another thug had taken his place, smoking a cigarette like nothing was wrong in the world. "Sokolov... is he a–"

"Worker's union head."

Gang lord.

"What's he doing putting people into Hana Song's territory?"

"We aren't drug dealers. We don't have territory like that, where we fight over where to put pill pushers and pimps. Our territory is virtual. It's people and businesses, the connections between them. Someone has to hold the dregs of society together after the corporations cast us aside. So, again, what are you here for, Detective?"

If Kyte has talked his way into protection, I shouldn't tip my hand...

"Haven't you been tailing me? I'm walking from one complaint to the next. Just doing my job. It's what I do. It's my late night hobby."

The man with the micro-blade shook his head and pulled a small phone out of his pocket. It was a dumb phone, no real processing to it. He tossed it over. Elliot caught it with his free hand. "I invite you to use that, in case you're about to get into trouble."

Elliot woke the phone up. It had a single number saved. "This Sokolov?"

"Don't be stupid. That's one of his subordinates. His name is Vlad. You got a problem with randos, the kind that could become an issue for everyone? Vlad will see that it doesn't become a raid. Understood?"

They're underestimating how much firepower I have right now.

Elliot nodded. "Alright, but no more following me. I can't do my job feeling like someone's going to pull a filet knife on me."

The man across from him took a step away. "We have to keep an eye on you, Detective. But, no more following. We got a deal?"

Elliot relaxed his shoulders. "For now. If I get a call to come after you though, I'll have to take the call."

More retreat. "You won't. We don't make mistakes like that."

Elliot took his hand away, and the micro-blade vanished. The shadows swallowed the man, and the detective turned to the smoking thug. Before the tension could melt from his body, he saw Ram standing, one arm up behind her back just like he had been.

What does she think she's bluffing? F-ranks don't carry firearms.

The smoker didn't know what to make of it either. He couldn't take his eyes off her, and held his burning stub of tobacco pinched in his fingers. Elliot could see the strain in the man's knuckles, ready to flick it.

Elliot strode between them. "Where'd you get those anyways? No one ever tells me where I can buy an actual cigarette. They just offer vape pens nowadays."

The smoker shot a glance to the darkness and straightened up. He sucked the cig and said, "I do some trading with the Isles. They still grow the stuff fresh."

"Yeah? They got filters in them. I hear that's the silly thing. One of the plastic companies makes the filters and sells them to 'em, but no store will stock the cigs."

The smoker grinned and snuffed his cig out. "As long as I can still get them, I don't mind much."

Elliot nodded, inching closer to Ram who had only then lowered her hand. "Makes them a bit more special, right? Maybe I should get a pack, in case I meet with your boss."

The thug laughed. "If you want him to hate you, go right ahead." He gave a yellow grin and walked away.

Ram cleared her throat. "What the heck just happened?"

Elliot dusted his jacket off just to straighten it out, straighten his mind out too. "I told you I was being followed, didn't I? I went noodling and caught a big fish. The only question is who the hell it is." He held up the burner phone.

Ram looked at him, at the phone, and back at him. "Oh, congratulations! You almost got yourself gutted in an alley in exchange for a phone number."

Elliot rolled his eyes. "You know, some guys would risk a lot more for the right phone number."

Her faux concern immediately switched to annoyance. "There's a reason those kinds of guys can't get phone numbers."

"Come on, you can finally tell me about your date from Hell, while I put in a tap warrant request."

Elliot got halfway through the warrant application when he had to stop, so he could listen to Ram. The two of them were at a coffee shop transitioning from sobering up drunks to waking up first shift workers, drinking decaffeinated coffee.

"The guy was completely insane. He actually thinks the Bastard is real. I made the mistake one time of muttering 'Bastard's blood', and he went on for like twenty minutes about how there is serious evidence that the new age sasquatch is still alive based on aerial photography of blighted horde movements. He almost started talking about Operation Holyfire, but had the gall to say that I wouldn't believe him, and even if I did, it could get me fired. Did I mention that he's trying to buy his way into New California? He got discharged from the occupation forces, dishonorably from what I could tell, and thinks he can still immigrate to the coast. He acts like it's some kind of dissident exile. Like he just has to find Mustapha Mond and get sent away to some artistic retreat on a ranch. Did I mention he's an artist? Does digital illustrations with a mix of simulation."

Wetting her throat slowed her down only momentarily. "I mean, we started by talking about that, because that's actually cool. You know, that's doing something with your life and it's a skill that not many people have. Like, a million people tops, and only a thousand any good at it. Way better than auditing the AI accounting at some place like–" she glanced at her mug, "Ajitatsu. Those people strut like peacocks because they get to work up on the top floor. Horrible. I'm not a prude you know, I don't look down on trade work or anything. I'm totally fine that he gets his paycheck doing internal gardening work for Phoenix Construction. He called it hydroponics. I'm pretty sure that's how he found out about the restaurant by the way. Ran into my parents while they were perusing for spicy peppers. On the bright side, I know my mother didn't set him up to say hi to me, because she would have sniffed out this train wreck of a brain from five minutes talking with him."

Elliot felt compelled to say something, to nudge the conversation forward. "I mean, was he mean? Or just insane?"

Ram scrunched up her nose and thought it over. "I wouldn't call it mean, but it's kind of annoying, you know? When someone just keeps talking? They take an innocuous comment and then give you a whole lecture about something and act like you know nothing about it, even if you know everything about it? I went to New California for training by the way. It was great. It's government through and through, though. You don't get to just go there unless you've bought off Congress."

Elliot nodded. "MPs get dispatched there every now and then, depending on jurisdictions. The port workers have gone native, made a little enclave last time I checked, but they aren't keen on artists."

"Same difference. Head-in-the-cloud creatives spend too much time dreaming up places they'd rather be. And you know what's the craziest part? He preemptively told me that he wouldn't be able to see me again for a few weeks. Not that I was ever planning to return his messages in the first place. But get this, it's because he's starting a pro-gaming group and they're doing a reality show live stream thing where they all live together while practicing for a tournament."

Elliot's mug banged against the table, splashing coffee. He swore and grabbed some napkins, mopping it up and cleaning his hand off. "Sorry, sorry. Hey, did he say what game?"

The look on his face must have been obvious, because Ram stopped rambling and eyed him. "[Zom-Fortress]... why?"

"Do you still have his number?"

She pursed her lips. "Technically. Why?"

"No real reason. No good reason to reach out to him. Shouldn't even think about it. Don't even know what I would do if I spoke to him."

Ram leaned in. "Mr Blackstone, what's going on?"

He cleared his throat. "I think my wife is in the same gaming team, and will be living there for three weeks."

She blinked, looking as dumbfounded as he had felt a moment prior. "Your wife is moving to live with sweaty gamers? As a publicity stunt for her stream?"

Elliot found that he was looking at the remains of his drink. He nodded. "Told me this afternoon."

"When we spoke and you came down here?"

"Yeah."

The silence of their conversation hung, surrounded by the city noise. Elliot didn't break it. Ram said, "You could tell her you don't want her to."

"I could. It would just make it worse though. We've had these kinds of fights before. Whenever she feels like her dreams are being held back, she digs her heels in. Like, the other day, she only helped with [The Faceless Well] because it was interesting content for her stream."

"How many views did that get, anyway?"

"Like, fifty thousand last I checked. When all the companies pumped out knock-offs, the views cratered."

"Okay, well..." Ram stretched her legs out, leaned back, and made a point of glancing at the clock on the wall. "I don't think walking around Gamma until you get a knife stabbed at you is a particularly healthy way to respond to this. And I don't want to have to reach out to her teammate just so you can keep tabs on him. You've got a few days before they do the thing, so let's try to wrap up this investigation in time for you to take some time off before their event?"

Elliot downed the last of his coffee and crumpled the cup. "Hey, maybe we could get lucky, and the kid will do something stupid, like access one of his accounts."

11

The Boys Of The Gang

2140/10/06

Kyte talked his way into meeting one of Sokolov's tech specialists, so he could get to his father's data. Vlad had wanted to toss him out the moment he heard it, but even he didn't want Fumi complaining to her father about something as trivial as the police potentially finding Kyte. It wasn't really theft anyways, and Raz had been assigned to him like glue, to make sure he got Fumi the song.

From the moment Kyte stepped in, he started trying to build a profile on the techie. There were tricks that could be used on people he knew nothing about, but only the most rudimentary of things. To really get into someone's good graces, to make them amenable and cooperative, he needed to know exactly who they were and what they wanted. It was a predatory way of thinking his father had taught him, but he couldn't deny its effectiveness.

He didn't even get through the door before everything his father taught him failed. He had learned how to deal with normal people, who had normal desires and normal weaknesses. The inside of the techie's workshop looked like a cybernetic horror show, with heaps of trash and robotic limbs. The air stank of solder and ozone and hydrogen peroxide and more. The techie wasn't a normal person, he was an artist.

Dealing with an autistic sociopath would have been easier.

"It ain't gunna bite you," Raz said, and shoved Kyte inside so he could close the door.

He had been expecting some kind of enormous processor, maybe built out of refurbished cores bought secondhand from one of EVE's relays. Maybe a guy suspended in an isolation tank, hooked up to the machine and speeding through data matrices. Instead, he stumbled over loose cables and forgotten boxes. He passed dozens of computers running training simulations or grinding through 3D modeling. Some of them seemed to make sense, based on the images, but most were nothing but lines of code spasmodically updating.

"You're a new face," a female voice said.

Kyte jumped back and put a hand to the void mask he had on. Getting to the workshop had meant passing through a few train stations. His heart still hadn't slowed down, but he knew rationally that his face couldn't be seen. It just made the woman laugh.

She was seated on a desk in a tight, white dress that trailed off into poofy lace around the legs. Legs that didn't have skin, nor feet; the plug-in joint dangled exposed. Her left arm had been removed at the joint so a charging cable could be stuffed in through the auxiliary port. If that all hadn't been enough, there was no rise and fall to her chest, no breathing.

"Looking for Miccolo?"

"Speaking. Real body is indisposed. To what do I owe the interruption?"

Raz nudged what looked like a robotic hand that was balancing a tablet stylus. The finger wiggled, the stylus wobbled. It didn't fall. Kyte's escort shrugged and turned to the robot. "Need your help getting something for the princess."

"Privately," Kyte added.

Miccolo, by way of the robot, said, "Privately? You aren't doing anything private with my stuff. I thought I already told you idiots that I don't make sexbots. That's disgusting. What is wrong with you?"

Kyte's mask hid his reaction. "Not what we meant. I need a VPN, a proper one, so I can get into some files without anyone snooping it out."

"Look kid, if you're trying to get your ex's nudes or something–"

"No! Bastard's blood man, can you just come out here and I'll explain?"

A toilet flushed in the back of the silicon jungle, and a man came walking out as he buckled his belt. Once again, Kyte's expectations were shattered. The man was tall, built like a super soldier, and kept his hair groomed with a buzz on the sides, flow on top. Miccolo nodded. "This had better be worth my time."

Raz gave a half-hearted wave. "It'll be easy."

Miccolo frowned. "Take that stupid mask off. EVE ain't in here. Now come here, to my client desk." He and Kyte sat down next to the one computer in the whole workshop not presently engaged in some processing activity. "What are you trying to do?"

Kyte pulled the mask off and brushed his sweaty hair back. "Just need to log into my father's storage drive without getting caught."

"You need me to hack it? What kind of encryption does it have? How big of a file are you taking out?"

"No, I have the passwords, or at least can get them. I just need to get them without EVE finding out."

Miccolo raised an eyebrow. "And why would EVE be looking for you?"

"Does it matter?"

"Yes. I need to know the degree of scrutiny to prepare for. If the old girl really felt like putting the light of God on me, there's nothing I can do about it. So, you wouldn't be here if you hadn't pissed somebody off. Are we talking rich corporate guy? Or does the Tribune want to know where you are?"

Kyte cleared his throat and tried to work up some spit. His mouth felt very dry, in contrast to how sweaty his palms were. He glanced back at Raz, and Miccolo got the message.

"Hey, go get me a six pack, would you?" Miccolo asked, tossing a credit chip to the young thug. "I'm not worried about this punk here, and he's not going anywhere without this." The techie's hand went to Kyte's void mask.

Kyte tensed, but as soon as the grumbling Raz left, Miccolo's hand let go of the mask. "Right, so, well, the police are after me for... aggravated assault." He tried to sound confident. It was harder to manipulate his tone when it was something like that though. "Guy was making out with my girlfriend, I hit him good. Maybe a bit too good cus he went down. There's probably a warrant out for my arrest, so I don't want to be seen logging in to things, right?"

Miccolo rolled his eyes. "That's all? Kid, I work for Sokolov, for most of my paycheck anyways. You could have just said so. You think I haven't done extractions for people on the lay-low before?" Out came an old laptop, he booted it up and got it connected with the rest of the room's networking. "Now, obviously, they'll know that the files were accessed. As far as the police will be concerned however, it was accessed by a defunct Russian satellite."

Kyte frowned. "Those are still in orbit?"

Miccolo paused the clatter of his mechanical keyboard. "Satellite state, not actual satellite. Come on kid, use your head."

Kyte kept his mouth closed and used his head to chase down the chain of interconnected profiles and recovery methods. "How much time do I have?"

Miccolo rolled his eyes. "Again, unless you really pissed off the wrong person, don't worry too much about it. I'm not the only one who uses this proxy. We've got this thing locked down quantum. Nobody is going to pay for the processing to break in."

Kyte ignored the knot in his gut and logged into his email. Then, he went into the family email account for all shared subscriptions. That happened to be the recovery account for his father's personal email address, which allowed recovery because it hadn't been used in over a week. With that profile enabled, he remote started the home computer and went directly to the local directory work files. The finished products were kept on individual hard drives, in a safe, in an undisclosed location. No way to hack those, but the difference between good enough and finished was a difference only his father could see.

"So, you've got a local drive I can save this too, right?" Kyte asked.

Miccolo held out a data card, and he slotted it in. One long download later, after encrypting and decrypting the package, he had Auroary's next song sitting in the palm of his hand.

"You done?" the techie asked.

He turned it over. "I guess so."

Miccolo reached over and jabbed a macro key, collapsing the internet connection back into obscurity. He smiled. "Congratulations, you're a hacker. How's it feel?"

"Like literally nothing."

"But you get to say you bested the strongest AI in the world, and that's worth something. Now get the hell out. I have work I want to do on Angela."

Kyte twisted in his seat and looked at the robot. "Her?" The techie nodded. "You know, I've never seen a personal robot so... actually I don't think I've ever really seen one, that wasn't a display piece. How'd you get it?"

"I made her. I've been collecting and tweaking parts for about four years now. I've been rebuilding all the control code from scratch and releasing it open source."

"You're not licensing it?"

Miccolo glared at his computer screen. His tone went flat. "Because it's the twenty-second century and we still don't have robot workers helping us. It's ridiculous. The government has all the technology to do it, but they won't. One mouth says they need labor protection to insure everyone has a job, another says it's national security risks, a third says it's unethical. So I'm doing it myself."

Kyte whistled. "That's pretty awesome man. Now that's what I call art."

Miccolo stared at him. "There's nothing artistic about muscle control algorithms. The only art involved was in the face mask I had printed off for her, and I didn't design that. This isn't art, this is engineering."

Kyte got to his feet and shuffled away. He mumbled, "Well, it is passion," just as the door opened up once more. Raz strutted in with a plastic bag swinging. He dropped it onto Miccolo's desk, the shape of a six-pack obvious.

Raz glanced at the computer going to sleep. "You done then?"

Kyte nodded. "We can head back."

"Easy. Nice and quick. Can finally stop baby-sitting you," Raz said, and jerked his head back towards the door.

Kyte followed him out after putting the mask back on. Before he left, he said, "I hope you finish your project and get it out there."

"Best thing you can do for me, kid? Never mention me again," Miccolo said, and waved him out.

Raz led the way down a circuitous path of halls, alleys, and abandoned shops. Kyte followed, his head down. He wanted to look around, to spot the cameras, but he put one foot after another and followed the pro. It took a few minutes for him to realize they weren't on the same path they had taken. "Where are you going?"

"What's it matter?"

Something was wrong. Kyte could taste it in the back of his throat. Something in Raz's tone belied him. "How am I supposed to give the song to Fumi if you don't take me back to her."

"Don't worry about that. All in due time."

With both of them masked, Kyte couldn't read the punk's expression. He turned his attention elsewhere. He tried to rebuild the path they had taken in his mind, spread it out and figure where he was. His memory of their trip to Miccolo's workshop had already grown fuzzy, the two mental snakes entangled with each other.

Then he realized he had stepped into an abandoned retail shop. The clothing had been looted, leaving behind bare shelves and mannequins, all cleared out in the middle. One panel of overhead LEDs illuminated the dance floor, washing the color from warped sheets of plywood. "The hell is this?" Kyte asked as someone else in a mask emerged from the shadows behind him and stood like a wall.

Raz spread his arms like a showman. "A teaching moment, free of charge."

Someone new stepped out into the clearing with Kyte. Tall, older, with a crooked nose and subdermal LEDs in his arms that made his skin scintillate like scales. Had his hair gelled up and dyed red, the kind of red only a chemical company could make. "Sup, new guy," he said, prowling back and forth.

Kyte set his face like stone behind his mask and squared his shoulders with him. "Who the hell are you? I'd remember a scalie like you if I saw one."

The guy sneered as some of the onlookers laughed. "The name's Drake–"

"You expect me to believe your mother gave you that name?" More laughter.

Drake planted his hands on his hips, flaring his elbows out like a cobra head. "You're new. You're acting too big for your own good."

Kyte rolled his eyes. "I'll be gone in less than a week and you'll never see me again. Why do you care?" His heart was hammering. It thumped harder and harder, but he didn't let it show. That would get him killed.

"Because you're making the wrong kind of waves with our princess! You're not giving Fumi the respect she deserves."

"And I can already tell you don't get even a drop of the attention you wish you got from her." Kyte smirked as he took his mask off and tucked it into the back of his pants. The smirk didn't touch his eyes, he wasn't that good at it, but in the gloom Drake wouldn't be able to tell. Putting the mask away was the perfect sleight of hand for what he had in mind. His stolen loot from the kitchen was still in his pocket.

The punk's face started to match his hair. "Well, I guess we can just get to the point. Give my apologies to Dr Bahtt when you see him."

Kyte looked around the room. "No hard feelings then? In your pecking order thing here?"

"Just like matchmaking. No one's gunna jump you," Drake said, shifting into a boxer's stance. He grinned and danced from foot to foot.

Kyte sucked in breath and held it. He used the pressure as a focus and set his mind. He locked eyes with Drake and braced himself. Putting up his hands, he hunched his shoulders enough to give Drake the invite. Then Kyte took the first punch to the face. It hurt so much it didn't even process as pain. Vision became a bright blur and his ears rang with shouts. It had been intentional though. Not only had he pressed in and taken it on the bone, but his mind was on the attack.

Blood squirted from Drake's thigh as Kyte stabbed the stolen kitchen knife into the thug, slipped from his pants before the fight had even started. Kyte recovered from the shock first and grabbed hold of his opponent. Fistful of shirt in one hand, a hypnotic steel wand in the other. Drake couldn't look away as the bloody edge stopped right in front of his eye.

The crowd went silent.

Kyte spat some blood onto the plywood. "Submit," he ordered.

"What the fuck is this bullshit? This was a fist fight."

"Really?" Kyte twisted his grip, making the fabric dig into Drake's armpit. "You never said it was a fist fight. You led me here, trapped me in the middle of your friends, and wanted to beat me. The only reason I haven't taken your eye out is because we both work for Sokolov. But maybe I should. I'd be doing him a favor, teaching you a lesson. Do a bit of research on who you single out, next time."

Raz hadn't quite blended into the crowd. As soon as the fight had gone wrong, they had pushed him back out, and he paced around the clearing. "Man, what the hell do you think you're doing? You think we're just going to let you go if you fuck Drake up?"

Kyte flared his nostrils and huffed. "No, but I think you'll back the hell off to get me to not kill this prick."

Drake had a tremble. No matter how he pulled away, he never got more than an eyelash's distance from the tip of the knife. "You wouldn't have the guts."

"Really? Wouldn't be the first time," Kyte said. The ache in his face made it easy to keep the scowl. Whispers started to go around. The young generation of Sokolov's organization asked each other who Kyte was, how he'd gotten in, why he worked for Vlad.

Someone in the shadows, with a voice deep enough to sound authoritative, stood up and said, "Tuck your tail, Drake. He got you." Others shuffled around, ducking behind shelves and making way. Drake put up his hands, keeping them wide and away from Kyte.

Kyte watched the gap form, saw the silhouette of the door, and took the knife away. The moment Drake closed his eyes and exhaled, there was a chance Drake might just think he had been unlucky. Kyte had to change that, had to make the risk of doing this again too high. He stabbed the knife into the punk's shoulder and ripped it through one of the subdermal wires. He screamed and half the lights in his arm went out. Drake moved to slug him, to grapple for the knife, but he stepped off with his injured leg and nearly fell.

Kyte strode to the door, grabbing his mask on the way. Before leaving the light, he pointed at Raz. "I'll remember this."

12

Catching A Lead

2140/10/06

Liberty Stadium buzzed as a hundred thousand people found their seats amid a bassy roar of rock-metal. Someone was playing someone else in a War Games match, repping some place or some corporation, to whip the crowds into a tribal frenzy. Ram had her face glued to the window, watching the thirty meter tall display above the main gates. It was all flash and fire, mixing player stats with advertisements.

That was all on the other side of the central plaza, well away from them. They were in the Military Police Central Command, a multi-purpose hub that could see Liberty Stadium out one window. It could see Capitol Hill out another. The tower was half built like a fortress and half an office building with ARU garages at the bottom, holding cells above, court rooms, meeting rooms, office rooms, every other menial kind of business room, all the way to the top where the rooms stopped having assigned functions. They were simply spaces for use, surrounding the various train stations along the edges.

MPCC buzzed with the perpetual grind of bureaucracy, and somewhere below, a judge was reviewing his warrant request. Without a warrant, his next best option was contacting the kid's mother. Her tone of voice was less than cooperative. "I've already given my statement."

This would be easier in person.

"Miz Vapor–"

"We're divorced. I'm Miz Nest now."

"My apologies. I want to let you know that I'm working very hard to track your son down, for his own safety. You understand? Given that he has avoided any kind of surveillance until now, he can only be in the lowest reaches of Gamma and Epsilon. That's not a safe place for anyone."

Miz Nest huffed. "Well, you should have done a better job tracking him down. Don't you police have little robot bloodhounds or something? But, I shouldn't be telling you how to do your job."

If only a QRS train had shown up to the club with one. This would all be over by now.

"Miz Nest, I know you were in communication with your son the day of the incident."

"I've already given my statement. If you have any further questions, I'd request you direct them to his father."

Elliot could feel the pack of cigarettes against his thigh. The days had begun to crumple the package, the creases rubbing against him as he paced beside the window. "I've already spoken with Seouljin. He wouldn't have the kind of information I need right now. EVE has already done a scan of his phone when we recovered it, but maybe he had a spare phone? I need to know if he had any contacts in less than legal spaces."

"You're just asking me to give you more evidence to arrest him with."

Elliot stopped and stared at the sky. He drummed his fingers on the cigarette pack in his pocket. "Miz Nest, your son is trying to escape Bastion, I believe. Assuming the blight doesn't kill him outright, do you have any idea what kind of life is in store for him? The Isles are his best bet and they're nothing like what he knows. There's no government, no system, barely any laws. They're anarchists and they aren't his friends. If he succeeds in getting to the Isles, they'll use him like a slave. You are never going to hear from him again and one day he will die and be left to rot where he fell. He'd be lucky if someone turns him over to rob his body. If you don't want that for your son, I need a bit more of your cooperation."

She sighed and when she spoke again, her words were much softer. "You don't understand, detective. You must be too young to have a teenager of your own. I've been preparing to never see him again for years now. My boy's eighteenth is just around the corner. He's an adult and responsible for himself."

"Never going to see you again? He's your son."

"Sixty percent of adults have no relationship with their parents nowadays, don't you know that, detective? Look, if you want to rip his room apart hunting for a phone that doesn't exist, you'll need a warrant or I'll have security escort you out. Have a good day, officer."

Elliot slowly put the phone back in his jacket pocket. He didn't move from the window, nor did Ram ask how the call had gone. Eventually, his ruminating was interrupted. "Blackstone," Cinder snapped as she strode into the room. "What the hell is taking you so long to pick up one teenager?" She looked like she had just come from a firefight, and knowing her, there was a good chance she had. She didn't spare a single thought for her unkempt hair or to button her uniform all the way up. No one was stupid enough to condemn her for it either.

I told you everything in the email this morning. Do you think hearing it from me in person is going to change something?

"Our working assumption is that he has talked his way into one of the local gangs. He's either looking for a forger to get a new identity, or he's looking for a smuggler to take him out to the Isles convoy in a few days. Either way, EVE hasn't gotten a whiff of his location. About an hour ago, his accounts were accessed and his family computer turned on. EVE says it was a relay cluster in the southern Ural Mountains."

Cinder listened and nodded, unwrapping a piece of chewing gum as he spoke. "Why haven't you had EVE crack it open then? That's obviously a proxy."

Why would I ask to do something that would get denied?

"Boss, I'm currently waiting on a communications tap based on a local gang lord by the name of Aleksander Sokolov."

Cinder froze mid chew. "Sokolov? How did you run into him?"

Ram said, "He found us, more like."

Elliot nodded. "I went looking in the area that Vapor Junior got his phone stolen and got noticed. Wasn't trying to hide, but I didn't exactly enjoy having a microblade brandished at me. A guy like that? With connections and control to hunt me? He's the best chance of snooping Skybyte out of the shadows."

Cinder chewed and thought and finally said, "Sokolov is on our watch list for the void mask investigation. It's a pretty short list of people that could orchestrate a hit like what happened at The Doll House, and he's on it."

Ram frowned. "The Doll House?"

Elliot grumbled and shrugged. "Strip joint. The owner got shot recently. Barely survived."

Cinder smirked. "No need to downplay yourself, Blackstone. You're the one who saved him."

"At the cost of the assassin getting away, just like Skybyte is currently getting away."

Cinder nodded. "Alright, you're going to have to get brought up to speed on some things. I don't have the time to do it myself, gotta get over to a Congress hearing about the Pyre. You said you have a warrant request in?"

"Yeah, number–"

"Found it," she said, eyes flitting back and forth, reading something from her neural implant. "I'll get it fast tracked. Put in the request to break that proxy, and I'll forward it to Ghos and see if he has budget to fund it. Colt will find some time to bring you up to speed on Sokolov. Now then, topic two. Ram, wonderful job with the Auroary program hack. Something like that? That's cost savings for the city. We get kickbacks for that. Once we get it sorted and blacklisted, I'll get you some bonus PTO."

Ram's eyes lit up and she smiled. "Really? I was thinking I could spend a day in the game, do some diagnostics and let one of EVE's shadows crunch through the isolated data."

Cinder nodded. "Sure. If it's after you get the Skybyte kid, make Blackstone do it with you. You're my game division afterall. Make him get better at the games."

"Yes, Ma'am!" Her hair flipped as she nodded so hard it looked more like a bow.

Bastard's blood. Maybe I should take my time getting the kid. Where's my PTO offer?

"I'll get the processing request in."

"Get it done," Cinder ordered, and marched past them.

Elliot darted forward and dropped his voice. He had to follow along before she vanished out the door. "You still haven't rescheduled our meeting."

Cinder glanced back at Ram. "If it hasn't already come up, then don't worry about it. She's a good kid. That's the problem, Blackstone," she said, and strode off. A single-car train slid past the windows and whisked her off to Capitol Hill.

Ram frowned. "Are meetings with her always like that?"

"Those are the good meetings. If she's making time for you, that means you fucked up. Come on, let's go meet with EVE," he said, and led her down to the main servers. He took her down the hall until he found an open room, and stepped inside.

"What? You're... volunteering for– I thought you hated VR?" Ram asked as Elliot sat down in a worn out lounge chair.

He picked up the ENU and gestured at the other seat. "Keep your voice down, will you? This is like a library, and it isn't a game. It's way easier to look over the data in simulation than on a computer screen. Meet me inside," he said, and slid the electrodes around his head. The sensations of the virtual world creeped into his mind and blotted out the MPCC. When vision returned, he was in the digital dream, looking at an endless expanse of white, like a marble field out to infinity.

Ram appeared a moment later, very obviously in her personal avatar. A head taller, a cup size bigger, and in some kind of fantasy silk dress adorned in glowing runes. She blinked and looked him over, then looked at the interface display hanging in the air awaiting their queries.

"You don't have a professional account to sign in with?" Elliot himself wore dress clothes in his natural avatar.

"What? It's not like we're meeting anyone important in here, right? I put a lot of effort into this one! I'm level eighty-seven in Arena!"

Elliot rolled his eyes. "As you will, it's not like she's going to care."

"She? Who's she?" Ram asked as Elliot got the interface working. A moment later, part of the ground slid up like an obelisk, and EVE stepped out. The effect reminded Elliot of pulling a corpse from morgue storage, but the department had general agreement to minimize the amount of bodies instantly appearing in view. It kept disorientation down.

EVE, sporting a similar button-down shirt and a pencil skirt shook her head. "I don't care. Wear whatever you'd like Miz Enna."

Elliot blinked. "I just realized you never told me your last name."

Ram planted a hand on her hip. "For good reason too. You could have looked it up if you wanted, but I got enough of people knowing it back in grade school. I can totally sympathize with Kyte wanting his name changed."

Ram Enna? Ramenna, Ramen, got it. That's probably it.

Elliot sighed, which just irritated Ram. "EVE, are you able to break that proxy station and backtrace it?"

The AI folded her arms and struck nearly the same pose as Ram. "Able to? Of course. I thought you knew me better than that, Blackstone."

He pressed his lips together and stared at her. Calmly and clearly, he said, "I do know you, EVE, I know perfectly well how many restrictions are placed on what you can or can't think about, let alone run processing on. If you have the free power to crack quantum encryption, I'll be amazed."

She huffed. "Alright, you got me there, but I was listening to your talk with Cinder. I've got the form ready for you already. I'd crack it myself, but I was actually thinking of routing it down to my sister on the Unnamed Hero. She could use more training on this kind of thing. Congressman Ghos should be able to stomach it as defense spending."

"Easy, where do I sign?" Elliot asked, and EVE sent over a menu for him to scribble his signature onto.

Ram looked around as he double checked the request, though there wasn't much to look at. "So, what kind of simulation is this, anyways? Why so barren?"

EVE glared at Elliot. "Because someone has no sense of fun. He won't even enable the base simulation we give to prison inmates!"

"I'm not here to have fun. I'm here to work."

Ram held up her hand. "I would like to enable that sim instead."

The world broke apart, massive slabs of ground material sinking and rising as EVE swept her hand across the world. Clouds and mist burst from the cracks, washing across the geometric monoliths like sea cliffs. The hue of the world shifted, from the sterile white of an interrogation room, to the amber hue of sunset. EVE smiled.

She did something to it. That's a smug smile if I ever saw one. She probably hid something in the bird's eye view or something.

Ram started chatting with the AI about what options were available, and what quality of life options the server had. Elliot couldn't listen in, because the main interface screen pinged him with a new message. The judge had approved his warrant to tap Sokolov's communications, on contingent that no action could be taken based on information gained from the tap solely. Elliot ignored the redirect request to Colt's investigation, and had the simulation recreate Sokolov's network.

A dozen more obelisk pillars rose from the ground and people stepped out. Lifeless avatars of real people. Sokolov stood before Elliot, nearly in the flesh. Overweight, sagging jowls, an appended note that he was a person of interest for nearly a dozen murders. The other people didn't have nearly the attention to detail. Some were rendered into avatars, but gave an impression of genericness, like features had been mapped to a standard template. A few just had a picture snapped from a street camera. A teenaged girl by the name of Fumi had a full avatar, more realized than Sokolov.

"What's the deal here?" Elliot asked, waving off the web of device interactions tying the people together.

EVE stepped over. "She just went through draft screening. We got a copy of her natural avatar there."

"So why isn't she in bootcamp?"

The AI waved her hand, and the data file appeared. "Rejected by decision of the recruitment officer."

Ram stuck her head over Elliot's shoulder. "Reason listed?"

EVE winced. "Emotionally unstable, reported as vaccine incompatible."

Elliot and Ram both stared at the AI.

Ram said, "Well that's bullshit and you know it. Who went to bootcamp and didn't find people having mental breakdowns in the bathroom?"

"She got rejected because her father is a gang lord, didn't she? Rather than bring her out of that mess and to a safe, healthy life, they trapped her in Bastion."

Ram frowned. "Wouldn't it have been better to separate her from him? Isolate her from the gang and keep the two of them apart?"

Elliot said, "There's a lot of reasons they might have chosen to do that. If I had to guess, they're afraid that she will end up inheriting his control, and if she's an upstanding citizen, a veteran with full access to the tops of the towers, that the gang might get out of hand."

"What? It's not like there's gates that stop you from going up to Alpha strata. You just have to buy transport passes and stuff. Literally anyone can go there, it's just hard to get employed up there. Also the people up there are pretty horrible. No one will smile at you."

"No one smiles at people they don't know. You're mistaking your neighborhood for normal. The difference between top and bottom is at ground floor the people around you are a physical threat, up in the sky the people around you are an economic threat. You never know who you might bump into."

Ram rolled her eyes. "Hey, I know this is obvious, but is it easy to cross reference the people here with people who were at the Auroary concert?"

"One moment," EVE said, and a moment later, one single indicator appeared. It floated like a golden arrow above one of the bodies that only had a picture for a face. "Vladimir Baker was present at the concert the night of the incident. Is believed to have been working with Sokolov for the last two years. Was originally a worker for an offshore oil rig in the Gulf of Mexico and was a victim of the Ono-Toba sabotage attack."

Elliot whistled. The Ono-Toba attack had set off the battery systems for the under-water mining gear. Decades old, they were still lithium based. One bomb in the wrong spot, and rather than temporarily inconveniencing the rig to manipulate plastic prices, they blew the whole thing up and left a burning geyser in the ocean. UAAF had been so embarrassed by it, the heads of Ono-Toba had been delivered to Bastion for justice.

EVE continued, "He had to use his insurance payout for facial surgery. Swapped out his eyes because the parent company, Myca, tracked their corporate security with retinal scans. Oh, I should have mentioned that he's technically wanted for arson after he torched the CEO's apartment."

"Why would he do that?"

"They didn't cover the insurance payments for long term treatment of his injured colleagues. Myca said it was the government's responsibility. Government said it was UAAFs. UAAF laughed."

What bastards.

Elliot shook his head. "Alright, I think we have our point of contact. EVE, set up an alert for us, will you? If anything suspicious happens to these other people?"

She cocked an eyebrow at him. "Would you like to be more precise than that?"

"EVE, you're the most advanced AI in the world. I think you can handle what suspicious means," Elliot said, and pulled up his personal interface. He retrieved a digital pack of cigarettes and lit one up.

"I thought you didn't smoke?" Ram asked as he took a drag.

"Not real ones. It's a point of principle with me and my wife. She thought I couldn't get off them. Guess what, I haven't smoked a cigarette in years. This? This isn't a cigarette. And I get my nicotine through food and drink. No need to tar up my lungs." It tasted like menthol. "We should get a hold of Colt, maybe take him with us to meet Vlad."

Ram said, "This feels like you're cheating your promise. Does she know you still drink Zeus energy drinks?"

Elliot smirked. "Not quite. That would require her caring about what I do on the job. Come on, no need to linger in here. Let's get ourselves some free time and do something about that video game." He shot a wink at EVE.

"[Auroary's Rhythm Apocalypse]?"

"No, [Sladder]."

***

They met with Colt in the abandoned wreck of a clothing store. The map had labeled it, "Prime Fitness Apparel (Permanently Closed)", but it looked more like a fashion designer's horror show. All broken mannequins and dirty rags. Officer C00173 outranked both Elliot and Ram, but his job wasn't too different. He was scraping blood off a sheet of plywood. It was the kind of work that normally went to the new guy, F00135, but the Fools of the department was Ram, and she worked for Elliot.

"You should just hand this investigation over, let it roll into the big investigation of void masks," Colt said, turning his little spatula over in the light of his phone's flashlight. It had a glint of brown on it, and he swabbed the blood flakes into a sample vial. The senior officer wasn't much older than Elliot, but had never quit physical conditioning. He kept his blonde hair buzzed tight on the sides and had cultivated a permanent scowl. Elliot knew exactly the kind of man Colt was on the inside though. "Would get the congressman off your ass."

Elliot strolled around the edge of the clearing, looking for cameras in the darkness. Every store had cameras. He found the sockets for them, empty. "Congressman Ghos has a point though, I'm involved in it. I'm the one who told the kid to go to that concert."

Colt rose. "No offense, Blackstone, but you don't exactly exude a presence of power and authority. You're the kind of guy who'll get shot if he puts his nose in the wrong spot."

That's why I'm trying to tread lightly. If that was enough to stop me, I would have retired by now.

Ram poked one of the abandoned mannequins. "How has this lot been forgotten? We're in Delta, isn't floor space at a premium?"

"Taxes," Colt said.

Elliot said, "The government is a stickler for their money. If the original company goes under without paying their taxes off, whoever wants the lot has to pay those taxes off to get it. Eventually, it builds up and the place becomes more radioactive than the ruins of Detroit. The IRS is worse than gang lords like Sokolov."

Colt scoffed. "From what I hear, Sokolov's actually a good boss to work for, outside of the crime. He doesn't pressure people into working overtime. Of course, that's because he has de facto slaves working off non-monetary debts, but the point stands. He and his little crypto-economy are an oasis."

Elliot cocked an eyebrow at him. "Thinking of jumping ship? Changing sides?"

"Not a chance," the investigator said. "My daughter is fast tracked to get into Daedalus Labs. I can't pay that tuition with Gamma Coin. Also, he intentionally let some of his people get killed last year so he had casus belli to destroy his neighbors."

"He's expanding?"

Colt shrugged. "He was expanding. He's gone quiet in the last few months though. If someone else was behind the attack on Mr Mink, then he'll have plenty to scoop up after we crush them. We're not exactly in the business of complaining about criminal groups not committing crimes."

"Hey," Ram said. "What exactly do you think happened here?"

Colt said, "All we really know is about a dozen people went into here, and one of them got stabbed." He shook the blood vial. "Two of them came from an affiliate of Sokolov, but they all had void masks on. Could have been a prelude to a territory war, or maybe just internal conflict. Once I get the DNA run on this, I'll know more."

"Who's the affiliate?"

"A techie by the name of Miccolo. Bit of a crazy guy. Works on robots. Might be a pervert, but he doesn't cause any trouble. We think he's the one who set up Gamma Coin, but we can't go after him for that. Nothing illegal about it."

"A techie? Like, a computer guy?"

Colt glanced at Ram, got nothing from her, glanced back at Elliot. "Yeah. That's what a techie would be. A tech guy. Guy who likes technology, is good at using it. Didn't think you'd need a slang explanation, for all the time you spend down in Gamma."

Elliot grunted and rolled his eyes. "Not what I meant. What time? Do we know when he was there?"

"Who he?"

"The two people who came here from there?"

Colt rolled his eyes and pulled out his phone. "EVE, do we have a timeline of where these people were and when?"

The AI responded, "Surveillance footage from around the area is still held in local storage. Would you like to authorize gait analysis?"

"Narrow it down," Elliot said, walking over to the other officer. "I just need to know about the people who visited this Miccolo guy. When was it, and did it coincide with my target, Kyte, ripping his father's data?"

"Yes, but–"

"Progress!" Elliot shouted, and pumped his fist. "I love a good breakthrough."

"But..." EVE continued, "That does not constitute reasonable evidence. You won't get a warrant to investigate Miccolo from that coincidence alone."

He snarled at the phone. "Oh come on, that's obvious! Hell, he's probably the one who got stabbed. New guy hazing or something."

"Hey." Colt shoved him in the shoulder. "You're not raiding Sokolov's techie on a hunch. You want to screw up my investigation?"

Elliot stepped back and calmed his voice. "Alright, look, Congressman Ghos is going to authorize breaking the proxy that accessed the files, the access that my guy Kyte used. If it comes back as this Miccolo, I have to go in. You know that. I'll run it by Cinder if you want, but if Kyte is taking refuge with Sokolov... we're not going to be allowed to do nothing."

Colt clicked his tongue and turned away. A moment later, he had his recon drone up and had it take a scan of the room. "If that happens, have the common sense to escalate it to Cinder. Don't just jump in. It's a bit too soon to be crashing ARUs into some hive of idiots again."

Elliot turned to Ram and tilted his head towards the door. "Of course I will. Sokolov is a big fish and I've got a tiny line. I just need the kid. Hell, they might just hand him over to keep us away."

Colt stopped and turned. "Why do you say that?"

Elliot stopped his escape. "They contacted me already. When I was walking around for leads. Told me that if the police had an issue, they'd resolve it for us... more or less. If I can prove that the Kyte kid is with them, they won't want that heat."

Colt blinked. His mouth gaped. "Are you crazy? You'd just give up your right to imminent discovery? You'd have the right to march right into the guts of his operation and arrest everyone you see."

Does he want me going after Sokolov or not?

"It would prevent me needing an armament of ARUs marching behind me, shooting anyone who has so much as sniffed CZAR. I'd get the kid peacefully. No one would have to die. Hell, the kid probably won't even get life in prison. Nice and clean. Everyone would go home happy."

Colt snarled. "Don't be an idiot Blackstone. Getting Sokolov's core could save lives, not to mention the justice of it. You're sworn to uphold that, you know?"

"I do," Elliot stated.

The recon drone flew back to Colt and he snatched it from the air. "Don't do anything stupid. I'll be reporting this to Cinder. You'll be lucky if she leaves you on the case," he said, and marched out the other side of the abandoned lot.

Elliot hooked a thumb, and he and Ram left the other way.

She cleared her throat. "That seems like a problem."

"To put it mildly." His chest felt tight. He had to rub inside his jacket to check if the rib brace was still there, but he had taken that off almost a week prior. He tried to write it off as ambiguous stress, issues he could deal with. Rationalizing didn't make it go away. "He's not going to do anything but complain to Cinder though. She's not going to change her mind. Doesn't change what we have to do."

They emerged onto an external walkway, sighted the nearest train station and headed that way. Ram asked, "And that is? Wait?"

"Yeah. Wait for the proxy to get cracked, and put in the new warrant." Elliot glanced around. "We should probably stick around the area. Something like that can be pretty quick. We'll be coming back here to talk to this Miccolo as soon as we get it."

"Assuming he doesn't bolt the moment that he realizes someone competent is attacking his proxy?"

"Assuming, yeah. Gambling anyways, that he won't just leave his gear behind."

"So... should we get a drink?"

The two of them sat down at a slider bar within eyesight of the train station, the kind of place where you could abandon your plate, get charged automatically, and run to catch your ride. It had acceptable beer, and a replay of the War Games playing in every corner. From what Elliot could see of the subtitles, it wasn't even an official exhibition match, but rather a trial run of a new arena layout. The rules commission was loosening communication restrictions on neural implants, specifically to allow teammates to see each other's visual feeds. To compensate for the extra information, they had built a labyrinth for the teams to fight it out in.

Shouldn't they have used an arena they were all familiar with? How are you supposed to know where someone is if you don't know what the place looks like?

Ram nodded along with the commentators. "I wish I had the time to track the players again, now that I'm old enough to put legal bets down. Back before the draft, I had a winning record."

"What? Were you betting with your classmates?"

"No, that would have been illegal."

And yet I'm sure you did.

"Well, on the bright side, I don't think this match is going to matter all that much. They're scrambling people for the next month, doing this weird pseudo tournament. I can catch up later, crunch the numbers, figure out who the rising stars are."

Elliot sipped his beer and cleaned his lips. "You know, I tried out for the War Games. Tried to rep the MPs when I was young. Thought I was hot shit with a gun because I could score high on the static tests."

Ram snorted and hid her face. "You and every other red-blooded male. Did you take it hard when you got your butt whooped?"

He leaned back, creaking the boards of the bar's stool. "It didn't eat me up too much. I had other things on my mind. I was working by then, was the department Fools. One of my superiors got killed around that time. Playing with super-charged, tactical paintballs stopped mattering for a while."

Just as well too. I sucked. The players, they have something I don't. A danger sense? I've heard people say that hardened killers can sense other hardened killers, a sixth sense. Telepathy of a sort. Me, I blunder into places and get surprised. Though, I have killed people. Never quite got that talent some people have.

Ram had been speaking, rambling something about the War Games. Elliot listened back in as she said, "We're entering a phase where the only people able to win, to put up points, will have primarily gaming backgrounds. The verisimilitude of simulations like Arena is going to get paired with haptic responses, maybe electric pulse restraints? Imagine a player who spends all day running games against AIs, his muscles actually getting trained at a scientifically controlled rate, while doctors can dope him up with whatever steroids they can conjure. Amateurs will never be able to compete again."

"That would ruin the sport though."

She shrugged. "Depends on how expensive it is, doesn't it?"

"Money... always comes back to money in the end, doesn't it?" The beer tasted worse when he sipped it again.

Ram put an elbow on the counter and turned her attention to him. "Money is why you get things like Seouljin signing a contract with that micro-cult."

"If we can get away with never visiting them, I'll be happy. They don't have anything to do with Kyte, I hope."

She groaned and rolled her eyes. "Now you've jinxed it. Now we're going to have to track them down, you know that? Should have known better than to say something like that."

Elliot's phone beeped. Ram flinched away, catching her breath. He rolled his eyes and checked the message. He didn't recognize the sender. With a frown, he slid his beer away and read the message. It had come from someone named Paige Palmer and read, "Good afternoon detective Blackstone. I've reviewed your department's request for an analysis of [Auroary's Rhythm Apocalypse] pertaining to the energy consumption. I submitted a first order approximation and Mr Ryder's equipment is not capable of consuming the amount of power shown on the utility bill, not for the amount of hours he had logged on his profile. As such, it appears there is something flawed in your hypothesis, and I have put a hold on further analysis. Let me know if you have any further questions."

Who the hell is Paige Palmer?

A quick internal search turned up exactly who they were, the sysadmin covering the department's issues while they hired a replacement for the last one.

"Who was that?" Ram asked.

"Not the cult, I'll tell you that," Elliot said, and on a hunch, he wrote back to Paige, "Could you check if his playtime on [Sladder] would match it? Those were the two games he was playing. Thanks for the help."

Ram let out her breath and picked her beer back up.

Elliot's phone vibrated again. Not a message, but an alert of a new warrant issued for his investigation, a corollary search warrant. He rolled his eyes and drained his drink. "Alright, that was quicker than I expected. Let's go meet a techie."

13

Freedom Piece

2140/10/06

Vlad sat down on the lid of a deep freezer. Kyte wondered if there had ever been a body kept in it. Light was on. There might have been a body in it right then. The older man rubbed his temples. The skin tugged wrong, an artifact of his eye replacements. "You mean to tell me you fucked up Drake in a fight?"

Kyte wanted to shrink away and vanish, but for as dark as the room was, in the depths of Gamma, he didn't see any spots to hide in. The two of them were beneath the brightest light, and no one would so much as hear them speak. "He's the one who forced the fight."

"Obviously," Vlad said. "You wouldn't even know who the hell Drake is. How could you have picked a fight with him? But I find it hard to believe you hospitalized him."

Kyte cleared his throat. It didn't help, didn't put strength into his spine. "I only cut him a little bit. Wasn't much of a fight." He wanted to clear his head, to reset, to not think about the fact that he was assuredly speaking with a murdering gang leader.

Of course, he was a killer too. Didn't mean they were the same though.

"You stabbed through that stupid ass light-up tattoo he had and nearly cut his femoral artery. You had a knife. A little cut is just a little different from a big cut. You realize that, don't you? Did you get a big head because you fucked up that kid at the concert?"

Kyte pressed his lips into a frown. His father's voice whispered in the back of his head, memories and advice; enough conviction. "I did what I had to do. Should I have let them beat my ass?"

"Would have been safer for you."

"They would have taken the data drive and given it away. I couldn't let them do that."

"But now you've got bad blood. Kid, this is a mixed bag for me, you know that right? The old boys, that have been working here long, they're going to appreciate I brought in a fighter, yeah. But Sokolov is going to want to be rid of you even more. He doesn't want trouble under his roof. Not like this. Probably, you and Drake both are going to be on the street."

Kyte folded his arms and ran his tongue across his teeth. "The convoy to the Isles is just a few days away. He's got a due date for being rid of me. As long as he has that to look forward to, he can put up with a temporary annoyance."

Vlad rubbed his temple again and stared at the ground. "What data did you get anyways? I heard Raz was the one that took you over to see Miccolo?"

"I uh... got something for Fumi. In exchange, she's going to load me up a harddrive for bartering with the convoy."

Vlad rolled his head, a stand-in for rolling his eyes. "Well, that would be why Drake singled you out then. You know, you're lucky the boss found a good use for you. Now come on, put your mask on." He slid off the murder-corpse-hiding-fridge.

Kyte blinked. "Why?"

"Because, you numbskull, we're going to go get you your freedom piece."

Kyte had never seen the thick parts of Gamma before, not from the inside. Some districts in Bastion had a way of accumulating people and things. Even within the city, populations found a way to organize themselves like enclaves. Where it got thickest, the towers clung to one another like vines wrapped around tree trunks. A lattice of support frames reached everywhere, and anything could be a floor, ceiling, or wall.

They passed over welded sheets of corrugated steel, stapled on strips of aluminum sheet, plywood patches and chunks of construction foam blasted on the spot. People filled every corner, every window and door. Everything was being bought and sold, and Kyte didn't see one single corporate logo, not on the businesses at least. The goods had everything printed on them. Romulus food snacks. Ajitatsu silverware. UAAF shoes for men and women and everything in between.

"Stop gawking," Vlad said. He led the way, sucking on a cigarette. Kyte followed him by the smell as much as by the back of his field gray jacket. He took him into a chinese sort of wet market, chopping up fish that Kyte prayed weren't taken out of the river. Through the back, they entered some kind of secondary mall. He could tell because the LEDs were set to a different temperature and the hall didn't echo with people arguing about nonsense.

The people filling the hall didn't talk much at all.

Again, Vlad led the way, stepping into what smelled like a hookah bar, and glowed like a rave. Kyte almost lost track of him before stumbling into an entirely unrelated shop. Nowhere he looked could he see a storefront, no main entrance with latest wares out for grabs. All he saw was self-defense goods.

Swords mostly.

Like a kid to candy, he found himself about to pick up an oversized machete. He couldn't quite tell whether it was more like a European saber, or a Japanese Katana. The stamped blade, like a shaving razer, could only be military standard though. Old war, the blighted special.

"Jesus Vlad, you're bringing kids in here now?" the proprietor asked, planting a bony elbow on his counter and staring at Kyte from behind bone white, whiskery eyebrows.

"Nah, he's an adult," Vlad said, leaning on the opposite side of the counter. "He's proven himself, sort of. What you're looking at right now though is–"

"A kid who's going to hurt himself, or make a mess of my shop at the very least," the merchant said, and on cue, the rack of blades tilted and things started sliding.

Kyte grabbed onto it and righted it, quickly lining everything back up under the gaze of the shop owner. "Sorry," he mumbled.

Vlad shook his head. "Alright, still a bit immature at some things. But, he's got my boss's attention, you know? This kid is going to be going out with the convoy. He needs a little heat to go with him."

The shop owner frowned and wiggled his eyebrows in thought. "He's leaving then? Never to come back?"

"That's right."

"And you can pay in Gamma coin?"

"Of course."

"Fine, just a moment," the old man said, and vanished through a door Kyte hadn't even realized had been there. He returned with a black polymer revolver. A six-chambered cylinder with a stub barrel and neon sights. The diamond grips had been filed down to take the points off for some reason. Kyte knew the reason why the serial number had been filed off.

"You giving me a hot weapon?" he asked.

The old man shrugged. "So hot you should use an oven mitt to touch it. Be grateful you get anything at all."

"What's it matter to you? Four more days and you're out of here. A second hand gun isn't going to do you anything wrong," Vlad said, and waved him over.

Kyte found himself standing before the counter. He didn't recall having chosen to walk there, but his feet had carried him. Then his hand reached out and picked the thing up. It was heavy. The balance seemed off. Popping the cylinder, he saw there were no bullets in it. The old man grumbled and fished out some accessories for him. A holster and ammo, namely.

It came to his attention that he was holding something he had only ever seen before. It was something that in a few months, he would have been given by the government as part of bootcamp, but he wasn't eighteen. He was only seventeen, and a civilian. It was illegal for him to have it, because it was a tool of murder.

Some people in Bastion still had guns. They were grandfathered in from the days of the apocalypse, when the people showing up to Bastion considered themselves survivors rather than citizens. They were rare though. Most people saw them as too dangerous to have around in a city so densely populated. A bullet could rip right through the target, the wall behind the first wall, and someone on the other side.

People found it much more comfortable to allow military-grade cybernetic limbs that could rip down a door and tear someone limb from limb. People needed those limbs after all.

And now he had a gun for killing people, and blighted. Vlad had given it to him because he had killed someone. The act had predated the tool, and in doing so brought it into being.

"You there, kid?" Vlad asked, waving a hand in front of his face. "The thing's not magical. It can't hypnotize you. That thing right there is your best bet for protecting yourself."

"By killing other people?"

"Damn straight. Kill them before they kill you," Vlad said, and stuffed some kind of hacked credit chip into the merchant's reader.

Kyte shook his head, like the thoughts were a bit of dust on him. It just reminded him that people in the Isles settled everything with guns. Allegedly, no one there ever went anywhere without a gun and bullets for it, to put down any blighted they encountered. Or people they would say after the fact were blighted. It was so different from Bastion he could hardly wrap his head around it. Was it though?

He tried telling himself that it was just a tool, a higher efficiency tool to inflict violence and people were more than capable of being violent with nothing but their bare hands. He'd just gotten mugged the other day, by people with their bare hands. A gun would have stopped that.

"So are you going to load it, or what? You do know what you're doing with one, don't you?"

Both of the older men were looking at him. "Obviously. I play shooters like anyone else." He dropped the cylinder with a flick that sent it spinning and whizzing against its slip bearing and slotted one bullet after the next into it before flicking it shut. He reached for the holster, remembered to set the safety, and stuffed the gun away.

"Smart ass," the shop owner grumbled. "Now get out of here. You're a ticking timebomb if I ever saw one, and I want you going kaboom far away from me."

Vlad patted him on the arm and started walking to another exit. "Come on kid, now to put you to work, my motivated employee."

Kyte hooked the holster onto his hip and covered it up with his hoodie. Not the easiest to get to, but hidden. "What? Now what are we doing?" he asked, following Vlad out the other end of the shop. He stopped dead when he looked at the place they had entered.

Black.

Not shadowed, but blackened. Soot, dirt, grime, mold, everything filthy in the world had coated the depths of the tower. It stank like ash a thousand times worse than the hookah bar. The overhead lights didn't even work. People had cobbled together bulbs and cables that dangled here and there, casting shards of light across the gutted world.

"What the hell is this place?"

Vlad stopped and grinned. "A kid like you wouldn't know. This is a remnant of the world from before, of a sort." The gangster spread his arms out to behold the sponge-like mesh of exposed girders and broken walls.

Kyte wanted to plug his nose. There was something wrong with the air that he couldn't put his finger on. "Of the world before? You mean the first America? What kind of shit are you telling me. Bastion was built in the middle of nowhere, between big cities. That's why they were able to build here at all."

Vlad clicked his tongue and wagged his finger. "No, no, that was the world before the world from before. I'm talking about the intermediate. The world of the damned, of people who showed up to the government's protection with nothing but hollow hearts, sin on their souls, and grave dirt beneath their fingernails. This is where the loners of the apocalypse arrived."

Kyte looked around and saw a part of the city that the government had simply abandoned. An uncontrollable, and unlivable rot buried at the heart of the hive. It was the kind of place that would have killed him on his way out to the walls. "What are we doing here?"

"Didn't I tell you? Putting you to work."

Kyte's chest tightened and his mouth went dry. He kept his face calm, still. "What kind of work?" If he refused, they had no reason to not turn him over to the police. Maybe they'd wait for the vaccination thing, but no longer than that.

Vlad smiled. It bared his fangs without shame. "What else would a bunch of lowlives like us be doing? Clearing out the wrong kind of drug dealers. Come on, some of the other guys are meeting up with us. Hope you're ready to put that toy to use. You might need to."

Kyte didn't step forward to follow, even when Vlad started down a hall and pulled out a phone with some kind of map on display. The gangster noticed his hesitation and turned back. "One question," Kyte said. "Are you the CZAR dealers? Or are they?"

"Does it matter? Either way, the people down here are on it. By choice, more often than not. But come on kid, you can't rule people on CZAR. It's as bad for us as it is for the government."

Kyte nodded. It felt like the weight of the revolver was going to drag his pants off his hips it was so heavy. So he took a deep breath and breathed in the filth and let it into him, and he followed behind Vlad to do the job he had been hired for.

14

Business Ventures

2140/10/06

"You don't have to answer anything they ask, Mr Benjamin," said his lawyer, by way of miniature hologram.

Elliot rolled his eyes and leaned against the doorframe to Miccolo's tech shop. "We do get to come inside, and I'd rather not kick the lock in."

The techie, Miccolo, frowned and looked him up and down. "You'd probably hurt yourself trying."

I probably would.

The lawyer sighed. "They are permitted entry."

Miccolo glanced over Elliot's shoulder and looked at Ram. He shook his head and stepped away, unlatching the locks and letting them enter his workshop. The place looked like a cannibal butcher shop, except there was no blood. A doll house at life scale fit better. The three of them walked over to what served as the techie's meeting room. He sat down like business as usual, but didn't say anything.

Elliot gestured at the chair in front of him. "May I?" The techie nodded. "As I'm sure your lawyer will corroborate, the warrant I was issued gives me the right to access any electronic device with reasonable probability of containing evidence pertinent to my investigation."

Miccolo's jaw tensed. It made his beard ripple slightly, but his eyes stayed cool on Elliot. Until Ram meandered to the wrong spot. She stood before some kind of female doll, and his eyes kept flicking over to her and back to him.

The hologram of the lawyer, the picture of a legal toad, cleared his throat. "The warrant only permits that, and was issued on unsuitable grounds. You lacked sufficient reasoning to attack a privately owned server like that. There's a thing called appropriate response you know. I'll be challenging this in court, and you know what happens if I get it thrown out, don't you? All evidence gained here will be forever inadmissable in court. Fruit of the poisoned tree."

Elliot's eyes half closed and he calmly said, "The case I'm working? It's going straight to federal court. One step down from SCOTUS. The person I'm looking for is wanted for the attempted murder of a sitting congressman's son."

That made the lawyer shut up and start reviewing his documents.

Miccolo cleared his throat and glanced around. He checked three different coffee cups and found them all empty. "Talking with a kid isn't a crime," he said, and stood up. Elliot nearly followed him, but the techie just walked over to a mini fridge and pulled out a beer. He thought better of it, and switched to a soft drink.

"Talking to him isn't. Assisting in his criminal activities is though."

"Mr Benjamin, I advise you don't say anything you don't have to. I am your legal consult here and–"

"Sokolov's, right?" Elliot cut in.

The wrinkled lawyer didn't flinch. "You know as well as I do that I don't have to answer that one way or another, Detective Blackstone."

"Look, I can do this the hard way and dig through all of your computers to find what I need, but I think it's pretty obvious you helped my target access his father's files this morning. The kid's name is Skybyte Vapor, goes by Kyte. Almost eighteen, tall. Is Sokolov hiding him? Because a whole lot of attention is going to come down to find this kid."

Miccolo glared at him from over top the rim of his drink. "I don't ask what Sokolov is doing. I just take freelance work from him. How do you even know it was me? I'm not the only one who uses that server. There's also the Humberts."

Elliot raised an eyebrow and glanced at Ram. She nodded and sent him a quick message. A glance at his phone confirmed, "That's the religious leader of the Holy Communion of Cyber-Wine."

Seouljin's business partners.

"We have associated evidence."

Miccolo's attention snapped onto Ram. "Please don't touch that. The control system isn't calibrated properly. You're interrupting my work enough as it is. I don't need you directly damaging Angela."

Ram yanked her hand back. "This? This is... Angela?"

"Yes."

"She's very pretty. I thought programmers like you tended to increment project names though. Angela to, I don't know, Beatrice? Charlie, and so on? Is this your first attempt?"

Miccolo stood across from her, one hand on his hip, the other in use to sip his drink. "It's a Ship of Theseus problem. The sub-projects get incremented. That's outside the scope of our conversation though."

She smiled and stepped away. "Right. I'm sorry. I'll let Mr Blackstone continue."

The detective nodded towards the robot. "Looks like a humanoid ARU. You know there's engineering reasons to not build the way a human looks, right? Silicon doesn't self-repair like flesh does."

Miccolo walked back over to his chair and sat down. "Officer, if you're going to confiscate my computer, I would appreciate it if you could stop wasting my time and get on with it."

Elliot turned from the techie and back to the robot. "You know, the warrant allows me to seize any recording device for investigation."

The lawyer interrupted. "Only the data within."

Elliot shrugged. "If I can't get the data digitally, I can take the device back to headquarters. And that? That looks to me like a non-standard recording device. Might take a real long time to dig through the on-board storage to see what it saw this morning."

Too far?

Miccolo and leaned forward, eyes locked on Elliot. His nostrils kept flaring. Then he killed the hologram of the lawyer. "Just ask me what you need to know, you bastard janissary."

"The kid I–"

"Yes, he came in here this morning. I gave him access to my proxy so he could log in and download a file. He walked out in under half an hour and I haven't seen him since. He came with one of Sokolov's guys. Kid by the name of Raz. If it wasn't apparent, I don't ask many questions. I also don't take recordings of those kinds of deals. Not that I save anyways. Nothing went wrong. It got purged."

"So, if something had gone wrong, you would have had video?"

Miccolo forced a smile. "A bit of protection for myself. You know, you probably think I'm some master hacker that works for the guy, that I'm breaking into competitor's email chains and tracking the movements of their key players, and who knows what else. But I'm his IT guy. I manage an internal messaging forum for people who do business with him and I fix firmware issues over in the clinic sometimes."

Elliot stared back. "You expect me to believe you aren't spying on your competitors?"

Miccolo snorted. "Bad example. That's trivial to do. Paid off one person to get access to their account and wormed in through there. Doesn't change the fact that I don't have your kid. The evidence you're looking for? You're not going to find it here. Especially not in Angela. That's not even where her visual data gets stored.

Elliot nodded, and pulled up a photo of Kyte on his phone. It had been taken as part of the kid's draft preregistration. Head on, well lit. "This is the kid you saw, right?"

Miccolo didn't bat an eye. "You know they wear masks right? They use masks like computers use proxies."

"But did he take it off while working with you? Or were you staring at a black void the whole time."

The techie shook his head. "Yeah, that's the guy. What more do you want from me? Can you leave now? Because if you're still thinking of confiscating my stuff and pressing charges, I will do everything in my power to bankrupt your department."

Elliot rose and nodded. "Thank you for the cooperation. If it all pans out, we'll never see each other again." He pointed his chin at the robot. "On a personal note, is that what I think it is?"

Miccolo nodded. "I'm bootstrapping up through full human automation. It's open source because you government bastards don't release anything."

"You know," Ram said, "I think I saw a media hit piece that Daedalus Labs got egg on its face that some indie programmer out did them at their own program?"

That put a smirk on Miccolo's face. "They tried hiring me."

"Tried? You turned down Daedalus?"

The techie shrugged. "They would have put me in a group. I would have had managers, not colleagues. Not collaborators. Corporations have deadlines, they have quotas and end of year reviews. They set targets that can be quantified because some schmuck from centuries ago said that was the best way to get a workforce motivated. They are accountants by design, and I'm an artist. Also, anything I would have produced afterwards would have been government owned. It would have been locked up and what's the point in that?"

Elliot turned to Angela, the robot that was plugged into some processor, getting a software update by his guess. He knew ARUs, the enormous machines of destruction that the military would send in to suppress riots and gangs. He knew the cybernetic prosthesis given out to amputees. There was a fashion to keeping the metal exposed, revealed through transparent silicon. Some people did it to show off the gear they had, like a fancy watch. Others simply didn't care to keep the fake skin color matched, UV was hell.

He knew that every time he had met someone with a fake hand, and learned about it by shaking their hand, it had been more off putting than seeing it first. A cybernetic hand simply didn't squeeze like a human hand, and there was no way to fix that. The joints couldn't be engineered to squeeze and collapse the way knuckle bones do. Even with temperature matching and just the slightest film of oil, it couldn't escape the uncanny valley. And yet, Miccolo had stopped at nothing to replicate humanity, a million times more complicated than the sculptors of old.

We should get out of here. I can solve this whole thing by calling Sokolov.

Ram didn't look like she was about to go anywhere. She had stepped over to the programmer, staring into his eyes and wringing her hands as the two of them talked about... Elliot couldn't even catch up with their conversation. The two of them were bouncing jargon back and forth, drifting between pop culture, video games, and the artistic choices in his design of Angela.

"The fundamental problem," he was saying when he paused to check his phone. Before he continued, he smirked and produced a cigarette. Once he had it lit, he said. "Is the back end processing. I don't want to do it by heuristics. There's a lot of autonomous stuff that can be managed by rote, but if I want to design the idle programs to be indistinguishable from a real human, I need a data set of real humans, and only EVE has that kind of data en masse. You know, the unconscious things. The rate of breathing, the way people shift their weight and why, how often people touch their faces without thinking about it, that stuff is what humans key in on. Not to mention, I would need to get my hands on one of EVE's processing cores if I wanted to have a proper personality core behind that face. And I got blacklisted from purchasing any after I turned down Daedalus."

Spiteful bastards. That's not my problem though. Ram is. Bastard's blood, she's into him. Must be even more obvious to EVE, if she's pushing cigarette ads to him.

"So you're saying," Elliot said, stepping over to the two of them, "That you have a price if I ever need a favor. Because that's what I heard."

Miccolo's face set firm again as he put his attention on Elliot. "You can get processing cores?"

"I know some people. You've already done me a favor for today though. I'll reach out if I ever need your help, after the situation with Sokolov is sorted out. Wouldn't want to put you in that kind of squeeze. Detective, let's get the report in and pick this kid up."

She spun and frowned. "Detective? Since when do you call me that? My name's Ram by the way."

Bastard's blood, girl.

The techie bowed his head. "If only we had met under kinder circumstances. The name is Miccolo Benjamin, as I'm sure you know. You might be able to find me online as MiccolosAngel."

"Well, maybe if Mr Blackstone here gets his hands on a processing core, it will be better circumstances."

Elliot rolled his eyes and walked to the door. Out came his phone. He sent a message to Cinder requesting time for a call regarding Sokolov. Then he noticed the missed message, from his wife.

"Hey, the [Zom-Fortress] isn't for another week still. Are you going to have a night off from this investigation? We need to talk again. Sort this out."

He stared at it. All the noise of the workshop tuned out, all the chatter between Ram and Miccolo. He rubbed his thumb across the screen and thought it over. He messaged back, "I'm on an important case. Lots of publicity. I'll find the time but I don't know when." He sent it off and stuffed his phone back into his pocket.

I gotta wrap this up and get this Kyte kid.

"Ram, we need to roll."

She nodded. "Right, thank you for the help, Miccolo." she said, and scurried after Elliot. She couldn't keep the grin off her face until she took a deep whiff and realized it suddenly smelled like canal water. "Where are we going?"

"Hell if I know," Elliot grumbled. He headed for the nearest train station. "We can't move on Sokolov without clearing it by Cinder. I messaged her a second ago."

"If we're on hold until then, why don't we finally reach out to the Holy Communion of Cyber-Wine?"

Come on, I can think of an excuse not to, right? I'm great at finding things to do. I just need the proper justification. Can't say we should take off, it's too early in the day. Already got food. If I say we should check the reports list, that would just obviously be making excuses. Do I have any other leads? Come on, there's gotta be something. Something to do besides go to that cult.

Ram charted the course with her WPS and led the way.

***

The Holy Communion of Cyber-Wine was officially recognized by the central government as an institution of faith. They lived in their church, or rather their church was where they lived. They had enough money come in through investment and so-called charitable donations that they had gotten a place all the way up in Alpha, where they had real sunlight shine through the windows. It gave the room an almost angelic look.

Elliot chalked it up to the pearl white everything. Walls, floors, sheets, cushions, all of it was as white as snow, whiter than most cocaine Elliot had seen too. Some throw pillows had color to them, about as much as the abstract art slapped on the walls. The impression reminded Elliot of the base simulation from the police headquarters, but without that thin layer of disbelief the neural uplink had.

Gregory Humbert met with the two of them, over a steaming pot of herbal tea in their living room. The complex had no doors, they had been taken out to improve the flow. It also meant every other member of the inner cult could be heard wherever they were. Elliot could hear one person tapping away on a keyboard, someone cooking, and at least two, if not three, people having sex. Mr Humbert just sucked the steam into his lungs and smiled from behind his bushy grey beard. "How may I be of assistance, officers?" he asked, pouring them dainty cups of the stuff.

Elliot politely accepted the cup. "It's about your recent addition to your..."

"Family."

Ram glanced down the hall that led to the bed area, where people were going at it like monkeys. "Family?"

"You may find it easier to think of it as a group marriage, polyamory of a sort."

One of Gregory's wives walked through the room wearing nothing more than a shirt and underwear. Just a bit younger than Elliot and with the kind of softness to her frame that women in bootcamp lost. As rare as it was eye catching.

How this hasn't imploded is beyond me.

Elliot asked, "Is everyone here part of the family?"

"No, not everyone. Peter is just an intern, though I think he's getting in bed with Amber. I haven't asked her about it yet. Officer, if I may, I'd like to clarify that we are not the entire constituency of our faith. Just the core, just my direct family. We support a handful of other enclaves like our own, surviving in this great epoch of apathy."

"So," Ram said, "there was a man by the name of Seouljin that–"

The cult leader's face lit up. "Ah! The artist. He could write the most heartbreakingly beautiful prose when he felt like it. I swear, he nurtures those pieces like flowers in his heart and it can leave some thorns on him. I do so hope he can extract himself from imprisonment soon."

Elliot sipped the tea. He couldn't taste anything in it, but it wasn't quite like water. A faint after taste of something he couldn't place that lingered on his tongue. He couldn't place what it reminded him of. He had drank better before, or perhaps he had acquired a taste for synthetic.

Ram led the conversation. "He developed a game while... partnered? With you. [Auroary's Rhythm Apocalypse]."

Gregory nodded. "We run the servers for it, but we exercised no creative control over it. Just a bit of networking stapled on top. It's one of our business ventures."

"Business? You're not charitable?" Elliot asked.

"Oh no, there aren't nearly enough people appreciative of our beliefs to live off charity, not without providing things in return. This isn't a hierarchical faith. We don't collect tithes or anything. Most of our money comes from people who think we're crazy," Gregory said, and laughed.

Elliot looked over as someone left the fornication area to strip down in the bathroom and take a shower. He could see their bare back in the mirror before it fogged with steam. "Most people regard any sort of faith as crazy."

The mirth in Gregory's face transitioned to a serious and intent look, directly into Elliot's eyes. "Well of course, the world tried to kill us all. It's hard to have faith in a creator that attempted genocide. But, that wasn't the first time it happened. The flood came before, and perhaps a great many destructions we don't know about. We here don't advocate for the will of God, but for the good of God. I understand that the difference can seem a bit opaque."

Ram frowned. "If you're defining those two separate from one another, isn't that defining them to be two different things? One a moral actor and one not?"

Gregory shrugged. "Perhaps they are two separate things. The God who acts, and the God who Is. You can twist yourself into beautiful knots if you try to understand whether an action is good or bad in the view of the creator. The old books say that God transcends time, he is immortal and eternal. To a being like that, what would killing a few billion people matter? If he's omnipotent, he can bring them back in a better future. Why should a life in the past be worth more than a life in the future?"

Elliot held up his hand. "Sorry, but we should keep the theology for after the mundane. You run the servers for Mr Vapor's game?"

The cult leader nodded. "And several other games. We also operate an internet archive that we keep insulated from EVE. It's very difficult for her to get in and meddle with our records. Makes people feel safe that the past isn't getting rewritten."

Ram asked, "And those people donate to you?"

"Some do. We also skim advertisements through the games, where it makes sense. You'd be surprised how much corporations would pay for the kind of access we have to eighteen to thirty-year olds."

Why do I have a bad feeling about this?

Elliot cleared his throat. "Do you run a dating app or something? Job placement after military service?"

Gregory blew wind past his lips and shrugged. "Well, our most popular simulation, though not by our design, is a game called [Sladder]. You might have heard about it. In truth, that game was a bit of a misfire. We tried so hard to satirize the digital facade of sexuality that we see in society today, that apparently we wrapped all the way back around to being something of an icon of it. Unironically appreciated by the very people we hoped would be repulsed by it."

Elliot set the tea down and folded his hands together. "If that's the reaction you're getting, why haven't you taken it down?"

"What can I say? Money talks, and some people come to the light, come to the understanding of what's wrong with it all. We can't save everyone, but we can save some."

"Hold on," Ram said, glancing down the various halls. "You mean to tell me that you're against flagrant sexuality?" At least three undressed people were visible.

I need to get out of here.

Elliot checked his phone, but Cinder still hadn't gotten him a meeting time. Amara hadn't messaged again. Gregory ignored his discourtesy, and said, "There's a difference between sexuality in person, and online. You can mingle your soul with another only if you're together. No machine simulacrum will ever be more than masturbation."

"Unless the machine has a soul," Ram said.

The cult leader laughed. "That would require direct intervention from God, I would think. Not a common thing to say the least. Did you know that the age of marriage has been going up over the years? And the rate of marriage overall has decreased to a mere quarter of people? Most children are raised out of wedlock. They aren't given that lifetime of example of what the beauty of the world has to offer. Detective–"

"Elliot."

Gregory nodded. "Elliot, you're married?" he asked, gesturing towards the simple band of gold around Elliot's finger. "Do you have kids?"

"I'd rather not say." Elliot rubbed the band, suddenly feeling it on his finger again. Years of habituation to it, the weight of it came back to his mind like being reminded he could feel his tongue in his mouth.

"That would be a no then. Never met a father who didn't speak of his children."

"Mr Humbert, I'd like to circle back to something else. You run the servers for the Auroary game? And for [Sladder]? So you're the distributor of the files? You authenticate them and so on?"

The cult leader blinked. "Yes, that's correct. Why?"

"So, if the files were doing something untoward, it would be your responsibility, isn't that correct?"

Gregory straightened up and leaned back in his chair. "Officer, if this is about personal privacy or something, I assure you that we take no data whatsoever. People get to see each other's avatars, but steps are taken to prevent the saving of that data in any way, and we don't collect anything. We understand that it is a very intimate game, and act accordingly."

"Well, that's good that you do. Your consumers surely appreciate it," Elliot said, and pulled up his phone abruptly. Excusing himself as though he had gotten a message, he stood up and moved back to the front door. While Ram pressed the man more on his connections to the proxy server shared with Miccolo, Elliot realized he actually had gotten a message.

Mikey d'Angelo had messaged him to ask, "Amara just reached out to me. Didn't even know she had my info. Asked if you had been over. What the hell kind of fight did you two have this time?"

A guilty knot formed in Elliot's throat. He couldn't place the reasoning for it. He swallowed it and sent back, "Don't worry about it. Just been busy with a high visibility case."

When he turned his attention back to Ram and the cult leader, they were in a discussion about pheromones and whether or not human beings could actually smell them. Biology had never been Elliot's interest and the latin started blotting out the meaning for him as he considered walking back over.

For someone who doesn't believe in hypnotism, she sure does chat with people who use it. Does she think the technical nature will help?

Given the time he had, he called up Paige Palmer, the stand-in sys-admin. After a few rings, they picked up. "Hi, this is Blackstone. I needed to check on if you had any progress with that initial assessment we discussed over text?"

"Officer Blackstone, nice to put a voice to the name. Let me pull up the report generated," she said. Elliot mentally rebuilt his image of who they were, and waited. "Seems that yes, your suspicion was correct. This... game, [Sladder] as well as [Auroary's Rhythm Apocalypse], based on Mr Ryder's play time of it, would be responsible for the inordinate processing power. I suppose, given the content of the game, he didn't notice or mind that his computer was nearly on fire."

He smirked. He glanced at the cult leader and had to turn away to hide his smile. "Can we break in and find out what exactly it's doing?"

"I can queue it into the system for EVE's attention, yes. Just a moment. Now, I should warn you that this kind of thing can take days if not weeks to... that's odd. EVE promoted it. You'll have your answer in the next few hours."

More like the next few minutes. You're welcome, EVE.

"Thanks. Send it over when you can. I'll wrap things up on my end," he said, and Paige said bye as well. The conversation between Ram and Mr Humbert didn't seem to have gotten anywhere during his exchange with the sys-admin. Elliot groaned and walked back over to the table. One of Gregory's wives, at least he assumed it was a wife by how little she had on, passed him by to ask if he wanted anything to eat. "No thank you," he mumbled, and strode up behind Ram. "Mr Humbert, is there anything you'd like to tell us about [Sladder]? Anything that wasn't properly disclosed?"

The cult leader frowned. "Officer, you know as well as I do that there is no reason I would ever answer that question, be there something or not. I'm happy to be polite, but I do know better than to speak to police about such matters."

Elliot nodded. "Just wanted to give you the opportunity, before any electronic search warrants get issued. Ram, are we wrapped up at this point? Any last questions?"

While she thought that over, Humbert narrowed his gaze at Elliot. "You're avoiding something, aren't you?"

Avoiding dragging this out.

"Always plenty of problems and not enough time."

"I don't mean your job," Gregory said. "I can see it in you clear as day. What are you avoiding?"

"I don't see why I should answer that question."

The cult leader grinned. "I am something of a priest. And I must say that I'd have to be blind to not notice the imprint of a pack of cigarettes in your pocket. Barely crumpled, I'd guess you haven't opened them yet. Very curious for a man that doesn't smell of cigarettes. If I had to guess, I'd say you quit some time ago but you're under a deal of stress. I'd say it had something to do with your investigation, but you're more irritated with me than stressed by me, so it has to be personal. Wife or family, and we've already ruled out children..."

Elliot's jaw tensed. "Nobody appreciates cold reading. You got a little detective program stuffed in your neural implant or something?"

Humbert laughed. "No, no, this is all natural. You're a tough one to crack though. Normally people flinch a little when the problem is guessed. Either you've had a bit of psychology training too, or everything is your problem right now. If so, you have my condolences but it's not professional to take it out on a civilian, you know."

"I know perfectly well how to separate my private life from my professional life, thank you very much."

Humbert smirked. "So which is it? Wife or family? I want to guess wife but there's something wrong about walking about with cigarettes that your wife surely doesn't appreciate, so it must be your family. Parents? Siblings?"

"None of your business," Elliot said, his voice rising.

"On the contrary, marital advice is my primary trade!"

He had to force his jaw open as he planted his hands on Ram's chair. "Mr Humbert, I will not be taking marital advice from a hedonist. I have one wife and that's it. We don't have a small committee on hand to sort our issues out. We have each other."

"Maybe you should," Gregory said. "I'll ask that you keep in mind you are in my home. I expect accordant respect, officer."

"This place is registered as a church, not a home. You sell sexual degeneracy to children. Act holy all you'd like, you're filthier than the lowest slum in Gamma." That felt good. It hammered the cult leader back into his chair. Even his wife stared in shock as her coffee machine hissed steam.

The cult leader pointed at the door. "Get out of my home."

"Elliot, we should leave," Ram said.

He threw a hand up, swiping it through the air. "Don't be like that Ram. This bastard doesn't deserve the respect. He should be behind bars just like Seouljin."

She rose. "No, we need to leave. Check your phone."

The seriousness in her face made him pause. The casual grin she always had was gone. He checked his phone. A general alert had gone out to all QRS personnel. There was a shootout ongoing in Survivor Canyon. It bordered Sokolov's territory and was normally a No Go zone even for QRS.

Cinder had called everyone in.

15

Survivor's Canyon

2140/10/06

Kyte was hyperventilating. He kept puffing and rebreathing his own panic, but it was all hidden behind his void mask. No one could see how wide his eyes were, how pale his cheeks were, only that he looked like all the others Vlad had assembled in this pit of hell he called Survivor's Canyon.

His ears still echoed with the gunshot from Vlad's gun. It was enormous. Kyte hadn't believed it was a revolver at first because the cylinder looked like the size of his fist. Shotgun shells the size of his finger were packed into it, and one of them had turned some guy's face into hamburger. The blast was so much louder than anything Kyte had ever heard in a video game. The report bounced off all the walls, slamming back at them as blood rained across the rusted sheet steel.

"You people, you just don't seem to get it, do you?" Vlad declared. "Your leader? Your alpha pack master? That degenerate with a fetish for wolves? He was the reason you could peddle your filth and. We. Killed. Him." Vlad marched around, strutting from platform to platform, crossing bridges made out of I beams and welded ladders. He moved with no fear of falling, and he never did.

The audience of Vlad's speech were on their knees. They shook and cried. A few were too doped to even respond. They weren't the danger.

The danger was the CZARheads. Kyte racked his memories, trying to dredge up what his father had taught him about CZAR. It had been a combat stimulant first. Not a coping mechanism like heroin in Vietnam, but an enhancement. More like methamphetamine in World War II. A disinhibitor first and foremost, of pain primarily but also fear.

People could fake being afraid, and CZAR would give them the clarity of mind to fake it without feeling it, if they were smart.

Kyte turned away from Vlad. The gangster spoke for the sake of the victims, to drive the new pecking order into their brains and exert Sokolov's influence. Kyte tried to tell himself that was a good thing. Sokolov was getting rid of CZAR, and treated his underlings well enough. The people who would go away and passively submit weren't the danger though. He kept telling himself that as he turned to one of the other gangsters. No idea who, just another body in a void mask, rifling through a bag of paraphernalia. A click click click like a Geiger counter followed the man around. Kyte assumed that was a blight detector, looking for contamination.

He paced to the side when he lost sight of Vlad, keeping one eye on his boss, temporary as it was and as he hoped it to be, so Vlad could keep one eye on him. Kyte's attention moved to another of Sokolov's thugs. Chatting up a prostitute, guessing by the latex dress. Perhaps she had been attractive once. Now, her eyes looked like she had taken a beating, half her hair was shaved for some foreign fashion, and her lip had a gash through it the size of a piercing. Ripped out was Kyte's guess.

Vlad started listing off edicts, rules, policies. He talked about Gamma Coin and about registering their businesses illegal or not. Kyte only half listened. It wasn't for him, it was all long term stuff, longer than he would be around. The beating of blood in his ears was louder anyways. He could feel the weight of the gun on his hip, the way it caught against his hoodie, dragging against the cloth when he moved his arms.

The thought that he might have to use it terrified him.

Part of him said he wouldn't really have to use it. He might have to fire a shot off, sure, but for as long as guns existed, people had aimed a bit too high, a bit to the side. They feigned jams, or worried about crossfire. They made excuses to not kill. Vlad would understand that kind of thing.

Then he saw someone acting wrong. He didn't consciously place it at first, then he realized they were too still. Their eyes didn't flicker around the alley as they listened. Too much tension in their body to be doped, not enough tension to be afraid. Kyte's mouth dried out. The person was a woman, late thirties. She had a factory jumpsuit on, with the kind of dirt and grease that came from regular use, not from living in the slums. A tourist of sorts.

And she was almost certainly high on CZAR.

He swallowed, felt like he had sand in his throat. She hadn't noticed him, and before she could, he looked away and kept her in his peripheral. He didn't know what he was supposed to do. He glanced around and saw that none of the other thugs were paying any attention to him, like he wasn't even part of the team. He shuddered to think of himself as part of Sokolov's team, but he was. Vlad couldn't even see him.

The woman rose. Before Kyte could come up with an idea, she moved like a predator through shadows and between rusted utility pipes. All the facades of pleasant living had been torn down in Survivor's Canyon, laying bare the essential structure. Abandoned appliances dotted power outlets, and she moved to one and then the next as Vlad circled the group of cowed prisoners.

She had a knife, or something like a knife. More like a short spear. A knife had been grafted onto the end of a baton, razor sharp.

"Hey." He didn't know what he was thinking, but she was far enough away that she couldn't charge him. Like some kind of ancient cowboy, he put his hand to the grip of his pistol. He tried to tell himself that CZARheads weren't people. They were people, in a physical, flesh and blood sense. Just not in a mental sense. Not moral, not trustworthy. But neither were most people, CZAR or not, down in Gamma.

Kyte shook his head. Realized she had looked over at him, then sized up the distance to Vlad. She stopped paying attention to him.

That meant she didn't see him as a threat. Kyte didn't know if he was a threat, because that would mean shooting them. The police did it, to CZARheads. Shoot on sight, because any one of them might turn into a blighted if their drug fix ever went wrong. The police didn't even investigate the deaths of CZARheads, not for prosecution anyways. Everyone knew that.

She moved.

"Fuck, hey!" Kyte shouted. The gun was in his hand. He darted after her. She scrambled up a staircase towards Vlad, blade first, crossing shot, short distance. She was going to kill Vlad and escape. Where would that leave Kyte? Dead in an alley.

He fired. The blast erupted in his hands, in his ears. It thumped his chest and blanked out his mind. The bullet went into her leg. She buckled and went down, breaking her teeth on the steel. Kyte blinked and tried to rationalize. He figured it must have hit a bone, because pain couldn't bring a CZARhead down. If pain stopped them, she wouldn't be spitting teeth out and hopping back to one foot.

A second gunshot went off, not from Kyte but from Vlad. Point blank shotgun blast to her chest. It put a hole through her, and she still tried to stab him. She got the thin edge thrust into Vlad's coat as he fell back. The two of them hit the ground. He drove his knee up and shoved, throwing her off of him and the walkway. The CZARhead grabbed for the railing, for the edge. Got her fingers on them too, and ripped her nails off before she fell three stories to the ground way below.

That was another thing about Survivor's Canyon. For as gutted as it was, there were lots of long falls.

Vlad rose, drenched in blood and panting. He ripped the blade out of his jacket. The tip had broken, but there was no blood. Armor in his coat. "Fucking crazy bitch. I knew that would happen! Didn't know who it would be but knew that would happen. That's what happens when fuckheads like that–" He pointed his gun at the first corpse. "Don't have proper supervision! Now then... who's the one who saved me?"

"It was new guy," one of the other thugs said. "Saw him taking aim, thought he was going to shoot you, Sir."

"It was you?" Vlad asked, pointing at Kyte.

"Me? Uh, yeah." He still had the gun. There was an empty casing, smoking hot, in the revolver's cylinder.

Vlad grinned. He nearly danced his way down the steps and clapped a hand on Kyte's shoulder. "I knew there was something special about you kid. Knew it the moment I met you." He smiled, and looked at him with those silicon eyes, and he squeezed Kyte's shoulder. Then he leaned a bit closer. "You didn't think you could do that, did you?"

Kyte forced himself to scoff. "What do you mean? That was the second time."

"That was intentional though," Vlad said, and patted him on the back. "I owe you one, kid. And you don't need to act tough. Hell, I'll trust you more when I see you break down and cry. All the good ones do, after something like that."

"I'm not going to cry." He really wanted to. He could remember the kind of release a good cry could give, but his father had taught him to keep his emotions in check, subordinate to his will. He couldn't cry anymore.

"Good good, just make sure you have your breakdown in private, okay? Or with a girl, but not Fumi. If these guys see you keep your cool, you'll have way more respect than Drake ever had. If they don't see cracks in you though, they'll be afraid."

Kyte nodded and listened, and pulled himself back together. "Don't I want them afraid of me? After what happened this morning?"

Vlad pulled away and shook his head. "Not if you want them to save you when you need it. People don't save people they're afraid of."

Vlad left Kyte standing there, and shouted some other orders at his subordinates. The men fanned out and changed tactics. He couldn't keep track of what they were doing. It was the most he could do to find a wall to slump down against and breathe. He still had the gun in his hand. Knuckles still white. He couldn't quite put it down. His eyes stuck to the end of it, wavering between his knees and trailing a line of wispy smoke.

Then, other shots started echoing through Survivor's Canyon. Not the monstrous boom of Vlad's gun, but a pop pop of something smaller. A lot of somethings smaller. People started screaming, people who actually reacted to pain and to fear.

The abandoned, rational part of his brain pieced together that someone was shooting. Sokolov's men were under attack, somewhere on the other side of one of the walls. He could hear the whizzes and bangs, the pinging of metal on metal as slugs pierced through walls and floors and flesh. He knew he was supposed to help, but he didn't have the strength to stand up.

Good thing too.

Another noise caught his ear. The whir of a drone, the buzzing of blades chopping through the air to send a camera bobbing through the halls. He turned to see it, and it got a full shot of his face. He panicked before he remembered that he still had the void mask on. Then it, the police recon drone, carried on towards the shoot out.

That got him to his feet. Gang fights were one thing. The police were another. "Fuck! Police! Police are here. Gunna be a SWATBOT!" he screamed. It was all he could do, to cast his echoing voice into the chaos. That, and holster his gun before one of the machines thought to do something about him. Then he ran. He didn't know where he was going, just away. He put his back to the shootout and charged. Other people ran, and he followed behind them. He prayed they were locals, and knew the way to go. Like a flock of birds, or a school of fish in a river, they herded one another down the alleys and walkways.

"This is the Southern Missou Police Department, Armored Response Unit Two. Cease all unlawful activity and combat." Loud, clear, inhumanly calm.

Kyte saw the steel behemoth before any of the gangsters. It looked like a tank, but with all-terrain climbing treads like big triangles that rolled over and crushed anything in its way. There was a woman atop it, riding it like the prow of a ship into the firefight. She didn't even have a helmet on, and he could see her blonde hair billowing behind her. She had no reason to be afraid, not with a suite of auto-turrets in front of her, already blasting concussive rounds across Survivor's Canyon.

Billowing meant there was wind. He paused and blinked. Saved him from getting a hand cut off by a fire door slamming shut just in front of him. Up and down the ghetto, he heard the slamming of fire break doors to herd everyone in, to trap them with the police. An inch of steel plated plastic stood before him, all yellow and black caution.

The crowd roared curses, and broke, they surged to either side, splintering. Kyte followed the oldest person he could see. That got him a pistol barrel stuffed in his face. The moment he crossed a hole in the wall, circumventing the fire breaks and headed who-knew-where, someone on the other side stopped him. "Who the fuck are you?"

Kyte reared back, and took his eyes from the gun to the man holding it. Well fed, reasonably cleanly dressed, no colors showing of gangs nor companies. "You got time to be asking that?" Kyte asked, and jerked his head back towards the ARU storming through the ghetto and knocking people down one after another. It made the gunman look away, and Kyte darted forward. The moment he made it through the wall, he was back in the shanty town, where walls were everywhere and made out of metal as thin as paper. But there were walls, enough to conceal him. He barreled through people and crowds, finding the mass of people more sluggish as it mixed with confused bystanders.

Then he was out, he was on the street and beneath the gaze of EVE. But, he had his void mask on and the police had better things to do than track him down. He took off running for the Greco Grotto.

16

Ordered Home

2140/10/06

"Level 2 contamination level. Proceed only if fully inoculated against the NZ-Virus."

Elliot glanced over his shoulder at Ram. They nodded to each other, the gesture nearly hidden by the bulky respirators covering their faces. The shooting had stopped by the time they had arrived at Survivor's Canyon, so they didn't bother strapping into QRS armor before entering. The place wound through Gamma, like an enormous snake had died and been left to rot. Everything had rusted and been painted in blood.

Cinder had rounded up the local leaders. She and her firefight squad squared off against the kinds of people Elliot avoided. "Did they catch the perps?" Ram asked.

Elliot pointed to another corner. It looked vaguely like a cafe setup. The overflowing trash chutes had takeaway boxes piled up. Paramedics were treating three thug-looking men. EVE had already confirmed them as known associates of Sokolov. "Some of them."

"Are they the victims? Or the ones who caused it?"

"Don't know. That's a victim though... I think." Before them was the most mutilated corpse Elliot had seen in years. Not rotten, like Nguyen had been, but butchered. He tossed up his own recon drone and got the feed recording. "Let's see here. It's October sixth, nine seventeen PM," he said as he squatted beside the woman's body. "Compound fractures through both ankles, split skull, both from a long fall." Out came a flashlight, a cone of white against the aging LEDs. There were a couple of places the woman could have fallen from, but the shortest was three stories. He made a mental note to check for more evidence, and continued, "I'd say the death blow was the shotgun blast to the chest. Took out most of the woman's right breast."

Elliot squinted when he saw the red on the woman's hand. After putting on gloves, he picked it up. Broken nails. "Fools, have you gotten an ID on this woman?"

Ram stamped a foot. "Why are you using my badge number?"

"Because I'm recording," he said, and twisted around to look at her. She hadn't gotten within fifteen feet of the body, like she wanted to hide in the shadows. "Are you okay?"

She brushed her hair back, tugging a few strands out of the seal on her respirator. "I'm fine, Mr Blackstone."

"Elliot," he corrected. "I'm recording."

"I'm fine Elliot. I'll get her face ran by EVE. No neural implant?"

Elliot's hand felt around the back of the corpse's head. Everything squished. Nothing felt like silicon. "Guess not," he said, wiping the blood off with an evidence towel. Then, he pried the corpse's lips open. The gums were black. He nodded. "Come take a look."

Ram inched closer and peered over his shoulder. "She was a CZARhead?"

"Yeah. Probably was high on the stuff when she got killed. Would explain why they needed such a large caliber."

"Gauge."

"What?"

"Caliber is bullets. Gauge is shells," Ram said.

Elliot rolled his eyes and took his fingers out of the corpse's mouth. "It was a figure of speech."

Ram planted her hands on her hips. "That's what people say when they confuse clips and magazines. Also, the ID has come in. Her name was Raya Castano. Was employed as a bar waitress over in one of the Rommie Blocks. No known criminal history. Not much of a history at all. Maybe she didn't like technology?"

"The real question is whose side was she on," Elliot said as he started checking pockets. He found a phone, and dropped it into an evidence bag. Found a credit chip, but no crypto chip. "Have EVE run a check if Miz Castano here was ever flagged in an illegal purchase. I want to know if she used Gamma Coin. I don't think she did, and if so, then she wasn't working for Sokolov."

"Already did, came as part of the identification. Like I said, no criminal history."

Elliot sighed. The respirator made the noise raspy. "A local then. Hold on." He turned one of the legs sideways, though the onsetting rigor mortis fought him. Blood from the thigh, pouring out of a small bullet wound. "Come here, Camera." He forced the recon drone over to get a picture of it. "I'll have to ask the coroner to take some measurements on that. I dare say she got shot in the leg before getting her breast reduction."

"Oh my god, Elliot. That's horrible."

Elliot chuckled and rose. "A bit of humor always helps you know," he said and gestured up towards the walkways. "We should get up there and look for the fight scene. With any luck, these guys have mismatched guns and we'll be able to figure out who shot what and can charge them accordingly. Sokolov's lawyer will probably fight like hell; but, that's not our problem."

When he looked down, and back at Ram, she wasn't looking back at him. She had staggered away to lean against a support pillar. She had her arms wrapped around her chest and didn't say anything.

I keep forgetting how fresh she is. She's too smart and quick with the tools. I forget.

Elliot put a hand on her shoulder as gently as he could, after taking the bloody glove off. "Hey, let's take a step back."

She blinked and looked up at him. With a little shake of her head, she said, "No, I'm fine. We can continue. Up to the, uh, up three stories right? To where she got killed?"

"No," Elliot said. "You're going to step back from this and take a breath. Come on, let's go over to the ARU and sit down."

She didn't protest, and followed him over. Something like a picnic table had been pilfered and laid out with water bottles. Elliot sat her down and handed her one. "That was your first, wasn't it?"

First corpse.

"I saw some in training," she mumbled, and picked at her respirator. "Is it okay to take this off?"

Elliot nodded. "It's level one over here. You're safe."

She popped the mask off and fiddled the lid of her water bottle off so she could drink some of it. "I saw some, before. A few blighted got close to one of our camp trainings. The sergeants took them out. No one was in any danger, or anything. Just a big surprise. Three in the morning, you know? Bang bang in the distance. They called us over to take a look. But, that was different. They were, the blighted were…"

"The infection changes the corpse. They usually look nothing like the people they once were. You're lucky though. Some people go their whole service without encountering a blighted. They're the ones that come out thinking the whole thing is made up."

"Still though," she said, and bit her lip. The water bottle crumpled in her grip as she rubbed her thumbs against it.

"It's different. Why don't you take some time. I'll handle this. You don't need to push yourself, not this time."

"I can–" She lifted her head, and words failed her. Eventually, she looked back down. "Thank you," she said, and chewed her lip.

Elliot left her beside the ARU, at the center of all the police activity, and climbed up to the walkway Raya Castano had been shot on. He took some extra video, some highlighted pictures, all enough that the scene could be rebuilt in simulation if needed. He didn't think much as he did the work, just lost himself in the routine.

He didn't notice Cinder approaching him, until she spoke. "Sokolov's put me in a tough spot."

Elliot glanced around. No sight of Colt. "How so?"

"Because I don't like people expanding, but I also don't like CZARheads and they were here to kill the dealers."

"Why didn't they just put in a report and have us deal with it? One ARU and they could have swept in through the aftermath."

Cinder sighed and tried to brush some of her hair out of her face. She had a bit too much smoke and gunpowder to keep it all under control. "Probably, because they wanted to assimilate the locals. Sokolov's building an economy. He needs people. He needs them using his currency and spreading it. Can't do that if we shoot all the CZARheads, now can he? Still though, I'm fucking pissed we didn't get Vlad. He was here. We caught him on camera and then by the time I got the ARU over, he had vanished."

"You could always just raid their headquarters, couldn't you?"

She shrugged. "Maybe, if we brought in some other departments. It would be bloody though. Not pleasant business. For now, we'll stick to trimming the extremities. Anyone we spot, we pick up. That includes the one the congressman wants. Figure out how to get him."

Would Sokolov still hand him over to keep us off him?

"Now's as good a time as any, Boss. When I was looking around for clues–" She snorted. "One of Sokolov's guys approached me. Gave me a contact number if I needed anything from them. Like if I needed them to hand over their new arrival."

She frowned. "In exchange for what?"

Elliot glanced around at all the armored police officers processing people, stripping void masks off, confiscating weapons, searching for CZAR. "Presumably, for not doing something like this."

"Well, you can't make any promises there, now can you? It's less and less likely that he's the one sending hitmen around, but that doesn't mean he's off my radar. Find another way to get the kid, or we may be handing him over to Ghos as a corpse. How's the new girl?"

"Ram? A bit shaken up. She needs to take the rest of the day off."

Cinder arched an eyebrow. "And what good will that do? She needs to get used to this. There's going to be plenty more. This is our line of work. If she can't hack it–"

"She needs to go home and deal with it that way," Elliot said. "Nothing we say here is going to help her. She needs time to help herself."

"Or," Cinder said, her gaze shifting over to the table Ram sat at. "She'll end up quitting. And won't that be a shame for her ideals."

"Nothing you can do that will change that. The last thing you want is someone on the force who can't handle it. What would you do? Keep her in the office at a desk?"

Cinder snarled, crossed her arms and pouted. "Look, Blackstone, you're her partner. If you say she needs to go home, I'll believe you."

Elliot nodded. "I'll help with the report filing tonight."

Cinder kept staring at him. "You need to go home too."

"You think I've never seen a dead body before or something?"

"No, I mean I'm well aware of the situation with your wife. You should go work on that. Take some time for yourself. Keeps you out of Sokolov's business while I make decisions on how to deal with the new wannabe warlord. So, go home. Consider that an order."

What am I supposed to do now then? Go home?

Cinder left him there, and after a moment, Elliot walked back to the ARU. "Cinder dismissed us for the night. Show's over. Let's get out of here," he said as he started dropping evidence bags onto the table.

She turned her head up and nodded. "Alright, yeah I think that would be nice. It's been a long day. I think I could use some sleep." Somehow, she managed to smile.

"Make sure you get some good food in you before then. We've been living off junk."

"You're the one that picked the restaurants," she said, following him out of Survivor's Canyon.

Maybe I should take my own advice. But, not yet.

***

Elliot went to Mikey d'Angelo's apartment to decompress. His friend had just gotten back from third shift at the factory, and the two of them sat down with a bottle of imitation scotch. "So, this is about Amara, right?" his friend asked as the two of them settled in.

Elliot swirled the glass. The dye in the liquor smeared around the edge like an oil spill. "She wants to do this three week long streaming event thing. I don't know, I guess it sounds reasonable. A bunch of them will all be in the same homestead type place, practicing for a tournament. It probably is a good idea for her streaming career that she wants."

"What do you mean? Like, they're going to be physically in person with one another? What's the point in that? Isn't it a VR game?"

"It's for stuff outside the game, I assume. Crossovers and silly things for entertainment."

Mikey looked flat at him and toasted his glass. "They're going to do a lot of drinking, aren't they?"

Elliot pressed his lips into a line and nodded his head. "And probably reactions to funny videos and stuff like that."

"Well, why don't you go with her?"

"I don't play video games, much less stream. And come on, do I look like I would be funny on camera?"

Mikey shrugged. "Then do behind the scenes stuff. Take some time off and do the cooking for them. You think they're going to complain about that? And if they do, just start running background checks on them and see how quick they change their tune."

"Okay, well, I can't do that. The background checks that is," Elliot said.

Though, EVE still owes me that favor. Probably a bad idea to call it in for that.

"I think you've got the right idea though. I could do that. I haven't had a vacation in months. Years maybe. So what if it's sort of a working vacation? Theoretically, they're entertaining people to be around. All their content is candid and done live, so it's not like they're actors on a script. There's gotta be worse people to have a drink with."

Mikey shrugged. "I say go for it. If you can't stomach it, you can just leave. You do have casual clothes, right? No way they'll let some working stiff in the door."

Elliot looked down at himself, still in uniform. He frowned and thought over his wardrobe. "Has fashion cycled back to ten years ago yet?"

Mikey's empty glass hit the table and he poured himself another drink. "That, my friend, is not something I can help you with. I don't even get it second hand from Dom. That kid just wears whatever bulk order clothes are cheapest. Great for my bank account, but... I don't know, maybe that's an influence he's missing from his mother?" Mikey's gaze had settled on the door to Dom's bedroom. The dingy thing, with faded paint, glowed from within. Not enough to be room lights, just the glow of computers and game consoles. Screen savers and charging lights.

Elliot sipped his drink. "He's probably awake and he probably knows what's in fashion. I bet you he designs his VR avatars."

"Let me check." Out came Mikey's phone.

"You're friends with him?"

"Under my name? Not a chance. He would block me in an instant. He doesn't know who I am though. Thus, I can see when he's logged in. Yeah, he's up. He's playing some kind of platformer by the looks of it. Never heard of it. Have you heard of [Crumbling Castle]?"

"Not at all. As long as he isn't playing [Sladder]."

"Why? What's that?"

Elliot worked up some spit and tried to wash out the chemical taste from his mouth. "Competitive matchmaking sex. Anonymous too. Met this one kid, spent so much time jumping from one random pairing to the next that he nearly starved himself. Just kept getting that dopamine hit and never left."

"What happened to him?"

Aside from getting hospitalized because he took my advice?

"Long story short, apparently he has a girlfriend now. Upside for him, he had the confidence to go get actually laid."

Mikey folded his arms and nodded. "Damn, maybe I should download this game. Could get an hour here and there while the kid's at class."

"Bastard's blood, Mikey. If you're trying to date again, there are better ways."

"Like what?"

Elliot's mouth hung open for lack of an answer, once again. He solved the issue by getting another glass of scotch and drinking most of it. "You know, this is the kind of thing that EVE should solve. It's a matchmaking problem, right? She has all the data on everyone. Why couldn't she just crunch the numbers and tell people who to get together with?"

Mikey laughed. "You serious?" He laughed harder. "Because how you meet someone, and what you intend when you meet them, determines whether you'll be interested in them. That's why women still bother with makeup, even when they're just running errands like getting food. Some guys too, though that's not what I'm looking for. They never know when they might run into the right guy. Might, I don't know, find themselves standing in line behind them at a burrito joint. And then a casual conversation turns into an invite. Everyone's got fucking music playing nowadays though. Worse too, they'll be playing games in their neural implant instead of looking at the people around them. Got a billion people in this city, and less connections than a farming hamlet."

The memory of how Mikey had met his wife rose up in Elliot's mind, and he nodded. High schoolers, but not the same class. They'd gone to boot camp at the same time, and somehow kept their relationship in one piece, then gotten married the moment after discharge. All from meeting each other in an art museum they had both been forced to go to. Mikey had gotten a recreation of the painting they had been looking at when they met, and Elliot only then realized he hadn't seen it on the walls in ages.

"Anyways," his friend said. "I'm not looking to date again, not till after Dom gets into the military. And I swear, if he wastes away playing video games, I will smash the damn thing against the wall. But after he's out of the house, I guess I'll start looking around for some other empty nester. I'd take a younger girl too, if she'd have me, but I don't think that's in my cards. Probably not even interested in that. I don't need a second kid."

The thought of having kids made something inside Elliot's chest ache. It was a familiar pain, and it hurt all the more because he knew he couldn't even think about it without first fixing the issues with Amara. "So? Your solution is to go cyber-fuck your way to happiness?"

Why did I say that? That was way too harsh.

Mikey chuckled. "I'll at least give it a try. Way I see it, at my age there are worse vices to have. There will come a day where it won't even be an option, without medical intervention, so may as well enjoy it while I can. A perk of being single!"

Elliot shrugged and shook his head. Fatigue had begun to droop his eyelids and nod his head. The liquor helped. "For as long as it stays up at least. EVE wants to nuke it for being a blight on the youth."

"All the more reason to enjoy it now! [Sladder] you said it was called?"

"Yeah, but I really don't recommend it. I think the religious nutjobs that distribute it packaged some malware on the backend or something. We've got an investigation into that right now. Pick one of the less popular ways to have sex in VR."

"You mean with all the people who turn into anthro animals and stuff? Pass."

Elliot suppressed those memories, shoved down that knowledge he would have preferred never learning. "I should get back to my house. I bet Amara is still awake. I'll talk to her about joining as tech crew or whatever."

"Hell yeah. Glad I could help you. For all the help you've given me, keeping Dom out of trouble, I finally get to pay you back a bit. In more than booze too."

Elliot sighed and smiled. "Mikey, you don't need to think about it as paying me back. Friends don't have a tally of favors between them."

Mikey waved and topped off his drink again. "Yeah, you know what I mean though. It's not a friendship if it's all one way, either."

"You're helping with [The Faceless Well]. There's that."

Mikey stared back at him. Didn't even spend the energy to say how ridiculous that was. "Are you planning to release more games posthumously or something?"

"God, I hope not," Elliot said as he rocked back in his chair. His hand brushed against his thigh and stopped when he felt the pack of Nico-Pure cigarettes. With a somber grimace, he pulled the pack out to look at it again. After days in his pocket, it was a crumpled mess that should be thrown out if he wasn't going to smoke them.

"I thought you quit?" Mikey asked.

"I did."

"Having second thoughts?"

"No, I'm not going to smoke them. I get plenty of nicotine through my energy drinks. It's just that these were my brother's favorite brand."

"Were? Did he quit too?" Mikey asked.

Elliot sighed and tossed them on the table. "He's been missing for... about six years now."

His friend nodded and made a few apologies out of consideration. Then Mikey said, "Never much hear you talk about your family. I didn't know."

Elliot swirled the dregs of his beer. "Like I said, it's been six years. Not much chance of him showing up again. I just wish the Draft Administration would unseal his records. Hell, maybe I should call in my favor with EVE to get them."

"Not a bad idea. It would get you closure, wouldn't it?"

"It might."

I might not want to see the truth though.

Elliot continued, "That's why it's just me and Amara though. You know, I might be a piece of work right now, you know that? I blew her off today. I shouldn't have done that. I should have heard her out. Alright, it's like two in the morning," Elliot said, and pushed himself to his feet.

"What? Isn't it still like an hour before your bedtime?"

"Yeah, but I need time to talk to Amara, don't I?"

"Fair. Maybe just make sure you can get the time off first? You got any hot investigations that would stop you?"

Elliot got as far as putting his jacket back on before he slowed to a stop. He found himself staring at the wall, like the worn down movie poster for some animation belonged in a museum. "Oh, shit. Oh shit. Oh shit. I do. I do have a hot investigation that my boss just put a freeze on until further notice. She forced me to go off the clock because she's meddling with other stuff, but if I don't get this kid in time, I'm screwed."

"Kid?"

Elliot shook his head. "Seventeen year old. Just shy of the draft. Screwed his life over because of an accident. Now he's making a run for the hills."

Mikey frowned. "Seems a little... what's the term? Synchronicity?"

Elliot stopped and shook his head. "No, this is different."

"How so? Young kid, right? Made some kind of mistake instead of climbing the ladder."

"The difference," Elliot said. "Is that this kid won't be vanishing. He's not going to slip through my fingers."

"You're going to put him in prison?"

Elliot turned away from his friend, slowly zipping his jacket and straightening his attire. "That's what you get for assault with a deadly weapon, isn't it? You don't get to just move on with your life."

"You do if you're already drafted. I know a guy who got promoted for winning a fight like that. Said he had guts."

I bet that guy didn't hospitalize a congressman's son.

"I suppose that's for the judge to decide," Elliot said. "He's young, smart, and fit. From a veteran family too. Maybe they'll go easy on him if he doesn't make himself more of a criminal. The kid's with a bad crowd right now and I don't have the power to haul him out of there. Not yet. This kid is sliding down into the guts of the underworld with no brakes. The best thing I can do for him is probably arrest him sooner."

"Or, let him escape to the Isles." Mikey looked at him from over his shoulder, illuminated by the glow from inside his refrigerator.

"I can't do that. Even if I did, it's Hell to live in the Isles."

"You'll do what's right," Mikey said, as Elliot finally moved to leave. "See you around."

"See you around, Mikey."

Elliot returned to the streets, to the walkways and bridges between towers and train stations. The unchanging glow of advertisements and the stench of the Mississippi. He started walking, his feet taking him back to his own apartment. Along the way, he took out the burner phone that Sokolov had sent him. He stared at it, but didn't turn it on. Eventually, he pulled out his own phone and called EVE.

"How may I be of assistance?" the AI asked.

He sat down in the seat of a train and hung his head. "You still owe me a favor, right? Two if that scan on [Sladder] pays off, right?"

The phone buzzed a hold tune for a moment. When EVE's voice returned, there was something more lively about it. "Did you finally think of what you want to ask of the great me? Judging by your talk just now, do you want your brother's records?"

"Not this time. Do you have any way for me to get this Kyte kid legally?"

"The one working for Sokolov and seducing the guy's daughter? That the Kyte you're talking about?"

Elliot pinched between his brows and closed his eyes. "He's doing what now?"

"He's a bit too involved for you to just extract him, unless you can catch him right when he tries to go to the convoy out. That would be your last opportunity though."

He hung his head and listened to the creaks and groans of the metal box around him. The hum of electromagnetics and the whistle of riveted seams in the wind. Some few others mumbled into their phones. Drunks blathered about their prospects and workers bemoaned their upcoming shifts. A dozen people surrounded Elliot, and not a single one looked at him. Their own lives blinded them to everything else.

What the hell is wrong with me? Was it the comparison to Dom? The bait and switch of joining Amara? Was it something that cult leader said?

"Do I have any options before then?"

The AI paused, thinking over her own options. "I'll check on it," she said. "Give me a call in the morning. I need to check what kind of snooping I can do within Sokolov's territory. Your boss is making all kinds of demands as well. I might be able to piggy back something for you. But you know, I'm already helping you prove your point to Ram."

That put a smirk on Elliot's face. "I know that. Just make sure she doesn't realize it yet. Alright? Chalk that up as officer training."

"Of course, of course. You're a very greedy man with your favors. You know that? I thought we were becoming friends, Blackstone."

"If we're friends, then why are you counting favors you owe me?"

She laughed. "Big favors are different from little favors. Now, why don't you focus on your own issues?"

Elliot felt drained, like his insides had drained out and left a shell of tension. He needed sleep. "Everything is tied up with the other things. My life is a mess."

"Obviously," the AI stated. "All life is. The trick is focusing on the things you can change, and more importantly, the things you can succeed at. Now go get some sleep. You humans need it to sort your brains out of all the gunk thoughts."

"And you don't?"

Elliot sat up. The line hadn't dropped, but EVE hadn't answered. Eventually, he took it away from his ear to check that it hadn't dropped. The call was ongoing. When he put it back to his ear, she said, "You are so easy to mess with. You know that?"

He hung up on her.

What was that though? Was that all?

17

Fumi's Home

2140/10/07

When Kyte stumbled back into the Greco Grotto, he didn't even know if that was where he should have gone. He felt like his head had cracks through it and all his thoughts were draining out. The Grotto's customers had been forced out. He passed dozens of them absconding with drink glasses and chicken wings into the night. Other people flowed in, all in void masks like him. It wasn't until he found himself standing halfway to the backroom that he took his mask off and looked at it.

"Where the hell is Vlad?" someone demanded.

Kyte turned. It was a woman. A well dressed woman, with curves in all the right places and green hair done up with a pin at the back. Kyte didn't know her. He would have remembered a figure like that, the kind of expression that should have been a sultry smirk and yet seemed all the more attractive for the panic. "I don't know," he mumbled. "He sent me off before the police showed up. I ran."

"Useless kid!" the woman in the dress shouted and stormed past him. She left nothing behind but some confusion, but it was something Kyte's brain could grapple with. He could handle the idea that Vlad had relations, that there were people who cared about that guy. That meant he likely cared about them too. The pieces twisted around just like they would have for his father. He did it just like his father had taught him.

The exercise was slow. It took ages and it made the time pass. While he sat down on a sofa, forgotten game console idling to his left and congealing queso to his right, the adults in the room went about the business of fixing the mess. No one came looking for him to do anything. Not until–

"New Guy, you made it back," Fumi said, hopping the railing. She landed on her tight pumps and planted her hands on her hips. She had her hair in loops now, the locks shooting out in either direction from behind cyan ribbons. It made her look really cute, but the reaction was entirely in his mind and not in his emotions. "If you survived, that means you have it, don't you? I spent all evening at the bar waiting for you."

Kyte shook his head. He gestured around the room. "I got held up a little. Sorry."

She pouted and crossed her arms. "So did you leave me waiting on you for nothing, or what?"

Kyte wanted to go back to his shitty apartment, curl into a ball beneath his sheet and vanish. "Yeah. Of course I have it. I said I would, didn't I?"

"Then let's get out of here."

He must have heard that wrong. Fumi should be interested in him, willing to spend some time, some resources. He was the new guy, an anomaly worth thinking about because he could be of benefit to her in ways that were hard to see through to the end. Fumi was supposed to know that he was going to be gone soon, that was supposed to create a tension of time that would make her act fact and irrationally–by extension, predictably. She wasn't supposed to prefer him to her father's gang.

Kyte blinked as she held out her hand to him and he took it. Somehow, she pulled him back to his feet and tugged him along to the back hall. She said some things, explained where they were going, but it all went in one ear and out the other. What stuck in his mind was the little dig between the palm of his hand and her painted nails, the way it pressed against him. Memories surfaced because it felt like Akane's hand.

Akane, who Kyte hadn't thought about since the concert. It hurt inside him, like the empty fear had been set ablaze. He knew they were through, would never date again. Even if he stayed in Bastion and didn't go to jail and didn't have any of those consequences. He and her would never be together. The relationship had been torn apart, a bond ripped and left ragged inside him.

Fumi dragged him in by the hand to an apartment above the restaurant. "Come on, I got a sound system over here." A nice apartment. It didn't stink like shit. It didn't have that dampness that pervaded Gamma. The air had proper climate control and, while sparsely populated, it had a homely decoration to it.

Kyte looked around, his head pivoting like a hungry bird's. The realization that he was in Fumi's home set in. Not just Fumi's, but Sokolov's. There was even a family photo on the wall. The gang lord, Fumi, and who must have been Fumi's mother. She looked ten years old at most in the photo, nearly confirming that Fumi's mother had died.

"So, do you have it on a USB stick or something?"

Kyte pulled the little data drive out that Miccolo had given him. "Solid state," he mumbled, and tossed it to her. He didn't have the strength to keep his voice tempered. She didn't need to be cowed or manipulated though, not anymore. She vanished into her bedroom and came back out with a tablet that she plugged into the living room's display screen.

"You can sit down, you know. Though, you should really take your shoes off," she said as the system booted up.

Kyte shuffled back to the door and kicked off his grimy treads. Then he went back and sat down on the couch, next to Fumi. It was soft. Reminded him of the time his father had gone up to a concert hall in

Alpha. Open air, open bar. A ritzy place beneath the stars. The ceiling of Fumi's house just had cameras. Closed circuit, he was sure.

For a moment, Fumi's homescreen colored the room pink with one of Auroary's original album covers. She wasted no time in pulling up the file and getting it running. "Why is the file called Reject_17?"

Kyte sighed. Thinking about his lying, manipulative father was the last thing he wanted to do. "The producer labels all his work in progress files that way. They're rejected until they're finished. Even if there's a deadline."

Fumi nodded, as though she approved of that. "Must be why Auroary's songs are so good."

"This is just an advance copy, you know. The songwriter, he's in jail. He'll finish it when he gets out. This is just as close as it gets until his lawyers spring him. It might have audio artifacts left in it. The voice synthesizer still has some issues that have to be manually tuned. He just does that after he's happy with the words and the cadence."

Fumi rolled her eyes and hit the play button. After a moment, a metronome started up. It syncopated. A drumroll kicked in. Auroary began in her soft voice. "Today is the day, I wanna hear you say. Look me in the eye, or I'll say bye-bye."

Kyte closed his eyes and sank backwards. He tuned out the kitschy electropop lovesong. The beat was fast, the thump would keep a dance floor in step, and he could already picture the idol's earnest gaze right back at the listener. He felt the music bounce off of him and push him down. He wanted darkness. He wanted isolation.

Fumi grabbed his hand, grinning from ear to ear. "So I'm like, the first person to hear this?" The earnest glow wasn't something he deserved.

The killer and liar in the room said, "Unless the lawyers and police snuck a listen." His arm felt numb, like dead weight reaching from his shoulder to her grasp. The work file had booted up the stock image of Auroary that his father used as default inspiration. The original fabricated idol, and one that hardly looked like her hologram.

Then he heard the rest of the lyrics. "Who's that girl over there? When I've laid my heart bare. I'm the only one for you, I always thought you knew. The only one, who can say, I love you."

The warmth, what little there was, drained from Kyte's face. It only took that line for him to realize what his father was doing with the song. It wasn't a love song at all, it was a candy sweet lie to suck people in before twisting it through the lens of an obsessive stalker. The beat never switched from bubbly pop, only the tempo increased as the lyrics twisted, and it went right over Fumi's head. Of course it had. His father had designed it that way. It would make people talk about it, because some people would realize it and others wouldn't and then some would get to gloat and others would be shocked. It was bait for media algorithms.

"Hey," he said, giving her hand a tug to bring her attention back to him. He stopped, mouth open, hesitant about what to say. His mind and his instincts weren't lining up.

"Come on, the song's almost over."

He winced. "You did get that harddrive, right? The payment? You said you would. I held up my end of our deal. I didn't do this for nothing."

"I'll get it, I'll get it. Why are you doubting me? You're worse than Georgie today."

Kyte leaned over, nearly to her shoulder, close enough she would smell the sweat from running for his life. He had to get out, and that meant going with what his father taught him. "Georgie and Raz and their friends tried to work me over in an alley this morning, because I got this for you."

She snarled at him. "They did what?"

"Their buddy Drake wanted to have a boxing match with me. They got a little lynch mob together to put me in my place. They bit off more than they could chew, but next time they'll know better."

"I should have them fucking killed," she hissed. "These people! They're always meddling with me! Second guessing me. Saying what I can and can't do. They put me on a pedestal like I'm made of fucking porcelain. Like I'm a fucking egg to be kept in my father's rotten nest."

He let out some of his breath, relaxed some of the tension. He could almost feel how Fumi's impulses were shooting out away from him. Felt like he was in the eye of a storm. "I won the fight with Drake. I bought myself some time. Now, I'm guessing they all have bigger issues than me to deal with, now that the police are looking at your father."

She paused, not catching the last lines of the song. She looked down at his chest and back to his face. "You beat Drake in a fight?"

"Street fight, yeah." The emptiness inside him made it easy to keep his face straight.

She grinned. "I hate that guy. You couldn't have picked a better target." Then she kissed him. Not on the lips, but she planted hers to his cheek and pressed her chest against his shoulder. She smelled like vanilla. Akane had always smelled like fruits, like she had dived into a tropical market and come out chewing bubble gum. Fumi had just a touch of a maturity to her, just enough to be noticed.

How much she knew what she wanted also helped.

"So," she said, batting her eyelashes at him. "Turns out there's a co-op mode to [Auroary's Rythym Apocalypse]. You're not doing anything tonight, right?"

Kyte fought down the urge to laugh. Laughing wouldn't do, it wouldn't make her help him get out of Bastion. She smirked at his effort. "That's your big request? Was stealing the next Auroary song just to get me in the door or something?"

"Sure was," Fumi said as she spun away and leapt to her feet. "Now come on, New Guy. We're playing video games."

"If you say so," Kyte said, and felt his pocket vibrate. The phone Vlad had given him had a new message for him.

"Report to the clinic tomorrow at noon to get your jab."

Vlad had sent it. At least he was alive and not in police custody. The message didn't say whether his blood test had been positive or negative though. He realized they probably wouldn't tell him at all, lest he back out of being their guinea pig. He needed the shot though, if he was to survive in the Isles. He needed that, and Fumi's harddrive to buy his way into employment, and he needed the gun hidden inside his hoodie to be of any use to them. Useful like he had been for Vlad.

"Here's my old ENU. Get yourself set up, yeah?" Fumi said, tossing the headset into his lap and breaking his thoughts.

"Sure," he mumbled, and went through the motions while his mind conjured up for him the blighted outside the walls of Bastion, and the police hunting him within. The glow of Fumi's screen fought to wash the image out of his mind. In the darkness he could circle the drain of his memories and fears, but the glow of Auroary was a mental onslaught demanding he relax, that he smile and enjoy his time with Fumi.

His tricks, his faux attitude, were working better than he could have hoped for. She was smiling, oblivious to the kind of guy Kyte really was. Deep down, he knew there was something even more effective than the right lies at the right time. It was the way she laughed and smiled and pulled him along without a hint of deceit or ulterior motive.

Hours later, all the gaming had come to a stop. Their bodies were exhausted and sweaty, pressed against one another in the dark. They didn't move, merely listened to a chill remix of Auroary's first album. Fumi had fallen asleep on the couch and slid onto him, her head pressed against his chest. He didn't dare move and he wasn't tired enough to sleep. His mind refused to slow down and allow that. Even though it was the last thing he wanted to inflict on himself, his brain meticulously documented everything about the moment—everything about her.

She was strong and honest, but under so much danger because of her father that a regular person would have snapped. As far as bad fathers went, Kyte couldn't decide who had it worse between them, but Sokolov probably didn't lie to his daughter. That glare which had told Kyte to stay away was still in his memory, but recontextualized into a challenge rather than a warning.

In just a few days, a girl obsessed with the worst idol in the world, one that he might get shot just for talking to, had slid her hand into his and hooked her fingers between his. Laying there, his nose full of sweat and strawberry shampoo, Kyte asked himself just how much would get ripped out when he pulled himself free.

But he didn't have to do that just yet. He could enjoy the night even if she was pressing herself into his life with every soft breath.

18

The Draft Administration

2140/10/07

Elliot cooked breakfast.

He wanted a traditional, continental style breakfast, so he spent the first two hours of the day trying to find what he needed in the grocery stores, all while handling reports and emails over his phone. After more than a few calls to Ram, who had offered to help with her restaurant expertise in shopping, he managed to get the requisite supplies.

The act of cleaning the dust off every tool he needed took him another half hour, but eventually he had bacon sizzling, eggs frying in the run-off grease, and waffle batter prepped. He had no idea whether the Belgian Waffle maker they had gotten as a wedding present still worked, but he only had one way to find out.

"What are you doing?" Amara asked, standing in the doorway to their bedroom. "You're not even dressed."

Elliot had on one of his old t-shirts. It was black and had originally born a graphic for the Tenn Samurais, but he no longer even knew if they were competing in the War Games. "I don't have to put on my uniform until I go to the office."

She scanned the kitchen again. "Is this an apology or something? Is there something I should know about? Other than you leaving me in the park?"

He winced and shoved the spatula under the splatter of egg. "No, no it's not an apology. I'm glad I can still get your attention through your stomach at least. Do you want cinnamon in your waffle?"

"I add cinnamon to my pancakes, not to my waffles. That's gross," Amara said as she sat down at the table and watched him.

What the hell is the difference between a pancake and a waffle?

"Food will be done in a second. I don't know when I'll get forced into the office, but it could be any moment now."

"You should have done breakfast burritos then, in case you have to leave."

He smacked the griddle with the spatula, stirred up the bacon some more and stepped over to hack up the melon so they could have some fruit with the spread. "Look, Luck-E, I–"

"You can call me Amara. That was really... embarrassing of me to say. I'm not on stream. You can– I want you to use my actual name," she said.

He twisted around to look at her. She wouldn't meet his gaze. "Amara, you're still doing that training camp retreat thing, right?" he asked as he dumped some batter into the waffle maker. He flipped it, and electricity blasted out of the joint like a ball of lightning. He jerked his hand back from the crack and blinked.

This thing is going to burn the apartment down.

"Do you not want me to?"

"What? No, no I don't want you screwing up your plans. I know it's important to you."

She twiddled her thumbs. "I've been thinking about how thoughtless it is of me. We haven't spent any time together lately, and I know what anniversary it more or less–"

"Amara," Elliot said, tossing the cooked eggs onto a plate as fast as he could. "We don't need to talk about the distant past, do we? I must have been a little more somber than usual, but I shouldn't be letting emotions like that change me, you know? So, I've got a proposal. An idea. Assuming I can get this current case wrapped up, let me take some time off and join you. You'll need behind the scenes help, won't you?"

His wife perked an eyebrow at him, then looked down at the gathering food on the table. "You mean as like? A chef? Is that why you're doing this?"

Elliot puffed out his cheeks and blew. "Partly . You know me though, you know I like home cooking. I always have. You're happier with proper food in your gut. Makes everything better. You know, I'm still hurting in the chest from that beating I took the other day. I could use the time off."

"Shame your mother doesn't do any cooking any more. I miss the cookies she used to make."

That's another thing I should fix, isn't it?

Elliot pulled himself up from his slump when the waffle maker dinged. He pried it out and onto a plate for Amara, dumped in another for himself and finally got the bacon. "So? What do you think?"

"Hun, it's a breakfast. It's not gourmet."

"I meant about me joining in the background, giving some help," he said, and drizzled some syrup across his bacon. A little burned, but he enjoyed it regardless.

Amara quietly poured syrup onto her waffle and smeared on some butter. After carving a piece off and chewing on it, she said, "I guess I don't actually know what the schedule entails. I don't know whether that would work. I think you'd be expected to be in some of the shots."

"It's not strange to have crew in the background with these kinds of things, is it?"

"No, but this would really be putting you out. It's not like we could pay you. None of us make enough money to be full time."

Elliot shook his head. "Are you looking for reasons to say no? Come on, I thought this was a good idea."

She huffed. "I don't know. I'll think about it, and talk to the others. I haven't exactly advertised that I'm married to a police officer, and that could cause some... controversy to say the least." Elliot's fork clattered out of his hand. He stared at Amara until the waffle maker dinged. She looked up at him and shrank back. "Babe, your thing's gonna burn."

You think I fucking care about that right now?

"You... what? Are you embarrassed to be married to me?"

She shrank. It looked like she tried to pull her shoulders into herself and tuck her chin. "It's not embarrassment. It's just that, well, the people who watch my stream, they're mostly from Gamma, since half of Bastion lives in Gamma. No one down there likes you. You know that better than me."

Elliot didn't know what to say. The waffle maker buzzed again and he brought his plate over. It too had blackened, but he drowned it in syrup till the only thing he could taste was butter and syrup. The two of them ate in silence, chewing their thoughts as much as the food. "I've gotta head into the office soon. If I don't catch this kid, a congressman is going to get me sacked," he mumbled, stirring the last piece of waffle through some spilt egg yolk.

Amara slipped away from the table and set her plate next to the sink. "Yeah, you need to do that. Uhm, sorry. I'll try to figure out a safe way to reveal it or something. You know how it is when you put something off for too long, don't you?"

Elliot didn't clean the kitchen, he just left it all to dry. A mess to be fixed later, he pulled on his jacket and left. When he reached the train station, he pulled out his phone. No messages, no summons to the office, no word from Cinder nor EVE. A train came and went as he stood there, mindlessly going between his phone calls, to his text messages to email and back again. Eventually, he sent a follow-up email to the sys-admin about the investigation into [Sladder] and checked his list of open tickets.

The meaningless paperwork drew him back to the police office. He took a corner workstation, one of the hidden ones that people didn't go to often. Little foot traffic, little means of distraction. It also meant he didn't expect to get press ganged into QRS. One by one, he went through the process of finalizing the various police reports he had addressed the other night.

The system threw an error at him when he tried to close out Miz Ryder's complaint that her son had been hypnotized. Something he had said in the paperwork triggered a follow up requirement. It wouldn't let him say the report had been finalized without a wellness check at least one week after the initial visit.

Bastard's blood, why? Because he's a politician's son? How the hell do I void this? Can I report it as an error? Maybe I can list it as wellness check confirmed by surrogate? Or would that require meeting with Akane again?

"Blackstone."

Elliot blinked and pulled himself away from the computer. Lizard leaned against the wall with a can of Zeus fizzing in his hand. The man was in normal clothes, not QRS armor. He had a certain and judging frown on his face as he looked Elliot over.

"How are you healing?" the senior officer asked.

"You mean after Gaia the other week? It's nothing much. A few aches now and then."

"Have you been hitting the gym? Getting your physical therapy in?"

Elliot spun his chair to face his original partner, and returned the inquisitive look. "Wasn't required. Why are you asking?"

Lizard drummed his fingers on the can. He glanced around, and pulled over a chair to sit down with him. "You don't look like you've been hitting the gym much. I think it would do you good." Lizard looked fuller in the face than usual, like he had started hitting the gym himself. Guessing by the nicotine infused drink in his hand, might have been cutting down the cigarettes too.

Yeah, it probably would. Maybe I should have gone for a run instead of come here to do busy work. What's going on though?

"Wyatt, did something happen?"

Lizard said, "Not yet. It's going to be cranking up though. Last night? In Survivor's Canyon? That was just an opening sortie. The rumor

I'm hearing is that they've got some new ARUs coming out. Cinder is getting pressure to put them to use, to show results with them."

"New? What's going to be different?"

Lizard shrugged. "You know how it is with Daedalus, don't you? It'll be sleeker, stronger, faster, something more. Probably will have new guns on it. Congress was demanding rail guns."

"Rail guns would pierce through three walls. That's not safe."

His colleague scoffed and grinned. "When do their demands ever make sense? Still, who knows, maybe one day even the big ones will fly. Shame we'll never get proper giant robots. We're stuck with these mid-sized things just so they fit between buildings."

Elliot rolled his eyes. "You're never going to get giant robots until we're in space. It doesn't make engineering sense."

A fire lit in Lizard's eyes. He leaned in. "Hey, that's not quite right. The thing is we won't get humanoid giant robots. But those mining machines? The ones that look like enormous worms and are treating Alaska like termites? Those are giant robots. There's been some leaked photos on the net, that us and the asians are working on undersea leviathans to replace the nuclear submarines. Make the whole thing nearly autonomous aside from a pilot to authorize the strikes. That's... that's a subject for another day though."

I wonder, did the robot fascination predate his daughter becoming half-cyborg?

Elliot let out his breath and nodded. "Over a beer sometime. What did you actually come over here for though?"

Lizard looked him in the eyes and said, "Do you have any desire to move back over to my department?"

Insurgent Response? Are these gangs really that bad?

"No. No, Wyatt, I don't have any interest in going back to that."

"You were good at it, Blackstone. Look at what you did back at Gaia? You kept your head and you survived. Not just anyone could have done that. Even better, you're not cocky about it. It doesn't make you boast. I'm not looking for the kinds of people who are happy to do the work."

Elliot leaned forward and put his arms on his knees. He frowned at his hands and said, "Cinder has me in charge of my own group now. I've got my own responsibilities, as much as I hate that she put me in charge of VR. You know my opinion changed when I got married to Amara."

Lizard shrugged. "Blackstone, you can't fool me. I know the hours you put in."

Elliot's teeth gritted together. His old partner was sounding like when they had first met, before his trip to California which should have settled his issues. Elliot had transferred out after that event. "Wyatt, look, QRS is as far as I'll go, and that's because everyone does QRS duty. I like working face to face with people, even if they're a bunch of ungrateful idiots. I get to bring things to a resolution this way, rather than just being a bit piece in power politics."

"Aren't you working on orders of Ghos right now? You didn't get away from politics at all."

Elliot recoiled back. "That's different."

"How? How's it different that you're headhunting some kid and driving the department on which gang gets made an example out of?"

"I'm not the one causing that! If Cinder wants a war down there, that's her decision and it sure as hell isn't my fault when she's ordering me away from it."

Lizard rose and put up his hands. "Alright, easy. I get your point. Just, think about it, will you?"

"Sure, I'll think about it," Elliot lied. The other police officer made a retreat and left him to stew in freshly agitated anger.

I need to get Kyte before a full on war happens. Just a kid. How can just a kid cause something like a full police crackdown? Just because the eye of politics has noticed him? Gazing down from the capital building? Come on EVE, I need a solution here.

He could only think of one solution without her help.

***

"Detective Blackstone, we meet again so soon," Seouljin Vapor said, smiling from the other side of the bulletproof glass. "I thought I told you a call would suffice. Did you have a fight? You certainly look the worse for the wear. I hope it's not my boy giving you trouble. I know he's smart, but you have the power of EVE at your disposal. If you wanted to, you could just send in some machines, couldn't you?"

Elliot stared back at the mindbreaker and said, "I need you to press charges against your son."

Seouljin's smug look vanished. He leaned onto the table and asked, "What for?"

Caught off guard, eh?

"Theft. He stole your unreleased song from Eden's Lyre. No idea what he did with it, but I need you to file the charges so I can start an electronic search warrant and watch for it to show up on the internet."

Seouljin narrowed his gaze. "And you can't get that approved under the current charges?"

Not with the investigation on hold because of Cinder, I can't.

"I'm pursuing all options to safely bring your son to justice. Preferably before he gets killed in a territorial dispute between gangs trying to peddle CZAR. Prison is better than dead."

"And worse than leaving Bastion for the Isles. Don't think you can make this a false dichotomy. Who do you think you're talking to?"

"A father who should be concerned for his son."

Seouljin smirked. "He's my son, don't act like you're supplanting my role. You know, last time you were here, I figured your issues were with your wife, but that's such a crude guess, isn't it? You wouldn't be interested in my son like you had a personal stake in the matter if your issue was your wife. Well, perhaps if you were homosexual, but that's even less likely. There are so many mundane explanations though. Are you going to get a promotion? Is the congressman breathing down your neck? Guilt perhaps? Though, I don't think you've let him slip through your fingers. Really, this would be so easy if I–"

"Stop trying to use your tricks. I know you're a mindbreaker. You worked overseas for almost ten years. I'm not going to give consideration to a single thing you say aside from whether or not you'll press charges. You should care that you're never going to see your son again. You'll never even have closure."

Seouljin grinned. "Who'd you lose, officer?"

Elliot gritted his teeth for a moment. "I already said no tricks."

"Family? Ah, but you're too young for a kid. That's already been established. Your brother then?"

"Shut your mouth! Focus on the case or I will find ways to ruin your life."

Bastard's blood, he got to me. Never let a mindbreaker get to you. Stupid.

Seouljin just grinned and sat back in his chair. "You know, it's not very professional to project your own issues onto a case like this. My son would be better off in the Isles. You're not helping him by capturing him. You're helping yourself."

Kyte is not Luke. I'm not delusional. It's just right to bring him back and make him face his mistakes. Make him face justice. He's a kid and it was a mistake. The courts will have mercy.

Elliot leaned back in his chair, put distance between him and the mindbreaker. His mind went to Evan, in the hospital grinning because he had a girl who liked him. Hurt but would heal. Dragged out from his house and not eager to go back to it. Kyte had arguably helped Evan, but Kyte was doing worse to escape arrest. He was pushing himself into the swamp beneath Bastion.

"Look, Seouljin, the way things are going, it's not even a question of whether I arrest him or he escapes, it's whether or not he gets shot during a full scale police raid on the gang he's shacked up with. He's not important, not in the eyes of people with power. He's the kind of person who becomes collateral damage, a victim of circumstance. He can't get out of the city until the convoy arrives, and the raid team? If they go in, it'll be before then. The best thing for him would be if I could pull his ass out of the fire. The judicial courts and some time in juvie are better than getting shot like a blighted."

"My son knows how to do what he has to do. He's smart and rational and would have made a great soldier. He would know better than to get caught in that kind of fight. He's not loyal to a gang, he knows better than to give his loyalty like that. It's not safe. Loyalty is something to cultivate in other people, not in yourself."

"Like you and your wife?" Elliot asked, glaring back at Seouljin. "I'm sure you gave your son a great example, a real northern light in the darkness. She thinks of the two of you as divorced, you know that? She's not even using your last name anymore."

A flicker of irritation touched Seouljin, nothing more than a momentary clenching of his jaw. The mindbreaker composed himself, but it had been enough to show how open and raw the wound was. "My son will know well enough to run away rather than stand and fight. I'm not concerned. The only way he'd get stuck like that is if some righteous-minded fool forces it on him."

"Then you know what?" Elliot asked, and rose from his chair. "I won't get your help then. And maybe by the end of this, your son will be dead and you'll have to live the rest of your life knowing that you could have helped me protect him. That's going to sit on your soul, not on mine, because I will have done everything I could to do what's right."

That didn't even put a crack in Seouljin's stare. "You're in a rush. Something is making you impatient. Something other than the convoy, other than the raid. What did your wife do? Why do you need this wrapped up so soon? Divorce seems to be on your... no, in the back of your mind. Not everyone knows it as the hungry beast, brother of fear, like we know it. Yes, that's it, isn't it? You're trying to have your cake and eat it too. You need to keep your job, but also need to soothe the missus. Terrified to sacrifice one for the other, because you might end up with neither. And in so doing, you're looking at my son as a virtuous little feather to put in your cap and make yourself feel good as you face your two bosses. How close am I?"

Silence prevailed, so complete Elliot's own breathing sounded like a wood rasp working against the table between them. By millimeters, Seouljin smirked at him with all the certainty in the world he had seen true.

"You're despicable," Elliot said, and left the interview room. One of the guards gave a knowing chuckle and when he made it out of the penitentiary, he called up EVE for a query. "Seouljin and his wife aren't yet legally divorced, right?"

"Correct," the AI answered.

An hour later, Elliot buzzed the door of a homestead on the tenth floor. It was a nothing special kind of place, one of thousands throughout the district to simulate what suburbs had once been across North America. Kyte's mother answered the door and looked him over. She looked like a wreck. Disheveled clothes, bags under her eyes, messy hair, stench of booze and body odor, and a certain slowness to her reactions that, coupled with her dilated pupils, indicated she was mixing an antidepressant.

"What do you want, jannis?"

The trauma teams must have ignored her.

"Miz Nest, I would like to talk to you about the situation your son is in."

She sneered. "I thought I told you security would have you out of here without a warrant."

Elliot shrugged. "I'm not here to search his room. I need your help before your son gets gunned down."

She stepped back from the door and led him quietly to the common area. At least six residences connected to the central room, just tiny things for bedrooms and bathrooms while communal amenities were meant to be shared. No one else had come out of their partitions, and the kitchen sat quiet, populated only by dirty dishes. Miz Nest sat down at the dining table, on the half that wasn't covered in boxes from online shopping.

Elliot sat across from her and smiled. He tried to make it warm. "I'm Detective Blackstone, I'm the one in charge of bringing your son in for aggravated assault–"

"That all? I heard it was murder charges."

"Who said that?"

Kyte's mother slumped down, her cheek in her hand. "Akane, that harlot who caused all this."

"I would think that the underaged drinking had more to do with his impulse control than a high school relationship falling apart. Either way, your son is doing a very good job of avoiding arrest so far, but the way he's doing that is going to get him in a hell of a lot more trouble than a fight in a club."

"And? What do you expect me to do about it? I've called him probably a hundred times. He doesn't pick up."

Elliot grimaced. "That's because his cell phone is in an evidence locker, not with him. What I'd like you to do is sign an official complaint of digital asset theft. I believe your son remotely accessed your husband's computer and downloaded some files. If I can get a warrant based on that, I should be able to track him down and arrest him."

"So you can pile theft on top of assault? Why the hell should I do that? He's my son."

"Because if he doesn't get brought in soon, he's going to do something he can't take back."

I just wish I knew whether that would be escaping to the Isles, or murder.

She didn't answer the question, she just went over to one of the refrigerators and got herself a beer. She finished most of it before sitting back down at the table. "I can drop the charges later, right? And you'll have to just let him go?"

Elliot let out his breath. A bit of tightness in his chest went away and he nodded. "On the theft grounds, yes. He'd still have to stand trial for attacking the kid in the club."

Miz Nest shook her head. "Fine. Just, get him somewhere safe. Please? I don't care if that's custody or the Isles anymore. I can't sleep at night knowing he's still on the run."

"Of course. Thank you for the cooperation," Elliot said, and sent her a link to the web portal where she could file the complaint. After a few minutes helping her through the process, Elliot rose from the table with a smile and headed back to the police station to file the warrant request.

No sooner did he have that in, than two officers from central MPHQ showed up next to him. They were in suits and carried themselves with the kind of self control that made them look like robots. Elliot knew the type. Rumor had it their spines had bypasses built in from their neural implants that overrode reflexes and stopped fidgeting. He wasn't sure he believed that, but he did believe they outranked him. "Detective Blackstone," one said, smile as smooth as botox. "We're from the DA."

Draft Administration?

Elliot rose from his chair, so they couldn't look down on him. "What brings you here?"

"We believe there has been a theft, and some falsification of records, and the parties involved are part of your ongoing investigation. So we would like to request your assistance as we begin our own investigation."

How would Kyte be involved with the DA? Did he get his hands on a vaccine dose somehow?

"What assistance do you need? I'll have to get it cleared through my boss–"

"Captain Cinder has already been brought up to speed on the matter, and many other assets are being brought in as we speak. We at the DA take these things very seriously."

Elliot frowned and crossed his arms. "Can you tell me what exactly happened?"

The DA officer smiled again and nodded. "Aleksander Sokolov illegally stole a shipment of NZ vaccine doses. We are concerned that he might be attempting some form of un-controlled efficacy trial. Bastion has many people like him, who don't understand probability and safety margins, and will look at a lucky outlier as proof of their hypothesis. This kind of misinformation could undermine trust in the DA, and we can't allow that, now can we?"

They're going to raid Sokolov. It's going to be a bloodbath.

Elliot forced himself to smile. "No, we can't have that."

What can I do? How can I get Kyte before he gets shot?

19

Adverse Reactions

2140/10/07

Kyte was in trouble.

He liked Fumi, and had tricked her into liking him.

She was trouble, no getting around that, but in her situation where she was surrounded by gangsters and punks, trouble was the rational response. Her father cared for her, but didn't know how to show it, and so created a protective shell around her, reinforced by cruel men who treated her like a pearl of beauty when they didn't want to think about the violence they had perpetrated. All she wanted was normality, to have friends that treated her as an equal.

That was what had made it so easy to make her like him. It came at the cost of people like Drake jumping him, but it had been like reaching down through an oil slick and finding someone drowning below. And he had saved her for his own selfish needs. Had faked his smiles and poked at her weaknesses to get her to unfold like a puzzle box. It was all exactly the way his father had taught him and it had worked perfectly.

He had poisoned their relationship from the start, and she didn't know. He didn't even have a way to backtrack, to make it up to her, to turn it into an honest relationship. Not that he could stay in Bastion. Identity forgers weren't something he had access to, and her father was more likely to kill him than to help him.

Under different circumstances though, he would have clung onto her and not let go. He would have gotten in fights for her, and the thought of that made him sick to his stomach.

"You alright?" Dr Bahtt asked, bringing his mind back to the present, back to the clinic.

"I'm fine," he mumbled. "Unless you're about to tell me that I'm incompatible with the vaccine."

Dr Bahtt turned to him, needle in hand, and grinned. "Why would I tell you that? You're getting the jab either way. It's too late for you to back out now."

Kyte shook his head. "How did you get that anyways? The government doesn't sell them. Well, they sell getting the jab, but not the actual vial. Only government nurses and doctors give them out, if you pay for it outside the draft process."

The doctor shrugged. "That's just what they tell you. There's thousands of clinical trials going on at any given time. People need to know about cross-compatibility. If you're testing something else, you just need to file some paperwork and you can get a batch. Those researchers are far more susceptible to corruption, or just common, every day incompetence. Now then, I hope you've got a show worth watching lined up. This here will put you on your ass for the night."

"If it doesn't kill me."

"Oh, it'll put you on your ass if it's killing you too," Dr Bahtt said with a chuckle. He swabbed Kyte's shoulder with some alcohol and checked the measurement on the injection once more.

"Wait, wait wait!"

"Wait what?"

"I mean, what if it is a bad reaction?"

Dr Bahtt stabbed the needle into his shoulder and squeezed the icy vial of chemicals into his arm. He smiled at Kyte as tendrils of pain seeped through his arm like it had to take root in him. "If it's a bad reaction, I'll treat the symptoms. You're the guinea pig. You knew that. We have every interest to keep you alive, so don't worry. It just might hurt a little. And I'll tell you now, that the government said you were incompatible with the vaccine. So buckle up. We can get you a bottle of whiskey if it will help you sleep through it?"

Kyte jumped to his feet, staggering until he bumped against the wall. "Bastard's blood, really? You really did that? You've killed me! You can't unvaccinate someone!"

The doctor shrugged. "Of course you can't, that's why we didn't tell you the results. Now then, put this monitoring strap on and begone with you. If you don't have that on, we won't know if you're dying in there, so keep it in place. Remember, the government is very conservative with their safety margins for these things. They're in the business of good PR, not in letting people leave. You'll probably be fine."

Kyte took the proffered device and stared at it, his heart already racing and thumping. Whether that was from the jab or in his own head, he had no idea. "Fuck." He tore his shirt off and strapped the thing around his chest and upper left arm. He cinched it and tightened it till he felt like he could barely breathe.

Dr Bahtt shook his head. "The readings will be off if you don't give it some breathing room. The sticky parts, they have to stay put," he said, and tugged at some of the adhesive parts to loosen it up on him. "Now get out of here and do nothing strenuous. Doctor's orders. Vlad will get you some food for dinner."

Kyte tugged his shirt back on. "Vlad's back?"

"So I'm told, get. Get," the doctor ordered, waving him away. Kyte stepped out into the hall, was met by several glares from people more obedient to the doctor's orders, and fled the clinic. He descended the steps as his shoulder ached more, and he tried to tell himself that it was all imagined, but that didn't help. He staggered into the darkness of the apartment room he had been given and dropped to the bed. He was hyperventilating, but he knew how to bring that back under control. With an effort of will he slowed everything down and brought quiet to his mind.

Out came his phone, and he messaged Vlad. "Can we meet?"

Rather than sit and rub his thumb across the screen impatiently, he did as the doctor suggested and turned the television on, streaming some mindless cartoon. Eventually, the gangster responded. "Of course. You like burgers?"

Kyte had never had a good burger in his life. "Sure."

Hours later, when sweat had stained through his shirt completely and the episodic cartoon had merged into one fuzzy string of punchlines, Vlad knocked on his door. Standing made Kyte's head light, feet numb. Had to grab onto the wall and stagger open to pop the deadbolt.

"You look like shit," Vlad said, pushing his way in. A shuffle of feet away in the hall, and Kyte was sure some bodyguard had left. "That from the good medicine? Or because you shot someone last night?"

"The medicine," Kyte mumbled, and sat down at the counter that acted as both a divide for the kitchen and the dining table. "Too tired to even circle the drain on shooting that CZARhead last night."

Vlad ripped open the bags and laid out a couple of steaming burgers from The Greco Grotto for them. "Good, that means it'll pass."

"Or I die."

"Or that, but Dr Bahtt knows what he's doing. We think. Why don't you sleep?"

Kyte shook his head and took a bite. It tasted like real meat , but it was probably synthetic. "Ever laid in bed for so long, trying to sleep, that it's like you were asleep? Then, you know, you can't actually fall asleep?"

Vlad nodded and swallowed. "Yeah, happened a lot before I got these put in. Have you tried reducing your blue light exposure? Nice thing about these cameras is you can set it to a simulated daylight cycle. Doesn't matter where you are, what you're doing, you can just program in when you want your sleep cycle to be. Gotta cover a few nerve patches here and there, so you don't get mixed signals to your brain, but it works wonders. Complete control over your melatonin and everything."

"I don't think it has anything to do with the light."

"Yeah, it's probably because you shot someone, but hey, you did the right thing. Ain't no shame in being a bit shook up. It'll pass. And you've even got a great excuse to black out on liquor and collapse to oblivion."

Kyte glanced back over at the bag of foodstuffs Vlad had brought, and the older man slid the edge down to reveal the neck of a vodka bottle. He nodded and chewed, thought it over, and swallowed. "Sounds like a fucking good plan to me."

Vlad laughed and got some shot glasses out of the cabinets. Tap tap, slosh slosh, toast. It burned, but it was a fresh kind of pain and Kyte didn't mind it much. "Hey," he asked. "How did you end up working for a guy like Sokolov? Or, I mean, I guess Sokolov doesn't seem like that bad of a guy to work for–"

Vlad scoffed. "Better than any corporation in this God forsaken city."

"How did you end up a gangster?"

Vlad shrugged and poured himself another shot. "Bit like you, started with an accident. Things escalated. Ending up burning all my bridges back to a regular life and found myself at the bottom of society. But, it's not too bad down here. Like the ocean, the fish on top look down and see only darkness and empty void, but the seafloor has its own kind of ecosystem who in turn look up and see nothing but vacuous space above them."

Kyte nodded. "And what? That makes Sokolov a volcanic vent?"

"Spewing out his blessed Gamma Coin for all of us to get by without the light of EVE above."

"Well, I don't think I can cling to Sokolov like you can."

Vlad set his empty glass down. "If you wanted to, I could arrange it. After what you did in Survivor's Canyon? Getting back on your own? No police on your ass and still with your gun? You're as good as any thug we've got. If you're worried about the police tracking you down, we can get you a new ID. Hell, we could probably start by just reviewing the legal case against you. Might even be able to get it dropped on a technicality."

"No, no, Sokolov isn't going to let me, not after what I did." His heart was beating harder. His breathing had gotten shallow. He took another shot to try and smooth it over, and didn't know whether the burn in his gut helped.

"What? You mean stabbing Drake? Fights between members happen all the time. It's not a big deal. We'll just keep the two of you apart. Easy."

His head throbbed, and his gut twisted. With a grunt, he lurched around the counter and to the sink just before he spewed half the meal back up. Vlad shouted and jumped up behind him, one hand to his back and the other to his phone. "I've poisoned the well, salted the earth, I can't stay here."

"Bahtt, check the kid's vitals, will you?" Vlad barked into the phone, holding Kyte up by the scruff of his shirt. "Come on you, back to the bed. You need to lay down. On your side, fetal position, come on."

Kyte let himself get manhandled onto the bed, the fever turning his body into one numb ache. "I can't stay man, I can't stay."

"Why? What the hell are you talking about, kid? What did you do?"

"I tricked Fumi into liking me."

20

Auroary's Rhythm Apocalypse

2140/10/07

Cinder was working remotely and called the meeting in VR when she got the report from Paige Palmer on [Sladder]. Rather than the sparse construct of the headquarters server, she had her own simulation setup. Elliot had it on good authority that it smelled like salt water and flowers, with a hint here and there of coconut. He had no idea whether it did because his ENU didn't have the fidelity to even try processing that. He contented himself with the sight of the lapis lazuli waves, the wash of tide against concrete and the tropical birds flitting through the air.

Anything to look away from the bikini his boss had on.

"Is this based on someplace real?" Ram asked. She at least was sensibly dressed in bootcamp fatigues.

Probably just loaded into her default outfit. She's lucky she disabled situational wardrobe logic.

"Caribbean, vaguely. I had a stint overseas and just... the pools up at the tops of towers, they're not the same. Even the ones that use salt instead of chlorine. There's something wrong about the experience. VR isn't much better, but it's something at least, if I use my isolation tank."

Elliot cleared his throat. He faced toward her, but turned his eyes directly away from her. "We're here to discuss the [Sladder] report, right?"

Cinder tilted her head and squinted her eyes at him. "What's... oh. Right." She swept her hand through the air, pulled up her menus and a moment later, her outfit updated. Instead of just a bikini, she had a buttoned shirt tied off around her chest and a skirt that didn't actually cover her thong straps. "Better? You dinosaur prude."

Elliot grimaced. "Might actually be worse, but so be it." Ram fidgeted, and looked about to change her own outfit to something more fitting for the tropical island. It wasn't really an island though—no sand to walk out on—unless oil rigs counted. The whole thing looked like an apartment building had been sunk in the water. Vending machines and game tables sat a few meters from ladders down to the water.

This is the kind of luxury that billionaires used to vie for. If it were real.

"Right, so you're my VR investigation team," Cinder said as she summoned the report like a wad of papers to wave at them.

Elliot said, "Yes, that's why we looked into what we suspected was a VR related crime. I'd say we hit gold."

"I'd say you missed the mark," Cinder shot back. "Just because you showed that this sex thing is using background processing to process Gamma Coin transactions doesn't mean we can tie it to Sokolov. This is a symbiotic relationship, not a culpable one. So what if someone else is skimming money off these transactions? How am I supposed to use that to take this smug bastard down?"

Elliot frowned and felt the urge to just call in EVE and have her join the conversation, but didn't think he'd be able to. Ram spoke up instead. "If we throttle the processing power of Gamma Coin by removing [Sladder] from the equation, his sub-economy will grind to a stop. The moment people can't actually pay each other with his currency, they'll have to do something else. It would at least pressure him, right?"

That works.

Elliot said, "He'd have to get his own processing farm going. It would light up in energy consumption like a flare in the night. You'd know exactly how to hit him when the DA makes their move."

Cinder snarled. "Nothing I can do to shut down [Sladder] without crushing those cultists, and that would get tied up in a Freedom of Religion investigation, and I'm not doing that until after Sokolov is arrested. Those vultures in the justice department would be drooling the moment they saw me do that."

Ram frowned. "So, because [Sladder] can't be directly tied to Sokolov, it's on hold until after the raid?"

"Right." Cinder nodded.

Ram said, "So, if we could tie it directly to him, then we could shut it down? Because I think the exact same hack is in [Auroary's Rhythm Apocalypse]. I think it's built into the loader program and just gets glued onto the download. If that's true, that's a direct tie to Sokolov, isn't it? Since he's harboring Kyte?"

That's more of a stretch than Cinder's bikini.

Cinder flatly said, "Ram, that would never fly in court. However, it doesn't need to fly in court to get an injunction on the program and root out instances of it. If you're correct, then it would also catch [Sladder] and would cripple his crypto without getting me in trouble with the Bill of Rights police. Can you prove it?"

"I think so!"

Cinder planted her hands on her hips and nodded. "Right then. Blackstone, help her do it. Oh, and Ram, you're welcome to use my simulation from time to time, if you want to take a dip. I know you're supposed to be on a bit of R&R after last night. Don't feel like you're in a rush, okay?"

Ram beamed. "I'll have to book some time in an isolation tank and come back. I don't think it's quite the same when my real body is sitting in a chair."

"Oh, you totally should. Isolation tanks are amazing!" Cinder said, and Elliot mentally retreated.

He pulled himself halfway out of the digital dream, enough to feel his own body once more, to see the computer before him and smell the leftovers. He let Cinder and Ram have their small talk while he started a request to EVE to rip through [Auroary's Rhythm Apocalypse]. He had just finished the sentence when a chat message appeared, from EVE. "I can't double prioritize that kind of crack. I'm going to need you to isolate the game and prove it's happening first hand."

No. No, please God, no.

"Surely there's another way," he responded.

EVE said, "Just do it. It'll be good for your health."

"It's a game about an idol for teenagers."

"The music is pretty good though. You'd like it if you gave it a try."

"I have no internal metronome. I suck at those kinds of games."

"Then learn and get better. Have someone teach you. This is your job, Blackstone."

"Not by choice."

"Most people would kill to get paid to play video games. Especially popular ones. Your wife for instance."

"I get paid to help people."

"And playing this game will help people. It will help break up a criminal organization and will help extract a kid who maybe can still be saved."

"If he doesn't die to an improper vaccine dosage that they stole."

"If that, yes. Now stop complaining, and if you send this to Miz Palmer, I'll make you regret it."

With that, the chat box terminated, and Elliot buried his face in his hands. He disconnected from Cinder's simulation and huffed. For a moment, rather than the wash of gentle waves, all he could hear was rustling of dust in the vents.

"Elliot, you there?"

The voice came from inside the simulation, more like a muffle in his ear. He leaned back in his chair once more and sank back into the virtual world. Cinder was waving her hand in front of his face until she saw his eye blink and his focus return. "Welcome back. I want your word that you're not going to go back down to Gamma. Even if you're not going after Sokolov, or the kid, or whoever, it will look to the DA like you are and they'll demand your badge."

Well, lucky me, I just got signed up for an all-nighter minimum of video games I hate. Couldn't go down there even if I wanted to.

Elliot smiled. "Would be happy to get some sleep and time with my wife."

That made his boss blink and narrow her gaze at him. "Okay, now I know you're up to something."

Sharp as ever.

"Actually, now's as good a time as any. Recall I requested a meeting with you the other day?"

She folded her arms. "Yes, it's been getting delayed. Stuff like the DA keeps making me postpone it."

"Well, here I am, to let you know that I'd like to request some time off next week. Personal time, to spend with my wife. She's doing a streamer event thing, and I am going to volunteer myself to help. No badge, no uniform, no nothing like that."

Cinder took a moment to respond, "Good for you. You'll need to get Congressman Ghos satisfied first though, without pissing off the DA. Figure out how to do that, and you've got, what? Like, two years vacation now?"

"Something like that. I'd have to check."

"Get everything wrapped up with a bow on top, and take all the time you need. Ram could use some time working QRS, get her exposed to the other officers and other fields of work. Just submit the request through the system and get it in on time."

Elliot glanced around, no sign of his partner. "Did she disconnect already?"

"Yeah, she's arranging for an investigation room for the two of you."

It was Elliot's turn to narrow his gaze. "Investigation room? For a VR hack?"

"Yup."

"As in, outside of headquarters?"

"Yup."

"As in, she's getting us a VR cafe room?"

"Spot on."

Elliot did not join her in laughing.

"She's something else, you know that? It's not often that someone joins the force because they were a victim of it, you know?"

"What's that mean? What happened to her?"

"She got trampled by a bit of garden variety corruption and never let it go. Instead of becoming an anarchist or something, she enlisted."

Elliot pressed his lips into a line. "So, that's what your concern was when you realized the kid was a Congressman's son."

Cinder nodded. "You've got the day with her. Ask her about it."

***

"You're gonna love this place," Ram said as she guided Elliot into the VR cafe she had booked. Sword Art Connect bustled with people despite the early morning hour. Half a dozen virtual assistants managed payments, room timers, log-in rewards, coordinated trainers and power-levelers, and one was in charge of tournament brackets. Arena, though Elliot didn't know the full title, took center stage that day, with fantastical fighters replicated in hologram form like a boxing ring. They darted and spun, hacked and slashed with magical boosts. Most of the fight moved faster than his eyes could keep up with, but whenever something important happened, parries, blows, counters, a freeze frame of the fight appeared next to the scoreboard overhead.

The buzz of people talking drilled into Elliot's skull worse than the deepest pit of Gamma. Not because it was louder, but because of the things they were saying. Build guides, and tier lists, and synchronization numbers, and launch dates and a million other things. Their chatter beat all the rest and recuperation out of Elliot, like he hadn't slept at all that night.

"Our room's this way," Ram said, leading the charge through the milling mass. On the second floor, she swiped a key card and opened up a private gaming room for them.

"So, does this have those deprivation tanks or something?" Elliot said, stepping in and only finding some couches around the perimeter of the room.

"Not this room, but you can book them. This is just for augmented games, so people can play together, in the same room."

"And people pay for this?" Elliot asked, sitting down next to the computer.

"It's a popular date spot," she said, standing in the middle of the room with one hand on her hip. "I learned about it when looking up common places to go on first dates and stuff. There's actually another location of Sword Art Connect which has a giant rolling ladder for infinite rockclimbing. It just keeps creating new holds and you're never more than a meter off the ground. So, you know, you can be in the game, scaling up the dark lord's tower or whatever, ready to swan dive and assassinate him, but if you fall you just hit some pads."

"That sounds exhausting. Why would anyone want to use their actual body to do that? Aren't games for escapism."

She shrugged. "It's fun to use your body though. They're coming out with resistance systems so that if you're fighting in Arena, you can actually activate your muscles in real life to train them. It's getting pioneered by streamers and competitive gamers, but was developed by the military. Pretty cool if you ask me. Up here in Alpha, there's a bit of a, uh–"

"Body worship," Elliot finished.

Would be nice if Amara got one of those resistance systems. Seeing her in tight shape again, like after bootcamp, damn... that'd be nice.... Damn, maybe I should get one. Sounds better than the gym.

"Anyways," he said, "EVE is hooked in here? She'll see what the program does?"

Ram gave him a thumbs up. "Yeah, that's why I wanted to use this place. They have the latest and greatest processors. Way more than what [Auroary's Rhythm Apocalypse] will need, so if they are using background processing to crunch their blockchain, it will be super obvious."

Elliot groaned and shook his head. He resigned himself to it, and stuck the ENU onto his head to let it interface with his brain. It stank of both sweat and lemon-lime cleaning solvent. Not being in his police uniform made him feel almost naked as he stood beside Ram, like the old t-shirt didn't fit him just because it was a decade old. But, the door was closed and just because he could hear the crowds outside, didn't mean they cared in the least what he did or looked like.

"Hi there, welcome new player. What's your name?" Auroary asked as the game booted up into AR mode. The idol's figure appeared before him, projected to his vision through the ENU. Young, cute, as bubbly in appearance as she was in voice.

"Elliot."

"Welcome to my idol training course, Elliot! It's a little intense, but I'm sure you're up to the job. Shall we get you started on the tutorial to learn the basics?"

Elliot glanced over and saw Ram stretching like she was about to go for a run, and he accepted the tutorial. Auroary clapped, a little delay so the program could map out the room and build the scenario accordingly. "Okay, first thing's first. Let's get you familiar with how to use the knife."

What?

The game put a virtual combat blade into his hand and one by one, a swarm of cartoon bats floated in from the edges of the room, flapping stubby wings and darting around. "What the hell? I thought this was a rhythm game?"

Ram said, "It is. The bats move to the rhythm. You have to slash them on the beat or they'll be too quick." With a few deft thrusts, she evidently cleared up the enemies appearing near her.

Elliot took a slash, missed, hacked again, and popped one of the note bats, only for a second to smack him in the back of the head with a gunshot explosion. Auroary groaned. "You gotta be careful Elliot! If the note bats get you, it'll be game over. Listen to the music and find your groove!" Then the tutorial reset, and once again a half dozen note bats flew towards him.

Just what the hell is this game?

Half an hour later, and drenched in sweat, Elliot collapsed onto the couch. He had finally beaten the tutorial, which included the gun section as well as knife and gun. Note bats weren't the only enemy, far from it. There were exploding birds that had to be shot at a distance, lest he take damage. Armored boars that could only be finished off by precision cuts, but could be stunned by sustained gunfire. The worst of it, however, were the laser attacks, which couldn't be defeated, only dodged until he was contorted around them like some kind of movie vault robber.

"Good God, isn't that enough? Shouldn't that have been enough for EVE to check the program?" he asked, pouring himself some ice water and downing it.

"One sec," Ram said, hosing down a line of fire on her virtual foes. She didn't even have dampness around her armpits. After a spinning flourish, she blinked out of it and looked over at him. "How far did you get?"

"Through the tutorial."

"We need to get to the expansion content, which means beating the campaign on expert difficulty," she said, redoing her hair tie to keep it all up in a ponytail.

Elliot blinked back at her, nearly dropped his empty cup. "You've got to be shitting me? Why would it only do that part of the time?"

"Because, that's how they snuck the extra code in, I think. Part of the download, you know? Come on, it's not that hard. You know how to shoot a gun."

I know how to use a gun for self-defense, to neutralize human targets. This is a mess of a game with almost nothing to do with actual guns.

"Ram, I don't know how to say this, but I don't think I am physically capable... no, not even mentally capable of beating this game on expert difficulty. This is some kind of hard core, no-lifer game addict game. I don't even play casual VR games."

Ram frowned and rubbed her chin. "I mean, we could just get some robot go juice and force you through it."

"Robot go juice?"

"Yeah, vodka and Zeus."

Elliot stared back at her, and felt all the issues and concerns tied to him like they were lurking monsters in the shadows of his mind, ready to pounce and trip him up the moment he let his guard down. "Fuck it. Sure. Just like bootcamp," he said, and pushed himself back to his feet.

They headed out of the private room and queued in line at the adult-only section of the game cafe. Ram chattered about the strategy to the game, how to get in the groove, and Elliot tried to absorb it all. He reminded her several times that he did actually understand video games, just only from the console and computer era, not VR. He chose not to plead injury over his dislocated ribs. After the few weeks since Gaia, it wouldn't have been convincing.

"Robot go juice," Ram said when they got to the front of the line.

The bartender arched an eyebrow and got glasses for them. "Long day of gaming?"

Elliot grimaced. "Apparently we have to beat an entire game in one day."

"Speedrunning?"

"If that includes learning how to play the game in the first place, then yes.

The bartender set two drinks down for them, and he and Ram picked them up. After a quick toast, they both drank the majority of their drinks in one go. Ram meekly turned back to the bartender and said, "We're going to need more."

"I'll set up some refills for you," the bartender said, and waved them off to take care of the next people in line.

The drink tasted like a sugar bomb with bite to it. Fizzy, invigorating, and enough to take the edge of fatigue off. "Been a while since I've had this."

"Kind of a dangerous drink, isn't it?" Ram said.

"Depends on when you need to sleep. It's got like four different ways to get addicted to it, too. But hey, it does what we need it to, right? Just can't drink too many."

"I think they water them down the drunker you get? To keep you from getting too annihilated. It's a liability thing."

The glass had just a bit of an orange tinge to it, entirely from the energy drink and growing ice melt. He shook the glass and drank the rest of it. Went down like water. "As long as it maintains a buzz, it's fine by me."

"I say, just think of it as good exercise. More fun than lifting weights."

Less helpful than weights though. Maybe I should just think of this like hell week back at bootcamp? Physical torture to prove I can do it? Might get me stuck in this department for good. Might get more people added if we keep making ourselves useful like this. It's better than ending up working for Lizard again, grinding shifts of QRS. Yeah, this is better than that.

"Come on, let's get this over with," Elliot said, and the two of them returned to the play room. Fortified with drink, he put the ENU back on and booted [Auroary's Rhythm Apocalypse] back up.

"Want to put a bet down? On which of us will get to the expansion content first?"

"Not a chance, there's no way I'll beat you and we both know that."

She pouted and took her side of the room. "You're no fun."

Elliot rolled his eyes and focused on getting the campaign started and set to expert difficulty. "I don't gamble on sure things. Let's just focus on doing this and proving your theory. We'll be in trouble if you're wrong about this, you know?"

"I'm not wrong," Ram said, and began slashing enemies.

"I sure hope not," Elliot mumbled. "Still, it could be worse."

21

Fever Dream

2140/10/09

Kyte couldn't have been worse.

Body chills. Headache. Sleep paralysis demons. He had everything bad possible, short of a congested nose. It hurt to breathe, like the inside of his chest was on fire, but he still felt cold. The pile of blankets just absorbed his sweat. Exhaustion led to a haze, one waking dream to the next. Dr Bahtt saw to him at some point. He vaguely remembered swallowing pills. At some point an IV had been put into his arm.

He felt like he was dying, and figured he was damn close to it. The only comfort he had was the knowledge that it wouldn't last. He'd either get over it or die.

In the times where he couldn't sleep, he found plenty of time to think, but not coherently. He couldn't bring his impressions to the fine point of a conclusion. One moment he was contrasting the way Vlad could be calm and comforting, supportive even, while the next he killed people without batting an eye—not that he could. Then he drifted back to his father, that monolith of stoicism. The way his father could stare at him until everything had been picked apart and his childish attempts at lies became nothing more than something to scoff at. Even when the lies mattered. Even when it was about school, and relationships, and what to do with his life, his father would just listen and tell him that he needed to figure it out on his own.

Fumi too. He thought about her, and Akane, and at times he couldn't tell them apart. Maybe it was their laugh, that hidden gem they kept for private. The rest of the world got a canned, cute giggle designed to endear people. The kind of thing that could be used on demand like an actress' tears. He had been able to catch them unawares, with their guard down, and squeeze out a peal of laughter. Nothing at all like an idol, but so real, and just for him who had provoked it.

"You're still alive, right?"

Kyte couldn't tell whether he was awake or dreaming, not until he felt Fumi's hand on his sweat drenched neck. It took all his effort to roll, to flop on his back and feel the sticky sheets beneath him. The room was a neon haunt of appliance LEDs, barely coloring the girl's figure. He wanted to ask if it was really her.

Fumi slid onto the bed, the foam collapsing beneath her weight as she leaned towards him. "Vlad told me what happened, what my father cooked up. You're not doing this for me, are you?"

It was hard to breathe, hard to focus. He couldn't muster the words from his lips. He wanted to tell her that he had hardly known her at the time, that he had everything to gain for himself by agreeing to this stupid stunt. He didn't even know what they would learn about vaccine compatibility anymore; exactly what the government had said would happen had.

Fumi bit her lip and brushed some of his hair off his forehead. "You look like shit. Shouldn't you be in an ICU or something? At least the clinic? You look like you're in so much pain."

"Not too bad," he croaked out. Strength returning, he tried to push up on his elbows. It didn't work. The moment his blanket shifted off his shoulder he felt the chill air right down to his core.

"Such a tough guy," she said with a smirk. "But not too tough. If I liked tough guys, I would be with Drake right now."

Kyte winced for a new reason. She was judging him by the standards a gang would use. Not the building fondness after sexual attraction, the support gleaned from one another and the pleasure of company, or whatever it was people got married for, but purely strength and composure. His father had never given a good answer as to why people got married. Kyte hated how well his actions had worked on her.

"Well, let me tell you," she said, dropping her voice to a whisper as she loomed over him. "I don't care that I didn't get drafted. If my father offers me a stolen vaccine, I won't take it. I don't want to follow his plans. I don't want to stay in his little kingdom. I'm going to leave."

That gave Kyte pause. "And go where?"

She shrugged and brushed her hair behind an ear. "I don't know, somewhere. I have to get a job first. I know that'll be harder without military service, but I don't care. I'll ask EVE for help. They say if you beg, the government can always find a place for you. And that's better than working for my father, don't you think?"

Sounded like trading one overbearing parent for another. Kyte stuffed away thoughts about what he had been planning, or failing to plan, for a career. With Fumi's hand resting on his chest, it was a lot easier than sitting across from a school counselor or the like. Her hand was so softly on his chest. She didn't even mind the fever sweat.

"I should get you something to drink." She rose from the bed, her absence sucking the warmth from the room until she returned and cracked open a bottle of some pop. Kyte couldn't read the label, but the sugar on his tongue was like ambrosia.

Fatigue hit him anew, his brief respite of wakefulness ending with his eyelids closing. When they next opened, his fever had broken. The bed felt like an oven, the blankets a sauna. He tried to pull them off, but they tangled on his body like a net. Someone had turned the lights on, and the faded apartment walls seemed more real than in the fever haze.

"Hold up, hold up," Fumi said, walking back over to put a hand on his forehead. A moment later, out came an ear thermometer. It beeped and she shrugged without telling him the reading. She grinned instead. "Looks like the doc was right, you'll live."

"Great," he gasped out. "Can you get me something to drink?"

She returned with a bottle of cream soda by the time he had extricated an arm. He sucked it down and felt that sickly syrup gut wrench of no solid food in his stomach. "What time is it?"

"About midnight."

Kyte frowned and turned that over in his head. "It's been an entire day? How long have you been here?"

She smirked. "Not the entire time. Been coming and going. Don't want Vlad catching me, but I think he suspects I've been slipping in. If you're up and awake now, we might not have very much time before Dr Bahtt shows up to check on you. But, hey, you're not trying to stay with these people, right?"

Kyte sank back down, propping himself against the headboard of the bed as he squinted at her. "What do you mean? Didn't I tell you? I'm going to join up with the convoy, leave Bastion. I've gotta get out of here before the police catch me."

She squeezed his leg through the blanket. "Lots of people live on the run from the police. You don't have to flee. You can just take over someone else's identity. You just have to get the records to match, do a little tinkering, and EVE will never know. If she doesn't know, the police won't ever know. The only thing you can't do is get drafted, but you weren't planning on doing your military service anyways, right?"

Kyte had no idea where she had gotten that impression from. "Fumi, it's too late for me to make that kind of switch. I'm a known face around here. I've got blood on my hands too. I helped kill somebody!"

"To save Vlad, and there's nothing wrong with shooting a fucking CZARhead. The police do it all the time, and they don't feel bad about it, do they? So why should you? Kyte, why don't you work with Miccolo and change your identity? Me and you could leave this mess behind. You're the only one that can still get out because you didn't choose to be here."

His mouth was dry. He didn't know whether it was from stress or the sickness. "Miccolo? He's the forger?"

Fumi rolled her eyes. "Of course he is. Forging is all about the databases. It takes tech skills, and he's the best we have. He's got a whole list of dead people that EVE doesn't know have died. She just knows she hasn't seen them lately, just like you. People who live down here in the shadows. Just like how the masks hide your identity from her, but this time it'd be permanent. Fresh start."

Fumi had offered water in a desert. He almost didn't see the problem. "He wouldn't do that for free."

She grinned. "I'll take care of that. You'll just owe me instead."

"How are you going to do that? Your money comes from your father. He's not going to let us run away. He doesn't even want me near you. Said he'd–"

"I don't give a shit what my father said!" Fumi snapped, then composed herself again. "The point is to get the hell away from him, to get out of this sort-of sort-of-not criminal mess before big sister government crashes down on us."

"But how are you going to get Miccolo to change my identity? And if he does, how are we going to get away?"

She groaned and shook her head. "We start by going away and finding work! It's not like these gangsters can roam around looking for us freely. The cameras? EVE? All the scary surveillance you've been hiding from? The moment you have a new identity, that becomes a shield to protect you from them. That's the whole point."

"Fumi, I don't see how that's going to work, and I don't think you understand how much danger that would put me in." He wasn't making his case right, he could tell. He was being honest, but it wasn't the way to convince her. It wasn't what his father had taught him, and that's why it wasn't going to work, but he couldn't put the pieces of the linguistic puzzle together in time.

"Stop," she said, putting a delicate finger to his lips. "You're just sick and in pain right now. And I just so happen to know what makes pain go away for boys like you."

Her hand trailed from his chin to his chest and down. Kyte sucked in breath, but his body felt like dead weight. "Fumi, your father will kill me."

She smirked. "My father makes more threats than he can follow through on." Her hand went below the blanket and tugged open the button of his pants.

His heart raced. He had really gotten her to like him—no, not him. He had gotten her to like the facade he had constructed and she was about to reach past it. He had done the exact kind of bullshit his father had done, and he knew exactly how that ended. "Fumi, stop, please. You don't want to do this." He let out a shameful noise as her hand reached inside and found between his legs.

"Come on, this is way better than VR, right? It's the whole point of getting to know someone. If this wasn't what you were looking for, you'd just be happy with virtual relationships, with playing sex games like [Sladder], with imagining a relationship between yourself and some fictional girl. But you know, they make chatbots nowadays that can welcome you home and ask you how your day was. Miccolo's even making a body for those things to inhabit, but it's not the same. They can't do what I can do."

Kyte bit his lip and tried to shut out her voice. He tried to clear his head, but all he could think about was the touch of her fingers, the smell of her breath and her vanilla perfume. The brush of her fallen hair against his neck as she stroked blood into his member. It made his stomach roll, but other systems were taking charge. "I'm a bit sick still."

"Doesn't feel like you're sick to me." She tossed the blanket off, exposing everything to the light before she jumped atop his legs and planted one hand on his gut. "Don't you feel special? At least a dozen guys are going to be seething that I've done this for you."

"They're going to try and kill me! Again!" he blurted out, but she just laughed. He stared into her face and didn't find a shred of doubt, of embarrassment or shame. Not an inkling that what she was doing was wrong. It was exactly the kind of poisoned relationship he had sown. "Please, stop. Stop, this isn't what I want. This isn't what it's supposed to be like."

"I can use more than my hand–"

"Stop!" He rolled, breaking out from beneath her and flopping onto the apartment floor. The shock left her dumbfounded and staring as he scrambled up to his feet and buttoned his pants back up. He darted for the table and got what he needed. The harddrive, the Gamma Coin chip, the burner phone, the gun, and his coat to hide it all.

"Kyte! Are you fucking serious right now? What the fuck is your problem?" she screamed at him, waking up half the hall as he tore the door open and went stumbling out. "You're going to regret this! I will make you regret this. You stupid fuck! I can't believe you just did that!" Her embarrassment to be seen chasing after him was all that kept her back in the room as he fled to the stairwell out.

Three flights down and he had to stop. He had to keel over and press his shoulder to the wall as he heaved up bile. He emptied his stomach of the acid, only to feel more empty than ever. He staggered out into the depths of Gamma, no notion of where to go.

22

Blockchain Shutdown

2140/10/09

"How is this possible? How is this even a rhythm game? This is a bullet hell survival game! You could brand the damn thing as survival horror if it wasn't for the bubblegum bullshit pop music!" Elliot paced the room, his shirt ran through with sweat.

Ram, who had partaken of a few more drinks than she had planned, laid sprawled across the couch, eyelids fluttering halfway between reality and dream. "What the fuck is this difficulty curve? This is just the smallest brain way to increase difficulty. It's just endless enemy spam! Who thought this was a good idea?"

Elliot downed another cup of water and crumpled the plastic in his hand. "A fucking government created sociopath is who. Why would expansion content be skill-locked behind expert difficulty? Does he seriously think it will get more people to play the game?"

Ram rolled onto her side, and nearly fell off the couch. "Mr Blackstone I don't think we're actually good enough to do this. Not in one day. Maybe give me a week and I can beat that. I'm so tired I don't think I could even imagine swinging a sword right now."

Elliot chucked the cup at the trash chute. "We should have just found someone who has already unlocked it. What about that Evan kid? He's out of the hospital by now, right?"

"He was just playing [Sladder], wasn't he?"

"He also played this so-called rhythm game. Pretty sure he beat it. Let's just call him up, get him to open his account, and have EVE scan it while he's active. Easy, clean, done. Let's get him on the phone."

Ram groaned, the room surely spinning inside her head.

Elliot pulled out his phone, continuing to pace as he dug through the database, through the reports and contact info until he found Evan's number and gave it a ring. A moment later, he heard the kid answer and he said, "Mr Ryder, this is Detective Blackstone. How are you doing?"

"I couldn't be better, Mr Blackstone. Is this some kind of wellness check or something?"

Son of a bitch, I was supposed to schedule that, wasn't I?

"Something like that. I'd actually like to request your assistance with an ongoing investigation, pertaining to the initial call placed by your mother."

"Sure, but I don't know how I can be of any assistance to you."

"Should be very easy. You beat [Auroary's Rhythm Apocalypse], right?"

"Yeah, why?"

"Could we have you boot up your account on a monitored computer? We have a hypothesis we're trying to test."

"Oh, sorry, Detective. I deleted all my accounts yesterday."

Elliot stopped pacing. "I'm sorry, you did what?"

"Yeah, Akane and I talked it over and we really found all this faux interaction, this parasocial stuff, it's just really demeaning to the human spirit and doesn't offer anything real. It's like getting fed aspartame when what you need is sugar, or you know, honey. So we deleted all of them and couldn't be happier for it. Feels like I tore off chains on my soul."

What the hell kind of hippy shit is this kid on? I can't tell if he's right, or if this is that fucking cult leader being proven right, or what.

"But... can you recover your account? We just need you to run the expansion content for a little bit."

"Sorry, Officer. The game's not too hard though, you know? Just don't try to beat it solo. The final mission is designed to require co-op, unless you're absolutely cranked out of your mind."

Elliot looked over at Ram, who had begun snoring. "Didn't you beat it solo?"

"Like I said, absolutely cranked out of your mind. I was good at the game, but you realize there's a meta narrative about groupies and people fawning over Auroary, right? It's actually pretty clever, but you won't understand until you play the game."

The last thing I want is to play the game any more. If this thing got nuked off the internet for the rest of time, I would be happy.

He brushed some sweaty hair back and asked, "I don't suppose you'd be interested in starting a fresh account and doing that all over again? A speedrun attempt or something?"

"Maybe another time, Detective. There's actually a corporate contest thing we'll be going to tomorrow, if we win first place, it has a month long paid vacation to California for two. That's really what's on our time, but I might be able to help you out next week?"

That's too late. God damn it.

"That's alright, Mr Ryder. I'm glad you've recovered from the attack and landed on your feet. I'll manage some other way."

"Right, well thank you so much Mr Blackstone, for giving me that push. I know it, uh, nearly got me killed, but overall worth it. Feels like my life is on a new trajectory now, and I just have to not fall into bad habits again. Thanks."

Elliot couldn't hold onto the anger, that knot of frustration that had propelled him into one attempt after another at the final mission of the game. "Glad to hear it."

"Let me know if I can help you out next week."

"Will do," Elliot said, and ended the call. He stared at his phone for a moment.

Is this when I call in the one favor with EVE? Seems like a waste of the favor. I wonder if Dom has beaten this game? I could call him up, see how he's doing. He's probably up right now. Only other person I could bet on would be Amara. I should probably start with her. Maybe I should have started with her before even coming here. Should have at least tried co-op with Ram.

"Mr Blackstone," Ram said, having rolled over and sat up. Something had woken her up, but not quite sobered her up. "If they raid Sokolov's, there's going to be a lot of deaths, aren't there?"

Elliot put his phone away and sat down across from her. He leaned his elbows on his knees and nodded. "Yeah. Groups like these, they don't go down without a fight. Most will turn and run, and we'll probably round them up one way or another. But some can't run, and when we knock on their door, they're cornered so they lash out. But it's not us. We're not the ones that will go in and do that. We're not that department."

"Were you ever the one to do it?"

He nodded. "I was, when I first started. The captain at the time talked it up a bunch. He put it in my head that it would be a quick way to get promoted, to make a name for myself, to get on pension plans and a dozen other things. I was too young to really understand the issue. You know, all the training you get at bootcamp? Basic PT and mental conditioning? That's so you can deal with the blighted. Those things aren't human, and we treat them as such. But at the end of the day, it's not so different from war, or raids, or just violence in general. Even in the investigations I do, there's always the risk that somebody charges me with a knife, that the people I'm talking with turn out to be CZARheads. There's always a certain kind of risk."

"Not exactly why I signed up, now is it?"

"Why did you sign up?"

She smirked. "Would it surprise you to learn it was because I don't like the government?"

"Ram, you're part of the government. Are you a reformist or something? This isn't exactly a ladder climbing career for that sort of thing."

She shrugged. "But it is the spot where bad people can be brought to account. When I was in high school, we had a bit of a scandal. The kind that got hushed up and faded into the obscurity of rumor. You know? One of the department heads turned out to be bribeable. I was the one that found out, because I did a group project with this rich girl and I failed the project but she passed it, when I did most of the work. She outright bragged to me that she just had her parents take care of it with money, that grade school didn't matter so long as she made it through the draft."

"Did you confront him?"

"Yup. You know, in hindsight, I'm really surprised he didn't say it was just a mistake, and then adjust my grade to match? That definitely would have been enough to make me put it out of mind, but you know, those kinds of people don't think like that. Not the ones that get caught anyways. He accused me of lying, threatened to get me suspended, expelled even. Really had it out for me the rest of the year but I couldn't prove anything because all the faculty sided with him."

"But he did get caught?"

She frowned and shook her head. "Yeah, but it was kind of weird. Wasn't for the bribes at all. One day an MP showed up and hauled him off to jail with no explanation. Rumor got out that he had been approaching students online, posing as a classmate. The weird thing was I think I had met him without realizing it, and shut him down, because he came across as this weird political reactionary with a huge chip on his shoulder. Distinctly the kind of armchair socialist that just hated he had to work a job? I think maybe that's why he had it out for me? Maybe? As weird as that sounds?"

Elliot blinked and frowned. His eyebrows pulled together till they nearly touched, and he had to ask, "Did he have a corruption checklist he was trying to work through, or something? Was there an abuse of power he didn't commit?"

Ram snorted a laugh. "Well, he didn't manage to keep that position, though he did graduate a lot of idiots just because they agreed with him. But, that MP kind of saved my entire future. So you know, this is a position where I stand a chance of taking down people hiding behind power. Also, I get to work with EVE, who's just right there with me, which is super encouraging. I just... I'm scared that there is just so much mess and violence out there that there isn't time to deal with people like him."

Elliot nodded. "You're in the right department then. I mean, don't get me wrong, Cinder is the literal first person to charge in guns blazing, but she knows that's not for everyone and is rarely appropriate. Just tell her, and she'll keep you out of the raid."

Ram turned her gaze on him. An exhausted slouch, drooping eyes, hardly a shred of strength left in her. "And you? Will she keep you out of the raid?"

"Let's get you home, Ram. It's late, you need to sleep, and we need to cover the bill for this room. I've got some ideas on how we can beat this game in the morning, but first is sleep," he said, rising and offering her a hand. She frowned that he didn't answer, but took his hand with a sigh.

I'm going to end up there whether she wants me to or not.

"What about you? Do you have some story about why you joined?"

Because I was an idiot who thought it would help me find my brother?

"It's the only military job that lets you live in Bastion year round. Simple enough, right?"

She frowned, but her eyes didn't flit to the pack in his pocket. She wasn't a wannabe psychic like everyone else he seemed to be meeting lately. The lie left something foul inside him, but he figured he'd explain himself when they were both sober, if ever.

***

Elliot gave himself one sleep cycle after Amara agreed to help. She had been awake, of course, and had already beaten the game on stream; but, not in an isolated manner that EVE would have been able to verify. Thus, Elliot slipped an ENU back on at three in the morning and joined his wife inside [Auroary's Rhythm Apocalypse] to beat the final mission on expert difficulty together.

She looked exactly the way he remembered first meeting her. Slim, blonde, and the kind of smug grin that invited a challenge. It nearly took his words away. "So this is the avatar you use for your content?"

"Default one, yeah. Are you allergic to fashion?" she asked, folding her arms and looking over his military fatigues.

He grinned and shrugged. "Never had a reason to update. With the new assignment, maybe I could use some pointers. You know, for professionalism."

Amara shook her head. "Well, whatever you do with the clothes, I'm sure there's some kind of protocol on what MPs are supposed to wear, right?"

If there was, I wish Cinder would give it a read some time.

"I'm sorry," he interrupted and held up a hand. He looked her over. Amara had on what should have been quite modest clothes, a shirt and pants; but, chunks of material had been removed. He wasn't going to complain about the midriff, that little span of belly flesh and navel colored by the straps of her underwear. He could even understand the purpose of the window across the middle of her chest, right across the valley between her breasts. What drew his attention were the holes in her pants, along her hips. "Who thought that was a good idea?"

She frowned and looked away. With a meek shrug, she said, "Flavor of the week. Can't always be in skirts and long socks, right? Trend chasing?"

Elliot stared back at her. "Someone popular wore that as a joke, and the viewers decided they unironically liked it, didn't they?"

She nodded. "Pretty much."

He frowned and looked at it again. "You know, at least in the flesh, I can understand that there's something to get your hand on, but here?"

She cocked her head at him. "If you had a neural implant, you'd be able to feel me."

"But it's not the real you."

Amara clapped her hands together. "Right, then, let's do this? Me and you, first time playing VR games together in over a year? I just spent over an hour speedrunning this stupid game to help you, so let's put it to use. By the way, I'm going to turn on my recording software when we get to the DLC. I haven't actually played the new content. I'll edit you out of anything I release though, don't worry."

You know, maybe Mikey had a point about something. Just that it should be me and Amara, not some anonymous hookup. There's something to be said for variety, for fantasy. Not really fantasy, though, is it? She's just using the body she always has, ever since I knew her.

"Honey?" Amara asked, hand hovering over the start button.

Right, business first. Still have to fix this Kyte situation so I can put in the work for her event. One step at a time.

"Let's do it. I've spent twelve hours today learning how to play this stupid game. Let's beat it."

Co-operative mood turned out to be far more difficult than anticipated. Not because the enemies were stronger, the map more challenging, or the music faster. It was the same frantic dance beat like Auroary was dancing on a piano, but he and Amara were completely out of sync. Note bats swirled around them, each of them thinking the other would deal with it. Some heavy enemies got their combined fire, others got missed completely. Neither ever warned the other of the incoming obstacles.

Nothing worked.

"Don't you ever play games?" she hissed at him as the word failure hung in the air over them for the third time.

Elliot snarled and glared. "I've been playing this fucking game all day. And you damn well know that I don't play VR. Shouldn't you be the expert? You do this for a living don't you?"

"I'm an entertainer, not a competitive player."

"And yet you're doing a training retreat for a contest!"

"For entertainment purposes!"

It was Auroary that interrupted them. "Hey now, players. Fighting is no good!"

"Shut the fuck up!" they both roared at the virtual idol.

He hadn't been this competitive with his wife in years.

Both of them spun away from the other, sucking in breath which only did a little to temper moods. Not nearly as much as doing so in the flesh. Elliot grunted and said, "Again, again. We're getting closer. Fuck the teamwork. Teamwork isn't actually needed. You were able to beat this mission on your own, right? Just pretend I'm not here, and I'll do whatever mediocre amount I can to make it easier. It's only a matter of time."

"You're screwing up my rhythm though. Ah, you know what, whatever. There's no strategy to this game, it's just reflex and skill. Again, boot it again," Amara grumbled, and the mission launched.

Without using augmented reality, his actual physical condition didn't matter, only his mental reflexes. Regular gamers found it easier, but he wouldn't have spent the entire day in AR had that been the case for him. To make matters worse, the alcohol had begun fading, leaving behind a hangover that colored everything with a tinge of frustration.

What had been tripping him up was the need to use the knife, a clumsy tangle of his two hands, switching from one mindset to the next as the situation demanded it.Instead, he tried ignoring the virtual idol's advice, and everything the previous missions had reinforced as proper play. He ditched the knife and took the pistol in both hands. The moment the enemies spawned, a swarm of note bats like an arcade alien invasion, he started firing. The gun had nominal recoil, well within what he could ignore, and no need to reload. He dumped ammo at the enemies like he was showing off for the drill sergeant after bootcamp.

Beside him, Amara joined in on the live fire whenever something stronger than a note bat appeared, the boars and such, but her attention stayed on the blade in her hand. Rather than a knife, it moved more like a conductor's baton. Edge alignment didn't exist in the game, and she flicked it around like inertia also didn't exist.

Their respective kill counts cranked up on pace, neck and neck with one another, until the song shifted. The frantic piano notes switched to melancholic chords as Auroary sang something sentimental and meaningless. The meaning of the love song didn't register with Elliot as he started twisting out of the way of the flying obstacles. A moment later, the playing field had been sliced apart and he and Amara thrust to opposite sides.

But, neither of them had taken much damage.

The song progressed again, interlacing hopeful spurts of melody with more of the longing chords, matched with waves of enemies and fresh sweeps of lasers to be avoided. Elliot started taking hits here and there, his health pool chipping away. But it was only a six minute song, and he could see the timer winding down.

"Fuck!" Amara shouted.

Elliot spun, saw her get body-checked by a boar and knocked into one of the barriers. Elliot's will shattered.

We lost. She's down.

Amara's body didn't disappear, didn't void out though. She landed on the ground next to him, rolled and came up swinging. Stabbed her knife right through the boar's jaw and killed it. "Finally saved enough health to not lose to that. Stupid fucking ambush," she grumbled.

What?

It took him a moment to stare at her and understand, a moment where dozens more enemies swarmed into the fray. She grabbed him by the arm and yanked him to the ground as a fan of lasers swept through where his head had been. The two of them rolled and up came his gun. He couldn't even hear the music or the rhythm. The hints of movement meant nothing to him as he fired at anything he could. Strategy vanished, just instinct. Amara did the same, their combined fire almost drowning out the music until it did.

There was no music. The mission had stopped. No more enemies spawned. The only other noise was the sound of Auroary clapping her hands on the other side of the playing field. Both of them popped off and ended up laughing. Elliot flopped on his back, staring at the digital stars. "Bastard's blood, so we can finally access the expansion? We can finally prove it's siphoning power?"

Amara nodded and sat up. "So the internet says."

"Congratulations," Auroary said, but something was different about her voice. About her figure too. Like an actress had been hired instead of simulated.

Amara blinked. "Oh my god. That was the first video game we've played together in a year. And won anyways. Co-op."

No, no we've done other stuff in the last twelve months, haven't we?... have we?

Elliot shrugged and glanced away. "Well, maybe we should get up to some more of it, right? Maybe homestead thing?"

"Training camp," his wife corrected.

Auroary didn't give them any time to talk though. The idol continued on. "You've beaten the game on the highest difficulty. That means there's nothing more for me to teach you. You've proven yourselves to be the next music sensation. And you know what that means? You've gotta brace yourselves for fans! And for hate."

For what now?

The playing field had been a very sparse thing of flagstone tile. The ruins of a pre-apocalypse city around them. Bits of grass lit up by spotlights in the night. The spotlights went out. The little shimmer that denoted the edge of the playable space, the boundary of the simulation, vanished. With the change, so too came wind noise, and on the wind there were voices.

Elliot didn't know much about games, nor about pop music, he did know what a crowd sounded like, and the type of noise they made when they were looking for someone. "Babe, we're in the expansion," he said quietly, getting up to his feet. He swung his hand through the air and directed his focus to get the interface menu.

A message from EVE popped up. "Good work, now survive for a few minutes so I can isolate the background program."

Survive?

Amara stood up beside him. "If we're in the expansion, shouldn't there have been some kind of explanation? A thank you for your purchase? Rules? Objectives?"

Elliot frowned and gave his pistol a test fire. It still worked. "It's not that kind of game. This one's trying to send a message, and we have to survive for the next five minutes."

"Five minutes? Why? Do you see a timer?"

"That's how long EVE needs," Elliot said as the darkness became a sea of silver eyes looking back at them. "We should move, come on! Go!"

An army of so-called fans charged at them from the weed covered streets. They laughed and whooped, but for all their giggling, they were also shouting, "Kill them!"

Not much room for misunderstandings there.

Amara didn't need to be pulled along, she took the lead. "Fuck fuck fuck, is this a fucking horror game suddenly?" Before Elliot could think she was afraid of it, she added, "I didn't start my recording!"

"Oh for fuck's sake," he grumbled and spun. Up came the gun. No request to stand down, not for NPCs. He fired. Like taking bottles down at a range, he worked across the road, blasting the charging crowd. Their blood hit the street neon green. It put an even more alien hue to the scene.

"High ground," Amara shouted, jumping up on an old rust bucket car, then up to a second story balcony. She had to cut down a pair of hands grabbing at her, but Elliot followed quick. The balcony wasn't safe, not enough room to put a gun to use, but up on railings they were able to run across the face of the building. The corner was no good either, nowhere to go.

Elliot spun and put down protective fire behind them. The apartment balconies turned green with bloody slime before Amara said, "This way," and leapt down. Elliot followed, hitting the pavement in a gap created by Amara's blade through the clamoring crowd.

"Where?"

She charged ahead, leading him to a slope of debris. Broken concrete and beyond gravel stuck to tar paper. The whole structure had been square, but collapsed to one corner. The far corner lifted high, narrow approach. It made for a holdout spot. The two of them got to the top and turned their guns on the crowd like a hoard of blighted were charging at them.

"Shouldn't we be trying to escape?"

"Escape where? It's just one big city! They're everywhere. The game has a timer. This is infinite survival," she shouted back, her spaces covered up by the blast of her gun.

Elliot snarled and tried to pull up the interface with one hand as he fired with the other. He tried to read how much time had elapsed. They had run around blocks and more, but the way adrenaline pounded inside him, he didn't trust his own sense of time.

A hand closed around his leg and pulled him down, one he should have seen if not for the interface menu. He roared and pulled out the knife, but that just made it a bloodbath, a frenzy of limbs and laughter. Up close, he finally saw that they all looked like Auroary, all the females at least. None quite right, but each trying their part. People casting aside their own identity to assume that of the idol, the famous girl, the one who could sing and everyone liked. And they were trying to kill the two of them, the winners, the ones with the skill to do what Auroary did.

It was enough to make him want to vomit, even before they tossed him off the side of the roof. He hit the ground hard, sound like bones cracking. His limbs stopped responding and he had to watch as more of them surrounded him. He could still hear Amara fighting. She shot and stabbed and exalted in the fight. The fan girls kneeled down and ripped Elliot apart.

His eyes opened up in the gloom of his apartment. "Bastard's fucking blood, EVE, tell me that was enough time."

"Four minutes, fifty-nine seconds, I'm afraid," the AI responded. He lunged out of his chair and looked for the speaker EVE had used, but couldn't tell. Her ensuing laughter was worse than the crazed fan girls. "I'm joking," she said, and he fell back into his seat.

"Never again."

"No promises," she mused. "Your wife is actually still going strong. I was giving myself some leeway when I said five minutes, but she's actually going to do it."

"Wait, what? How long did I last?"

"About two," the AI stated. She commandeered the monitor of his computer to display her avatar, purely to shrug at him. "It was good enough for me to capture a full transaction calculation to their block-chain. I'll shut it all down once Amara is done recording. And that includes that horrible cesspit of filth and destruction of innocence those cultists also put out! Ah, how wonderful!" She swooned and hugged herself at the thought of deleting [Sladder].

Elliot rolled his head back over his chair and stared at the ceiling. No stars, digital or otherwise. Just a layer of painted foam, and above that another apartment with another layer of painted foam. Again and again at least twenty times.

Well, the pressure will be on. Now I actually have to go get the kid. I wonder if I can still call them for that favor of cooperation? I don't really have anything to offer them anymore. One way or another though, not much time left. The convoy is the day after tomorrow. He's going to smuggle out tomorrow night.

23

The People Smuggler

2140/10/10

Out of Sokolov's shadow, Kyte had ended up in the same place he had started, the Worm Tunnels. The only difference was he didn't get woken up by an overweight man watching nearly pornographic videos next to him. He felt a hand slide into the pocket of his coat. He woke, but only by opening his eyes, impossible to see through his void mask. While the pickpocket had his attention on sliding out the Gamma Coin chip, Kyte shifted. Then he had the barrel of the revolver against the would-be thief's crotch.

"Take one, lose the other," he said.

The thief froze, retracted his hand, smiled and patted Kyte on the leg. He spread his hands wide to show nothing was in them, and backed off. A few steps later, Kyte hid the gun again, and the thief bolted.

Rather than consider how natural that had been, how calm he had done what he needed to do, he pulled out the burner phone and checked the time. He had messaged the human smuggler before passing out. Not particularly well written messages, but enough to arrange a meeting. Vlad had given him the contact info earlier, and after fleeing Fumi, he had put it to use. Still fifteen minutes.

There was also a message from Vlad. "Come back to the Grotto. All hands on deck."

Kyte wavered, then ignored the message. He had what he needed from them. Nothing had changed. He still needed to leave the city before the police found him. He put his focus to the area around him. He hadn't slept on a train this time, but rather one of the old station benches. Out of sight from the cameras above, but close enough to the stairs.

A passing girl caught his eye. She had hair like Fumi and the same height, not her though. Wasn't Akane either. She was just some girl that had nothing to do with him, hadn't been hurt by him nor returned the favor. His mouth went dry, not just from dehydration. He couldn't take the mask off to get a drink though, so he just ignored it like he ignored the empty pit in his stomach.

Above the Worm Tunnels, the wall loomed before him. All the way at the edge of the city, he came out adjacent to the circle road: the one strip of asphalt in all of Bastion. It wound between the towers and the wall, a big military highway. He could even see one of the buildings slapped into the edge. Possibly a draft processing center. A gateway to the world outside. Not that he'd be using it.

The meetup spot was around the corner: a brunch diner named Spacey Boy covered in vintage UFO paraphernalia. Smelled like frying butter and cigarettes as a grandmother slapped potato hash and flipped eggs. Every table had a liter of maple syrup and the menus were printed into the plastic tabletops. His stomach growled, but one of EVE's cameras could almost stare him in the face no matter which table he took, so when the waitress looked at him and his mask, he said, "Just waiting for a friend. He'll order."

She rolled her eyes, but left him be. Ten minutes after the meetup time, the smuggler finally walked in. Styx, zero percent chance he had given his actual name, didn't have a mask on and apparently didn't feel a need to blend in. As gangly as an alien and puffing a thin cigar, he sat down and stared at Kyte from behind mirrored aviators. "So you're the one?" Styx asked, pointing his cigar at him.

"I'm the one."

Styx sucked on the tobacco till the waitress came over. All smiles and laughs, he put in an order that could have fed a family of four. The waitress went away with a grin, nearly skipping, and Styx turned back to him. "Kid, you do understand what life is like out there, don't you? Don't get me wrong, I'm going to take your money. I don't care."

"If you don't care, then why are you asking? I can pay, that's all you care about right? The less you know about me the better."

Styx shrugged. "Whatcha wanna call it? Professional curiosity? An inkling of the good Samaritan? Have you even been outside at all? Ever touched grass?"

"I've touched grass. It grows down here in Gamma, if you haven't noticed. Maybe you can't see well, wearing sunglasses inside."

Styx bit off the butt of his cigar and chewed it as he lifted his glasses. His eyes were bloodshot. "Keep your voice down. I was up late with a lady last night, you understand? You old enough to understand?"

The similarity was more uncanny than his own reflection in Styx's glasses. "Like you wouldn't understand."

"Sure you do, sure you do, kid. But, the grass in here? That's just weeds, and not the fun kind of weed. Totally different from outside. It gets thigh high and even gets hard to walk through. Gotta wade and brace yourself. Gets run through with burrows and warrens. Sticks and holes. Rolling stones. Buzzing insects–"

"What's your point?"

Styx sneered and puffed his cigar. "My point is just walking around is hard outside. Not like in here, where all the difficulties get cleared away. You don't even realize how hot the sun is. You've probably never been to Alpha, let alone gotten sunburn or heatstroke. Been living your life in climate control. You're like veal. You know what veal is?"

"Expensive."

"True that. You ain't wrong there. But, you know, basics of the basics man, they got blighted out there. You're literally volunteering to live where the monsters live. We didn't build these walls for nothing." Styx hooked a thumb out the window at the black bulwark.

Kyte shrugged and held his tongue when the waitress started putting down plates. Cheesy hashbrowns, sticky pancakes, a heap of scrambled eggs like gold foil. Kyte's stomach was too empty to even growl. He could still taste the vomit acid. "It's not like people don't live out there. And you know what, there's less of them. I've been thinking just how many problems are in this city because there are so many of us. So many people there isn't enough room for each other. We're like a bunch of fuel and oxygen getting squeezed together."

Styx laughed and swallowed. "Kid, this city ain't no diesel truck. Did you read some mopey poetry after a girl dumped you or something?"

"No," he stated, but he couldn't deny the burn in his cheeks. Thankfully, the mask hid that.

Styx just laughed again. "Well, I hope you're not going out there because of a girl. Some romantic idea of the rugged wilderness. I'll tell you one thing about the Isles, there's not many women out there. Or, if there are, they keep em' back home. I hardly ever see a pair of tits walking around at the convoy. If you're going there to get yourself a girl by your own sweat and strength, that ain't gunna fucking happen. Them cowboys are tougher than steel and you ain't shit."

"I'll adapt. You sure talk a lot for someone who doesn't care about me though."

Styx, who had managed to eat almost half the food despite the amount he was talking, shrugged. "Sure, sure. Whatever you say. You won't be the first person I've taken out to their deaths. I'll sleep fine. Convoy's tomorrow though. That means going out tonight. Early morning at the latest. So you gonna pay me now, or what?"

Kyte pulled out the Gamma Coin chip, and the smuggler nodded. Out came a receiver, like he was running an above board business, and the device got plugged in. An error sign showed up on the screen. Styx furrowed his brow and ran it again, to no success.

"It has money on it. Your machine is broken."

Styx glared at him. "I ain't saying you ain't got money on this, now am I? This error says it can't read the blockchain. It's queued. Can't reconcile the wallets. No big deal. Lag happens some times. This ain't my first rodeo, even if it is yours." But, he ran it a third time and got the same error message. Styx licked his lips, drummed his fingers on the table, and waved over the waitress. "Sarah sweetie, could you run my bill with this?"

To Kyte's surprise, she didn't even bat an eye at the almost-illegal payment method. He had just chalked it up to Sokolov's reach when the waitress called back, "System's down. You better have another way to pay me, Styx."

"Down? Like, down down?" the smuggler asked.

Kyte's chest began to thump and drum. It was a heavy, uneasy beat that mixed up all the rot in his gut left behind by the vaccine. "What the hell does that mean?"

The smuggler pulled out his phone and started sending messages. "If Gamma Coin is down, we've got a lot bigger issues than me and you, kid. Couple thousand people just had their life savings deleted."

"What, did it get hacked or something?"

"Don't be stupid. You can't hack a blockchain unless you're EVE herself. It's got other vulnerabilities. Quantity limitations. Mining chokes. That kind of thing. Fuck, the forums are lighting up. Fucking thing went down for everyone."

Kyte grabbed onto the table. He could almost feel the rising panic in the city as people caught on to what was happening. One fact was inescapable: the police were behind it, and they'd be using the chaos to move in. "Look, can't you just take the chip? Not like Gamma Coin spends out at the Isles, right? Take the whole thing. It's useless to me."

Styx cocked an eyebrow at him. "And what? I'm supposed to just take your word that enough payment is on there?"

"Yes!"

The smuggler scoffed. "Maybe," he said, and set about devouring his food like his mouth was a garbage disposal. "Right, so, meet me there," the smuggler said, cheeks packed, as he pointed at a rusted out access hatch across the way from the diner. "At midnight. Hopefully, the system is working by then. I'll take a rain check on payment till then, okay?"

"Okay, sure, so I just wait all day then? What am I supposed to do?"

"That's your problem, not mine," the smuggler said. He slid the useless chip back over to Kyte. Then he bolted from the table.

Kyte blinked, caught on when the waitress started screaming at him, and he bolted too. He took off running, but by the time he got out the door, the smuggler was nowhere to be seen, and he had to pick a direction and go. He'd never dined and dashed before, but wasn't about to get grabbed because of that after everything he'd gone through.

His sprint came to a stop when he saw the bright red holograms of caution walls. Police milled around the burrough, dropping virtual walls and pinning in the neighborhood. Recon drones buzzed through the air, up and down through the towers. He also saw the big ones. Not as big as ARUs, but with all the onboard computing to analyze entire crowds. Kyte knew exactly what the robots were there for. Behind the mantis-like observers was every kind of analysis from magnetic imaging, to wi-fi mapping, to what would get him immediately arrested: gait analysis.

A little novelty government education liked to talk about, human gait was as unique as a fingerprint. His father had always scoffed at it and would say they'd never get the margin of error down low enough for use in Bastion. Kyte wasn't in a position to test it, not when he could see a dozen police officers ready to cuff him for an easy warrant grab.

"What the fuck is happening?" he whispered to himself, and backed away. He retreated to the heart of the enclosure, bringing himself closer to The Greco Grotto.

24

Thrill Kill Train

2140/10/10

Elliot stood ironclad in the midst of over a hundred other police officers, riding a train to Hell. Not everyone had QRS armor on. Some had standard issue military body armor, like they were getting deployed against the blighted, or against some terrorist cell in the Caribbean zone. They all stood in line, rank and file, even as they tightened straps, checked ammo, and tested their HUDs. Two people stood separate from the formation; Cinder and some spook from the DA. They were at the front, with a camera drone buzzing before them to echo their image down the length of the train.

"Ladies and gentlemen," Cinder said, her voice broadcast across the entire battalion. "We are a mere thirty minutes from war, right here in our very own city. Of course, it won't be a very long war, not when we've got the best fighters in all of Bastion right here on this train." Even Elliot smirked. A few men whooped and clapped their hands for the so-called Blonde Devil. Cinder grinned and waved for them to quiet down. "We'll be going into an area of Missou the locals call Aemos. The whole burrough has been cordoned off for us. They know we're coming, but they won't be getting away. We've got some special reinforcement this time, which our friends at the DA will tell you about."

Someone shouted, "Who needs reinforcements?"

The DA spook stepped into the spot Cinder had been speaking from, with a dry smile. "Hello everyone. I don't mean to hurt your egos. Captain Cinder was just talking me up. What the DA will be providing is simply some auxiliary, robotic support. We've deployed thirty spotter drones, which will synchronize with your HUDs when we arrive. The integration AI will automatically highlight active threats and your allies in red and green respectively, just like in the War Games." As he spoke, the display banners overhead split down the middle. Him on the left, an infographic on the mantis-looking machines.

Shoot the bad guys, don't shoot your friends. Who is who? They get to decide. Love it.

"This will be a quite extensive operation, because the man, Aleksander Sokolov, has built himself an empire beneath our feet. Normally that wouldn't be worth the effort to stomp out, but he got it into his head to steal a batch of NZ-virus vaccines. That, and he has de facto declared war on his underground neighbors. Our latest tally has fifty associated deaths with his expansion, and no sign of it stopping. His latest stunt in Survivor's Canyon resulted in twelve deaths and over forty hospitalizations. He also deals in drug distribution and human trafficking, the very channels which bring CZAR into the city."

You lying weasel. He trafficks tobacco, not CZAR. It just gets smuggled the same way. What kind of propaganda bullshit is this?

"Oh," the DA agent said with a shrug, and glanced at Cinder as though he had forgotten something. "We're also providing this." At his command, the infographic switched. Gone was the well-known spotter bot, and up came a rendering of a steel beast. Shot after shot panned across the sleek curves, the lustrous panels of chrome, the gleaming rifle barrels. Not an infographic, but an advertisement for the four-legged machine. The name blasted onto the screen, Manticore. Bigger than an ARU, and that was before including the steel tail like a dragon.

The crowd of police and soldiers whistled and cheered, popping off like a bunch of fans at a game launch. A moment later, the train shuddered, and Elliot heard people jumping and swearing. A shadow passed over window after window as the train cars rocked with newfound weight. No one took aim though. Elliot saw why when it reached him. The Manticore was climbing across the outside of the train, headed to the nose.

I guess Congress wants to see what their money can buy.

The DA spook laughed and gestured for Cinder to take the stage once more. She puffed out her chest and barked out, "Op in twenty-five. Get ready. Y'all like the Unnamed OST?" No one seriously refused, and she turned on some music. A bass line like a drum beat. Kick drum like a dog fighting its chain. By the time the lead guitar started, the entire atmosphere on the train had degraded. The ordered lines dissolved and attack squads clumped to one another. Everyone knew the music. They looped it in every rec hall throughout bootcamp. Government owned pump-up music. It was a chorus of building drums and chanting that drilled into the subconscious to latch onto the primitive hunter's instincts to violence.

A hell of a lot more than fifty people are going to die today. The DA is going to make Sokolov's crimes look like child's play, and they're going to enjoy giving everyone the reminder.

A soldier tapped Elliot on the shoulder. Four of them stood there, faces hidden behind opaque white facemasks. Unlike void masks, their eyes were exposed behind polycarbonate inserts, and the rest of the material was similarly bullet proof. "So you're the VIP?"

Elliot's mouth went dry and he nodded. "I'm the detective, yeah. The one Ghos is yelling at. So you're my bodyguards?"

"Yes, Sir, Mr Blackstone. Just stay behind us if there's resistance."

"I'll be happy to," Elliot said. He looked into the soldier's eyes, tried to get a read, but there wasn't enough. The bodyguard was just some person assigned to him from some other department working for people he didn't know and they couldn't care less about what he was doing.

Something buzzed against his thigh. It took him a moment to realize it was a phone call. When it didn't auto-connect to his armor system, he frowned and went digging through his pockets. It wasn't his own phone ringing, it was the one the thug with the micro-blade had given him. Sokolov's phone. When he finally got it out, he saw the caller ID labeled as unlisted. He accepted the call, popped his helmet open. "Hello?"

"Mr Blackstone, it seems we have some kind of misunderstanding with a bit of urgency to it. I thought my man told you to call if there was anything wrong." The voice was older, male, had a bit of a wheeze to it, and unfamiliar to Elliot.

Is this Sokolov? Am I talking to the leader himself right now? Cinder...

Elliot knocked his fist against his bodyguard's chest and pointed at Cinder. The soldier got the message perfectly, and delegated it to his subordinate. The other man took off running to get her, and Elliot put his attention back to the call. "Who am I speaking to right now?"

"Don't play games, Mr Blackstone. You know exactly who I am. You people have laid siege to my establishment. For what? Because of a squabble over CZARheads? Is that what tipped you over the line?"

"Sokolov, I take it? The problem is talking to you wouldn't have helped. This is all over my head. You understand how that works, don't you? It's politics."

Sokolov scoffed. "Is this about the kid? The one who hurt the congressman's son?"

He knows about Kyte?

There wasn't music good enough in the world to keep the ice out of Elliot's veins. He glanced over. Cinder was on her way, but not there yet. He hung his head, dropped his voice, and asked, "If I said it was, would you even be able to hand him over?"

"I am a very powerful man, Mr Blackstone."

Cinder had gotten the message. She had almost made it to him. "Look, Sokolov, I don't have much time here. I suggest you surrender and cooperate as best you can. You pissed someone off, and they're using you as an experiment. They're sending a monster for you. Think of your daughter."

"You don't understand pride, do you, Mr Blackstone? And I have a monster of my own."

Cinder reached over and snatched the phone from Elliot's ear. She flipped it to speaker phone. "Well well well, is this who I think it is? I heard my boy here say you're Sokolov."

"Ah," the gang lord said. "You must be the Blonde Devil. The one who arrested my men in Survivor's Canyon."

"Yeah, that's me. You wouldn't happen to be calling to surrender, now would you?"

Do you have to ask that with a grin?

"Respectfully, I do not recognize your authority to do this, you uniformed tyrant. Do you wipe your ass with the constitution you pledged an oath to? You come to my property and we will retaliate with full discretion."

Cinder laughed. "I think I like you, Mr Sokolov. That's because I like a fight. They used to have me overseas, fighting it out with UAAF proxy forces, but now I'm here. So I'm looking forward to going back to the good old days. Now, let me be clear. If you want to surrender, you and your boys had better put your hands behind your head, put your face to the ground, and present your asses for us; because, we're coming in hard and fast. But, I really hope you fight it out. I've got these new toys to test out."

Sokolov answered, "You're disgusting," and hung up.

Cinder threw back her head and cackled. Elliot snatched the phone back with a snarl. "Do you want this to be a bloodbath?" he asked.

His boss shook her head. "We're the government, Blackstone. We are and must be the final authority, the monopoly of violence. We are here to make an example of Sokolov and tell everyone that there are lines not to be crossed. We're here to destroy his operation, and they are welcome to try and stop us. If they don't surrender, they're consenting to the fight."

You're not exactly giving them a choice in the matter. Do you think the people who work for him can just hand themselves over? I'm sure plenty—hell, most of them are more mired in their own mistakes than Kyte is. His influence is built on trust and un-taxed currency, not on fear. These aren't terrorists, they're domestic separatists.

"You're going to make it harder for me to safely arrest Kyte. Do you think Ghos is going to just accept getting told the kid got shot and killed in the firefight?"

Cinder's laughter faded. The mirth vanished from her smile as it became cold, ruthless. "Better than him escaping. Death is a justice of a kind. It's honest at least. It has finality. Don't like it? Get in there and get the kid. That's your job. Just pray your partner is doing a good job buttering him up, eh?"

Ram had been assigned liaison to Ghos during the operation. Demeaning for her qualifications, but she had requested to be taken off the raid, and that was her transfer. Elliot didn't know if she'd handle reporting on the fighting well. Distance only sanitized violence to an extent. Elliot didn't know what to do but grumble, "Yes, Ma'am," as Cinder walked to the other end of the train. The bodyguard didn't seem to have an opinion of the exchange. Strict professionalism, he stared through Elliot like he was watching a rerun of a movie.

Ellliot slapped his helmet back on and accessed his own phone. He dialed up the one person who could help him.

"How can I be of assistance, Detective?" EVE asked.

He turned away from the crowd of soldiers, and faced out the window. He let his eyes glaze over the towers flying by, filled with millions of people oblivious to the chaos being brought into existence. He said, "I'm calling in the favor."

After a moment, he heard her voice again. The little delay was him getting transferred to her central consciousness. "Oh my, oh my, the stingy Detective Blackstone is finally calling in the grand favor of mine. Whatever will it be? What is your wish that you would make to the most powerful being in the whole world?"

"I want one of two things. Either I get my hands on the kid safely, or he escapes to the Isles. Do whatever wizardry it is that you can do to make sure he doesn't get killed in this raid." A tension released in his chest. He found himself breathing quicker and harder, pumping air into his body as he set his gaze. "Can you do that?"

EVE said, "Can I do that? Look at you, asking stupid questions. I was just surprised by your altruism. Spending your favor on someone you've never met."

His lips pressed into a frown. "No, I haven't; but, I know what's happened to him. This has all spiraled out of control from one immature accident."

"It was poor luck for him that he fell in with a gang that caught the DA's ire," the AI mused. "Was it because of his father? I know you have a soft spot for kids like Dom, but there are kids like Kyte every day. Thousands of them even."

Elliot's helmet thunked against the window as he leaned against it. "Maybe, but I'm tied to this kid, like it or not. Proximity breeds affection."

"Even if his crimes didn't stop at the concert? Even if he stabbed another thug? Even if he willingly shot someone?"

"Doesn't mean he can't be saved, EVE."

"No it doesn't. I was just checking. I wanted to make sure you understood what you were getting yourself into. I'll see what I can do. Consider us even, as far as the Devson affair is concerned."

"You pull this off, and I'll owe you one, EVE."

"I'll hold you to that, Elliot."

Back into Hell I go.

25

The End Of The Grotto

2140/10/10

"Have you gone insane, Kyte?" Vlad screamed.

"Don't give yourself a heart attack, babe," Mary, the green haired woman seemingly in a relationship with him, said.

"What are you even talking about?" Kyte asked.

The three of them were in the backrooms of The Greco Grotto. The whole place vibrated with stomping feet as people piled in and rushed out through the back. There was a path down to Epsilon hidden away. Not quite the Worm Tunnels, but enough for non-combatants to turn tail and flee before the police arrived. Kyte kept wobbling from foot to foot, anxious to join the crowd. The Greco Grotto was the crux of the raid, but it was the last place that would get swept by the police. It was the only place that he felt he wouldn't get immediately arrested in, and had ways out from, but the moment Vald turned on him he ran out of friends to rely on.

"Fumi; you fucking idiot," the gangster shot back at him.

The words hit harder than Drake's fist had. Kyte winced back, feeling like he was about to vomit again. "Look, that whole thing, it was a mistake. You were right. I shouldn't have gotten involved with her. I should have found another way to get what I needed and steered clear. Everyone told me to stay away and I should have listened. Sorry."

Vlad's anger tempered down. He paced and stopped, squinted his silicon eyes at Kyte. "Did you do it?"

"No. I didn't do anything. I mean, I talked her into liking me enough that she volunteered to be my sick nurse…"

Vlad stepped closer and cut his hand through the air. "You didn't touch her?"

"Me touch her? Vlad I could barely move. I mean, we kissed before I got the jab, but what are you asking?"

"I'm asking if you touched her, you numbskull. Did you cross the line?"

Mary frowned. "Fumi showed up crying at her father's office maybe fifteen minutes ago."

Kyte fell down, landed on one of the worn-out couches and composed himself. "I didn't do anything to her. I turned her down."

"What do you mean, you turned her down? Sokolov's got a kill order out on your ass. Says he wants you castrated!"

Kyte's head shot up. "What? Hey, she got handsy with me! I shoved her off and ran! What the hell else was I supposed to do? I was almost an invalid. I puked in the hallway on the way out. The only reason I'm back here is because of the police barricades. I'd be out of here if I could be. I'm going to the convoy and getting the hell out of here!"

Vlad and Mary held their tongues and stared at him, watched his panic and his desperation. Kyte didn't need to fake anything about that. "So you didn't touch her?"

"No!"

"Then you need to get the hell out of here before someone kills you. Get ahold of the smuggler and get outside the city. You're better off camping than in this crossfire. I'm sorry, but I can't offer to make you one of us anymore. You would have been great, but this ain't no good anymore."

Kyte's shoulders slumped. "What do you expect me to do to get out of here? They've got the whole neighborhood on lockdown! They've got spotter bots checking everyone. They'll pluck me from the crowd.

I can't even pay the guy because Gamma Coin is down. Transactions aren't processing."

Vlad snarled and went back to pacing. "Those jannis bastards. They took down the miners. Cut off the processing power this morning. Gamma Coin isn't down, it's just clogged and they're going to raid us before we boot up the backups. Threw everyone into a frenzy. It's got everyone running with their tails between their legs."

"From a police raid? I would too!"

He threw a hand in the air. "For the non-combatants, sure. There's nothing special about that. Why everyone's acting like they've never had anything to do with us, that's what's got me."

Mary sighed and lit up a cigarette. She leaned on the couch arm, much more casual than her dress implied. "Cowards is all. Rats flee sinking ships, you know that. They think we're going to get stamped out like an old cigarette butt."

Vlad paused and put a finger to his ear. He turned away from the two of them and took a call through his neural implant. All Kyte could hear was some grunts and acknowledgments, before the gangster turned back around. "Sokolov wants me manning Zathial."

Mary leapt her feet, and faltered. She grabbed onto the couch to steady herself, and said, "He's putting that burden on you? I thought he was going to use... that thing... himself."

Vlad shook his head. "He still hasn't learned how to use it well enough. He's better use coordinating people and I agree with him. It just makes sense. Besides, Zathial is the only thing that can stop an ARU."

Kyte found he couldn't hold it in any longer. "What is Zathial?"

Vlad smirked. "Nothing you need to worry about. You won't be fighting. Much as I'd like to have you helping me out, the chances of someone shooting you in the back to make my boss happy are too high and too risky." He sighed. "Kid, just go with the others and get out of here. With everyone ditching Gamma Coin, transactions will be working by tonight, regardless of if we get the backups working. Good luck out there, alright?"

Kyte nodded and lowered his head. He felt empty as Vlad left the room. It hurt just as much as Fumi had hurt him. Like they had reached in, put down roots, then ripped out a part of his insides. Bit by bit, he was becoming nothing but a shell.

He jerked upright when Mary put her hand on his shoulder. "Come on, no point in going straight to the crowd. Let's get you in some new clothes, yeah? Ones that don't smell like fry oil."

Kyte gave her an embarrassed smile and followed her to another of the backrooms. The clothes hung across rickety racks gave him the distinct impression that it was a prostitute's dressing room, a staging ground for women making their money with their bodies. The back half had the same, but for men. He frowned as she started rifling through to get him something.

"What? Not to your liking?" she asked, holding up a tight black shirt in one hand, and a maroon leather jacket in the other.

"So is this all... for a theater?"

"It's for hookers. Are you going to take the clothes or not?"

Kyte changed into the clothes, and Mary nodded approvingly. It all fit perfectly, and to his surprise the jacket seemed to be genuine leather. "You're giving this to me?" It was possibly the most expensive thing he had on him, even more than the gun.

Mary nodded. "Vlad thinks you're a good kid. You'll need it, if you're going out to live in the Isles. Not much climate control out there. Winter is coming and you don't want to be begging."

The coldest Kyte had ever been had been in simulation, through the filter of an ENU. That had made the arctic survival game as chilly as stepping into a fridge, but not more. He was pretty sure he'd need more than a leather coat eventually, but he would have a few months to get that in order. "Thank you."

"Go on, before the police arrive."

Kyte didn't know her well enough to hug her, so he bowed out of the room and stuffed his void mask back over his face as he stepped into the flow of people. They poured down the halls, a few people in-the-know explaining how to navigate the tunnels. He had just gotten to the staircase down when the music arrived. Far ahead of any soldier or police officer, the thump of too-familiar music made everyone lift up their head and look around like a herd of chickens.

It was jingoistic boot-thumper music, made by people like Kyte's father. The kind of mind numbing thrill kill music that brought out the savage in people. Kyte's spit began to taste like the previous night's vomit just listening to it. Other people had a more energetic reaction. They charged down into Epsilon. The crowd became tighter than a mosh pit at an Auroary concert. Kyte threw himself to one side, pressed himself flat to the wall as people charged past. The fear and panic hit him too, but his fear didn't reach past the crowd of people before him. The kind of instinctual flight driving them away, just like in Survivor's Canyon, when he had gotten a gun stuffed in his face.

He was afraid he wouldn't slip by a second time.

It wasn't a gun that ended up in his face though, but a camera. First thing he saw was the high powered light shining from it, just enough time to rear back and squint his eyes. With huge, blue smears in his vision, he backed away, even further from the staircase down to Epsilon level. The perpetrator jumped back, attention fixated on the digital display. It took him only a moment of confusion to realize what had happened, that they had photographed his face through the mask.

He hissed, grabbing at the rim of his void mask just to feel that it was there. Obviously, some amount of light could go through the mask, enough to see by. He hadn't considered just how much light it would take to get a picture of his eyes.

The thug with the camera grinned. He was so young he had braces on, but his frame had enough muscle he must have been using steroids. "We got a match, boys!" he shouted.

Kyte backed away, put distance between him and the thug. Others started to appear, lurking around the edges of the crowd. It was just like when they had trapped him in the retail lot. Sure enough, he made eye contact with Drake. The thug had been patched up. Bandages could be seen from his shoulder sleeve, but Kyte didn't have the spare time to think about that. His mind glued onto the glint of steel-that-wasn't-steel extending from Drake's grasp.

The bastard had a micro-blade pointed right at him.

"Come here, Kyte, you piece of scum. I just want to talk."

Kyte blinked. His mouth gaped. He didn't know what to do but to reach inside his coat and grab the handle of his gun. The moment he did, he froze. His arm locked up and the memory of shooting the CZARhead flashed through again and again. He felt the blunt recoil. Heard the muted bang. There was a distance to it all, like he was a mere observer to it. But he wasn't just a viewer in a movie theater for it, he was chained to the seat and unable to close his eyes.

Drake moved closer, taking his steps as deliberately as he could so no one would run into him and lose an arm from knocking into the micro-blade. That kind of accident might let Kyte escape, and Drake couldn't have been more obviously riled up on righteous fury.

Like a schoolboy and a bully, he was saved by a bell. Specifically, an ear-splitting, world-filling buzz that went straight through every wall, door, and floor to suffuse the entire neighborhood in head-splitting pain. People all around them fell to their knees from the shock of it, only regaining themselves when it waned slightly. The acoustic warfare had its desired effect immediately, non-lethal displacement of every person not committed to the fight. People like Kyte.

He took off running, but not down to the tunnel where hundreds of other people pressed shoulder to jaw. He went against the flow, to where the crowd thinned. He ran to where he'd be able to get away from people, and perhaps use his gun for a second time. Additionally, Styx's meetup spot was inside the police cordon.

26

Engagement

2140/10/10

Police and soldiers streamed off the sides of the train, raining down from rappel cords. Beneath, the Manticore had landed and unleashed a sonic attack. Elliot's QRS gear filtered the noise, it was just a sine wave, but he still felt the vibration through his boots. It made his feet numb as he followed the bodyguards to the boarding station. Already, people by the dozens were getting walked through the barriers. They got cuffed and mag-tied to support beams for processing.

The sight reminded Elliot of livestock, or possibly a slave market.

"So everyone here, you've scanned their faces?" he asked. He didn't even know who he was talking to. In his vision, the officer in charge was simply green and labeled with a 'B', the highest rank he could spot.

"Yeah, most have arrest warrants and outstanding fines. The judges are going to love this little flood we're dumping on them. You're the one manhunting, right? For Skybyte Vapor? No dice here."

"Message me if he does show up. I don't think he's going to turn himself in though," Elliot said, and got a nod from the B-rank. He turned from the processing team and headed for stairs down, to get to ground floor. The bodyguards followed behind, white-faced shadows. Through his armor system, he rang up EVE. "If you'd spotted him by now, I'm sure you'd have told me. So do you have any guesses? Suggestions on where to go?"

"No, not quite. Too many people too tight together. He's got a void mask on and I don't know what he's wea–oh, hello."

"What?"

"You know I'm amazing at this, right?"

"What did you find, EVE?"

"Someone took a photo of him just now. I set up a scan for any photos taken since the moment you called in the favor, and someone just snapped a picture of his face. Now that I have a timestamp and a router geo-location, I can just play it back to get a picture of the picture. He was in The Greco Grotto."

Elliot hissed and turned towards the Manticore. He could see the chrome tail twisting in the air, and could hear the gunfire exchange. Half of it at least sounded like concussive rounds. Less than lethal, but not where he wanted to walk. "Is he fighting?"

It's only been a few days. He isn't that enamored with these people, is he? I'm not too late, am I?

"Technically?" EVE said. "He's running away at the moment, but his fight is with Sokolov's men. They appear to be trying to filet him for some reason. Getting a view inside this place is entirely reliant on stupid people forgetting to turn their devices off, so it's a bit choppy. However, go here."

A waypoint appeared in Elliot's HUD, like a quest marker for a video game. Thankfully, he didn't need to explain anything when he changed direction and headed straight into an apartment building owned by Ajitatsu. Whether they actually owned it, or just had a licensing deal with some nebulous real estate investment firm, Elliot neither knew nor cared. The raid had all private security checkpoints disabled, and he breezed through the halls.

Good God, it's nice to not have to listen to corporate mascots and advertisements wherever I go.

One of the bodyguards grabbed him by the shoulder when he rounded a corner. The soldier threw him backwards, spinning and landing atop him as a burst of gunfire pounded in the hall. His vision had been only on the waypoint, not on anything else. The soldiers returned fire, barking call outs to one another. They activated stun-beams and bathed the hallway in flashing laser light.

Then, as fast as it started, it was over. They pulled Elliot back to his feet and surveyed the damage. Four women sprawled across the carpet, turning the brown mat red. Two of the soldiers wandered over them, kicking the bodies with their boots. One flinched, so they pumped some coagulating foam into the bullet wound through her hip and took her gun away. The rest of their attention stayed on the man who had saved Elliot.

"Damn, ripped right through the fabric," the squad leader said, digging out most of a bullet from his subordinate's shoulder. Right in the gap between chest and shoulder plates. "Fucking bitches."

Elliot walked past them, tuned out their conversation on injury. One of the dead women stared up at him. Her face looked like the one who had died in Survivor's Canyon. Or maybe he was remembering that one with the face now before him. The memories blurred together, mixing with all the other corpses he had seen and made. It wasn't the shock of death so much as a sudden reflection on himself that nearly took his legs out from under him.

Maybe Ram had the right idea. I think she had the normal reaction. Fuck, am I still normal?

"Are you alright, Detective?" one of the bodyguards asked.

Elliot realized he had slumped against a wall.

They must think I got shot.

"I'm fine. Let's go. Longer we stay here, more likely they'll come around to get us, right?" He started following the waypoint again and didn't think about whether his claim made sense. He could hear the erratic popping of gunfire echo. Distant, mute, stripped of its murderous potential. It grew faster, like the crescendo of music, mixing with the noise blasting out of the deployment train.

The emergency line, the open channel on everyone's frequency, blew up. "We got armor!"

They have fucking what?

The soldier didn't mean body armor. That wouldn't have been worth an announcement. Only something on the scale of an ARU or a tank got called armor. The realization had the same stifling effect on the bodyguards. Otherwise stoic, implacable, even they shifted around and glanced at one another. "Doesn't concern us," Elliot said. "Besides, that's what the Manticore is for, right?"

As long as it's more an advanced design, rather than a proof of concept.

"EVE," he said on the private line. "You'll navigate me around that, right?"

The AI laughed. "Uhm, about that. You see, the thing is–I just cracked their comms by the way–that this thing, Zathiel, kind of immediately set off emergency analysis procedures? Let me get back to you after I figure out how they built a robot without me noticing."

Elliot slowed to a stop. He turned to face the line of bodyguards trailing behind him. "We should move quicker. The target is moving towards the wall, away from The Greco Grotto." He didn't need to add, 'So, let's get the hell away from this thing.'

For as large as the Ajitatsu apartment building was, they eventually had to leave the sprawling tower to get to the next one. Something black and burning flew over their heads like a meteor. Elliot threw himself to the ground as it roared past. He hit the dirt with flames above him. Then he rolled back to his feet. The soldiers had nearly done the same, they had their guns up, pointed at the thing.

Elliot blinked, but all that remained was the reflections of light off windows. "The fuck was that?"

Someone answered him over the general. "It can fly. Repeat, the armor can fly."

Cinder took over the general and barked out, "All teams, repeat. All teams, prepare for operator neutralization. EVE is going to find where this bastard is. Closest teams are to move in with full prejudice and eliminate the target."

"Come on," Elliot said to his bodyguards. Other teams started barking back the acknowledgement across the comms, but he just shook his head. "That's not us. We have a goal. We're leaving." He ran, the QRS suit bogging him down and sapping the wind from him after only a single block, but he chased the waypoint regardless. With his back to the main fight, he put as much distance as he could between him and it. The sound of sustained gunfire haunted him through a rundown shopping mall, through a stretch of pay-by-the-week apartments, and caught up with him when they finally announced a location for the operator.

A second waypoint appeared in Elliot's HUD, along with a measurement. The squad of bodyguards stopped and stared at it. Everyone could see the reading, "87m". The squad leader turned to Elliot. He might have been frowning, but there was no way for Elliot to tell. The man inclined his head towards the waypoint. "No one but the security detail is closer than us, and they can't dispatch to it."

They could... she did say all teams.

"We can't just abandon our mission either."

"You can go on without us then. We will be taking the fight to them. You're just going after a kid. I'm sure you can manage."

Elliot found his teeth gritting so hard he couldn't respond. Instead, he pulled up the video feed of the fight. He took a look at the mayhem and for a moment, couldn't even comprehend it. The quad-copter recon drone struggled valiantly to videotape the occurrence, but couldn't put enough distance between itself and the mechanized monsters to keep up. The Manticore kept leaping about the valleys between the towers. It sprang into the air and twisted, landing on bridges and walkways. Mounted rifles at the hips and shoulders fired in a broken, random pattern. They constantly tracked, swinging around, but only let loose whenever the backstop wouldn't kill anyone.

The thing it fought had no such concerns. The thing zipped around like a fiery bird. Wings like a phoenix, body like black soot. Not quite a machine gun, but it hammered the Manticore with armor-piercing rounds. The thing was so large the flying robot barely ever missed. Whether the bullets actually damaged it at all, Elliot could only guess.

What turned his stomach was the half dozen corpses strewn about the street beneath the robotic rampage.

"Fuck." He slammed a fist into the wall hard enough to crack it.

"Are you going? Or coming?"

"I'm coming! Bastard's blood. Come on, before anyone else gets killed by that thing."

He glared at the waypoint marking Kyte. From how fast it was moving, he could tell he was nearly on the kid, but if that flying thing beat the Manticore, there would be no end of damage.

God damn it. Don't get yourself killed, kid.

27

Auto-Hypnosis

2140/10/10

One day after being bedridden was not much time to recover his cardio. Kyte had never had much cardio in the first place either. With Drake and company charging behind him, every step ate up what little headway he had. Here and there he had a breakaway. He vaulted railings, took unexpected staircases, and had the balls to sprint across a firefight. Not directly in the line of fire, above it by one story, but it was close enough to make the other thugs think twice.

Some of them even gave up the chase. Whether they started shooting at the police, or ran for the Epsilon tunnels, Kyte didn't look back to check.

His lungs set on fire and gave out one block from the diner. The pain became too much. The first doorway he saw after turning a corner, he ducked into to pant and pray. The one step he took proved too much, and he tumbled into empty air. The spot where a staircase should have transitioned to floor had collapsed, and he went right through the gap. "Fuck!" He hit the floor half a story down, banging himself up something fierce but not rolling an ankle. His body throbbed, but he checked himself over one ache at a time. The worst injury proved to be a swelling lip.

"You okay, kid?" a man asked. He had a can of spraypaint in one hand, and a respirator in the other. He wore what looked like an oversized kimono, flecked with paint like confetti. Bushy hair down to his shoulders, mirrored goggles that reflected Kyte's sorry state right back at him.

"What? What are you– Don't you hear what's happening?"

"My ears work fine, kid. You're the one in a panic about it, not me."

Kyte didn't have the breath to argue with the painter. He pushed himself up and stumbled. Slumping against a wall, he focused on regaining himself. The painter shrugged and went back to his work. With the help of mixers and applicators, and other tools Kyte could only guess at, he blasted down gradients of blue and white. Stroke by stroke, he turned a barren wall into a sky so vast it felt like he could fall into it. There was ground too, rolling fields of grass and dirt, illuminated by a rising sun.

The painter stepped to the side, pushing the edges of the mural further and revealing the figure. A man sat in the shadows of one side, but it wasn't a human. It was something like an android or a cyborg, with cables plugged into its spine and skull, trailing off into the darkness and terminating at the wall's power outlet.

"You know, this wasn't meant to be seen before it was finished," the artist said, glancing over his shoulder.

Kyte blinked, realized he had caught his breath, and pushed off the wall. "It's really good."

"No it isn't. It makes me sick to look at, but all I can paint nowadays is the kind of dreck that makes me want to throw up," the artist said, spinning the paint gun around in his hand as he sneered at it.

Kyte shook his head, glanced back at the door he had fallen through. Drake's silhouette didn't blot the doorway behind him though. "Well, I like it. Glad I saw it before I left," he said, and tried to walk out a door the other way. The room had once been some kind of retail store, with an open front three stories high, sweeping balconies covered in trash like snowdrift.

"Leave? Where the hell are you going? Jail?"

"The Isles."

The artist whistled. "Wish I could join you. Man wasn't meant to live like this."

"You should get out of here before the raid…" he trailed off when he saw something flying through the air between the towers, burning and trailing smoke. It was headed right at him. He shouted, spun and sprinted. The painter was slow to turn, but quick to panic as well. Kyte barreled into the man, knocking both of them beneath the crumbling staircase just before the burning thing smashed through the window and into the store.

It crashed into a wall like a cannon shot and didn't move.

The painter shoved Kyte off of him and ran back over to his mural. He fell to his knees, tugging at his hair and wailing because the surface had cracked. Kyte ignored that and peeked around the corner to see what had happened. The burning thing was a metal figure little bigger than a man, broken in the middle and oozing oil. Just like the painting, it was meant to be an android, an imitation of a human, but the fighting had burned and marred it horribly.

"Zathiel? Vlad?" He had no doubt it was born of Miccolo's work. The government didn't make anything like it.

The machine turned its head to look at him; but, when it opened its mouth, no noise came out. The robot realized the issue, and shook its head. Struggling out of the debris resulted in the bottom half ripping free. The wings that had been the source of the fire, some kind of jet thrusters, sparked up again and ignited the oozing oil. For a moment, fire engulfed Zathiel.

It flew back out of the abandoned store just as fire retardant spewed from rusted pipes and snuffed it out. Zathiel blasted out as the giant police robot chased after it, the two blasting gunfire at one another and fighting for domination. Emotions fought inside Kyte. Awe, fear, and a crushing sense of smallness. The scope of it threatened to overwhelm him.

"There you are," Drake hissed, stepping out on a balcony over Kyte's head.

"Oh, fuck." He'd spent too much time staring. He'd basically been standing next to a fireworks display; of course he would get spotted. Kyte spun for an exit, only to find other guys in void masks closing in. They panted and heaved as well, but still outnumbered him three to one. The chaos hadn't pulled away enough of them. One by one they dropped down to the floor Kyte was on and circled round him like wolves to prey.

He knew his only option was the gun. To pull out that revolver and kill one of them. The thought made his hand shake. Again, he could feel the recoil from the CZARhead he had shot. "Don't you people have something better to do?" he pleaded.

Drake spread his arms out, micro-blade in one hand. "Why would you ask that? Now that we've got you, this will only take a moment. Ain't nobody going to ask questions about how a punk like you got killed in this mess. I bet Sokolov will promote me afterwards."

"Sokolov is going to die, you stupid idiot! Everyone who fights is going to end up shot, or jailed if they're lucky. There is no more Sokolov. There is no more Gamma Coin. Everything you people had is getting torn apart. Your lives are over."

Drake shrugged. "Long as I don't die, there's always tomorrow. Hell, if we have to rebuild, I might end up second-in-command. After all, Fumi will be real thankful to me that I'm here, dealing with you."

The punk's words hurt like a knife in Kyte's chest. "There are cameras everywhere. EVE will know if you kill me here. You think Sokolov would have been able to build something if the police could have picked him up and put him away as soon as they felt like it?"

Drake shook his head. "Who knows? Maybe. One way to find out. I'll worry about tomorrow's problems tomorrow." He stepped closer and gave the micro-blade a twirl.

Kyte's heart pounded so much he wanted to puke. It throbbed in his ears as the din of fighting faded. Everything tunneled in on him and

Drake. He did what he'd been taught to do, what he had to in order to survive. The moment he made the decision, his actions became mechanical. Drake was close, almost three meters away, but the stab to his leg hadn't healed. Running on it had broken the stitches and Kyte could see blood seeping through his pants. So when he drew the revolver he fired a shot into the ground before taking aim. Drake flinched, faltering one step away from him. The involuntary jerk of surprise, the need to see if he had been hit, bought Kyte the breath of time necessary.

He shot Drake in the chest, then didn't let himself dwell on it. He spun, blasting another round at the second thug. He had no idea whether he hit, just that his target turned and fled. On to the third and Kyte froze.

The third thug slumped, knees hitting the ground before his eyes rolled up and he collapsed. The painter shook his hand out and frowned at the blood pooling from Drake's groaning body. Kyte blinked, his consciousness falling back out of the tension. He asked, "What happened?"

"What's it look like? I punched the guy. If they killed you, they woulda tried to kill me too. I would have been a witness," the painter said as he bent over and picked up the micro-blade. He sneered at it and produced a roll of masking tape from his supplies to wrap it up.

"Thanks?"

"What did you do there? Looked like auto-hypnosis."

Kyte stared at Drake's body. Thoughts barely moved through his head. "Just something my father taught me," he mumbled.

"Your daddy taught you to kill? Must have been a real bastard. I guess you're lucky though. I had to learn to fight on my own," the painter said, wagging the bound micro-blade. "Still, you better be careful with that. Pushing it all down inside you? It doesn't make it go away."

"I gotta go," Kyte said, and wandered over to the broken window the Zathiel had flown through. For a moment, he surveyed the city. He only spent a minute at it, before either of the thugs could get their bearings. He could see the police ARU and the Zathiel swiping at one another, and then the big robot exploded. Or, something that hit it exploded. A plume of fire and slag went up from the middle of it, which could only mean the fighting would get worse, bloodier, deadlier.

So while everyone else's attention was there, he slipped off to the rendezvous Styx had shown him, and vanished into the darkness of Epsilon level.

28

Dropped Charges

2140/10/10

"All teams, Manticore is down. They hit it with some kind of IED. Bogey still live. We need that operator dead, now!"

Elliot arrived at the target location the same time as another squad, much more heavily armed. They were the ones to pull out breaching charges and pop the doors off the apartment building. Though, Elliot had never seen an apartment building need inch thick steel bars. Recon drones swarmed in first, disposable ones. They mapped the place out as fast as they could, before the people inside shot them down or smashed them with clubs. Doing so marked them all in red within Elliot's HUD.

The soldiers stormed ahead of him, the radio lighting up with chatter even louder than the exchange of gunfire. The only thing that didn't light up was the location of the operator. EVE didn't know a precise location, all she had was the data cable sending the transmission, and the power outlet fueling it. The two locations were offset, and created a general area where the operator could be.

While the soldiers cleared room to room, sweeping through guns first, Elliot stalked behind with a short-barreled shotgun. Low-velocity shells only, nothing that could punch through a wall. Typically, they weren't even lethal. While the soldiers followed habit, moving in an algorithm, Elliot meandered the building as his intuition told him.

His main bodyguard hopped on their squad channel to say, "Spotter bot coming soon. We'll get a sweep for thermals."

"No need," Elliot said, facing the only plus sized bed in the entire complex. The apartment was wrong in every minute way he could think of. The trash can had wrappers but no stench. Empty beer cans dotted the living room, but not the kitchen. It smelled wrong too.

He grabbed the bedframe and gave it a tug, the headboard peeling away from the wall. Behind it, an improvised door. The moment he stood up however, the door flew open and a man dove through. He hit the ground rolling, sprang up, and got shot in the face by Elliot's bodyguard. The body crumpled to the floor, dropping a micro-blade that had nearly slashed into Elliot's neck.

"Thanks."

"Good work, detective."

Elliot bent over and took the micro-blade as the rest of the soldiers piled into the room, lined up at the door, and stormed the hidden room. Thermal imaging cut through the walls and exposed only two people within the room. Elliot followed behind, listening to the confused screaming of the soldiers for surrender.

The room was nothing more than a boarded up bedroom from the adjacent apartment. Furnishings went no further than the computers and some chairs, in front of which stood a trembling, green haired woman. She had her eyes closed, tears trickling down her cheeks as three different stun beams blasted her in the face to blind her. The soldiers had been trained to deal with the unconscious man behind her, the one plugged into the machine, not her.

Get out of my way.

Elliot walked in front of the soldiers, put himself between them and her, and took the pistol from her hand. She dropped to her knees and buried her face in her hands. She tried to look up at Elliot and asked, "Why did it happen like this? Please, don't kill him."

Asking me to save a killer?

"Blackstone! Move," the squad leader barked.

He didn't move out of the way. He let go of his shotgun, let the strap hold it to his chest, and grabbed the operator by the hair. The man was Vladimir Baker, but his mind was three city blocks over. Elliot hacked the micro-blade into the back of the man's skull.

Vlad convulsed. His muscles spasmed and locked up as he fell from the chair. Silicon eyes bulged as he writhed from the induced seizure. He grunted and moaned, barely able to open his mouth. The man thrashed, kicking away the chair and grabbing for cables, for a weapon, for anything.

The soldier stepped up beside Elliot and looked down. "Fair enough," the man said, nodding at the micro-blade. Then he shouldered his rifle and pointed it at Vlad

The woman screamed and Elliot grabbed the barrel to shove it away. "This is a police operation."

The soldier's cold eyes turned on him. "This is an active firefight."

"Not for him, not anymore. Can't operate a drone with a broken implant."

The soldier stared back, then touched a finger to his ear and asked over the general comm, "Operator neutralized, please confirm."

Cinder said back, "Bogey crashed. Neutralization confirmed."

Elliot let go of the gun. "Get some cuffs on them and call in medical. He's going to be wanted for questioning," he said, glancing back at Vlad.

The man's convulsions had eased. He was left breathing like he had run a marathon and staring at his hand. "What did you do? What did you do to me? Why can't I see?"

Bastard's blood... better than dead at least.

He turned from the criminal with a shake of his head. "Just remember; if your lieutenant finds out you killed this guy, when he could have been interrogated, your career will be over." When he stepped away, the green-haired woman threw herself around Vlad. Elliot didn't stay to see them get pulled apart and arrested.

"Where are you going?" the soldier asked.

"I've still got to get the kid."

The entire tone of the neighborhood shifted. Elliot could tell the moment he emerged from the tower. People weren't fighting back anymore. They were running away or surrendering. Their symbol had been crushed. The fight had been won.

Elliot focused on the waypoint. He followed it from bridge to staircase, to hallway, all without comment from EVE. It led him to what his HUD told him had originally been a formal wear shop, a place for ball gowns and suits and the like. Nothing of the glamor and luxury remained, and in the center was a corpse.

No... no, don't be him.

The corpse wasn't Kyte. The kid was about the same age however. Tall, muscular, looked like he would have been a perfect fit for the military and yet he had ended up in Sokolov's domain. Bullet wound to the gut, hit something that gushed. Wasn't the kid's first wound, he had bandages on the thigh and shoulder.

Elliot sighed. "EVE, is this the one that got in a fight the other day with Kyte?"

"Most likely. There's a certain degree of uncertainty because of the respective locations, but it's the assumption I would make."

"Where is Kyte now?"

"Working on that. Sorry, Miz Palmer is breathing down my neck because of this Zathiel thing Sokolov built. They've filed a dozen different investigation requests, and it's triggering automatic alerts over to Daedalus, and ugh, it's awful. You wouldn't understand."

"Sounds like the kind of bureaucracy I deal with," Elliot mumbled and stood back up. Out the broken window of the derelict store, he could see a recon drone looking at him. It could see the corpse too, so he figured a mortuary team would show up eventually. Before he could glance around, he saw another bullet hole in the ground. It had chipped the plastic tile just in front of the corpse.

Elliot frowned and reoriented himself. He stepped around, putting himself where Kyte would have been standing. In his head, he rebuilt the events. Instinct told him there would have been others, else Kyte would have kept running. Then he finally saw the mural.

"What the? There's no way..."

This is the guy. This is the artist. The Ay-maze guy from the Devson case.

He blinked, his mouth hanging open inside his suit as he gawked at the cracked mural. The focus was a figure sitting at the edge of shadows, and yet able to see the world for what it was beyond. The roboticized figure didn't look out to the fields of nature beyond, but turned to look back with longing and sadness at the viewer themselves. Chains that looked like cables meant the figure would never be able to reach the fields, but he could see them.

I need a picture of this.

"Detective, what are you doing?" EVE asked as he fumbled out his personal phone and tried to snap a picture without taking off his suit gloves.

"Just a second."

"Kyte is crawling down a maintenance hatch to Epsilon."

"Bastard's blood." He got the photo and spun. The AI had put up a new waypoint, and he started jogging after it. "Tell me one of these spotter bots saw the artist that made this thing."

"Is that really what's important right now?"

"I can multitask, can't you?"

"I'm already multitasking! All the camera feeds are getting sent to temporary storage. If you think I'm reviewing something not immediately combat critical, you're delusional."

"Well, please!"

"In like a week, maybe. If you're lucky. And you ask nicely."

Elliot didn't respond. The run in the weight of the QRS armor, despite the weight assist, had sapped the breath from him.

I really need to hit the gym more. Too much walking, not enough running.

"Blackstone, he's getting away from you. Are you seriously going to lose him because of a footrace?"

"Oh shut up. What do you... expect me to do?" Elliot wheezed out.

I shouldn't have asked that. That was a stupid question.

"Well, for starters," EVE began.

"Please don't."

The AI sighed. "Pick a machine and learn how to use it next time. You could have powered wheels in your boots. You could just get artificial muscle fibers inlaid. You could even learn how to ride a cityboard."

Elliot rolled his eyes. "That's a magnetic death trap and you know it."

"For you maybe."

Elliot was saved from more of her opinions by a phone call. It rang in through his suit, and the name made him slow to a stop. Congressman Ghos said, "Detective Blackstone, you make for some entertaining television."

Elliot grimaced. "Been watching a feed?"

"Yes, we have," Ghos said. "I'm actually sitting here with a little group, much to my surprise. You're on speaker phone."

"Hi, Elliot," Ram said.

Great, Ram saw me maim that guy.

"Mr Blackstone, that firefight was awesome," a younger man said. Belatedly, Elliot placed it as Ghos's son, Evan.

I hope EVE is able to track Kyte through Epsilon. If she tells me she's lost him after all this...

Elliot hung his head, and didn't look at the access hatch to Epsilon level directly in front of him. If he went down, the call would drop. "What do you need?"

With a huff, Congressman Ghos said, "Regarding the charges against the boy who hospitalized my son–"

Evan cut in to say, "Can those be dropped? Not pursued? I don't want it on my conscience that he helped me out and I got him put in jail."

Elliot sagged. He felt like a burst water sack, taken too far on a march and ruptured. "You're saying this now?"

Ghos cleared his throat. "My son came to visit when he heard about the raid, and we've talked it over. I have been forced to agree that it wasn't my place to demand charges on behalf of my son. He's a grown man. It should be his choice."

Elliot shook his head. "Sure. Easiest thing in the world to do. He'll never see the inside of a courtroom for the beer bottle."

"Thank you, Mr Blackstone," Evan said. "I can't thank you enough. Ever since we met, I feel like my life has been back on track. It took getting in a fight, but, hey, that's a manly thing to do, right?"

Elliot walked forward. "I'm glad it's worked out for you, Evan. You had the courage to take a risk."

"So, you'll stop pursuing him?"

"I can't do that, Evan." The words nearly made him cry at the tragedy of it.

"What do you mean? I just dropped the charges! It's over. He can go home, right?" Evan asked, and his father laughed.

Well no wonder the two of them weren't getting along, an attitude like that.

"Ram, I've gotta head him off. The call is probably going to drop once I do. Why don't you explain it to him?" Elliot asked as he pulled up the rust coated slat of steel and stared into the damp abyss of Epsilon. He reached down and took hold of the ladder rungs and sank down, one step at a time.

"Sure," she said. "Evan, at this point, the pursuit has nothing to do with the initial charges. From what we've tracked, in the process of evading arrest– a crime itself– he has taken illegal possession of a firearm and used it in two incidents, both of which resulted in fatalities. Even if those were waved as self-defense somehow, we'd have to pick him up as an accomplice to an organized crime group. Extortion, intimidation, monetary crimes... if you picked up a book of legal codes for reasons to arrest someone, and flipped to a random page, you'd probably hit an accurate accusation."

Sounds like with a bit of distance between her and the violence, she can handle it. Well, Ram, I hope you're getting something out of this, playing liaison to Ghos. You're getting a behind the scenes look at how our government functions. It's an elected aristocracy. They make decrees that ruin people's lives.

The call broke into static and died.

Elliot stepped down into the tunnel. Sewage flowed behind one wall, and steam pumped across Bastion behind the other wall. The floor was coated in rust and mud that stuck to his boots as he walked and the air stank like stagnant canal water. He had to duck his head to get around crossing pipes, and squeeze around retro-fitted support beams. His QRS armor had a front facing light, and he could see Kyte's footsteps headed out to the rim of Bastion.

29

Out Of The City

2140/10/10

Kyte sat huddled in the darkness, shaking. The tunnels echoed with indistinct voices. He could hear footsteps near him, around him, over him, but never within the tiny room he had crawled into to wait. The air was damp. A cloying type of wet that stuck in his throat and sucked the heat from his body. No matter how much he clutched the blood-colored jacket around himself, he couldn't warm up.

He heard gunshots too. He heard the pings of creaking pipes fighting their joints. The little shifts of thermal expansion that chimed off beneath the city like insect mating calls in a forest. The actual insects stayed quiet, crawling through cracks and grime and fighting over scraps of trash pilfered from wayward people like him.

He had killed Drake, and he had done it on purpose.

His stomach lurched and he threw himself onto all fours to vomit. All that came out was a bit of acid and such a rot of pain inside him that tears flooded his eyes. Nothing more would come up. He couldn't get it out of him.

"Well, I'll be damned. You did make it here," Styx said, leering in from the darkness. The tepid emergency light barely colored the smuggler.

Kyte deflated. "Thank God I'm in the right spot."

"Not quite, but close enough, kid. You're lucky I'm good at my job. There's a jannis down here too, you know?"

"What would a police officer be doing down here? Don't they have more important things to do?"

"Who knows. Maybe they're looking for someone," Styx said, and stared at Kyte through his mirrored glasses.

"Maybe," Kyte said. "So, you got your chip reader?" He held up the Gamma Coin chip and the smuggler quietly nodded. They put the devices together and squeezed out the one transaction they needed. "Let's go. Come on, I need to get out of here. Out of this city."

"The toll's been paid, let me lead the way," the smuggler said, bowing himself out of the room and back into the darkness. The man picked up an electric lantern and held it up before him. He led the way, his light bobbing and swaying. Shadows danced and leapt, jumping out at the two of them as they squeezed through forgotten tunnels and broken walls.

The closer to the wall they went, the colder it got. His entire body felt like it had been drenched in sweat, enough to make him shiver and pull into himself. Every few steps, he felt a surge of raw emotion well up and fought with his mind. It made him cringe and shirk away, but he forced his feet to follow the smuggler through the darkness.

"You okay, kid?"

"I'm fine."

"You're crying. Did you leave someone behind?"

Kyte clawed at his face, wiping the tears away. "No. I mean, my mother I guess."

Styx frowned. "Judging by your lack of a mask right now... kid, are you alright? Did you get in a fight?"

"I'm fine!" he snapped. "Lead the way."

Styx clicked his tongue and shook his head. The smuggler was just a ferryman though, and resumed taking Kyte out of the city. Suddenly, he stopped at a grimy slab of concrete. "Grab a seat."

Kyte looked around. Wooden pallets and oil drums had been arranged into a sitting area beside the wall, but they were in a dead end. "What? Why?"

Styx stretched and sat in a corner, the lantern before him like a campfire. "Because, we have to wait. That's part of the canal lock. Nothing I can do to move it. The path is on the other side. Won't be but an hour or so."

Kyte stared at the smuggler and saw no deceit. He stared at the wall and saw horizontal scrape marks, the surest sign he could think of that it did slide. He shut his mouth and took a seat. He rubbed his hands together and stared at the lantern and tried to quiet his mind. He wanted to pull out his phone, to jump on a video game, to watch a cartoon, to drown himself in social media. He wanted a mindless escape. There was no internet reception in Epsilon, and he couldn't have logged in regardless. He had nothing but himself and the smuggler, and that was a lot of company.

"So, tell me," Styx said. He had lit up a cigarette, the smoke trickling through the unseen cracks in the room. "What are you going to do, when you get out there?"

"Sign up for work. Do what they tell me to," Kyte mumbled.

"After that. Work ain't life. What's drawing you out there?"

"Nothing. It's what's pushing me out," Kyte said, and quiet draped around the two of them once more. The smuggler sat and smoked. Kyte wondered whether the man had a neural implant, and was drifting through some internal simulation, but Styx never adopted the slow breathing that came with the digital dream.

The wetness of the room seemed to get worse. He wondered if something was leaking over from the artificial river. An ooze of sludge through a pack of algae and lubricant. He would have preferred bitter cold, the kind that made fingers and ears burn. He would have preferred a parched desert, sun baking in the sky. What he had was damp, dark, and forgotten.

"So, who'd you kill?" Styx asked.

"What?" Kyte couldn't look at the man, that would have meant seeing himself in the reflection of his eyes.

"That's what you did, isn't it? You got the blood splatter on you and everything."

"It was some punk. Came after me because of a girl, because of what I did to her. I couldn't get away. What was I supposed to do?"

Styx frowned and rolled the butt of his cigarette in his fingers. "Did you try running away?"

"Obviously."

"And he caught you? Trapped you?"

"Yeah."

"Sounds like you didn't have a choice then."

"That's not all. I shot a drug addict. Someone else finished them off, but I'm accomplice."

"And why'd you do that?"

"They were charging him with a knife. Not that there's any proof of that. We... Sokolov's men, they got rid of all the cameras. We went in, we left corpses behind."

"Still sounds like you might have a defense, kid. You're young too. You'd get tried as a juvenile, wouldn't you?"

Kyte sighed, and his face twisted in anguish. "And I'm definitely at fault for breaking a beer bottle over this guy's head because he was making out with my girlfriend."

Styx didn't have a response to that one. He nodded and smoked, and the two of them resumed waiting for the door to open up. Neither of them slept. It was too cold to feel exhausted. The shivers woke him up whenever his head started to droop. Whenever his eyes closed, he saw Drake looking back at him; not in pain but confusion, surprise.

Kyte found himself looking at the wall, yet to move. Beyond, the open world outside Bastion. "What's it like out there?"

"You're just now asking?"

"Yeah, I am."

"It ain't exactly a mystery. Anyone who's ever served in the Great Lakes Region knows what it's like, more or less. Cold, mostly. I don't think you'll have to worry much about the blighted for the next few months. Where you're going, it's going to start snowing any day and won't let up till March if you're lucky. You're so used to climate control that I doubt you can even imagine what it's like having to go out into the woods, on your own, to cut some deadfall and bring it back to burn. It gets real quiet out there, when the snow falls. If the wind stops, the whole world holds its breath. Nothing but you and the world."

"I don't think I've ever had a quiet day in my life."

"Of course you haven't. You grew up here. This right now is probably the furthest you've ever been from another human, myself excluded. We're beneath the wall, on the far side of the ring road. You've got a whole thirty meters or so. But, if you listen carefully, you still hear the pipes. The echoes. The everything. The silence will be the loudest thing you've ever heard."

Kyte smirked. "Louder than a full blast Auroary concert?"

"Whoever that is, yes. The people are different too. They talk less, think more. Comes from having to hold their tongues if a blighted shows up. You don't make noise to avoid hearing your own thoughts, not when you've got a monster staring back at you. But, hey, at least you know you won't lock up when you see one, right? That's a big benefit. You might actually survive long enough to find a girl willing to put up with you."

Styx's laughter echoed through the tunnels, and when it died away, the two of them heard the grinding gears, the cramping stone. The wall began to shift inch by inch. Like a giant through a swamp, it pushed over till the muck squelched and then Kyte saw the tunnel beyond. There was a dim, nightly glow. The weight in his chest lifted, and he pushed himself up. His legs had an empty pain to them, and he teetered for a moment as he struggled with fatigue, but he started to walk.

Styx didn't follow. Kyte turned back, one hand on the cold wall. "What's wrong?"

"Nothing kid. This is as far as I go. Convoy is that way. I'm not leaving Bastion, just showing you the way."

Kyte left the smuggler behind and left the walls of Bastion. Behind him, they spread from one end of the world to the other, vanishing into the horizon. The once great wall now bore rust and patches. Wind tunnels honeycombed the surface like giant bullet wounds, the turbines not even turning anymore. At the foot of the barrier, Kyte couldn't see over the top, to the spires of the city. He couldn't see a real way back in either. Even the canal was gated shut.

Kyte stepped out from the shadow of the city walls, out from behind shrubs and weeds, and then dirt was beneath his boots. Grass covered the world before him. Dawn light swelled to his left, swallowing up the stars in the sky. Beneath the sky, crawling across the ground, Kyte saw the trucks of the convoy, the swarm of traders down from the Isles to set up shop. They had come to trade, to offer up their surplus food, the kind of luxury only the richest in Bastion could afford, and scamper off with the overflowing amenities of modernity.

He could hear them in the distance already, blasting music, drinking, and partying. They had vehicles circled around fires where they danced and partied, their shadows like titans in the early morning. They exulted in their freedom and in the wealth they would escape with, and Kyte headed towards it because he needed to find someone willing to hire him.

30

The Convoy

2140/10/11

Elliot sat at a table along the main strip of the convoy. He had lost Kyte's footsteps in the darkness, but so close to the wall that he knew where the kid would come out. He figured it was better to step outside and wait than to play cat and mouse, so he visited the festival.

All the big merchants of the Isles lined up like a hall pointed at the gates to Bastion. Soon, the doors would slide open, and approved shipments would get dragged out and hawked to anyone with some credits. It was never anything special. Shirts and pants, toilet paper by the metric ton. Imports from Asia and Europe. Things that people within Bastion took for granted. The convoy wasn't poor though, they just had to stock up quarterly.

Elliot sat with his back to a barbeque smoker. They had brought down barrels of chipped mulberry and fed the wood in scoop by scoop. The smoker radiated heat, billowed salty smoke, and taunted Elliot. He knew that a hundred pounds of pork had already been hung inside, dry rub seasoned and set to slowly cook all through the morning. By noon, they would be shredding burgers off of it and slathering on spicy cole-slaw the likes of which he could never get inside Bastion. But, it would be hours more, and he couldn't stay that long.

He faced the scrub-covered crack in the wall, the exposed gulch down to Epsilon, the known escape hatch. Eventually, Kyte would walk out of it, and he would get his last chance at the kid.

A woman sat down across from Elliot, folded her dirty hands together and stared at him. "You're a cop, aren't you? What brings you here? You've got some people concerned."

Elliot slid his helmet off the table and onto the bench beside him. "Nothing to worry about. Just need to pick up a kid."

"You're only supposed to be here if you're buying or selling. It's part of the agreement, you know?" She had her brown hair tied up in back, strands poking free like a pinwheel that waved in the October wind. There wasn't an ounce of fat on her, but she didn't seem frail in the least.

She'd do well as a streamer. Maybe. Maybe this attitude would stop her.

"Unfortunately, I won't have the time to buy some of your cooking; but, can I ask a question?"

"Seems to me like you already have."

"What happens when a kid sneaks out and tries to leave with you?"

The woman shrugged and glanced around the convoy. "Depends on if he can make a friend quick enough. Somebody has to vouch for him or he'll get left behind and you police will come pick him up... if he's lucky."

Elliot nodded. "Say he does make a friend. You're anarchists of a sort, aren't you? Do you let in immigrants or something?"

She scoffed. "You can't have immigrants if you're not a nation state. It would depend on who they fall in with, what work they can get. Someone on their own will probably end up forced to the frontier, probably in old Canada. Only tough sons of bitches survive up there, and tough sons of bitches are more likely to integrate with us, to not end up living with the blighted. Why do you ask, Mr Policeman? Looking for somebody?"

"I am, yeah. A kid about eighteen. Male, average height, short brown hair and fit enough for service. Fully vaxxed against the virus, no injuries. Not stupid either. The kind of guy that would be useful out here."

The woman nodded along. "I have to be honest, most people who sneak out here to run away, and there's not many, they've got something wrong with them, you know? It's easy to live in the city when you're functional–no reason to run out here."

Elliot said, "I assume he had his reasons, and I'm hoping word would have gotten around about him or maybe you know somebody who would know."

"That's a big ask, Mr Policeman."

"You want barter for the information? Creds?"

"You got a name for this kid? Asking me to rat out a friend will be expensive."

But you'd do it for the right price?

Elliot nodded and looked to the wall of Bastion; the strip of steel that separated the city from reality. "Yeah, Luke Blackstone. This would have been about six years ago. I've got a picture right here of him," he said, turning over his phone to show his little brother.

The woman frowned and picked his phone up. Then she called over some old man who frowned and squinted his eyes at the picture. "Six years ago, you say?" the man asked, tonguing a missing tooth as he stared at the picture. "Do you know which season?"

"It would have been this one, the winter convoy."

"Luke Blackstone, I can't say it rings any bells. You know, these kinds of kids have it rough with us because we get rustled by the GLR every now and then. They come in for a shakedown of deserters. It's easier to sneak into the convoy, but most people who join the Isles come from the service. You've got headhunters that come around to court martial the runaways."

Elliot felt himself slumping into the table. "And you don't stick up for them? You're independent, aren't you?"

The old man shook his head and set the phone down. "We don't much care for oathbreakers, you see. It's easiest for us to put 'em up till the headhunters arrive. Keeps 'em from causing trouble, you see? Did this Luke fellow, and I'm thinking the resemblance isn't just a chance, have one of them neural implants?"

Elliot's head perked up. "Yeah, he did. Cheap one, but he had one."

The old man tutted and grinned. "There you have it then. He didn't join us, or he's a clever son of a bitch. We out here don't have neural implants. That's one of the things the headhunters check for. You know how it is, yeah? Turn around, lift your hair? Real straight forward check. Maybe someday the little skin flap will grow hair again, but it's pretty obvious at the moment. So, I say because I don't recognize that face, I don't know the name, and he would have been arrested if he were with us, that therefore he ain't."

So that's how they scoop up deserters... if that's the case, only a sadist or an idiot would bring on a kid with an implant. Luke's not... probably was never with the Isles. Then where the hell did you go, little bro?

The old man nodded. "Happy to help," he said, and headed back to his truck."

The woman shrugged. "You're grinning. I guess that was good news?"

Elliot wiped the grin off his face and glanced back at the ravine: no movement. "You know, can I ask you something? How do you people deal with crime?"

She folded her arms and straightened her back. "If the two people in question can't sort it out, we call a moot."

"Rudimentary court of peers, yeah? How do you keep the punishment proportional? Can the person in question appeal to a higher moot?"

She frowned and scratched her cheek, where a bit of smokey gristle had gotten on her. "I suppose, but I can't remember that ever happening. Not since the founding at least. That's why we have moots. The bigger the issue, the more people you gather round to hear it out. Unless it's too big an issue. Then, likely as not, someone in the moot will shoot the bastard and go on trial himself."

"What if it's a kid, who made a mistake?"

"Depends on the father, assuming you're talking something violent anyways. You know, we do things different up in the Isles. We don't hide death from our kids. We don't make it digital pretend where you can make-believe butchering one another. It's custom that before even a kid hits puberty they have to be the one to slaughter a pig or a cow or some other animal. It's just a bit of stress, a growing experience. You can learn a lot about a kid's psyche and raise him proper by doing that."

So you traumatize them all. No, not traumatize, normalize. Killing animals for food is normal. We're the strange ones, living off insects and bacteria and vat grown meat.

"Well, this kid? That I'm here to get? He made a lot of mistakes. One after the next, they piled up on him and got worse and worse. He's here to get a job and join you all in the Isles, start a new life–"

"He didn't kill anybody, did he?"

Yes.

"No, but he did hurt some people and maybe they deserved it. If he stays, if I arrest him, he's probably going to jail for a long time."

The woman scoffed. "Jail is so disgusting. Primitive."

Elliot frowned. "And what do you people do?"

"Most often? Tell people to move on. If that's not enough, the one at fault has to apologize with his labor. Not money. It's never money. Money lets rich people get away with crimes. If it's something that you can't just apologize for? Like rape and murder? They get removed. If we're certain they did it, we kill them. If there isn't certainty, they're told to leave and not come back. Forever."

Elliot said, "Must be easier for you, since there's a big world of crap out here."

The woman waved her hand, at him and at the convoy and everything around them. "Humans are social animals. When you put them in jail, in prison, incarceration, it's just you exiling them to a room they can't leave. Often with the rest of the scum. Do you cops tell yourselves a pretty lie that you're rehabilitating these people when you put them in cages? Or are you just removing the problem from society? At least when we exile someone, they still have their dignity as human beings."

"Until they get eaten alive by the blighted."

The woman laughed. "Maybe, but that's the risk of freedom, ain't it? We don't turn people into animals like you people do."

But you do kill them. Well, so do we. At least they use a moot. How many people did we just kill in a firefight we started?

"Life is very different in the Isles, isn't it?"

"Sure is."

"Is it better?"

"Who can say. Some people like security more than they like freedom. And as we say in the Isles, they're free to do that, to put themselves in one big prison." The woman grinned and pointed a thumb over her shoulder at the walls of Bastion.

Elliot sighed. "There's something we're missing though. Sometimes, the problem isn't what other people think of what you did, but what you think of it. If this kid leaves Bastion, he'll never get closure. I doubt he'd ever come to terms with what he did. He's just running away."

"You know, you might be alright, for a cop. You want a beer?"

"It's dawn."

"Yeah, but I can tell from your eyes that you didn't sleep a wink. Do that often?"

Elliot hung his head and closed his eyes for a moment. "More than I'd like," he said, and she left the table. She came back with two bottles of something fizzing. No labels, but someone had used a marker to put some kind of code on the caps. Elliot had no idea what A38 meant, but he recognized the smell of hops. It was cold and the best thing he had tasted in weeks.

Can't tell Ram that though, can I? I was at her family's place just the other day. Wonder if I could bring a crate of these in? I should call Ram.

With a few recon drones buzzing in the sky like circling crows, Elliot pulled out his personal phone, set his gaze on the ravine, and rang her up.

She answered with a yawn. "Good morning, Mr Blackstone."

"I didn't wake you, did I?"

"You definitely did, but that's fine. Did you get any sleep?"

"No. I'm outside the walls right now."

"You're what? Why?"

"Because it's a dark, horrid, wet maze down there, and I'm reasonably certain Kyte got lost. Way easier to sit outside in some sunshine and wait here. I could use your report."

"Please don't make me fill out a report. I feel like I have to actively delete memories from last night. The things I saw. It was horrible. He was endorsing bills based on who wrote them instead of what they were about."

"Oh, don't worry about that, Congress doesn't have any real power. The bills are for show. I need your opinion on whether Ghos is going to personally pursue the matter with Kyte, or did he come to an understanding with his son?"

"What do you mean the bills are for show? They're how the government does things!"

Elliot closed his eyes and rubbed his temple. "I'll tell you about that later. Can you answer my other question?"

Ram sighed. "My honest opinion? He doesn't have the attention span to follow through with it."

"And can you look up the track record for his father's lawyer? I don't think Kyte will be able to use one of Sokolov's lawyers."

Ram took a moment to get her computer booted up once more, and Elliot sat there, drinking his beer and fiddling with the pack of cigarettes. The wood smoke made his mouth water, but he told himself to hold out on eating until he could sit down with Amara. Eventually, she said, "Mr Vapor's lawyer is Robert Polanskia. Specializes in divorce court but has a history of aggravated assault cases. He interned working for Romulus–"

"So he knows his way around self-defense?"

"Looks like it. You think he'll represent Kyte?"

"Seems likely, don't you think? Even if he and his father aren't exactly on speaking terms, it's obvious his dad cares for him and would act accordingly. And Kyte isn't so stupid as to turn down a lawyer. I think the important thing is, if shit really hits the fan for him, he needs a lawyer that will have kept him out on parole so he can do this whole escape thing all over again."

EVE cut into their conversation to say, "I'm going to forget you said that."

Elliot cleared his throat. "Please do."

Ram laughed. "That's certainly one way to look at it. Have you seen him yet?"

"No, not yet."

"He's not going to be happy to see you. You know that, right?"

"Ram, he just killed someone his age in a street fight. I'd be surprised if he was happy to see anyone. But that doesn't mean I'm not going to go get him."

"Do you think that's the best for him? Instead of letting him slip off into the convoy?"

"I don't think these people are going to take kindly to him escaping with them. I think he's come here on a delusion, a fairy tale."

"A fairy tale it might be, but it's one he's been clinging on to, to keep himself from falling apart."

"Well, he'll have to put the pieces back together," Elliot said, and he saw movement in the ravine. "There he is. Talk to you later." He hung up on her and rose from the table. His motion didn't go unnoticed. The woman from the Isles followed him without making a secret of it, and the two of them marched through the mesh of trucks and people, out to confront Kyte.

31

Interview

2140/10/11

The air was unlike anything Kyte had ever breathed before. Cold, fresh, dirty without rot to it. There was a kind of dry, plant odor to it, entirely unlike the canal dreck that oozed through Gamma. Something else hung in the air, the smell of burning gasoline and diesel; fossil fuels. The people from the Isles had come down in archaic contraptions of contained combustion. The economic sponge to eat up all the waste gasoline produced by the plastics industry.

There was no scent of people though. He could smell fire, and cooking meat, but not the jam-packed grease of human bodies that had been so infused into his senses that he had gone numb to it. For a span of space, between the walls and the convoy, he was alone. Him, grass, and a few insects bounding away from him. The noise of the wind in his ears drowned out the noise of people talking, a whispering from the world.

Kyte was alone, and trudged on to the convoy, to the people who lived outside of Bastion.

Two people saw him walking over, and they stepped out from the array of trucks and caravans. They seemed to be looking at him, walking straight towards him. Their gazes made Kyte's mouth go dry, and he glanced down at himself. He had Drake's blood still on him, mired in the grime of Epsilon. His heart started to thump, and he knelt down.

He tore off the bloody jacket and took a handful of grass to try and scrub it clean. Some blood flaked free, not enough. Even when streaks of green marred the leather, he hadn't gotten the blood off of it. He had been an idiot to sit in the darkness and do nothing. Hours had passed and he had done nothing.

"You okay?" It was a man's voice. He loomed over Kyte, back to the rising sun.

"Yes!" He stood back up and gave the jacket a shake. Grass blades fell away and left blood behind. "Just had to get something off this," Kyte said, and squinted his eyes at the man. The sun had crested the horizon and blasted light out across the world. Not one single photocell sucked the energy away. There were no shadows, no reflections, no competing LEDs, just the full brunt of the sun. it was like he had gone all the way up to Alpha, and yet there was dirt beneath his feet. It made it hard for his eyes to pick out the details of the man, his bulky chest and thick arms. After so many hours in Epsilon, the new dawn wanted to blind him. The man didn't seem affected, no more than a disappointed frown. Kyte could pick that out in his expression. He'd seen it all his life, adorning his father's face before the bastard moved out.

"You don't look okay, Kyte."

The chaotic tension of pain inside him cooled with fear. "How do you know who I am?"

A woman stepped out to the side of the silhouetted man. She put her hands on her hips and looked him over. She looked like she had just stepped out of a video game, a vivid tenacity of life amplified beyond reality. She had muscle and curves both, a sharpness in her eyes that couldn't exist in Gamma. "So, you're looking to move out to the Isles? Did you get jabbed? I hear city folk have to get vaccinated to survive out here."

"I'm clean. I'm not going to turn blighted on you. I made it out here, didn't I? You can't make it all the way out of Bastion half-assed. I'm good. You a merchant or something? A convoy leader?"

She smirked. "You could say that. You could also say I'm the good-will ambassador for the suits in Bastion. I make sure things are smooth, that things stay the way they are, because we like the current arrangement. That kind of thing."

Kyte tried to swallow, but couldn't work up any spit. "So what? You saying I'm trouble? I'm not trouble. I'm a hard worker. Reliable. I get things done. I'm valuable. I can pay too. Was told you people like payment in data?" He fished out the harddrive, the one Fumi had given him before he betrayed her. It felt like such a flimsy thing between his fingers.

"Did you get that while working for Sokolov?" the man asked.

Kyte stepped back. His eyes started to adjust, picking out the shape of the body, the jacket thrown over top. Then he saw the police badge. "What the fuck are you doing out here?"

"Calm down, Kyte," the jannis said.

"What the fuck is a jannis doing out here? Isn't the convoy managed by the military? Foreign relations or whatever? Why are you out here?"

The policeman put up his hands. "Come on, you know why. Take a breath, Kyte. Did you get all the way here by screaming at people?"

"No, I fucking got here by fighting," Kyte screamed, and pulled his gun. He hadn't reloaded it, but the cylinder wasn't empty either. He thrust it at the man, barrel swinging from face to chest and around again. "Why don't you just forget you ever saw me?"

Both of them, the jannis and the woman from the Isles, tensed, neither drew their weapons though. The man shook his head. "No Kyte, you got here by running away. You don't even realize that Evan is still alive, do you?"

"I... what? I don't even know who the fuck that is." Maybe Drake had lied about his name, but that shock of death had been certain. The blood had been enough.

"Evan Ryder! The kid you brained with a beer bottle because your girlfriend cheated on you. He's fine. He's not even mad at you! He dropped the charges. He didn't even want me coming after you."

Memory from the concert flashed back into his mind, the night distorted by darkness and blood. "You're lying. I know you're lying. Even if he is fine, you can't just drop charges. You government pricks can prosecute anyways."

The woman laughed. She had migrated away from the policeman, gotten herself out of the line of fire. When she saw him look at her, her hand shot to her hip where her own gun was. "Don't drag me into this, kid."

"Vlad didn't tell you that Evan survived, did he? That gangster stayed at the concert. Saw the whole thing, him getting taken away by EMS. He knew, and didn't tell you, because he wanted to use you. He did use you, didn't he? In Survivor's Canyon maybe?"

"You don't have any idea what happened in there. You don't even have jurisdiction out here. This isn't Bastion. I made it out. I'm free."

"Did you kill Drake?" the policeman asked.

"Fuck you, what kind of question is that?"

"Was it murder?"

"You people recorded everything!"

"Or did he corner you?"

"Do you think I would have shot him if I had a choice? I was on my way out! I was going to be gone!"

"You're the one who has to answer that, Kyte! You're the one who has to decide whether what you did was wrong. Forget me, forget the courts. Say you get out of here. Say you leave Bastion behind and never see your friends or family again, you have you. You have to live with yourself. You might be able to run away from your problems, but you can't run away from the consequences of running away. So tell me, did you murder him?"

"No, no I didn't. I fucking shot him because he was going to cut my head off with a micro-blade. What the hell was I supposed to do? What choice did I have? Die? Should I have laid down and died? Because that's no fucking choice and you know it."

The man seemed to let out his breath. His shoulders sagged but his hands didn't go down. "Kyte, you should come back. If you testify to what Sokolov's operation was like, you'll get let off."

Kyte's mouth hung open. He didn't know what to say or what to do. "You're lying."

"I'm not lying."

"You're just trying to get a promotion or something. A gold star for your record."

"Kid, if I cared about getting promoted, you really think I would be out here right now? Hell, I'm trying to take a week or two off to spend it with my wife."

Kyte gritted his teeth and tried to think it through, to build a profile on the jannis, officer E11107. Nothing fit, and he knew it wasn't because the guy was enigmatic. Kyte just couldn't make his mind work the way his father had taught him. He couldn't do what that bastard could do. "Just let me leave then. You wouldn't be here if you weren't getting something out of this. Do I need to shoot you too? Because going back and getting put in jail for life ain't a choice I'm going to take either."

"Kyte! You just said yourself that it wasn't murder. You don't have to run away. You can clear your name."

The woman was watching, bemused. She shook her head and looked down on him. Every word from the police officer's mouth dug him into a grave. Made his chances of joining the convoy slimmer by the sentence. "Just shut up. What are you even going to do? Force me? Going to tackle me and cuff me and drag me back inside to sit in front of a judge?"

The police officer sighed. "No, I'm not going to do that. Don't you realize you're never going to see the people you know again? You abandoned your mother, if nothing else. When I saw–

"Don't talk about my mother. You manipulative bastard."

The police officer's eyebrows rose, and he leaned his head forward a bit. The shallowness of the insult couldn't have been more apparent to the both of them. "What is it that you want, Kyte?"

"I want to leave."

"To start over?"

"Yes!"

"As a runaway murderer?"

"It wasn't murder, you fuck. You police are all the same, you know that? You're an offshoot spawn of the military. All you do is break things and kill people." That hit the jannis hard. The man took a step back, lost for words. "When's the last time you ever actually helped someone?"

"Kyte, if I was like the others, I would have shot you by now. We're still talking, aren't we? Or are you going to run away from me too?"

"Shut up."

"Come on, kid. It's obvious that you don't want to leave. You don't want to start over. Or do you expect me to believe you're this torn up over your girlfriend dumping you?"

"I said, shut up."

"We've got Fumi Sokolov in custody right now, and she won't shut up about you, you know that? We just destroyed her father's entire empire, and she's talking about you. You expect me to–"

"Does it look like I want to hear about Fumi?" Kyte snapped.

The police officer scoffed. "What, were you dating her too?"

"Get out of my way!"

"Kyte–" the cop stepped forward.

It caught Kyte by surprise and the tension in his body snapped. His finger pulled. The gun fired. The thing erupted in his grasp and almost tumbled out of his gab. Fire and lead belched forward, into the cop's gut just like how he had killed Drake. The police officer didn't go down, he lunged forward and ripped the gun from his hand. Kyte didn't even resist it. He stood there shaking and trembling. "I didn't mean to..."

"I'm fine, kid. I'm fine," the cop said, and he put a hand on Kyte's shoulder.

Kyte looked down and saw the black mark where the bullet had hit; right against the police officer's body armor. There was no hole, no blood. He hadn't accidentally done anything. He fell to his knees and couldn't see, not through the flood of tears. He finally ran out of the desperate strength that had pushed him out of Bastion. He wouldn't have been able to hold onto it had he wanted to. Wet tears streamed down his cheeks and off his chin, soaking into the policeman's jacket as the sun took the coldness away.

32

Pork Spending

2140/10/13

The smell of grilling meat did not make Elliot's mouth water. Even as he stood there, a few steps from Congressman Ghos' personal propane grill, he felt no compulsion for the slabs of red meat. It was good meat, bought from the Isles convoy for Ghos to grill up, a treat for him and his family whenever the outsiders showed up. There was even one for Elliot, but he couldn't find any appetite for it.

"You know, it's a good thing you brought that kid in," Ghos said, shoving the steaks around like they would stick to the grill. All he succeeded in was spilling grease into the blaze and smoking it up.

"The prosecutors appreciate it, yes."

"Well sure, there's that, but I was able to arrange a visit between that Skybyte kid–"

"Kyte."

"Right, him and my son. Evan was so tickled about it he agreed to this," Ghos said, spreading his arm across the eightieth floor patio. The congressman had the whole floor, and had even put down enough space heaters the October evening felt like July. A dozen people Elliot didn't know milled about, sipping beers and chatting. Mostly about bills and various corporate movements. The only table that appeared to be having fun was the table Ram, Evan, and Akane sat at playing a card game.

What a waste of time and money.

"I appreciate the invite," Elliot said.

"Least I could do," Ghos said, flipping one of the steaks like he was sauteing it instead of grilling it. "Can you believe that new ARU got destroyed though? What are those stooges in Daedalus doing with all the money we give them?"

"The Manticore was designed to withstand gunfire, which it did. No amount of armor in the world is enough to stop a dedicated explosive though. The real surprise is that Sokolov had one of sufficient yield."

"Still millions down the drain. That's taxpayer money wasted for a national embarrassment."

Who the hell pays taxes in this city except corporations?

"Well, I hear Daedalus has a new recruit and a few breakthroughs. Nothing wrong with scientific progress."

"True that," Ghos said, shaking his head. He stared out at the horizon, over the mottled peaks of Bastion like so many hills. "One step closer to the future. Never know when we'll finally have another war."

Elliot grimaced. "Let's pray it's not in our lifetimes. Can I ask though? What made you salvage that?"

"That? Spoils of war, I say. Looks pretty too," Ghos said, gesturing at the mural rest against one wall. The entire panel from the retail shop had been cut out and transported at his expense, looted from Gamma and brought to be part of his private collection.

Does this kind of art mean anything to a man like Ghos? Or did he just take it as a status symbol?

Elliot walked over to it, extracting himself from the conversation to admire the work. The painting hadn't been signed, but he was certain the artist was A-maze, same as the graffiti during the Devson case. "Wish I could have met him," Elliot mumbled. Some of the paint lines had streaked with dust and overspray, lines running down like tears. The artist must have barely finished it before the raid started.

"So, this is good news, right?" Ram asked.

Elliot glanced over his shoulder. The card game had been abandoned, and she was sipping some kind of neon green soft drink he didn't recognize. "As good as could be hoped for."

"This party is really stifling though. All these people, they're congressional staff and lobbyists and CEOs, and I'm just a junior officer. I feel so out of place."

"Aren't you happy for the chance to meet them? These are the people you're going to be attacking, soon enough, aren't they? This is the corruption. People on high sending out dictates while drinking and grilling imported steaks while their decisions drive people into corners and ruin their lives."

"That's what makes me so uneasy about being here," she mumbled. "Spending the whole day relaying updates to him while he argued about stock prices was worse though. It's that kind of low burn stress that builds and builds... I hopped on a treadmill for five miles afterwards just so I could fall asleep."

I need to hit the gym again. Five miles would kill me.

"Sorry you drew the short straw."

"Don't be, I asked for it. It kept me out of the raid, just like I asked for."

"Next time, let's try to avoid the violence all together, yeah?"

Ram laughed and nodded, but her gaze never made it up from the foot of the mural. She rubbed her fingers on her glass and glanced at Ghos the more the conversation dragged. Elliot pulled out his crumpled pack of Nico-Pure cigarettes. He opened it up, pushed a cigarette out and offered it to her. Her face lit up. "Oh, sure," she said, and in a moment, had the tobacco lit. She tried to hide it like a teenager in a school stairwell, but Elliot just laughed. She frowned at it and asked, "Hey, since when do you smoke? I thought you made a big deal out of that?"

Elliot inhaled, getting a lungful of secondhand flavor. "I don't."

"Then why do you have a pack?"

"Habit, I give them away usually. It was my brother's favorite brand, but he's been missing for six years now. That was why, by the way."

"Why what?"

"I joined the force. You asked me the other day and I dodged the question. It was because my brother went missing and we never got answers. It got under my skin, the injustice of it. I still don't know if my decision even made sense, but then it got in my head that this is who I am, so I kept going one day at a time, one case after the next. Now, I'm here."

"I think that's very admirable, Mr Blackstone. So could you tell me how an E-rank officer became the head of a department?"

Elliot barked out a laugh and shook his head and grinned down at her. "Maybe some other time, when I understand it myself. So tell me though, since when do you smoke?"

"Uh…" Her cheeks flushed. "Well, I've dabbled in nicotine for years! It's in the energy drinks and protein bars and stuff. Like Zeus."

"So since when do you smoke?"

"Past few days, I guess?"

"Hmm, that's almost like you changed your stance on it suddenly. Kind of like someone put the idea in your head without you even realizing. They changed your behavior without the slightest resistance from you… Sounds to me kind of like hypnotism."

Ram froze. She stared at the cigarette in her hand, smoke trickling like incense. Her gaze snapped onto him. "No. No fucking way. You did not do this to me."

"I definitely did. Ordered it anyway. The brunt of the work was done subliminally through your media feeds. Didn't even take a week to shift that habit of yours, Miz Hypnotism-Isn't-Real."

"You gave me a cancerous addiction to prove a point?"

"Okay, first of all, me telling you right now is enough to break the effect, so unless you were huffing hookah for the last forty-eight hours, you're not going to get cancer. Second of all, you're on government health care. They'll print you off a new set of lungs if you need them.

Third, it was a very important lesson that you needed to understand. Human beings are very easily manipulated. Book a visit with Seouljin some time if you don't believe me."

Ram's expression was somewhere between a pout and a scowl, and she stubbed the cigarette out in a plant pot before crossing her arms in a huff. "I can't believe you did that."

"That I chose to or that I was capable of it?"

"Both!"

Elliot sighed. "I'm sorry. We do it to everyone who joins the force. It helps build resistance to it in the future. For the record, all these techniques were developed by advertising agencies. They really wanted to know how to get inside somebody's skull and get them to willingly hand over money. Push notifications, friend networking, context interruption, comparative reasoning. There's a thousand things they do."

"Oh, really? Because I think you got pretty easily manipulated yourself. Seems to me that Seouljin, that mindbreaker got exactly what he wanted. His son is safe and sound and soon won't even have a blemish on his record."

Elliot's smirk vanished. "Maybe. That way lies the road of self-doubt though. I'd rather be ignorant. Makes it easier to put it out of mind. I've got a vacation to look forward to now. Work is the last thing I want to be thinking about."

Ram pouted at him. "You're sticking me with all the testifying and report checking. You know that, right?"

"I'll make it up to you. Just let me know how after I get back."

"I'm holding you to that."

"So do you have a date with him yet?"

Her anger vanished with a blissful grin. "Next Tuesday yeah– wait, who told you?"

Too easy.

"You did, just now."

Ram sputtered and finally said, "He's got an offer for contract work at Daedalus labs now! He's totally above board."

"Yeah, and you found a guy with passion, and who takes care of himself. Exactly what you were looking for. Ram, I'm not blaming you. I just wish I had been able to give you actual advice on how to meet someone. For us, work is not really a solution to the dating market."

"I'm fine with the fact that I got lucky! I think."

Behind them, Ghos bellowed out for people to come start grabbing steaks, and all the various groups disintegrated to queue up. Elliot gestured for her to head over, and said, "I wish you the best, Ram. Tomorrow, I'm going to have to suffer through seven clout chasing streamers stuck in a homestead together, so when I get out, I'll probably be happy to dive back into work with you."

"Try not to arrest any of them."

"That might be a struggle," Elliot said, as she headed to get her plate of food. He walked over to the upwind corner of the patio, away from the drifting allure of seared steak. While everyone else gorged themselves on the spoils of the Isles, he pulled out his phone to message EVE. "So [Sladder] is down, right? So you still owe me one?"

"Just the one, yeah," the AI responded. "You're not going to ask me to teach you how to play [Zom-Fortress], are you?"

He laughed. "Given what you can do? That would be a waste of a favor. Besides, my goal is to not play the game at all."

"Good luck. She's going to see you like a content gold mine."

"There are worse things that could happen."

"Enjoy your vacation, Blackstone. By the time you're back, Kyte will be walking free."

"If his tongue is half as honeyed as his father's, I'm sure he will be. For now though, I'm putting work on hold," he said, and sent a message to his wife that he was officially on vacation.

33

Recruitment

2140/10/15

The room was dingy and pounding with music. The guards had put on *Midnight Rider* and he had no idea whether they had done it on purpose. The very same song that had been playing when he got into the whole mess had looped back around as he sat beneath a flickering incandescent light and tried to hold his tongue.

"Mr Vapor, the–"

"Don't call me that. My father is Mr Vapor. Call me Kyte."

The man in the suit across from him smiled and nodded. He folded his hands on the interview table, mimicking the way Kyte was cuffed. Obvious emotional mirroring. "Kyte," the man said, "I'm sure you're aware of the attention your acquaintances have garnered from the American government."

"No, sorry, I must have missed the killer robot you sent in, and all the bodybags that came out. What does that have to do with me? I've already testified against them."

"Yes, you have; but, you are something of a special case, because you were involved in an illegal clinical trial of the NZ vaccine. That's a violation of several pandemic related policies. In fact, we have records–"

"Who the hell are you people?"

The man paused and smiled. "I'm from the Draft Administration. It's my responsibility to investigate matters of recruitment malpractice."

Kyte snarled, anger burning inside him. He wanted to jump up, but the cuffs on his wrists were barely an inch long. "Malpractice? The only recruitment malpractice that occurred was blocking Fumi from escaping her father. Why don't you go find which bastard caused that lie?"

"Fumi Sokolov's case was of special consideration, which can now be reviewed in light of her father's arrest and the dissolution of his organization," the man from the DA said, all with a smile. There was even a casual sway and bob to his head, in time with the music.

"You mean now that Sokolov isn't a political threat?"

"Domestic terrorist threat, to be precise. And as you saw, we were right to be concerned. That man built a cybernetic WMD."

Kyte laughed in the man's face. "So, for you people, the sins of the father fall on the child? I think you owe her more than just an apology."

"We would never say the sins of the father pass down."

"But you think it."

"It's quite inarguable that the father teaches the child though, isn't that right, Kyte?"

He slid back in his chair and looked for some hint in the man's face but found nothing. He wondered if, behind those smoked glasses flashing with HUD inputs, the man's pupils were wide open, doped out on some neurological down-regulator. "What are you getting at? Shouldn't I be free to go? Didn't I do everything asked of me? Reveal all the secrets, point all the fingers? Don't I just have a few more court appearances to make?"

The man pulled out a paper folder and spread some sheets around. There was a picture of a corpse that made Kyte's breath catch. "You don't need to have your guard up so much. I'd actually like to talk about the events the night of the eleventh, when you killed Drake Penrose... in self-defense. We aren't arguing that legal matter."

Kyte calmed his voice and asked, "What about it then?"

"It's how you did it, particularly while still fevered from the ill-advised inoculation. Unfortunately, we don't have visible spectrum footage of the event. However, EVE was able to isolate audio from the shooting. She triangulated the echoes quite well. And one of the wide spotter bots had you in its gaze. We can show you the video if you'd like."

"I don't see what the point would be. It's not like I've forgotten what happened. The nightmares keep reminding me."

The man nodded. "Understandable. The thing is, that from the looks of it, you were quite calm when defending yourself. Unnaturally so."

"It was fight or flight instinct, and I had been trapped. It's a normal human reaction."

"A normal neurological reflex, yes. But that wasn't reflex, now was it?" the man asked, smiling at Kyte. "You triggered it on purpose to keep yourself from getting hurt. Auto-hypnosis, as your painter friend put it. That's a trick very few can pull off. Kyte, we at the DA think you have more talent than you realize."

"What are you getting at?"

"Kyte, I'd like to offer you a position in the psychological warfare division. We think you could be a great asset to your country."

"You want me to be a mindbreaker, like my father was?"

"That's right."

"You're out of your fucking mind. I have nothing more to say to you."

The man scooped up the papers without losing his smile, and stood. "Well, we ask that you consider it over the next few days pending your release. There are many advantages to it. We could even arrange some special considerations for you, such as putting you in the same boot-camp as Fumi so the two of you can reconcile."

"Fumi wouldn't want to see me."

"You're a clever kid, Kyte. You'd be able to do it. You got her to like you in the first place, right?" The officer smirked.

Fumi just wanted out, a normal life. Kyte had, in his small way, destroyed the abnormal life she did have and even testified against her father. She had confided in him and reached her hand out only for him to run away from it. He still felt sick about it, but he wasn't in the Isles. He still had time and ways to make amends. It just wouldn't be easy and he couldn't use tricks.

Not if he wanted it to last.

Kyte planted his elbows on the table and buried his face in his hands. "Just get out. I have nothing more to say to you."

The man bowed himself out, but paused at the door. "One more thing. Your father asked me to relay to you something. He said, 'Good work, son. Couldn't be more proud of you.'"

"And you can tell him that I never want to see him again."

"Certainly," the man from the DA said, and left.

Kyte was escorted back to his jail cell, alone save for his thoughts and memories. His father's poisoned advice. Evan's laughing apology that twisted a knife inside his gut. The police officer that had given him a second chance. The hole Fumi had carved out in him. It gave him plenty of time to think about how to fix it all.

Thank you for reaching the end of Gamma Coin : BASTION/ Blackstone II.

Please consider leaving a review of this work on any platform. Word of mouth is the most important form of marketing and the easiest way to support an independent author.

If you enjoyed this book, you may enjoy these.

Ship of Fuls by James Krake
ISBN : 9781957599069
A tense sci-fi thriller aboard a civilian ship in hiding from a vicious army. Space Ranger Marcus must maintain order at all costs, while surrounded by murderous conspiracies, a starving crew, and rapidly diminishing resources.

Infinite Money Glitch by James Krake
ISBN : 9781957599090
A comedic heist orchestrated by the self-aware NPCs of an MMORPG to drain the in-game market. The System is rigged in favor of the players, but that doesn't mean there aren't exploits.

Five To Four by James Krake
ISBN : 9781957599007
It's five minutes to four o'clock on a Friday when a handful of office workers find themselves trapped in a nightmare maze version of their

building. All the doors lead to the wrong rooms, they can't find the way out, and they aren't alone.